Natasha Woodcraft has painted Biblical narrative, engaging the s(as she explores the development c thing to watch your child develop boggling to imagine if they were t

..... ~........ ever to be skilled at flutes and harps or the instructor of every craftsman in bronze and iron.

While only four chapters deep in the Bible, The Wanderer's Legacy takes place 800+ years after the world was formed, and it is easy to see the slide from honoring the Lord avalanching to depravity within a couple of generations. My heart hurt for the people who had only heard in passing the name of Yahweh. How will they know if they aren't told? How will today's culture know the ways of the Lord if we don't actively fight the landslide?

The Wanderer's Legacy is a warning we'd do well to heed. It is wildly imaginative and sent me to my Bible—the mark of a great Biblical Fiction. Readers of Biblical Fiction will not want to miss this book (and series!)

Naomi Craig, **author of** *Ezekiel's Song* **and founder of** *Biblical Fiction Aficionados*

Natasha Woodcraft transports readers to the ancient world, where humans live for hundreds of years and Leviathan swims the sea. The Wanderer's Legacy is an exciting, yet foreboding tale of love, betrayal, and adventure I couldn't put down. A must-read for all Biblical Fiction fans.

Dana McNeely, **Christy-Award finalist author of** *Rain*

This is the final book in a trilogy of ancient, pre-Noah times. This is one brave author, for she has tackled stories set in times that so little is known about and done a sterling job. Many of the characters reject their creator and make choices that lead them far from him, yet there is always a remnant of faithful folk. This third book also looks deep into a dysfunctional marriage bringing forth lessons still relevant today.

Christine Dillon, **Contemporary and Biblical Fiction author**

THE WANDERER SERIES

1. The Wanderer Scorned
2. The Wanderer Reborn
3. The Wanderer's Legacy

The Wanderer's Sister (A Wanderer Novelette)
Between the Rivers (A Wanderer Novella)

The Wanderer's Sister is available exclusively for members of the author's readers' club. You can join at:
natashawoodcraft.com/subscribe

ALSO BY THE AUTHOR

From His Heart to Yours and Back Again: *Scripture-based Prayers for Christian Writers*
Pray the Bible: *A 10-week prayer journey through Ephesians*

THE WANDERER'S LEGACY

The Wanderer's Legacy © Natasha Woodcraft 2025.
First edition published in Great Britain 2025 by Broad Place Publishing
https://broadplacepublishing.co.uk

All rights reserved. No part of this book may be reproduced or distributed in any form without prior written permission from the author, with the exception of non-commercial uses permitted by copyright law.

Paperback ISBN 978-1-91-503488-5
Ebook ISBN 978-1-91-503489-2
Hardback ISBN 978-1-91-503495-3

A catalogue record for this book is available from the British Library

Scripture quotations and paraphrases are from the ESV® Bible (The Holy Bible, English Standard Version®), copyright © 2001 by Crossway Bibles, a publishing ministry of Good News Publishers. Used by permission. All rights reserved.

Cover Image by Getcovers
Maps and interior images by Natasha Woodcraft

THE WANDERER'S LEGACY

Book 3 in *The Wanderer* Series

A standalone novel based on Genesis 4:17-24

NATASHA WOODCRAFT

BROAD PLACE
publishing
broadplacepublishing.co.uk

In peace I will lie down and sleep,

for you alone, Lord, make me dwell in safety.

Psalm 4:8

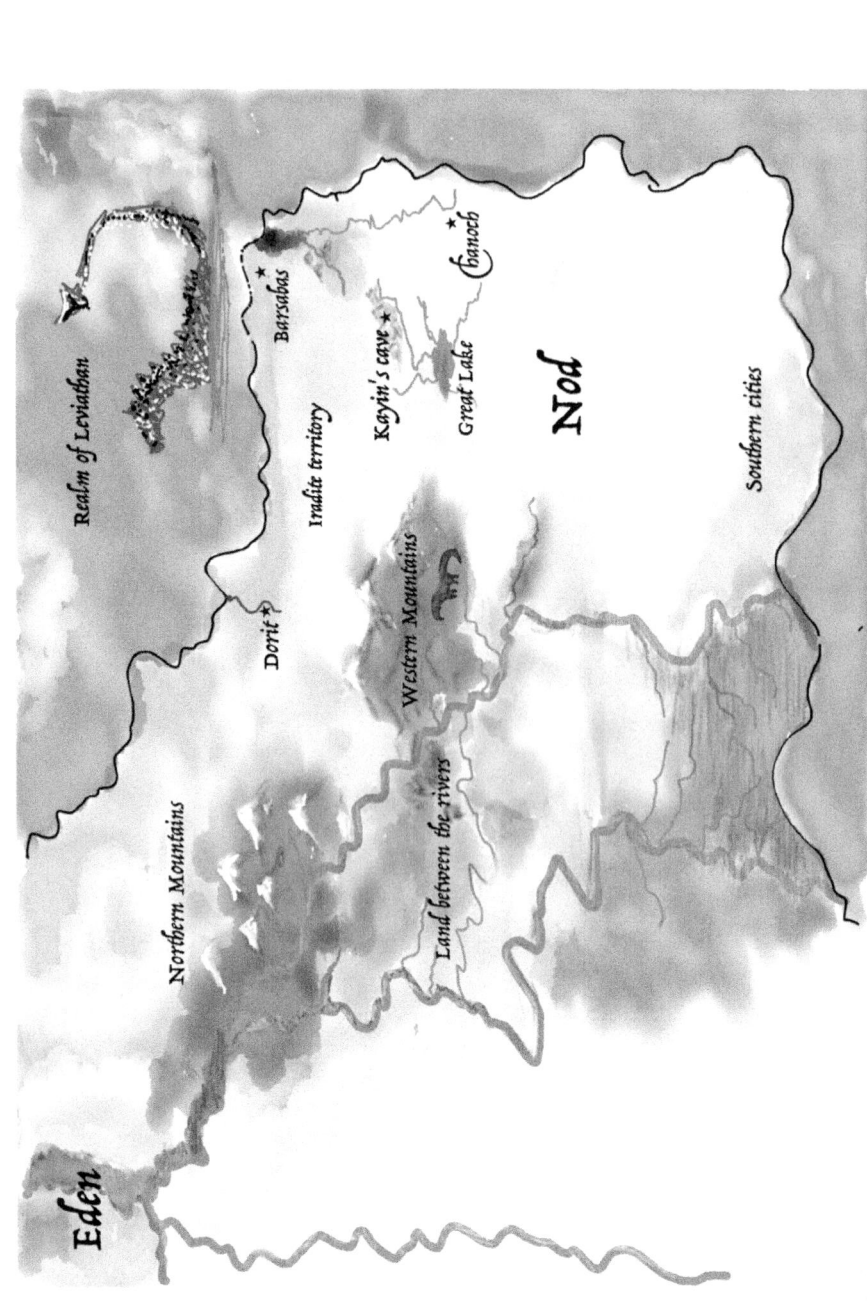

AUTHOR'S NOTE

Dear Reader,

This is just a little note to say that I'm British! This means I do things like realising an offence instead of realizing an offense, and using single quote marks, 'like this', instead of far more sensible double quote marks. I hope that if you are not used to them, you will forgive such eccentricities. They are not mistakes.

The Wanderer's Legacy is based on Genesis 4:17-24 in the Bible, but you don't have to be a Christian to read it. The human condition is familiar to us all, and I hope you'll find the story engaging and challenging, whether you have some faith or none.

This is not a light-hearted book. It explores the possible descent towards the Great Flood, when '*The Lord saw that the wickedness of man was great in the earth, and that every intention of the thoughts of his heart was only evil continually* (Genesis 6:5).' It contains violence, domestic abuse, baby-loss and infidelity. If such things are likely triggers for you, then please take this as a kind warning. I have tried to address them as sensitively as possible, whilst acknowledging that not much has changed in the ensuing millennia, and these issues are a reality many people still live with.

If you want to explore some of the ideas in the story further, there is an appendix at the back. May every blessing be upon you as you read.

N.W.

CHARACTERS

Clarifications

Abba means Dad/Father. **Sav** is grandfather.
Ima means Mum/Mother. **Sava** is grandmother.
Elohim means God, and **Yahweh** means LORD. They refer to the same being, **Yahweh Elohim** (Yahweh is God's name).

Cast of characters

Adah	Daughter of Shimiel, wife of Lamech
Shimiel	Adah's father
Lamech	Adah's husband
Tzillah	Lamech's 2nd wife
Yaval	1st son of Lamech & Adah
Juval	2nd son of Lamech & Adah
Naamah	Daughter of Lamech & Tzillah
Tuval-Kayin	Son of Lamech & Tzillah

Staff

Azurak	Lamech's second-in-command
Shua	Adah's housekeeper
Leah	Adah's maid
Tzel/Shadow	Adah's guard
Avram	The gatekeeper

Wider family

Noa	Lamech's mother, Methushael's wife
Methushael	Lamech's father, Noa's husband
Bekhor	Lamech's eldest brother
Dinah	Lamech's sister
Barsabas	Dinah's husband
Rivkah	Shimiel's 2nd wife
Levi	Son of Shimiel & Rivkah

Friends

Chanoch	City founder, Son of The Wanderer
Shiphrah	Chanoch's wife
Eliana	Adah's best friend
Ruhamah	Eliana's brother
Manon	Eliana's husband
Mela	Eliana's daughter
Nasya	Adah's friend

Wider acquaintances

Kenan	City elder, Chanoch's grandson by marriage
Eber	2nd son of Kenan
Gomer	5th son of Kenan
Anak	Son of Dinah & Barsabas
Tamar	Lamech's concubine
Nahar	Son of Lamech & Tamar
Naman	An elder
Selah	An elder, Chanoch's daughter
Yosa	A tanner employed by Lamech
The Wanderer	Kayin, Chanoch's father
Awan	Chanoch's mother

PART ONE

CHAPTER 1

City of Chanoch, 750th year of Wandering

Adah presses her back to the pillar, squeezing into its evening shadow. Her heavy breathing is almost as loud as the heartbeat pummelling in her head. *Surely someone will hear?*

Her chance to escape diminishes with every moment of delay. She is a desert jerboa - alert, aware of every sight and smell, yet frozen in place as she awaits her predator's pounce.

Azurak should be occupied. Her son arranged it when she pleaded with him on hands and knees, eyes streaming in desperation. But Adah is sure she hears him. His rasping breath and distinct blood-soaked-campfire smell linger, fusing her feet to the ground.

Unless it's someone worse than Azurak. Perhaps her husband will find her.

CHAPTER 2

Countryside near Chanoch, Fifty years earlier

There once was a time when Adah loved her husband. The memories of those days come vividly, with fondness even, if she's feeling generous.

She was young then. For four prolonged seasons, she'd been tending her ailing mother – a nineteen-year-old beauty restricted to the role of nursemaid. At first, Adah hadn't minded. She loved Ima, and the opportunity to sit by her bedside hearing legends from long ago was a blessing. Then Ima's voice and strength had ebbed away, until all Adah could do was hold her thin, frail hand, and mop her sweating brow. Then the simple hut they shared in the hills constricted her like the holding cells in the city, where the dangerous dwelt. When Ima's stories ceased, Adah's vivid imagination became her principal companion.

Mercifully, the daily walk to the well and twice-weekly trip to the marketplace broke up her days. Yet, even those, which she used to enjoy with her best friend, Eliana, lacked pleasure once Eliana married and Adah did not. Then she had to traipse alone, past the boulder-lined tracks that often hid people of nefarious intent. She pleaded under her breath, whispering all the way for Yahweh to keep her safe, imploring a name she knew little about, except that Ima had said it was powerful, protecting The Wanderer for generations.

She hoped to meet The Wanderer one day. He was said to be recognisable by the scar dominating the right side of his face. Some thought it made him look fearsome, others that it showed the vulnerability of the man who couldn't die. If she saw him for herself, she could decide. But she never had.

The day Adah met her husband rivalled her mother's death in its importance. Ima hadn't long passed away – into which life, who knew? The pit of Adah's loss was still cavernous. For two such significant events to occur within weeks of each other might be called peculiar, if her father hadn't planned it. Not that Adah knew so at the time.

She'd been to the well later than she should, for mornings dragged in sorrowful slumber. When she returned from the blistering hike, with a large, stoneware jar balanced precariously on her head (she'd never been very good at carrying it) she knew instantly that they had a visitor. The scent of nutmeg and cinnamon wafted from the hut, revealing a hospitality that her abba hadn't extended since Ima became ill.

She rounded the corner and lifted the jar from her head, nudging it down from shoulder, to hip, to floor. Then she saw the visitor, seated on a wicker chair – their only chair – to the left of her abba, who held a goblet of wine. *It is not yet halfway to noon. Since when did Abba drink so early?*

The visitor's shoulders were broader than Abba's by half and his height extended well above the back of the chair, setting Abba in the shade – for Abba was hunched on the three-legged milking stool. The visitor's hair, falling to his shoulders, glimmered with hints of red. *The Wanderer has hair that colour.* Or so she'd heard.

The broad man laughed at something Abba said. She hadn't heard Abba joke for many moons, but now the boom from the big man infected him, and he chortled a response. He was evidently pleased with this visitor. Tremors of excitement rippled through Adah's gut. A man who pleased her abba? That was a rare thing. A man he invited over—? Its significance impressed onto her heart.

Adah had been sought after before. As soon as she'd blossomed into womanhood at the tender age of thirteen, men noticed her. As she traded for supplies in the market, they would glance her way, stepping aside to make room for her, scrutinising her like they might do a cattle purchase. She would catch their whispers on the wind. They were saying things, not always pleasant, but she didn't understand why. Not until three years later, when Eliana laughed at her and forced her to look at her reflection in a bowl of water.

'What do you see, Adah?' Eliana had asked, in her birdsong voice.

Adah had peered into the water, seeing the face she hadn't considered for many years. She knew what it felt like – the lengthening of her nose and widening of her lips, and the bumps that sometimes pushed beneath the surface of her skin, irritatingly compelling her to squeeze them. They had accompanied the swelling of breasts and flow of womanhood that her ima had endeavoured to explain and hide from her abba. She hadn't known why. The bumps had lessened since, appearing now for only a few days a month. Also, her black hair had thickened. It required far more braids than it had when she was a girl.

As Adah viewed the features often felt, it became clear she resembled her mother—apart from her skin tone. Her eyes were darker too, though the colour was hard to distinguish in the earthenware bowl.

'What colour are my eyes?' Adah asked.

'They are like copper,' Eliana replied, 'The most precious thing to come from the ground. Precious like you, my friend.'

'Didn't The Wanderer discover copper?' Adah asked.

'You and that man! Is there any thought of yours that doesn't involve him?'

Adah's cheeks warmed and she glanced at her reflection again. 'What am I meant to be seeing?'

'You are beautiful, Adah.' The statement had come from Eliana's brother, walking into the corner of her vision at that moment.

Adah was stunned. 'Am I?'

'The most beautiful woman I have seen.'

She stared at Ruhamah with wide eyes, but he stood resolute, holding her gaze. His didn't wander like other men's. She noticed his simple tunic, much like hers except quite filthy, and the leather pouch around his waist from which tufts of fleece stuck out. Eliana jumped up and pushed him away, laughing.

'Her abba will never accept you, Ruhamah. You may as well give up now. Though—' and here Eliana dropped to her knees and squeezed Adah's hand affectionately, 'to have you as my true sister would be the most wonderful thing.'

Eliana was three years older than Adah. She knew everything, and everyone, and Adah relied on her for all the information she never got from her parents. As Ruhamah countered and her friends wrestled playfully, she felt a familiar pang. To be an only child was uncommon in their culture. Rare and lonely.

'I know,' Ruhamah responded, throwing his hands in the air. 'Adah is her father's prize. A mere sheepherder will never be worthy. I can still dream.'

Adah caught his wistful gaze and surrendered a small smile. Just two years older than his sister, they'd all grown up together and she loved Ruhamah like a brother – wished he was her brother. She hoped he wouldn't treat her differently now she'd altered into a prize to be won.

Ruhamah had married another woman the following year and seemed happy. He'd never acted inappropriately towards Adah but had remained a friend. Until the day his bride asked her not to visit again.

As Adah wandered back from her memories, the visitor noticed her. His head turned her way and his mouth twitched. He tucked his hair behind his ears, revealing strong eyes. *Dependable eyes*, her mother would have said.

Abba swung round, jumping off his stool and exclaiming a welcome. 'My daughter!'

Adah nodded in respect, watching the visitor from under her lashes.

'Come join us,' her father continued. 'You must meet my friend, Lamech.'

CHAPTER 3

Adah took two steps forward before Lamech stood, shifting on his heels. Adah halted. Now she wasn't sure what to do.

Her abba laughed at Lamech. 'Don't be embarrassed, my friend. She's a beauty for sure, but she doesn't bite.'

Was the visitor nervous about meeting her? Lamech's mouth twitched into a smile. His surrounding beard was perfectly trimmed.

Abba skittered behind the man, placed a hand on his back and gave him a nudge. 'You two must walk together; get acquainted. Adah, why don't you give Lamech a tour of our smallholding? It's nothing compared to his vineyards and properties I'm sure, but we love our land. I will follow along behind – eyes open, but not ears.' He chuckled.

'Of course, Abba,' Adah stammered. Lamech moved closer until she could have touched his cloak. 'This way, please.'

She turned and headed back the way she'd come, feet protesting at having to walk again when she'd only just returned from the well. *Stop it*, she told them. *This is important.*

Lamech walked beside her silently, though she could hear his steady gait. Steadier than her abba's, who scampered everywhere like he was in a constant hurry. What was Lamech doing here... was it what she thought? If so, why hadn't Abba mentioned his friend before?

'I was sorry to hear about your ima,' Lamech said. She almost jumped as his voice broke into her musings. 'It must have been difficult for you.'

Despite herself, Adah wanted to look at him. Peeling her eyes from the ground, she allowed them their desire. His dependable ones returned her gaze.

'Thank you. It has been.'

'Of course. I feel... inappropriate, intruding upon you so soon into your time of mourning. Yet, Shimiel insisted I visit when I met him the other day.'

Met him for the first time, or met him again? Adah scanned her memory for a time when Abba had been gone. Since the funeral, he'd only been out once that she could recall. He'd visited Chanoch the previous week – the elder the city was named after.

'Did you meet him at Chanoch's?' Though she didn't know him very well, Adah liked Chanoch. He'd always been kind to her and had never made her feel uncomfortable. He was the oldest person she knew – at least six hundred, Abba said. If Lamech was a friend of Chanoch's, then he should be a good man.

'Yes. I was seeking his advice on a matter of business when your abba arrived to do the same. We immediately got along.'

So, it *was* the first time they'd met. She didn't know what business her father might be asking advice about. Nothing had changed in their situation for years.

'These are our goats,' she said, having reached the pen. She bent to tug some ivy from the rough stone wall then leaned over it, beckoning to her favourite. The nanny goat jumped off her perch and came for the snack.

Lamech chuckled. 'She likes you. She's clearly a good judge of character.'

Adah felt her cheeks warm. 'I reared this one by hand, that's all.'

They kept strolling around her father's land until the sun was high in the sky and Adah sought the shade of their orchard. As Lamech relaxed, he graced her with his full attention, and when he smiled, Adah had to look away to prevent herself grinning like the madwoman who sat beside the pool near the city gate. When she glanced back at her abba, he gave her a brief wave before pretending he wasn't watching.

She mustered the courage to ask Lamech about his business. Having no siblings, she had learnt to talk to adults early in her life, and though she rarely felt comfortable with strangers, she knew people always liked talking about themselves, so she kept a set of questions ready. After all, the more others talked, the less she had to.

Lamech was no exception. He grew animated as he described his vineyard – apparently his pride and joy – and his flourishing construction business. He told her of his idea to start building houses for people who didn't want to construct their own.

'Won't that lessen the skills of our people?' Adah asked then felt embarrassed for doing so.

'On the contrary,' Lamech replied, unperturbed. 'If my workers build people's houses, those men have more time to concentrate on the skills they really enjoy and get better at them.'

As they ascended the last hill before their land ceased, and the land of Eliana's parents began, Abba's favourite tree came into view. A pomegranate.

'It looks like they're ripe. May I?' Lamech reached up and cradled one of the fruits in his hand.

Adah smiled. 'Oh yes; they are delicious.'

Giving the fruit a gentle twist, Lamech pulled it down, broke it in half and handed one part to her.

She nibbled the sweet seeds, trying not to let the juice run down her chin. 'This tree has been in our family for generations. It's very special to Abba.'

'Special and delightful. Just like you.'

She was sure her face matched the colour of the seeds.

When they arrived back at the hut, Lamech took his leave.

'Won't you stay, my friend? Adah will make us a meal,' her abba said.

'Thank you, but I must return to work. However, I would like to call again. Perhaps you can join my family for Shabbat?'

'We would be delighted. Wouldn't we, Adah?'

Adah's heart quickened. 'Of course.'

'Excellent. I will inform my ima. She enjoys any opportunity to show off her cooking. If I have time, I'll return before then to confirm the arrangements.' After tilting his head her way one last time, Lamech turned and descended the hill towards the city. With each step, his presence diminished and left Adah feeling cooler. When just his broad shoulders and shining hair were visible, Abba spoke.

'Well?'

Adah's heartbeat hadn't quite calmed. 'What do you want me to say, Abba?'

'Do you like him?'

Adah searched her father's face. She hadn't seen him this excited for a long time. The pressure of Ima's illness overwhelmed her again – not just the burden that had weighed her down, but the one that had dampened Abba's spirits as well. Was Lamech what they needed to finally be released from the pain? She grasped his hands, lifting them to her lips and kissing them.

'Yes, Abba,' she replied. 'I like him.'

ELIANA PUSHED ASIDE the beautifully woven linen hanging over the entry to her home and narrowed her eyes. 'You look different.'

It was the day after Adah met Lamech and, desperate to tell her friend the news, she'd left home early in the morning to visit. Having arrived, she didn't know where to start. She pursed her lips, trying not to give anything away.

'Something has happened.' Eliana balanced a baby on her hip; the little girl was just old enough to stay there with a single arm wrapped around her waist.

'Oh Mela, look at you.' Adah pulled the babe from her friend's arms and showered her with kisses. 'She's grown so much!'

'Stop avoiding my questions.'

'You didn't ask me any questions.'

Eliana stepped back, letting Adah inside. 'You know what I mean.'

Adah sat on a stool beside the loom, jiggling little Mela on her knee. Eliana's home was simple, much like hers, though it was inside the city. She had a good position though, atop a hill, and a small yard outside where a fire usually burned. The only luxuries were the beautiful fabrics, for Eliana's husband was a weaver and evidence of his profession hung from the walls and beams.

'I would say your ima's passing has changed you, but you look too happy for that,' Eliana probed.

Adah smiled. 'Abba introduced me to a man yesterday.'

'So soon?' Eliana put a hand on the hip where her babe had sat.

'I was surprised too.'

'But not surprised enough to be upset.'

'No.' Adah grinned and blew a raspberry on Mela's neck, producing a fit of giggles.

'Oh. You are incorrigible! Shall I have to wring it out of you?' Eliana grabbed a cushion and plonked herself on the floor. 'Tell me everything. I probably know him, and I can give you my opinion.'

'I have no doubt you'll do that.' Adah laughed. 'His name is Lamech.'

'Lamech?' Eliana stroked her chin, thinking. 'Is he old?'

'No. I mean, older than me, but perhaps thirty or forty – no more. He's the son of Methushael and Noa.'

'Methushael?' Eliana whistled. 'But they live on the east side of the city. They are *wealthy*, Adah.'

'I know. Lamech has his own vineyard. And some sort of construction business.'

Eliana's brows drew together.

'What is it?' Adah's voice rose. 'You know him. You disapprove…'

'I don't know Lamech. But I know of Methushael. I am just surprised, that's all.'

'Because he's wealthy?'

Eliana shrugged. 'I didn't think your abba valued such things. I would have thought integrity was more important to him.'

'It is. I'm sure their wealth is incidental. He met Lamech at Chanoch's.'

'Oh. Well, I suppose that makes more sense.'

Curiosity caused Adah to lean forward. 'Is there anything else you've heard?'

Eliana shifted about. 'I haven't had anything to do with them. They are in a different, what might you call it – social circle – to my friends. Certainly, there have been whispers about some of Methushael's activities. But that might have nothing to do with his sons. And I don't think Lamech is the eldest.'

'No. He has an older brother.'

'Hmmm. Well, I'll do some research tomorrow at the well. Though I'm sure your abba will have done his own.'

'Perhaps. But he hasn't been out much in the last few years and has little to do with the city folk. Still, given how cautious he's been in the past, I doubt he would throw me to the wolves so swiftly.'

'No, indeed; he would never do that. So, tell me what Lamech is like. You must be interested, or you wouldn't have that look on your face. Is he as *robust* as his name would suggest?' Eliana giggled.

'Very *robust*.' Adah bit on her lip, trying to suppress her own giggle. 'He has broad shoulders, strong arms, and lovely eyes. He seems so accomplished, so... secure. And his smile...' She could feel her cheeks warming even though she had nothing to be embarrassed about in front of her dearest friend. 'He is quite the most handsome man I've seen, Eliana. Added to which, he was kind, funny and intelligent. If a little overconfident.'

'I would think I'd be overconfident if I had such remarkable qualities,' Eliana smirked.

'But you are! And you do. And I love you so.' She grasped her friend's hand and squeezed it. Then dribble wet her shoulder as Mela chewed it.

'She's hungry,' Eliana said. 'She's so even-tempered, the only way I know is when she starts eating me. She never cries unless she's hurt.'

'She is wonderful, just like her ima,' Adah replied, passing the babe back for a feed.

Adah remained with Eliana for some time, enjoying the respite from farmwork and the renewed companionship. But her thoughts kept drifting to the man she'd met the previous day and by mid-afternoon, she'd decided to leave.

'Lamech said he might visit again, and I wouldn't like to miss him,' she explained as she excused herself, ready to make the long walk home.

CHAPTER 4

Lamech didn't visit again before Shabbat, but a messenger confirmed their invitation. It was only three days, but it seemed to last a lifetime as Adah waited to see him.

A servant met Adah and her abba at the western gate and led them to Lamech's family home. They crossed the city, passing by the marketplace and the elders' square before they reached the eastern side, where large stone houses were being built for the city's increasingly wealthy inhabitants, in stark contrast to the simple huts in the northern area where Eliana lived. Ornate pillars marked the entrance of Methushael's house, displaying carvings of wild beasts and pine trees, as if inviting guests into the mountain forests rather than a home.

Adah ran a finger along the carvings as a guard showed them through the gateway into a courtyard. 'What is that for?' she whispered to her abba, pointing at the huge, wooden gate leaning against the inner wall.

'It's for the entrance. The gatekeeper must slide it across the ground with all his strength to let people in and out. A needless hassle if you ask me.'

And very strange. At the city gate, men just stood in the way. 'Why does the gatekeeper need a weapon?' she asked, noticing the spear he carried.

'As you can see, Methushael has become rather wealthy. Not everyone likes it, so he guards his property from those who might threaten it. Lamech was telling me how his ima worries. He seems to be very fond of her.'

Isn't everyone fond of their ima?

'Shimiel. Adah. Welcome!' Lamech stood in the courtyard waiting for them. The sun was shining behind his head, casting him partly in shadow. Clearly more comfortable in his own home, he strutted over and embraced them both with a kiss. As his beard tickled her cheek, Adah's stomach fluttered.

'My ima is desperate to meet you, Adah. Come, I will take you straight to her.' Lamech tucked her arm into his. She hesitated, glancing at her father. How strange that Lamech should be so bold. However, Abba was happily wiggling his eyebrows and as Lamech led her away, he scampered along behind them. Adah almost laughed.

After passing through another archway to their right, they reached an open courtyard garden where a woman bedecked in a striped tunic and turban stood in the centre surrounded by servants. Tendrils of light, curly hair peeked out from her turban and floated down her neck, which an elaborate copper necklace adorned. She turned as they entered.

'Lamech. Is this her? Well now—' Lamech's mother stepped forward with arms wide. She briefly glanced back and waved at the waiting servants – 'Go! Do what I have said!' – then faced Adah again. 'Come here, my child. Let me have a good look at you.'

Lamech chuckled. 'Ima, behave yourself. Adah's father, Shimiel, is here also.'

'Of course, Shimiel. I believe we met some years ago. It is a pleasure to see you again. What a beautiful daughter you have.'

'Indeed, I have, Noa. I think we met before she was born. And the pleasure is all mine, of course.'

Noa surveyed Adah's figure, then ran her hands over her soft, sprung hair, continuing to trace the line of her face. Finally, she tilted Adah's chin so their eyes met. Glints of mischief and approval sparkled.

'Very good. Very good,' Noa concluded.

Adah glanced at her father again, who winked. Then Noa grasped her arm, pulling her towards the centre of the garden. 'You must come and see this. It's my favourite spot in the whole city. Sit.' Adah obediently lowered onto a bench and Noa joined her. 'Look up!'

Adah gasped. It was a walled garden, and the walls extended the height of two men. From them, weeping plants cascaded down, covering the stone in maroon and violet flowers. Water also trickled from above, bringing life everywhere it touched.

'How—?'

'My husband built the house into the cliff face. There are beds of soil on top of the walls. I commissioned men to find me plants that would grow there. They have journeyed all over Nod, selecting the best varieties for me. Isn't it wonderful?'

'It is. Breathtaking.'

'My son could build you this.'

Lamech's voice was at her shoulder. 'Ima!'

'It's true. Why not say it? You have an even better head for these things than your abba. Just don't tell Methushael I said so.'

'I meant assuming...'

'Oh, don't be ridiculous. Adah doesn't mind, do you?' Noa grasped her arm tighter. 'You are beautiful, and he is handsome. Don't you think my son is handsome?' Adah's mouth fell open. 'Of course you do. Lamech! I like her already more than I can say—'

'And you say much, Ima.'

'Ha! See how he abuses me. I hope your sons never treat you this way, Adah.'

'Ima, is there nothing in the kitchens requiring your attention?'

'He is embarrassed by me, see?' Noa sighed, rolling her eyes. 'Then again, I should return to the preparations. No one can be trusted to get it right unless I am hovering over them. I will see you at the meal table – daughter.' Noa stood and dropped a kiss on Adah's cheek.

'Ima,' Lamech cried. 'We have only known each other a few days.'

'Nonsense. She will be my daughter soon enough.'

With that declaration, Noa left the garden in a flurry. The space immediately altered without her.

Lamech sat beside Adah and dropped his face into his hands. 'I'm so sorry. She is... she is... ah!' He exhaled.

Adah pursed her lips, trying not to laugh. But a giggle soon escaped, and her hand flew to her mouth. Lamech studied her. His eyes began dancing as he saw the amusement in hers. More giggles escaped. Then Lamech's booming laugh filled the garden.

'You like her?' He wiped his eyes.

'She's wonderful.'
'Only when she likes you. Get on the wrong side of her and she is fierce.'
'I can imagine. What is your father like?'
Lamech's eyes widened. 'Oh, he is... well, you will see soon enough.' Lamech's gaze flickered beyond, then he reached for her hand, brought it to his lips and kissed the end of her fingers. His eyes suddenly burned with intensity.
A cough came from behind them. Adah jumped.
'Should we be going inside now, Lamech?' her abba asked.
Lamech jumped up. 'Of course. My apologies. Follow me.'

They entered the main house, and a room large enough for twenty persons or more. Patterned mats were rolled out around low tables and several people were already reclined, chewing on flatbread or olives. It was cool, and lamps flickered along the walls. How strange when the sun was glorious outside. Why did they hide in here?

Several people turned their heads as they approached. They varied in age, but most were of Lamech's generation. A young woman with ornately-dressed hair reclined at one end on several cushions. Lamech motioned as he introduced his family. 'That's my sister, Dinah. To her left is my favourite brother, Bekhor. My other brothers sit opposite, then on that end, my grandfather. The rest are stragglers.' He grinned.

None of them rose to greet her except the eldest, Lamech's grandfather. He hobbled over saying, 'Welcome, Shimiel. And your daughter, welcome. It's good to see you back in the city.'

'Yes, cousin. It's been some time,' her abba responded.

Almost everyone in the city were cousins of some description, but Lamech's grandfather looked at least four hundred, a fair amount older than her abba. Either he or Lamech's father, Methushael, must have waited some time to have their children. Unless Methushael was the youngest of many. Adah didn't know, but none of Lamech's siblings looked older than one hundred.

'I was sorry to hear about your wife,' the grandfather continued. 'She was taken far too young.'

'Indeed, she was. My heart might have departed with her, were it not for my daughter.'

'She is a good girl?' The older man considered Adah kindly.

'The very best.'

'Come, sit by me,' he said to Shimiel. 'We have much to catch up on.'

Adah didn't recognise any of Lamech's wider family, though her father had so many relatives that she couldn't possibly know them all. Though almost the entire city was related in some way, a few had found wives or husbands from other people groups. Abba being one. When she'd asked him if they were closely related to Lamech, he'd said they weren't.

Lamech and Adah sat on a mat to the grandfather's left. Lamech's sister – Dinah, with the elaborate hair – was scrutinising them, but trying to conceal it.

'What is the order of your siblings? Are any of them married?' Adah asked Lamech.

'Yes, Bekhor – though his wife never joins us, preferring to stay home with her many children. My other brothers are younger than me. Dinah is married, though. She's carrying a child but doesn't show it yet. Her husband has gone off to fight.'

'To fight?'

'He decided he wanted a piece of ground in the north that belonged to an Iradite. Who knows why? Once he got it in his head, he gathered men together to go and fight for it.'

Adah gasped. 'Fight for a piece of ground? Isn't there enough for everyone?'

Lamech put a finger to his lips. 'Of course,' he whispered. 'But Barsabas is a fool. My father chose him for Dinah because he's influential and wealthy. Not because he's wise.'

'Did Dinah want to marry him?'

'I don't know. I suspect not, but she had no choice.'

Adah glanced at Dinah. Tears sprang to her eyes. *To be forced to marry such a man? Poor Dinah!*

'My grandfather isn't happy either. That land belonged to his kinsman. He dislikes Barsabas as much as the rest of us. Only my father admires Barsabas' tenacity.' There was a hint of acid in Lamech's voice.

He soon changed the subject to his brothers, while Adah continued to study the scene. The decoration and fine clothing were impressive, yet several of the men wore expressions that made her want to hide behind her abba.

'Is Methushael not here?' Adah asked, just as Noa entered.

'Welcome family, guests, soon-to-be-family,' Noa said, winking at Adah. 'Dinner is served. Enjoy!' She lowered herself with a flourish at the central table – the place next to her notably empty.

'He should have been,' Lamech murmured. Before long, servants entered carrying various dishes of exquisitely cooked vegetables, breads of all shapes and sizes and some meats. Other people also joined them around the low tables. Adah noticed the elder, Chanoch, and they shared a smile.

'Why do you pick at your food?' Lamech asked after a while. 'Are you unwell?'

'Oh, no.' Adah responded. 'I'm just not used to eating such rich things on Shabbat. We usually have something simple prepared the day before. Do you always spend Shabbat this way?'

'Yes. Ima believes that for everyone to rest they should be made as comfortable as possible. Which to her means stuffing them full.' He grinned. 'Yet, you seem troubled?'

'I was just wondering when the servants get to rest.'

Was that a flicker of anger in Lamech's features? No, she must be mistaken.

'Don't worry yourself about them. They are paid well for their services and rest at other times. They are all here by choice.'

'Of course.' She inwardly cursed her wayward tongue. 'I would never suggest otherwise.'

Lamech's sparkle returned, and he smiled brilliantly, extinguishing her concern. Adah didn't look down as he took her fingers in his but kept her eyes focused on the room, trying to think of something harmless to say, as his touch battled with her breathing.

When he had finished eating, Lamech rose to greet others. Adah exhaled in relief, grateful she didn't have to talk for a while, until Chanoch came and sat beside her.

'It seems so long since I saw you, Adah. How are you? Oh…' Chanoch shook his head and partly closed his wrinkly eyelids. 'Dear me. That is a thoughtless question. I'm sure you cannot answer given the circumstances.'

'It is a little hard to answer,' Adah confided. 'The past few weeks have held such sorrow and confusion.'

The wrinkles around Chanoch's eyes deepened. 'Of course they have. To lose a mother is a terrible thing.'

'Have you lost a mother?'

'Oh, no, I have not. My mother is well. Though I don't often see her.'

Of course, his mother is The Wanderer's wife. How could I forget? I wonder if Chanoch would let me meet them…

'So, what brings you to Methushael's house today? I haven't seen you here before.'

'Lamech invited us.'

'Ah yes, Lamech.' Chanoch ran a hand through his beard.

'And you? Do you often come here? How is your wife – is she here also?' Adah didn't know Chanoch's wife well, for she was often confined to her bed.

A glimmer of sadness reached his kind face. 'Sadly, no. Her health wouldn't allow it. I come occasionally, just to keep an eye on things, you know.'

Adah wasn't sure she did know. There was a moment of silence while she ploughed her mind for further conversation. 'I understand Lamech met Abba at your house?'

'Indeed. Though it was quite unplanned,' Chanoch mumbled, 'Unfortunate perhaps—'

Adah caught the unintended words. 'How so?'

'Hmm?' Chanoch looked up.

'Why unfortunate?'

'I… I don't know… I don't know why I said that—' Chanoch closed his mouth and smiled, though it seemed forced. 'Perhaps a better question is, do you like Lamech, my dear?'

Her eyes flickered to where Lamech stood, strikingly visible against the backdrop of strangers. 'I do.'

'Then I suspect there's nothing more to say.' Chanoch patted her arm. 'Perhaps Yahweh has plans I'm not privy to.'

Chanoch dropped eye contact and began a conversation with her father. Adah returned to picking at her food, though she wanted to ply him with many more questions. *Is there something wrong with Lamech? What do you have to keep an eye on? And where is Methushael?*

CHAPTER 5

Soon a commotion from behind caught Adah's attention. She turned to witness a man entering the hall. He looked like Lamech, though she could tell he had a smaller stature beneath his excess of grotesque animal skins. Noa rose to greet him, and they kissed in front of everyone. Adah's face grew hot at the display. *This must be Methushael.*

After pulling back from his wife, Methushael scanned the room, fixing each of his guests with a stare. When he reached Adah, his eyes narrowed, flickered to her abba, and back to her. Then they burrowed deep inside her, like a worm getting to the thick of the soil. She feared his scrutiny would reach the centre of her soul.

Noa stole her husband's attention away. 'My dear, you're late. Come, sit and eat.' They reclined together, and Adah caught whispered rebukes about *working* and *Shabbat*. She paid them little heed, for she felt sure Methushael had left a gaping hole in her for everyone to see.

Adah remained conscious of Methushael throughout the next course, though each time he looked her way, his persistent wife reclaimed his notice with an anecdote. She longed for the reassuring touch of Lamech's hand, but he hadn't returned. He was hovering, trying to approach his father, but Methushael had turned away. Lamech's younger brothers snickered, then Dinah raised a delicate hand, beckoning her. Should she rise?

As she shuffled in indecision, Abba's firm hand warmed her arm.

'Stay with me,' he murmured.

Adah hadn't realised he was paying attention, but Chanoch and Lamech's grandfather had both moved on, and they were alone. She glanced at Dinah with an apology. Dinah shot a derogatory look back before joining her brothers' sneers.

'They all hate me,' Adah whispered.

Abba shook his head, rejecting the notion with no proof otherwise, for what had been awkward before was unbearably tense since Methushael had entered. As the servants cleared the tables, Adah looked around for Lamech. *Where is he? I need him.* Her feet itched to flee. She was on the verge when the servants brought fruit and yogurt.

This time Adah ate her fill, glad for the distraction. Just as she was devouring the last sweet mouthful, an upheaval broke out. She glanced to her right. Methushael was no longer with Noa. He had risen, and now pushed a serving girl out of the way in his haste. Heavy footsteps clomped behind her. Then different footsteps. Then the clash.

'Abba.' Lamech's voice spoke behind her. Hushed, but within earshot.

'I have nothing to say to you. Move aside.'

'Abba. Will you not greet them?'

'Certainly not.'

'But everyone is watching.' Lamech's tone changed as he pleaded.

'Precisely.'

More shuffling. 'You must acknowledge her. She is our guest. Ima has welcomed her.'

Methushael's breaths came loud and heavy. 'Why would I welcome someone I expressly forbade you from entertaining? I am the head of this household, not your ima. Yet you insist on disobeying me. In front of the elders, no less.'

Methushael had forbade her entry?

'Please, Abba. Come speak with her. I'm sure she will change your mind,' Lamech quivered.

Methushael raised his voice. 'I do not want my mind changed!'

Heads turned, lips sneered and more narrowed eyes shot Adah's way. She stared at the table, trying to resist the urge to crawl beneath it. Might those eyes focus on the argument behind her, without knowing she was the subject?

Abba tried to distract her with some conversation, but she could not hear him. Methushael's voice dominated all others.

'Why would you consider marrying a woman whose mother bore no sons and died before she reached a hundred years? What if the daughter bears the same curse?'

Methushael's words hit Adah in the chest. Lamech swore and drove his fist into the wall. She cowered, squeezing her eyes tight. Why did he have to make a scene?

Lamech approached. She could feel the heat from his body, but she did not turn. He spoke her name. *Don't draw more attention. Just let me disappear.*

Abba came to her rescue. 'My dear, you know, I fancy another look at that garden. What do you say?' Adah nodded and grasped her abba's offered hand. He pulled her from the room and Lamech trailed behind them.

'Please don't listen to him, Adah,' said the voice at her shoulder.

She said nothing. When they were safely in the garden, her abba turned to face Lamech, tucking her behind him. 'What was the meaning of putting my girl through that humiliation? Never in my life have I experienced such disrespect.'

'I was trying to get him to acknowledge—'

'I know what you were trying to do, boy. But to bring my daughter here, to parade her around without your father's permission—'

Adah stifled a cry.

'See what you have done,' Abba said, taking her in his arms.

Lamech reached forward. 'Adah. Forgive me. I thought if he saw you, he would change his mind. Adah, please…'

Abba blocked his way. 'You will not touch her again. Not until you put this right.'

'Of course, Shimiel. Of course.' Lamech paced across the garden, rubbing his fist in his hand. 'I will. I promise.'

Adah leaned forwards. 'What if he's right, Abba? What if Methushael's right?' The thought of everyone judging her for her mother's failure was more awful than Methushael's stare.

Lamech strode to her side. 'He is not right. He is a fool.'

Her eyes widened. 'You would speak that way of your own father?'

'Only because it's true! Any man who doesn't love you is a fool.'

'Enough.' Tenderly holding her shoulders, Abba guided her towards the gate. 'I am disappointed in you, Lamech. I hoped I'd finally found someone worthy of my daughter. It seems I was mistaken.'

'Please, Shimiel. Give me a chance – time to win him round. Allow me to make it up to you.'

They paused at the exit, and her abba looked back. His chest heaved. 'That is up to my daughter. Adah?'

Adah pulled her eyes from the ground to study Lamech. He was altered from the confident man she had seen earlier. He no longer looked so secure, but shifted on his toes, his expression pleading. She realised how little she knew him or knew about him. Her parents had married for love and now Abba was blessing her with choice. A choice that women like Dinah never received.

Wisdom dictated she should turn away and not get involved with Methushael's family. But wisdom was not on Adah's side. For the heart can be treacherous and demanding. Though her abba gave her freedom, her heart did not. As she searched the depths of Lamech's earnest expression, the longing for companionship, and the addictive reaction of her body to his, let him in.

'Adah, will you give me another chance?' Lamech took one step forward. He restrained his hand from reaching out, but Adah felt it anyway. She felt it stretch and grasp the heart beating furiously in her chest. Lamech possessed her desire. There was no use fighting it. She was his.

Adah nodded. Yet all the walk home, she felt like a shattered piece of pottery. She couldn't allow herself to dream of the future they might have as she had done the previous days. She mustn't consider the home Lamech might build her, nor what it might feel like to snuggle into the warmth of his strong embrace. Although Lamech owned her heart, Methushael would never give his approval.

When she returned to their modest home, her mother's empty sickbed – still in place, for they'd not felt ready to move it – stared at her, cold and lifeless. Adah's old self would never have entertained the thought that Ima could betray her. Her new self did. For Ima had left her alone when she needed her the most – when she needed her to disclose what it was like to fall in love, and how she should behave with a man. And Ima's premature death, with its associated gossip, may have ruined Adah's chance at happiness.

CHAPTER 6

City of Chanoch, 750th year of Wandering

As Adah hides behind the ostentatious pillar in Lamech's colonnade, she wishes she had heeded that warning: the warning of Ima's cold, lifeless bed. She wishes she had paid more attention to the snickers, the stares and Chanoch's accidental slip. He'd known Lamech was no good for her but had let her walk blindly into the marriage.

No, not blindly. She had seen Methushael. She should have guessed what Lamech might become. Yet, she'd been so young. What was it Chanoch had said? 'Perhaps Yahweh has plans...'

I hope Yahweh has a plan now.

Though Adah's initial terror has eased, the risk of discovery isn't over. She must think straight. The corridors behind her are quiet. The only movement is the shadow of her favourite grasses dancing in the wind that sneaks into the courtyard. She prefers the grasses to the wondrous displays in her garden. Just one part of her beautiful home. A home she must flee.

Adah glances one last time behind her, then scurries into the courtyard, heading towards the gate. The gatekeeper is there, but thankfully, he's the one loyal to her.

'Is Shadow away?' she asks.

He leans against the gate, sliding it along its recently installed tracks. 'Yes, mistress. He's not here.'

The screech of metal on metal makes her wince. 'And Azurak?'

'I haven't seen him.'

She presses a gift into the gatekeeper's palm, knowing that in letting her escape, he is putting his own life in danger. Then she is out.

Flattening her back against the exterior wall of their complex, she closes her eyes, breathing steadily. *In - two, three, four... Out - two, three, four...*

Slowly, Adah reopens her eyes and peers into the darkness at both sides of the passageway. Clear. She tiptoes northwest, always warily surveying the landscape. After she's passed a few streets, her breathing steadies. She allows her mind to wander to her destination and her heart lifts.

It's going to be alright.

Loud, drunken voices break into the silence behind the next corner. A human barrier between Adah and safety. She peers around the right-hand wall, praying she won't be seen. A gleam of light from a doorway highlights a crowd of men.

One of them is Azurak.

CHAPTER 7

Countryside near Chanoch, 700th year of Wandering

As Adah glanced towards the hill's ascent, a figure emerged, gradually becoming more distinct against the backdrop of the incline in the late afternoon sun. *Lamech.*

Her heart flipped. He held a basket, and some cut flowers hung limply from his sweaty hand.

Adah was grinding flax seeds. She too was sweating – the exertion causing beads to drip beneath her tunic and gather on her brow. Indecision held her fast. Should she run inside and freshen herself? Where was Abba?

As if he'd heard her thoughts, Shimiel materialised from the back of the house and skittered out to meet Lamech. *Thank you, Abba.* Adah released the grinding stone and stole into their hut. She splashed water on her face, neck and underarms, then pulled on her only spare tunic. A brisk rub of thyme over her skin, and she was ready.

She peeked around the entrance. Her abba and Lamech were deep in conversation. Abba kept glancing towards the house before answering, as if anxious for her wellbeing. Love for him flooded her chest. Oh, her precious abba, who had kept her at home, refusing to sell her off to the highest bidder. Whilst her mother's illness had forced her to stay with him longer than she might have wished, she would never begrudge him that. He'd needed her, and she'd needed him. They'd made it through together. She suddenly realised the bittersweet nature of Lamech's courtship. If he succeeded, what would happen to her father? It was a question she needed to ask.

Abba stepped to the side, widening his arms. 'Adah,' he called.

She stepped out, ready to meet the man who'd claimed her heart. In the heat of their last exchange, he'd been fervent with his apology. Now he bore a timidity that didn't suit his robust figure. It was like he'd shrunk.

Lamech took two steps forward. Adah took three. They stood, considering each other.

'Well. Tell her then,' Abba said with a chuckle.

Lamech placed the basket down. It contained cheese, bread and fresh fruit. Presumably a gift from Noa. Then he held out the wilted flowers. 'I apologise,' he said, 'they looked beautiful when I bought them.'

Adah quirked a brow. He'd traded for flowers readily available on all the hillsides?

Lamech was waiting for her to take them. 'Thank you, they're lovely.' She gave them a sniff. They just about retained their scent. 'I'm sure a little water will revive them.' Should she get water now, or was he going to say something else?

Her suitor rocked on his heels, motioning towards the basket. 'My ima has advocated for you. She knows how to win my father around to her way of thinking. She is much better at it than me. Abba and I have never seen eye to eye—'

Adah tilted her head. Was he embarrassed Noa had succeeded where he had not?

'Anyway, he has now given his permission for me to court you. Will you consider me again, Adah? Or have I displeased you too much?'

Could it be true – Methushael had consented? She'd dared not hope for it. Now, all the dreams of the days before Shabbat flew back into her mind. She wanted to run into the hills and indulge them, but Lamech was waiting. He looked so peculiarly vulnerable that Adah couldn't help but smile. She'd better put him out of his misery. 'I would like you to court me again, if you think I am worth the trouble.'

Lamech's face transformed. He grinned widely and his confidence returned, swelling his frame back to broad. 'Yes,' he said. 'Yes!'

Unease crept back in, and Adah glanced at the flowers. 'Let me put these in some water before they lose all hope.' She retreated swiftly into the hut as the humiliation of the night at Methushael's house returned. It wasn't the best move, for there, the stare of Ima's empty bed beckoned. *What would Ima think of Lamech? Will I end up like her?*

Adah poured water from a large earthenware jug into a smaller vessel as slowly as possible, then took her time arranging the flowers.

'Adah? Are you well?'

She looked up. Lamech's shadowed form blocked the entrance. Concluding honesty was the only solution, she took a few steps towards him. 'What if your abba is right about me, Lamech? What if I am cursed?'

His hand reached for her face; his stone-roughened fingers felt like sand on the breeze. 'He is not right. How can you think that? I don't believe in curses or any other superstitious nonsense. You, Adah, are perfect.'

But The Wanderer is cursed. Don't you believe that? She wouldn't voice her thoughts. She didn't need Lamech thinking she had an unhealthy obsession with an old legend. 'I'm not so sure,' she said instead.

'I am sure. I am sure you will give me a horde of sons and live for fifteen centuries.' Lamech grinned.

'But what if your father doesn't like me?'

'He might be awkward for a while, but he'll come around. Besides, you have Ima on your side, and she is the one truly in charge. Adah, I don't care what my abba thinks – I love you.'

'How can you know that after so little time?'

'I knew it the moment I laid eyes on you. You are the only woman for me. I could never love another.'

Tears threatened Adah's composure. What had she done to deserve such devotion?

Lamech stroked her cheek. 'I wish I could kiss you now.'

Adah almost gasped. Instead, her eyes flew to his lips. How delectably soft they looked. A pull she'd never experienced before drew her closer as Lamech's other hand reached the small of her back.

'You cannot, Lamech.' His name came out in a low groan. 'We must go back outside, or Abba will be angry.'

'Mmm...' He drew nearer, getting dangerously close to her face. Then he stopped. 'You are right.' After turning abruptly, he walked out.

Adah followed, hoping her cheeks weren't noticeably flushed. Abba watched them exit, with his brows drawn together in concern. He mouthed to her, *'Is everything alright?'* at which she nodded and smiled.

Lamech began to pace. Back and forth he went, churning up the dust. Once again, his distress was almost comical. Then he turned to her. 'Adah. Agree to marry me! Please. I cannot leave here until you say yes.'

Her chest tightened. He looked so fervent, so sincere; it was endearing. 'I already agreed you can court me, Lamech.'

'That is no longer enough. Say you'll marry me. We'll leave an appropriate time for you to mourn, of course. I can build our home while I wait. You must instruct me – I will give you anything you want. A garden better than Ima's. Name it and I will do it. Please, Adah.'

Adah glanced at her abba. He shrugged as if to say, *'It's your choice'*.

Her parents had loved each other deeply. She'd seen the devotion in their eyes, and in every touch. Lamech's dependable eyes held the same devotion. His touch was tantalising. Pushing aside all cautionary whispers that tugged at her heart, and all notions that this decision would change her life forever, she gave free rein to the excitement rippling through her. Here was her future.

'Alright. I agree.'

Lamech's face lit up. He reached forward, put his hands on her hips and lifted her, swinging her around like she was a little girl in her abba's arms. Adah laughed, letting her joy soar through the landscape and dance high into the hills. When he put her down, she gazed into his eyes once more. As his hand caressed her face, she believed no love could be sweeter.

'I must show you my vineyard!' Lamech declared. 'Will you come with me?'

'Now?'

'Yes, now. I want you to love it as I do.'

'But I was in the middle of—' Adah gestured to the grinding stone. 'And I have not made this evening's meal or collected the eggs.'

'Then I will help you.'

'Really?'

Lamech nodded, his face still beaming. 'Don't think me useless, Adah. I am perfectly capable of doing all your tasks. Just give me the order and I will obey like a humble servant.'

Adah giggled as Lamech ran over to the grinding stone and began scraping the seeds.

'Not like that. You will send them all over the ground.' She pulled his arm away, surprising herself with her confidence.

Remembering her father again, she turned to him. 'Do you have time to accompany us?'

'Not today, no.' His brows had drawn together and he wore a frown. Adah dropped her hands, realising he was unhappy with something. Had she acted inappropriately? Had Lamech?

'Excuse me. I have tasks I must address inside,' she said, then escaped once more. Let Abba take up his concerns without her. That was safer.

Although her heart longed for her beloved, Adah dragged out a few tasks as long as possible. She knocked back some dough and shaped it, then arranged the flowers several times, playing with the colours. After a while, she heard voices that sounded pleasant once more and deemed it safe to return to the men.

Abba immediately put her out of her misery. 'I will accompany you while Lamech is here helping with your chores, but the vineyard will wait until we next visit Methushael. I want to speak with Lamech's parents before proceeding further with this arrangement. And, in future, Lamech must ensure a suitable escort is present when he spends time with you.'

Adah glanced at Lamech. His earlier timidity had gone, and he did not look ashamed. Either he was brazen, or her abba was unusually kind. Knowing the latter to be true, she threaded her arms around her father's neck and kissed his cheek. 'Of course you are right, Abba. Thank you.'

CHAPTER 8

When Adah married Lamech three seasons later, he'd already constructed a dual-roomed house, situated on a huge plot adjacent to the south-eastern city wall, which looked out over his vineyard. Delight dominated their early years and Lamech soon extended the dwelling into the elaborate home he'd promised. He proved himself devoted, showering Adah with gifts, praising her to all his friends and giving her plentiful attention when he was home.

Yet Adah didn't quite know what to do when he wasn't there. Used to working hard, she disliked idleness, but Lamech employed servants for the daily chores and forbade her from doing them. So Adah visited Eliana frequently and also insisted her servants were given the day off on Shabbat. Lamech agreed to the latter on the condition they went to his parents' house, so he could follow his mother's tradition of feasting on the last day of the week. In this way, and others, they came to compromises and were happy.

Even Methushael behaved himself. Aside from a few scornful looks in Adah's direction – particularly at her breasts and midriff – he tolerated her presence.

'He will love you as soon as you produce a son, never fear,' Noa told Adah confidently soon after her wedding.

'But why should a son be so important? Why not a daughter?' Adah had asked, twirling one of Noa's flowers in her fingers. She'd never heard of one child being more valued than another.

'Methushael has visions of grandeur, my dear. I thought you would have gathered that by now. He wants many heirs to carry his name well into the future. Girls will not carry his name, you see.'

Noa sighed. 'My husband wasn't always this way, but success has filled his head with importance, I'm afraid. It is up to us women to keep these men firmly grounded – not always an easy task, I can tell you.'

'You seem to have achieved it remarkably well. I fear I don't have your strength.'

'Nonsense. You have spirit, my girl. I saw it in your eyes as soon as I met you. It's why I fought for you.'

This pleased Adah. She had worried it was just her looks that impressed Noa, seeing as she'd barely uttered a word during their first meeting. As time went on, the grief for her own ima slowly became less raw and she increasingly appreciated the astuteness of Lamech's mother. Though, she never felt entirely comfortable in Noa's presence. She couldn't share with her the depths of her heart, nor the fact that when she tried to 'keep Lamech grounded', it seemed to anger him. Noa invariably defended her son.

As for her abba, Adah needn't have worried. Though she'd invited him to live in her new home, he politely declined.

'You don't need an old thing like me getting in the way,' he'd said. 'Besides, who would look after the farm?'

'You're not old, Abba. You have barely reached your ninetieth year. Besides, the farm is too much for one man.'

'I shall not leave it, Adah. It is our family's ground. It will belong to your children one day. I'll hire help when I need it.'

He did so, though Adah didn't know how he could afford to; so, she went to help once or twice a week, enjoying the break from the boredom of kicking around a large house on her own.

Once Lamech created a garden space, Adah relocated her favourite goat to her new home and made it a special pen in the garden using woven hazel branches foraged from the woods a short walk away. When Lamech brought home some other goats after a successful trade, Adah at last had enough to keep her occupied. Unfortunately, elaborate planting became impossible. Every time the goats escaped, which was often, they ate almost everything, much to Noa's disgust.

'They devoured the palms I gave you,' she exclaimed one day.

Adah felt her cheeks warm as Noa inspected the garden, noticing plant after plant that was missing.

'You will have to control them better when you have a little one,' Noa tutted, her eyes flickering to Adah's slim waist. She said nothing more, but the comment hovered between them.

Around five years after Adah and Lamech wed, her abba rather shyly confessed he was marrying again. 'It's not that I didn't love your ima. It just gets lonely out here.' He scratched his beard. 'Rivkah is a good woman. I've known her all my life. She was recently widowed too.'

'Of course, I wouldn't think you didn't love Ima.' Adah took his hand and squeezed it. 'I know how much you loved her. I'm pleased for you, Abba. I remember Rivkah with fondness. She used to make raisin cakes and slip them to me when I was a girl.'

Her father laughed, commented on how good those raisin cakes still were, and they shared a prolonged embrace.

When Adah had been married eight years, her father had another child – a son. Perhaps it was the birth of Shimiel's son which sent Lamech over the edge of reason. Or perhaps Methushael was putting pressure on him behind the scenes. Either way, everything changed that year.

One night, the sudden crash of the outer door being kicked jolted Adah awake. Something in the hallway tumbled and smashed. She reached an arm across the bed. Lamech's side was cold. It was him then, coming home drunk. It happened often, but this time, he seemed more intoxicated than usual. He sang so loudly, the words carried to her bed.

My woman came home
With a behemoth bone,
I asked her how she had come by it.
She said that a man
Had asked for her hand,
And then she'd kicked up a riot.
'Married I am! And married I'll be
Unless something grand you acquire for me.
If you want my breasts,
I'll not settle for less,
Than a brilliant behemoth bone!'

Adah covered her ears as the song went on, becoming lewder with each verse. Lamech continued to clatter about. Eventually, he entered their bedchamber.

'Woman!'

Adah sat up and removed her hands from her ears. 'Yes, Lamech.'

'I want something to eat. Where are the servants?'

'They are in bed. It's halfway through the night.'

'Tell them to get up.'

'I shall not. I will get you food myself.' Adah staggered out of her low, wooden bed, rubbing her eyes.

As she passed Lamech, he grabbed her arm. 'Woman. I told you to wake the servants. You are my wife; you do not work.'

Adah took a deep breath and focused on his face. He was not in his right mind; perhaps she should do as he said. Yet, if she didn't stand up to him now, it might set a precedent. And, despite the tight grip on her arm, he had never hurt her before. Pushing down her indignation, she smiled, leaned forward, and kissed him gently on the lips.

'It would be my pleasure to serve you, my love.' She kissed him again. Lamech yanked her closer. His hands ran over her nightdress, his desire evident. Then Adah remembered. She mentally kicked herself as she drew away.

'My love, let me get you something to eat.'

Lamech groaned. 'Alright. I'm famished. That useless foreman of ours provided wine at his party, but no food. However, once I have eaten, we will have our fun.'

Adah smiled an apology, touching his arm gently. 'I cannot tonight, my love. The way of women is upon me.'

The face that had softened at her touch suddenly changed. Fury flashed across Lamech's eyes.

Pushing her away, he turned and slammed his fist into a wall. 'You bleed again. What is wrong with you?'

Adah moved past him, not wanting this conversation while he was inebriated. She padded down several steps into an antechamber, pulled out bread from a stoneware crock, and began breaking it. The downside of a large house was the distance to the main kitchen, but knowing Lamech's habits, Adah always kept food nearby.

In a flash, her husband was behind her, rubbing his hand. 'Why do you not answer me, Adah?'

'Because I don't know what I am supposed to say.'

Lamech grabbed her arm once more, hauling her around to face him. As her elbow caught on the work surface, she cried, 'Lamech! Please.' Never before had she seen his strength as a cause of fear, always as a comfort.

Her cry gave him pause. He released her and sighed. 'My abba says you are cursed; that I should have listened to him and not married you. Is he right, Adah?'

'Why would I be cursed? I have done nothing against Yahweh.'

Lamech coughed and spat on the ground. 'Why did your mother not have a son? Your father has one with another woman.'

'How should I know? Lamech, many people take years to conceive. It isn't unusual. Why does it even bother you? We are happy, aren't we? That should be all that matters. I love you, Lamech.'

His fierceness pierced her eyes, and the thick smell of wine on his breath churned her stomach. She blinked, gulped down any disgust and raised a hand to stroke his face, running her fingers around his cheek and into his beard. 'I love you, my husband. I-I love you...' She said it as much for herself, reminding her heart that once he hadn't believed his father's vitriol – had even called his abba a fool.

Lamech caught her hand. Drawing it to his lips, he kissed her fingertips one at a time. Adah relaxed again as his lips moved down her arm and groaned when he reached her neck.

'You are infuriating, woman,' he muttered. 'But despite this, I love you as well.'

Then he dropped her arm and stomped into the next room, collapsing on the bed fully clothed. Within moments, loud snores filled the room.

Adah replaced the bread into the crock. Her chest remained tight. She had a terrible premonition that the conversation was far from over.

CHAPTER 9

'm building you another garden!' Lamech declared when he returned from work the next day.

Adah looked up. She hadn't seen him since the previous night. He'd left for work before dawn, which had seemed odd given his extremely late night.

'Your goats are out of control. I know you love them, but you also want a garden like my ima's. So, I will build you another. What do you say?'

She smiled. The wine having worn off, he was once again his charming self, as if the previous night hadn't happened. 'That would be wonderful. But you will have to build a very high wall if you want to keep the goats out.'

Lamech's features broadened into a grin. 'Oh, I know. They can't bear being kept away from their mistress, just like I can't.' He stepped forward and swept her into his arms. Shivers ran her entire length as his lips caressed her and he murmured, 'Once these few days are over, I intend on filling your womb with my children. Do you object?'

'Not at all. Fill away.'

Lamech laughed. 'Good. Then when our children arrive, they can enjoy the new garden with their beautiful ima.'

Her husband made good on his promise, designing a garden more elaborate than the original. He created a new courtyard, entirely separate from the goats, which he banished to the area behind the kitchens. A new wall separated the garden from the main entrance, with access via a beautiful archway. At first, Adah feared walking under it – would the curved stone hold? In the centre of the garden Lamech created a pool, fed from the stream that provided their private water supply. The water supply particularly thrilled Adah – no more balancing jugs.

Unsurprisingly, Noa came regularly to inspect the work and boss the workmen around, particularly once planting began. Lamech himself was rarely on-site, always busy managing other jobs and far preferring time in his vineyard to hauling stone.

To escape boredom more than anything else, Adah often joined him at the vineyard. She loved climbing the watchtower. The view was spectacular, encompassing the dry plains of the east, the southern grasslands and the distant western mountains. She never looked behind at the city. The river sparkled at the edges of their land. Like his ancestors before him, Lamech knew well how to cultivate the ground, ensuring the continuous stream of water to his precious vines despite the red, flyaway soil.

Adah would watch him work – trimming here, tying there, plucking elsewhere – always relaxed, vibrant, and free. Occasionally, he would look up and wave at her, and her heart would fill with warmth and longing. If only he would be content to farm every day. But much as he loved the vineyard, he couldn't stop himself from directing business elsewhere. His mind was too active.

Lamech also made good on his intention to fill her with children. Her womb became another quest to conquer, another space to subdue. As promised, Adah did not object or resent his attitude, but chose to revel in the attention and join him in the quest. After another two seasons, their efforts finally proved fruitful.

'You haven't bled.' Lamech strolled into the room, rubbing his wet hair with a strip of linen. He came near the bed where she lay. 'I'm sure we've passed a new moon since. I'm right, aren't I? Answer me.'

Adah yawned and stretched her arms. His gaze was intense, but when she wrapped her arms around his neck and pulled him in for a kiss, he softened. 'I am late. But it's early days. Let's not jump ahead too soon, my love.'

'Of course. But is it safe to still, you know?'

Adah raised an eyebrow. He had never been bashful before. 'I don't know. Do you?'

'Didn't your mother tell you?'

'We never had that conversation before she passed. In fact, it was your mother who subjected me to a discussion before our wedding. Do you remember how meticulously she arranged every detail of our day? Part of that was pouncing on me, in front of her servants, when she realised I knew nothing.'

'Really?' Lamech's eyebrows raised. 'That does sound rather like Ima. But she didn't mention this?'

'No.'

'You should ask her then.'

Adah's cheeks warmed at the thought. If she asked Noa, their news would be paraded through Methushael's home in an instant. She thought fast.

'I will go to Eliana. I am due a visit anyway. She has many children so she will know. In fact, she used to love regaling me with details about marriage when I was far too naïve to understand what she was talking about.'

Lamech's nose twitched, but he didn't say anything. Instead, he grunted, pulled a tunic on and stumbled out of the doorway.

Adah visited Eliana that afternoon. The basket of provisions she carried to her less fortunate friend weighed heavy by the time she'd crossed the city and ascended the little hill to Eliana's humble home. Squeals and children's laughter greeted her as she approached.

'So, you're still alive then. I thought a bear might have had you for lunch,' Eliana called when she spied her. Several children gathered at her friend's feet. Another was throwing stones at the pigeons congregating in the small yard in front of the home. Eliana suspended a pot over the fire to boil, then pushed back the beautifully woven linen hanging in the entrance to the hut. 'Well, come in then, stranger.'

Adah smiled and kissed her cheek. 'It's good to see you too.'

After uncoupling a small girl from her waist and depositing her on the floor of the house, Eliana eagerly received the basket.

'Aunty Adah,' squealed Mela, running in and launching herself into Adah's arms. Now a girl of ten, she was vivacious, playful and a wonderful help to her mother, which was just as well considering how many children Eliana had. Adah counted three who'd followed them in, plus Mela and the one outside. There should be another somewhere...

'So, to what do I owe this visit?' Eliana asked, rifling through the gift. 'You didn't just come to bring us— Mmm, wine from Lamech's vineyard? Bread, cheese, dates... Perhaps you are a good friend, after all.' Eliana grinned.

Nerves gently tremored through Adah's gut. Lamech had kept her so busy, it had been a while since she'd visited. 'I have some news. Tentative news.'

Eliana stopped her rifling. 'Strip off your tunic.'

'Excuse me?'

'I want to see for myself. Come on. There's no danger of Manon walking in. He's never home before dusk.'

So, Eliana discerned exactly what her tentative news was. She shouldn't be surprised. Adah gingerly stripped and stood, feeling ridiculous parading her undercloth before the busy household.

'Hmm, how long?' Eliana strode around her with hand to chin.

'I am only late by a couple of weeks, at the most.'

Eliana put her hand into Adah's hip joint. 'Does that hurt?'

'No.'

'And this?' she poked the back of Adah's leg, under her buttock.

'Ow!'

'Good,' Eliana smiled.

Adah rubbed the sore spot. 'How is your hurting me *good*?'

Watching from a stool, Mela giggled.

Eliana then put both hands on either side of Adah's navel and massaged with her fingertips. 'It's far too early to see anything of course. But there is hope. Your hips have begun loosening. Do you feel nauseous?'

'No. But very thirsty. Is that relevant?'

'Perhaps. Some are constantly sick. But not me, so don't worry.'

'It's true,' Mela said. 'Ima never gets sick. We don't know about the babes until she gets fat.'

Adah blinked. 'Really? Don't you keep track of your—'

Her friend laughed. 'I am always expecting the next child before my body has the chance to bleed again. One of the benefits of so many pregnancies.'

'I wasn't expecting anything to show yet,' Adah confessed. 'Often women keep it hidden for a season or more. In fact, I intend to keep it quiet...'

'From Lamech?'

'Oh no, he has guessed already. He called me out this morning.'

Her friend's brows drew together. 'He won't keep it quiet.'

'But if there is a risk it's a false alarm, or something happens... I would rather nobody know.'

'Are you often late?'

'Never.'

'There you are then.' Eliana stopped her prodding and threw her arms around Adah's semi-naked form. 'Oh Adah, I'm so thrilled for you. I will see so much more of you when you are an ima, I'm sure.'

'Are you?'

'Oh yes. For you will join us – the women at the well. Won't you? We go there every morning. I know you don't need to get water yourself, but the children play, you see. It keeps them happy.'

'I would love to. If Lamech will allow it.'

'Why wouldn't he?'

'I don't know.' *He's just funny about things like that.*

'On the subject of water jugs, avoid carrying anything heavy until the baby arrives. You might injure your back.'

'Well, that's actually why I've come. May I get dressed?'

Eliana laughed again. 'Of course! Sorry.' She handed Adah her tunic. 'You are worried about your health?'

'Not mine. The babe's. Lamech wants to know if it's safe to...'

'To what?'

Her cheeks warmed as she slipped on her tunic. 'You know. Do what men and women do.'

Eliana lifted an eyebrow.

'In the bedroom.'

'Oh, Adah! You have just stood here naked before me. Why be so bashful? Oh, you are funny. I do love you.'

'Your children are present.'

'As they are *all* the time. Even after dark. Not all of us have a house like yours, my dear friend.' Eliana continued chuckling as she retrieved hot water and poured it over the tea.

'So... Is it safe?' Adah asked again as she received a cup and cradled it.

'It has never harmed ours. And there is no way Manon would wait that long, that often. I wouldn't worry. Let Lamech continue his fun. Though you could go to the healer if you are worried, I suppose. Oh, I forgot to tell you. Guess who I saw the other day?'

Adah shrugged.

'The Wanderer.'

Her heart quickened. 'The Wanderer! You did? When?'

'He came to Manon's stall. I happened to be there dropping off food as he was working late. I saw him, Adah.' Eliana took her arm. 'Manon stood there gawping like a lost rabbit, so *I* had to ask the man what he wanted. He said, "You are followers of Yahweh?" His voice was so deep I could practically feel the earth shake. When I nodded, he chose a wool tunic for his wife. Then he pointed to the kid goat tied up nearby and left. Just like that.'

'He paid with a goat? Not grain or fruit?'

'Of course not. He can't farm, silly. But Manon was thrilled with the goat. It was worth far more than the small tunic. I wonder why they didn't just make their own... Anyway, I digress.'

'No, tell me more!' Adah was desperate to know. *Was he as tall as everyone said? What colour was his hair now? What was his scar like? Did he have a look of kindness in his eyes or shame?* 'Tell me everything,' she pleaded.

With a sly grin, Eliana described him in detail: So tall – a head higher than Lamech – 'can you imagine?' His hair, as expected, had hints of red shining through the greying streaks. A long, unkempt beard – 'you would hate it, Adah' – but beneath that, a chiselled jaw; a handsome man still, even in his seven-hundreds. The scar was not as bad as everyone made out. 'One might not fixate on it unless so inclined. I would think it's quite a feature, really.'

'So, to you, it was a reminder of grace, not a curse?' Adah asked.

'He's still alive, isn't he? Now, how did I get onto the subject of The Wanderer...? Ah yes. Healers.'

'Healers?'

'His wife is a healer, remember?'

Adah did not. Her mother had barely spoken about the man's wife when relaying the bedtime tales.

'Well, she is. Awan – the mother of them all. Well, us all, of course. But especially the healers. The eldest trained directly under her, I believe. Anyway, if you are worried about your child, you could go to a healer just to make sure. That's all I meant to say before I got sidetracked.'

'I'm glad you did. Forgive me, but I am so envious. I wish I'd seen him.'

'I knew you'd feel that way,' Eliana chuckled. 'Now, back to Lamech. You must be pleased. This news will silence the gossipers.'

'I hope so. I thought everyone hated me the first time I met Lamech's family. Now they barely tolerate my presence. And the looks I get— I must pray it's a boy.'

'Why?'

'Methushael will not accept me until I produce a son.'

'Uh! What is wrong with that man? Praise Yahweh that Lamech doesn't take after his father.'

'Yes,' Adah whispered. 'Praise Yahweh.' *A name I have never heard my husband speak.*

CHAPTER 10

Adah prayed. As the weeks wore on with no sign of blood, she petitioned Yahweh daily for a boy. Sometimes Lamech walked in when she was on her knees next to their bed – arms wide and eyes towards the ceiling. He would kneel next to her and she'd thread her fingers into his as she prayed and he stroked her back. She felt closer to him in those moments than in their lovemaking. Perhaps he did trust Yahweh, though all supplications were hers. When her words ran dry, he would kiss her, working his way down from her lips to her swollen stomach, speaking to his *son* at the end.

'I'm so proud of you,' he murmured to Adah more than once as he made good on Eliana's assurances of the child's safety. Even so, he sent her to a healer, just to be sure.

'You are certainly carrying a child,' the woman said at last, once Adah had missed four bleeds, 'Can you feel anything yet?'

Adah shook her head.

'Not unusual at this stage. Some women feel nothing until they are halfway through the first time. Don't fear. You are young and healthy; the perfect abode for this little one.'

Adah tried not to fret, but when the fifth month passed with no movement from the babe within, vines of worry sprouted and curled through her mind.

'Your stomach is small,' the healer confirmed. She felt around Adah's belly, much like Eliana had done. 'Still no bleeding?'

'No.'

'And no pain beyond the expected discomfort?'

She wasn't sure what the expected discomfort was, but having no pain, shook her head.

'I wouldn't worry.' The healer patted her hand and handed her some fennel, mint leaves and ginger root, tied with twine. 'Make tea with these; they might get the little one moving. And rest. Sometimes we're so busy running around, we don't stop for long enough to feel what's within.'

I am not at all busy running around. I wish I was.

On returning home, she visited her goats. Though Lamech's workers had finished the new garden, and Noa's gardener had planted splendid multicoloured flowers from all over the east, Adah preferred the old one. She sat cross-legged on the ground and Berta, the goat she'd reared by hand – quite old now – joined her. Adah's lips twitched into a smile as her four-legged friend sat on her haunches like a man.

'They are beginning to accept me,' she confided to Berta, who stared back with amber eyes. 'Lamech's family, I mean. Last Shabbat, Methushael even patted my shoulder, though he wouldn't meet my eye. I suppose it's his way of showing approval. Yet I cannot help but feel…' She sighed and scratched Berta behind the ears. The nanny goat nudged her under the elbow. 'Something is not right, my dear. Something is not quite right.'

Her hand trembled as she drew it away. It happened often. 'I better make that tea.'

Nothing happened for the rest of that week. No bleeding, no flutters, nothing. Then the following Shabbat, sharp pains in her abdomen jarred Adah from slumber.

She bolted upright, clapping a hand to her mouth to squash a cry. On the bed beside her, Lamech lay on his front, fast asleep, with one hand grasping the bottom of her nightdress. She eased the fabric from his fist as the pain hit again.

Holding her breath, she reached for the edge of the bed, then, when the pain subsided, felt between her legs. Her nightdress was wet. Sticky.

Adah shuffled off the bed, a few hand spans from the floor. The moonlight shimmering through the opening in the wall had illuminated Lamech's pose, but it was too dark to reveal the colour of the sheet where she'd lain. She bent down to smell it. There could be no mistake.

Adah took a deep inhale. She placed a fist in her mouth. *Don't scream. Don't wail.* Releasing her hand to the floor, she bit down hard until she tasted iron – her lip now bled too. Desperate not to wake Lamech, she crawled across the floor, dragging her aching legs, then checked over her shoulder. He hadn't stirred, but a line of darkness snaked a thin trail from her clothing. She gasped. There was no escape. Death was stealing her unborn child.

Curling into a foetal position, she shook as another pain pierced her womb. Then the sobbing began. Tears joined blood as her groin continued its ceaseless ache. Loss – she would never hold her child. Anger – it would never suckle at her breast. Fear – what would happen with Lamech?

'Adah?'

He was awake. She shuddered, but with no strength to leave, she curled up tighter, trying to disappear.

'Adah?'

Lamech's arm wrapped around her side. He felt beneath her, then sniffed his hand.

As he kissed her forehead, he ignited a momentary flicker of hope. 'I'm going to get help. Don't move.'

As if she could.

By the time Lamech returned with the healer, the soft light of dawn had filtered into the room, highlighting the smears across the floor. A starkly visible, crimson accusation. Adah lay as he'd left her, with tears and blood congealing where she'd touched her clothes and hair. No amount of sunlight could warm the stony floor, nor her cold womb.

Lamech held her face and kissed her as the healer poked and prodded.

'You must still push it out,' the healer said at last. 'It won't take much effort; the babe is so small. Use the pain.'

Following the healer's instructions, Adah clutched Lamech's hand hard as she squeezed her stomach muscles with all she had left.

She glimpsed a tiny, blue, crinkled face before her babe, the size of the healer's palm, was untangled from her shrivelled cord, covered and removed.

'It was a boy,' Lamech said. Then he got up and left.

CHAPTER 11

Noa visited her that afternoon, but Adah couldn't speak. So Lamech's mother busied herself telling the servants what to cook for her health and moaning about how filthy their house was. It wasn't.

Before she left, Noa came and sat beside her. She patted her gingerly on the hand. 'Don't fear, my dear. You managed to create a boy. This is good. Many women experience these... difficulties. It's only temporary. You will soon be full again; I have no doubt.'

After she left, Adah burst into tears. *Full again? Full again with what? Nothing can replace my child. Nothing can remove the pain.*

Lamech returned that evening. He stood in the doorway with dirt-smeared clothes, fidgeting on his toes. *Have you been at work... How?* He hadn't looked so anxious since the day he proposed. His nerves reflected the ones restricting her chest.

'Are you... well?' he asked. Adah swallowed then nodded. He tiptoed towards the bed, then sat beside her. His strong arm settled around her shoulders and he pulled her to his chest.

'Forgive me—' Adah stuttered.

Lamech squeezed her and kissed her head. 'Shhh. Say nothing more. All that matters right now is you.' Then he leaned down and kissed her slowly on the lips. 'I love you, Adah.'

Relief flooded her body, trickling into all the extremities of fear and failure. She buried her head in his chest and clung tightly to his sturdy arm. Soon his tunic was wet with her tears and all-consuming exhaustion smothered her. Lamech shuffled down, lying prone and gathering her to his side. Not bothering to change from his work clothes, he remained that way until morning.

After that, Lamech appeared to recuperate quickly and never stopped working. Adah supposed it was normal for men to heal quicker than women. She asked Eliana, but Eliana didn't know – she had never lost a child. Despite this, Adah found comfort in spending time with her best friend rather than her husband's mother.

Eliana's daughter, Mela, became Adah's most precious companion. The girl instinctively sensed what her busy mother did not and often sat by Adah's side in silence, holding her hand. Sometimes they walked together. Once, they wandered close to her abba's farm. The familiar hill reminded her that Abba had tried to visit soon after she'd lost the baby, but consumed with grief, she hadn't felt able to see him and had sent him away.

Now he spied them from a distance and ran to them. 'Come in. Come in. You must eat with us. Now, who is this treasure? You must be Eliana's daughter. You look just like your ima. Come in. Come in!'

Adah sat and peered at her abba. He was on edge.

His wife, Rivkah, set a stew before them. 'It is so long since you visited, Adah. I was so sorry to hear of your loss. Such a terrible ordeal for you.'

'Thank you. It was.' She had been avoiding them and suspected they knew it. Seeing her half-brother's clothes hanging on the trees outside, and her ima's possessions replaced by Rivkah's, magnified her losses.

As they enjoyed their stew, Adah was unable to find words to fill the silence, but Abba made up for it by chattering between mouthfuls about the animals, crops and people Adah would know. It seemed he'd become far more sociable since his marriage. Rivkah was well-liked and had plenty of friends, and more importantly, Abba was happy again.

'Thank you for the lovely meal,' Adah said as she got up to leave. 'We had better go, or Lamech will wonder where I've got to.'

'Of course. And he must be hungry, too. It is well past the time a man should be fed,' Rivkah replied. 'Take some stew home with you.'

'Oh, he will have eaten. My housekeeper prepares all the food.'

Rivkah's eyes widened.

'It's not my choice. He doesn't let me do it, though I would like to.' Adah's sudden defensiveness scrunched her eyebrows.

Regardless, it had the desired effect, for Rivkah softened and put down her spoon.

'I should think it is harder to kick about that big house with nothing to do, than to manage a farm,' Rivkah said.

'Perhaps.'

Rivkah smiled and drew Adah into an embrace. 'Come again soon, then. We'll happily put you to work.'

With a smile, Adah squeezed her back, doubting she'd take up the offer.

'Where have you been?' Lamech asked when she arrived home at twilight, after walking Mela home.

'At Abba's.'

'Oh.' The tension left Lamech's shoulders. 'Is he well?'

'He is.'

'And his wife and child?'

'Also well.'

'Good. Have you eaten?' Lamech rose from the table and brought her a basket of flatbread and a cup of wine.

'I have, but it was a long walk. Thank you.'

After she'd had a sip, he wrapped his arms around her, and she snuggled into his warmth. He smelled slightly of sweat and baked earth. He couldn't have been home long.

'Did you go alone?' he murmured into her hair.

'No. Mela was with me.'

'Who is Mela?'

'You know, Eliana's daughter.'

Lamech stiffened.

'What is it?' she asked.

A deafening silence sat between them before he growled, 'I do not want you to see that woman again.'

'Eliana?'

'Yes.'

Not see her best friend, her comfort? 'W-Why?'

'It's her fault our son is dead.'

'What?' Adah's mind flew about, trying to latch onto something that would make sense. 'What can you mean?'

'She told you it was safe.' Lamech pulled away and paced to the other side of the room.

Understanding hit her in the stomach. 'She told me it hadn't harmed her children. That was true. It did not.'

'But did she have your difficulties conceiving?'

'No.'

'Then what right had she to give advice?' Lamech's face was glowing red.

'I asked her, Lamech.'

'Yes, you did. You asked *her* instead of my mother. If you'd gone to Ima as I told you to, none of this would have happened.'

'Lamech!'

'Do you deny it?'

'Yes, I deny it.' Surely his thoughts were nonsensical, driven by his assumption that his mother was always right? 'Why should Noa know better than Eliana, or the healer for that matter? There was something wrong with this child from the start. I could feel it.' As she could feel her chest and throat tightening now.

'You didn't tell me that. You told me you never felt it.'

'I-I didn't. I didn't feel the child. I sensed it in my heart; I cannot explain it. I just knew.'

'And still, you let me touch you? Adah! I don't know what to say…'

'Say it wasn't that, Lamech. This child was not meant for this world. It is heart-breaking, my love, but it is not your fault, or mine, or Eliana's. The cord was… The cord was—'

Adah broke down. She saw the tangle around the tiny neck, the contrast of blue against red, and caught again the stench of death. Her legs buckled and she slid to the floor, cradling her midriff.

After more moments of silence, she lifted her head. The starkness of her husband's cold expression penetrated her tear-blurred eyes.

She rubbed them, then forced her arms to open wide towards him. But his face did not soften. Rather it reddened further, and the vein on his forehead bulged. Her voice came out broken. 'Say you understand, Lamech. Please.'

His nose twitched. His colour lessened. Yet he could not relent. He didn't know how. 'I will not say it, Adah. You will not see that woman again, or her daughter. And next time, do not argue when I tell you to do something. I expect total obedience.'

Then he stormed from the room.

CHAPTER 12

As Adah battled her grief, she built emotional barricades around her heart to shield her from further pain. It allowed for an uneasy truce with Lamech, which comprised of never mentioning Eliana's name or talking about their lost child, in return for his continued favour. Though lonelier than ever without her friend's comfort, she took solace in minor acts of disobedience, like secretly assisting the servants when Lamech was at work.

One morning, the vessel Lamech's workers had installed in their courtyard to collect water from the brook, drew a miry filth.

'The channel must be blocked. I'll ask the maid to fetch water elsewhere,' said Shua, the housekeeper – a short, sensible, plain woman, whom Adah liked immensely.

'I'll go,' Adah declared, imagining grey-haired Leah struggling with the container.

'Not at all, mistress. If you don't want her to, I'll go myself.'

'You have far too much to do, and I would like to go.' She'd been looking forward to meeting the other mothers when her baby was born – another thing that had been stolen from her.

'But if the master were to find out—it is unthinkable!'

'If he finds out I will tell him the truth. It was my idea; I wouldn't take no for an answer. Do not fear.'

'I do fear, mistress. I see the way the master has changed. I am not blind.'

'It is not up to you what I do. I am the mistress. I shall take the consequence. Farewell.'

Adah grabbed the large, stoneware jar from the courtyard and placed it on her head. It wobbled. With so little practice, she was even worse at balancing it than she used to be. But she was determined. If she dropped it and it smashed, so be it. Lamech could afford another one. She needed to get to the well.

Mela ran to greet her before she was fifty paces from the women gathering to draw water in the cool of the morning.

'Adah!' Mela squealed, launching herself onto Adah's chest.

She instinctively grabbed the jar on her head, just stopping it from toppling. 'Careful, my dearest. I am pleased to see you, but useless with this jar.'

'Let me.' Mela placed her palms together under her chin and opened her eyes wide. How could Adah resist that face? She laughed and passed the jar to the young girl. Mela placed it on her head and strode towards her ima. The jar almost doubled her height but barely wobbled on her competent head.

'Adah,' Eliana echoed her daughter. 'I am so pleased to see you. Where have you been? You haven't visited us in weeks. I feared I had lost you. I wanted to come to your house but the children... Forgive me, I should have come.'

Adah embraced her friend. 'Don't fear. Lamech's gatekeeper wouldn't have let you in anyway.'

'You have a guard?'

'Yes.'

'You poor thing.'

Adah wasn't sure whether to chuckle or cry. She knew Lamech meant it for her safety, but Eliana saw the prison it created. Although the guard had never stopped her from leaving her home, his mere presence formed an unconscious barrier to making friends.

She sniffed. 'Lamech has forbidden me from seeing you.'

'What?'

'It is true.' She could no longer control the tears.

'Oh, Adah.' Eliana gathered her into her arms, and the floodgates opened. Adah didn't need to explain. Eliana would discern the reason; she would sense it.

Having fetched Adah's water, Mela placed the jar on the ground and joined them, wrapping her arms around Adah's middle. For some time they stood there, two women and a girl, bound together by understanding and sorrow.

THE WANDERER'S LEGACY

'What will you do?' Eliana asked at last, wiping her eyes. 'You can't stay in that house forever with no friends. We should disguise Mela. Lamech doesn't know what she looks like.'

'She looks exactly like you. Lamech will know she's your daughter immediately.'

'Hmm, true. Why don't you visit Ruhamah? He is your brother as much as I am your sister.'

'His wife doesn't like me.'

'Ach. It is ridiculous, but true. Then I will introduce you to some of the women here. You must make new friends. They can keep me informed about how you are.' Eliana winked.

'Thank you, I would like that.'

Eliana did as promised. Several women came to Adah's house over the following days. The guard at the gate lifted his eyebrows but did nothing to stop them entering. Having company was a breath of fresh air. They ate and drank in the garden, and Adah listened while the women chattered about ordinary things she rarely got to experience since she'd married Lamech. She played with their children, and surprisingly, it didn't make her feel sad.

One day, Lamech strolled in on a gathering. He did so just as she doubled over with laughter at one child's antics.

'Adah, what is this?'

Shame knocked on her heart as she momentarily feared his displeasure. She decided to be brave. 'My love, come and meet my new friends.'

Lamech ventured further into the garden. As Adah introduced three women in turn, they stood, and Lamech greeted them warmly. Then he took Adah in his arms and kissed her. Warmth flooded her body at his public affection. He was still proud of her, and as the women looked Lamech up and down, she was proud of him too.

'Have you all eaten? May I get you anything further?' An enchanting smile graced Lamech's features.

'We have had plenty, thank you,' one replied.

'In that case, I will leave you in peace. Adah, we are dining at Bekhor's this evening. Dinah is back for a visit.'

Adah's stomach tightened at the thought of seeing Lamech's eldest brother and his difficult sister, but she forced a smile. 'How lovely. We won't be long, then I will get ready.'

The boldest of the women, Nasya, giggled once Lamech left. 'He is so handsome.'

'Nasya. You are married,' Adah chastised half-heartedly.

'That doesn't make me blind!'

Another woman guffawed. 'I suppose we shouldn't have expected anything else of your husband, Adah. But to be fine-looking and wealthy—' She whistled.

'Oh, how I would adore a house like this with servants to do all the chores and a man like that in my bed,' Nasya said.

'Nasya!' All the friends chorused this time.

'I am only joking. I adore my own husband – when he's sober anyway. And I wouldn't trade these little rascals for anything.' Nasya caught her three-year-old son and tickled him.

I would far rather have a son and a simpler house. Adah's thoughts seemed too self-pitying to voice aloud.

Once her new friends had left, she went inside. 'What brought you home early?' she asked, as Lamech passed her a cup of wine.

'Bekhor sent a man to our site to inform me of Dinah's arrival. I thought I'd collect you and go straight there, but I didn't expect you to have company.'

'Oh. Sorry.' Adah drank half her cup in one gulp.

'You don't need to apologise. I am pleased to see you with other women.'

'You are?'

'Of course. You go about life like a creature removed from its herd, not knowing quite where to turn, nor when a predator will strike you.'

The cup almost fell from her hand. Lamech had never seemed capable of such an analogy. She glugged the rest of the wine, grateful for its fortification. She'd need it to get through the evening, which was likely why Lamech had offered it.

He pulled her towards him by the waist. 'Why are you scared, my dearest?' His lips were soft as they brushed hers. 'You know I want you to be happy. That's all I've ever wanted. Yet you looked at me today like I was that very predator.'

'I did?'

'You did.'

Tears sprung to her eyes. She had misjudged him. Of course she had. The man he'd been recently was not her Lamech, not her beloved. He was a man grieving for a child he had passionately wanted. Such grief had made him irrational, but that was not him. Not really. He was dependable and generous. Hardworking and passionate. And she loved him. 'I have been a fool. Please forgive me.'

His fingertips brushed over her back, pulled her closer then unthreaded her tunic. It appeared they would be late for dinner.

Adah had only been to Bekhor's home three times. Though unsure why Dinah was staying with Lamech's eldest brother rather than his parents, it wasn't her place to ask.

Lamech's sister greeted her coolly as she entered. 'How nice to see you, Adah.' Dinah's kiss on her cheek felt like the prick of a needle, the tone of the words betraying the opposite meaning to their content.

Though Adah knew some affection existed between them, Dinah greeted Lamech in precisely the same way. He threaded his fingers through Adah's and, as soon as his sister had turned her back, whispered, 'Now *she* is the wolf to your sheep, my love.'

Adah chuckled. She'd never had the chance to get to know Dinah, who'd left for the north shortly after their wedding, travelling to join her husband who'd succeeded in conquering his piece of land.

'Are your children with you?' Adah asked Dinah as she reclined before the table.

'Oh, no. I left them with a nurse. The journey would have troubled them.'

Lamech laughed. 'Would have troubled them? Or troubled you?'

Dinah glared at him. 'When you succeed in having children of your own, brother, perhaps then you can lecture me.'

The jibe was like a fire stick to Adah's womb. By Lamech's reaction, it was too soon for him as well. He bit his bottom lip and squeezed her hand tighter. She concentrated on that to prevent her own sorrow rising.

Lamech spoke his next words through gritted teeth. 'And how is Barsabas?'

'My husband is doing well. He has established his lands, and patrols suggest the Iradites do not intend to reclaim them. They seem to have crossed back over the Tigris. We have developed the farmland, and it is producing plentifully at last. The previous tenants had barely tapped its potential.'

'So, are you happy?' Adah's cheeks burned. Had she really asked that aloud? It had been playing on her mind, but she hadn't expected it to escape from her mouth.

'What has happiness got to do with it? We can't all defy our parents and marry for love.'

The retort transported Adah back to the night Methushael rejected her. It was difficult to determine whether Dinah shared her father's low opinion or envied her.

'Then you are still to be pitied,' Lamech replied. His fingertips stroked the palm of Adah's hand. 'I am sorry for you, sister.'

Dinah huffed and looked away. Fortunately, at that moment, Bekhor's wife appeared with a servant and several trays of food. A shy woman, she avoided company, but she had produced several offspring, so Methushael approved of her. No sooner had she served the food and greeted her guests than she disappeared. She rarely attended dinner, preferring to remain in the nursery while her husband entertained.

While they ate, the conversation turned to business, with Lamech and Bekhor discussing their father's lands and their joint affairs – for Bekhor was a wonderful carpenter and often crafted items for Lamech's sites. Adah remained silent, having nothing to contribute. Instead, she watched Dinah. Elegance radiated from Lamech's sister, even in the simple act of eating, but her brown eyes were heavy with sadness. She was the picture of Noa in every way – looks, intelligence and haughtiness. If Dinah had possessed a sliver of Noa's charm, they might have been able to get along.

CHAPTER 13

Six seasons after losing her child, Adah was pregnant again. This time, Lamech hadn't been keeping track, so, dreading another loss, she kept it from everyone until she was sure.

Predictably, Eliana noticed first. They were at another friend's home, where they had contrived to meet without Lamech's knowledge on a few occasions. Nausea had struck Adah particularly hard that morning, but she was trying to hide it, knowing it was a good sign.

'You are with child,' Eliana announced immediately after greeting her with a hug.

Warmth tickled Adah's cheeks.

'You are, aren't you?'

'I think so, yes.'

Their hostess jumped up and hugged her. 'Oh Adah, this is wonderful. How many weeks since you bled?'

'Twelve.'

'And does it feel different this time?' Concern lined Eliana's features.

'Yes. I feel awful.'

'Oh, Praise Yahweh!' Eliana said, clapping her hands, and their hostess hooted.

Despite herself, Adah laughed too. The release was beautiful. All the tension she'd been holding for weeks dissipated as hope broke in. 'If I have a healthy boy, perhaps Lamech will forgive you, my friend.'

Eliana nodded. 'I will pray for that every day.' At the mention of prayer, confusion threatened to break through Adah's reverie. Prayer hadn't worked last time; her baby had died...

Nasya chose that moment to burst through the doorway. 'Oh. Hello, Eliana; Adah. I didn't expect you here.' Nasya's gaze flicked over her then moved to her hostess. 'Would you look after my boys for the morning? I must help my husband.'

'Of course. There are enough of us here to watch them. Is everything alright?'

'Yes. We're just busy.' She ushered the little ones into the room, glanced at Adah again and left.

'Sometimes Nasya is so odd.' Eliana chuckled. 'So, have you told Lamech your news?'

'No. Though I suppose I will have to now that you know.'

When Adah returned home, she was surprised to find Lamech already there. He stood gazing through the aperture in their bedroom wall – no doubt at the vineyard – rubbing his wet hair with a linen cloth. Another cloth was tied around his waist. Unable to resist, she slinked in and ran her hands over his chest. 'This is a nice surprise.'

Lamech turned and kissed her. 'We got smothered in dust today. I left the boys to clear up while I came back for a wash.' Adah noticed the scent of thyme in the room. It didn't usually linger this long after her morning cleanse.

'So, you were at a building site?'

'Yes. It's a big project for one of the elders. His son is getting married, and they want an impressive home to welcome the bride into.'

'Hmm. Shall it be as impressive as ours?'

'I have designed something suitable for their status. But naturally, everything I do for you is superior. You inspire me to greatness.' Lamech grinned. He was in a good mood; this was the perfect time.

'Speaking of great things, I have something to tell you.' She chewed her lips as a smile tugged them.

Lamech drew his brows together, calculating. 'Are you?'

She allowed her smile to spread widely. 'I believe so.' Euphoria struck as her husband swirled her in the air. Until he put her down. Then the room swirled instead, and her stomach rose to her throat. She clenched it.

'Are you well?' He laid a hand on her back.

'Yes, just queasy.'

'Sorry, I didn't think.'

'It's alright.' Pleased with Lamech's concern, the pressure released, and the world righted itself.

'Ima will be so thrilled.'

Why was that his first thought? She didn't bother to ask. Seeing his joy was enough.

Lamech stroked her belly. 'May we go tell her now?'

She would far rather they spent the extra time together. It was rare to have an evening alone with Lamech these days; he so often worked late, visited Methushael or Bekhor about business matters, or went to the tavern. But denying him his mother again wasn't wise.

'Of course, my love. Let me just freshen up, then we can go.'

That night, Lamech didn't cradle her as usual. He slept with his back to her, and the resulting chill set her trembling. Several times during the following week, she wrapped her arms around him, but he never responded. When a fortnight had passed without Lamech initiating affection, she realised his intention – he would refrain through her whole pregnancy. Fear of losing the child had stolen their marriage bed.

Adah determined that their loss of intimacy wouldn't extend beyond the bedroom. Where she'd rarely taken an interest in her husband's work before, she now asked him each morning where he would be and was surprised to find he wasn't often at the vineyard.

Several times a week, Shua packed a lunch and Adah took it to Lamech, staying to watch him work well into the afternoon. From this, she observed some surprising things.

Lamech had far more workers than she had realised, and far more projects on the go. He rarely stayed in one place for long but moved about the city between sites. Though he didn't mind getting his hands dirty, most of the time he was directing foremen, who in turn directed others. Many of the workers looked thin and weather-beaten.

'Why are those workers so ill-dressed?' Adah asked, as they sat to eat one day.

Lamech laughed. 'Why should they be well-dressed for hauling stone and carving wood? It would be pointless.'

'But they don't even have sufficient footwear, and they seem to wear the same thing every day.'

'They are merely the lowest class of worker, my love.'

'What does that mean?'

'They have no particular skills. They do as they are told.'

'Why don't you train them?'

'Some of them do get trained if they show aptitude. But most are expendable.'

'Expendable?' Why did hearing that word make her gut feel heavy, like a building stone had settled in it?

'They work for me because they have little use elsewhere. No other skills.'

'But I thought your business was supposed to enable people to thrive? You know – if you build their house, they can weave, that sort of thing.'

'Oh, it does, for the vast majority. But some people are just not cut out for learning skills, or they have had that opportunity removed.'

'I don't understand.' Wasn't everyone made by the Creator and blessed with gifts to use for the benefit of all? At least, that's what Ima had told her.

'Some have fallen into debt. They must work to repay it.'

'Debt. What is that?'

'They may have borrowed something and not returned it, or failed to produce their portion of a trade deal.'

'To you?'

'Occasionally. More often, to one of my benefactors.'

'So, then they must work for you, instead of doing what they do best?'

'Until their debt is satisfied, yes.'

'And these are the men and women who look so weak. Do they receive anything for their labour?'

'Of course. I arrange food for them. I'm beyond generous, Adah.'

'How many are there?'

'Several hundred, I suppose.'

'Several hundred!'

'I think we should stop this conversation now. Someone might hear and get the wrong impression.'

'But Lamech, do you mean to tell me you are supporting several hundred workers who have no prospect for betterment?'

'Enough!' Lamech's face reddened. 'I do my best by them. Without me, they would be dead. This conversation is over.'

'Your best? They are threadbare. We live in luxury.'

Lamech stood abruptly. Supporting her swelling midriff, Adah stumbled up. He faced her and lowered his voice. 'Either you accept my affairs without question, or you do not join me here again. Do I make myself clear? I shall not withstand insubordination at my workplace. Least of all from my wife.'

Her visit was meant to keep them together, not push them further apart. She mustn't speak another word; her tongue had run far too loose already. Swallowing all indignation deep into her throat, she nodded. 'I understand. Please forgive me, my love.'

Lamech softened, put his hands on either side of her face and kissed her. 'There. Now they will all know nothing is the matter.' He made another show of affection, then stepped away and called to the foreman. 'Azurak. Come here and meet my wife.'

A man approached, clad in leather from the waist down, with a linen tunic beneath and dark hair tied in a knot. His beard was black, his eyes almost the same colour. Yet the darkness seemed to extend beyond his irises – further inside, like an infection.

'This is Adah. And this—' Lamech stretched forward and stroked her belly. 'Is my son.'

Azurak's gaze dropped to her naval. 'It is a pleasure to meet you. I have heard so much about you.'

'Indeed?' That was surprising. She'd never heard about him.

His eyes met hers again. Could the infection spread? 'Your beauty is renowned.'

'Oh.' It would be nice, for a change, to be known for something else.

'Her beauty belongs to me.' Lamech laughed and pulled her tightly against him. His fingers pinched her skin.

One corner of Azurak's mouth twitched. 'Of course.'

Lamech laughed again. 'Anyway. I just thought I should introduce you. You may go now.'

Azurak gave a stunted bow, then spun on his heel and returned to the workers.

'A strange name, Azurak,' Adah mused.

'Oh yes, he comes from the far west, well beyond the Euphrates. They worship other gods there, I think.'

'Other gods? What does that mean? There is only one Creator.'

'How should I know? It matters not. Azurak is an excellent worker. He keeps good charge of my men and doesn't insist on a Shabbat rest, which suits business well.'

'How sad for him.'

Lamech's eyebrows drew together. 'You are a funny little thing sometimes, Adah.'

'Sorry.'

A grin spread across his face. 'I must return to work. Thank you for lunch. Go home and rest now.'

Adah looked wistfully back at her husband as she wandered down the hill towards home. He was deep in conversation with his foreman while the other workers trudged on.

CHAPTER 14

City of Chanoch, 750th year of Wandering

That same foreman stands in the glimmer of light sneaking from the house in the next alley. *Azurak.* The day Adah discovered the slaves was so long ago, well before Azurak became Lamech's full-time enforcer, but Adah recalls it vividly when she sees his duplicitous face, which still makes her heart shrivel, as it did then.

She recognises a second man's features. He is of slighter frame than the beast who stands before him, and is holding a skin of wine. *No, not him. Not Naamah's husband. This cannot be. Naamah was my best hope...*

'You will not enter,' Naamah's husband says before glugging at his wine. He stands in the doorway with several others, barring Azurak's way.

Azurak whips round an angry face. 'It's not your choice.'

'She is my wife.'

'A wife who never loved you.' Azurak pauses and something between a chuckle and sneer escapes his lips. 'Besides, you cannot stop me.'

Four people lunge for Azurak but he is more than a match for their drunken states. Within the space of a wrestle and a couple of punches, Azurak is free and has a grasp of the slighter man's neck. 'You really think you can beat me? I made you who you are. I own you.'

Perhaps Adah should make a run for it while Azurak is distracted, but the events playing out are too significant. Her mind cannot think beyond them.

'I have given you everything you wanted,' Naamah's husband gulps. 'The best supplies and agreements, to the detriment of other customers. I've even spoken to my father on your behalf. You've had my loyalty. Why must you have my wife as well?'

The sliver of light increases as several more exit the house, presumably having heard the commotion despite the loud music and drunken cheers inside.

'What is this?' one asks. 'Master?'

Soon, the slighter man has a crowd of ten supporting him and Azurak's grip softens. Adah ponders which way her enemy will go if he leaves. Most likely, he'll head straight for her.

'We are done,' Naamah's husband says. 'You cannot fight us all. Now get away from my house.'

The route to Eliana's home beyond is now impossible. Adah pictures a map of the city streets, placing friend and foe like pieces on a game board. *Chanoch.* He lives near the western gate. It's not the way she planned, indeed, will likely fail. Moreover, it's quite a distance, but she could get there with a few careful runs...

Azurak emits a final, angry roar. He is giving up. She must decide. Pulling her scarf over her head, she prepares to dart forwards. No, she should not dart. It will look suspicious. Only one type of woman walks the streets at this time of night.

Adah takes a deep breath, adjusts her footing to the west and saunters into the opposite alley.

CHAPTER 15

City of Chanoch, 712th year of Wandering

Chanoch studied Adah from across Methushael's dining hall. Was she happy? He found it hard to tell. It was unbearably hot in this place. He wished Methushael would just eat outside. He had never understood his great-grandson's obsession with large indoor rooms and showing off. Young Lamech seemed to be following in his father's footsteps.

Chanoch sighed. How things had changed since the early days when he had built this city with his abba, scavenging red stone from the hills and forming it into houses. It had been so exciting. The first buildings that might outlast a person. 'No more rolling around in the mud for you,' his abba had said.

It was a joke at Chanoch's expense. Chanoch had been the messiest in the family by far. The eldest of seventeen children, he always preferred playing with mud, sticks and stones rather than growing things. Grand aspirations, he had not. He was content with the simple life. A steady fire and a warm bed were all Chanoch required. Still, someone had to watch over this city and these people. His people. For they all descended from him, one way or another.

He wished he'd listened to his ima better. After constructing the first few homes, they'd started on the wall. Wild animals were problematic at the time, and it had seemed necessary to protect the lives and lands within. His abba encouraged it, enjoying the extension of their building time together. Yet Ima said the wall showed lack of trust in Yahweh's protection.

They'd laughed at the time, thinking her overdramatic. However, as the space within the walls filled with homes, while farms were relocated outside the city, Chanoch couldn't help but feel remorse for the division the wall created and longing for the previous unity. Why should some be protected, and others not?

Yet, when he looked about him, the protected ones did seem to have disproportionately abandoned the old faith, while the farmers relied on Yahweh for the rains and their protection. The homes of Methushael and Lamech, which were built into the wall, stood strong and fortified, keeping others out. By contrast, Chanoch's own home was often insecure, for he typically left the archway to the outside uncovered.

Adah stroked her stomach subtly. She was with child then; that was good. According to his wife, Shiphrah, who always stayed updated on gossip despite rarely leaving the house, Adah had suffered the loss of a babe a few seasons ago. Poor dear. Chanoch remembered when Shiphrah lost a child. It still stung his eyes to think about it, even though they'd had several more children afterwards and it was some two hundred years ago.

'That's because everyone is a child of Yahweh,' his ima had said. 'Every babe is precious in His sight, whether it lives or dies.' Ima had relayed the story of his aunt Avigail and her distress during childbearing, about the child that had almost died until the breath of Yahweh raised it. Presumably she'd meant well, but the story hadn't aided Chanoch's grief.

He should have gone to see Adah as soon as he'd found out. Yet there were so many in the city now that he struggled to keep up with everyone, and he didn't even know them all. Still, Adah held a place in Chanoch's heart. Probably because she reminded him of his ima.

Adah still looked out of place in Methushael's household, as she had done the first night he'd seen her here, twelve years previously. Everyone else was pampered and preened, but Adah sat stunning in her simplicity. Not for the first time, Chanoch regretted holding his tongue when he'd first seen Adah here. He had failed in his duty, allowing Shimiel to select a man such as Lamech for his only daughter, without cautioning him against it. It was an unfortunate coincidence they'd met at his home, for Lamech rarely visited. Why Yahweh had allowed him to that day, Chanoch didn't know.

A gust of fresh air found its way through the opening nearest Chanoch, tickling his skin and bringing him relief. He should invite Adah to sit with him in the breeze. Shiphrah always ran hot when she brewed a babe, and Adah was likely roasting. She was playing with the thread on her tunic. Lamech had one hand on her, but he wasn't giving her any attention, rather he spoke loudly to Bekhor, facing away from his wife.

Chanoch hadn't been to Methushael's on Shabbat for some time. He hadn't missed it. But now he felt the creeping spider of failure crawl across his back again. If he'd visited earlier, he might have offered Adah better support. That would change today. Responsibility for the marriage of Shimiel's daughter lay with him. He must endeavour to put things right.

CHAPTER 16

Adah found them together a few weeks later – her husband and her friend.

She'd told Lamech she'd be at her abba's all day. Then she caught her hand in a tangle of thorns and, wanting Shua's poultice to treat the wound, left early. The look the gatekeeper gave her suggested something was amiss, but she barely registered it before catching the waft of thyme.

Shua blocked the doorway. 'Mistress. You're not meant to be here.'

From inside the main house, a giggle escaped. A woman's giggle.

'Who's here? Has a friend come to visit? I thought they knew I was going to Abba's today.'

Her housekeeper's eyes held guilt. 'Don't go in there, mistress.'

'Why? Shua, you are being strange. Let me pass.'

The giggle transformed into something else. Something more guttural.

'What—?' Adah pushed past her housekeeper and barged through the antechamber, descended the passageway and entered her room.

Lamech was in bed. His neck twisted and he cried out her name. Adah just stared as her husband jumped from the bed, and a woman pulled linen up to cover her nakedness.

My linen. My bed. My friend...

Nasya's face, smudged with makeup, reddened, then hardened.

Lamech threw on a tunic then, before Adah could register what was happening, he seized her arm and shouted something at Nasya. He continued shouting as he dragged Adah from the room and, once clear of the bedchamber, pushed her against the passage wall. Her arms throbbed under his grip.

Adah stared as his eyes bored into hers, just like his father's had done years ago. Was he going to speak? Apologise? Or hit her? When she cowered, he softened, released her arms and, turning his back to her, wandered several paces away.

As the realisation of what her husband had done dawned, disgust and envy coursed through her in equal measure. She couldn't decide what she desired more – to scratch the skin from Lamech's chest or force him to make love to her instead of that woman.

Yearning, hatred, fury, pain. Each warred for dominance, shouting behind her eyes. She screwed her eyelids tightly together, blocking Lamech's form as the pressure mounted and the shouts transformed to screams. But the cacophony was all within – from her mouth, no sound escaped.

Lamech said nothing either.

Adah's legs trembled. She leaned back against the wall and slid to the floor, unconsciously cradling the babe within as her stomach tightened. Shuddering ensued. When had it become so cold? Moaning escaped her trembling lips.

Lamech left the passageway, his familiar gait echoing away until it was only in her mind. He wouldn't even speak to her. What had she done to deserve this?

Then, another waft of thyme.

'Adah.' It was Nasya's voice. Why was she still here? After a pause, stinging fingers touched her face. Adah's eyes flashed open to find her betrayer's glinting, cat-like, before her.

'Adah, you need to calm down. You might endanger the child.'

Laughter assailed Adah's eardrums. Was it her own? What did she have to laugh about?

It was hers. A deep roar of something between anguish and mirth left her lips. 'Oh, now you care about us? You conniving vulture! You are meant to be my friend, Nasya. My friend!' Shudders spread from her chest to her legs as her speech rang in her ears from somewhere outside her soul.

'Adah, you are being overdramatic. Things like this happen all the time.' As she spoke, Nasya's face transformed. The cat eyes still glinted, but now Adah imagined a vulture's hooked beak dripping blood. Then its talons reached, sliding their way over her absent husband's skin before sinking into her own beating heart.

'You are so conceited,' the vulture said. 'Why should Lamech be faithful? No one else is. Poor Adah. Perfect, superior little Adah never expected infidelity to happen to her.'

A moment of clarity descended. Epiphany perhaps. Nasya spoke poison.

'What do you mean, no one else is?' Adah spat. 'I have never known this. Lamech is mine. "The two shall become one," united in flesh – not to be touched by another. That is what we promised. Your claws have claimed *my* property, beast!'

Nasya was not defeated. Indeed, she sneered. 'You didn't seriously expect Lamech to abstain for your entire pregnancy, did you? You should feel fortunate it was me he chose and not some woman from the tavern.'

There were women at the tavern? Adah had no head space to consider that. How could Nasya possibly think she was fortunate? 'I did expect... I-I thought—'

'Ha. You really believe this is the first time, don't you? The first time he's had a woman other than you.'

She did. For it was. Wasn't it?

'Oh my, Adah. You do! Did you also think Lamech was a virgin when he married you? He is a rich, powerful man. He's the son of a rich, powerful man. He can have whatever he desires. And he *has* had it.'

'But he desires me... He-He loves me.' The words came out as a squeal, forced from a throat so tight, her breathing stopped as soon as she'd uttered them. Tears filled her bulging eyes. *Breathe. I can't. Breathe.*

The woman before her transformed again as Adah's tears multiplied the scavenging vulture into a hideous, dancing kaleidoscope.

'Yes, you trapped him in your web for a time,' the vulture said. 'But think back to your wedding night, Adah. Did Lamech know what to do? Was he confident?'

He was. He had been. She hadn't thought anything of it before now. Adah's throat released just enough for one huge breath, and Nasya rematerialised.

She held a contemptuous smile. 'You see; you were not the first. One flesh. Ha! As if anyone believes that Yahweh-nonsense anymore.'

I knew you were naïve, my friend, but I hadn't realised you were this bad.'

Friend. Nasya still called her friend? After seducing the object of all her affections, stealing her hope, her life and now...

Adah failed to breathe again, as her stomach tightened violently.

Nasya wasn't finished. 'You'll get over this, Adah. After all, you get to keep him. I must return to my pathetic husband and pretend I'm not imagining Lamech every time he takes me to bed. Whereas you will give birth to Lamech's son, doing your duty. Then he will love you once more and all will be well. I have done you a favour, really. I have enlightened you to what men are. Perhaps now you can enjoy him without burdening him with your neediness.'

Nasya rose and left. As soon as she had gone, Adah could inhale. Yet she remained on the floor, clasping her unborn child, willing him to kick her, to prove he was real – that his conception in love was not a lie. *So long as I cling to him, Lamech's love must be true...*

At some point, Shua helped her to her chamber. Lamech was nowhere to be seen. She hadn't the strength to resist her housekeeper's ministrations, or she might have refused the bed. For in it, images of the betrayal penetrated the eyes of her heart, piercing her innermost being in rhythmic repetition.

She must have drifted to sleep, but it didn't last long. Adah woke before dawn with the sensation she feared most – the preoccupation of her nightmares. Though the bed was still cold from her husband's absence, there was a sticky warmth between her legs. She screamed.

CHAPTER 17

'I've come to invite them to dine.'

'It's not a good time. My master is absent. My mistress is... is not well.'

'Why is Lamech absent if Adah is not well?'

'He doesn't know.'

'May I see her?'

There was a pause. 'I'll ask.'

Shua entered the room. It was the guest room. They'd abandoned Adah's bedchamber once the healer had left and the mattress of straw, linen and a thin layer of feathers, had been declared fit only for the fire.

Adah tried to sit up and rubbed her eyes. 'Was that Chanoch's voice?'

'Yes, mistress.'

'How do I look?'

'Honestly? Terrible.'

Despite the gravity of her situation, Adah couldn't help a small smile. 'It matters not. Let him come.'

'Into the chamber?'

'I'm not sure I can move far. Stay with us?'

Shua nodded, then helped her to sit up and propped some rolled linens behind her back. Then she left and returned moments later with Chanoch in tow.

'My dear, forgive my intrusion into your private chamber. I didn't realise you would still be in bed—'

Shua hovered behind Chanoch as Adah replied, 'I requested you to come. To be honest, my heart warmed when I heard your voice. I think I need a friend.'

The word pierced her heart again. Nasya had been her friend. Suddenly, she felt as if lemon juice had been squeezed into her eyes. Then her cheeks were wet, her shoulders hunched and her hands trembling.

Chanoch rushed forward. 'Adah. My dear, what has happened?'

She wanted to tell him, but words stuck on her tongue as wails took over. How could she express the pain? The shame? She had lost everything.

Shua brought her a cloth to wipe her face. 'The babe is gone,' Shua told Chanoch.

'Oh, Adah. I'm so sorry. Not again.' Chanoch shook his head as he muttered under his breath. His fingers stretched forward, and he took hers. His hands were warm, like they'd been near a fire. Lamech's were usually cold. 'Would you like me to send someone to fetch Lamech?' he asked.

'No.' The word came out vehemently and Chanoch stood back in surprise. Adah took a breath, fortifying herself. 'There is more going on than Shua has suggested. I don't know if I should tell you…'

Chanoch's eyes met hers. In them, she saw compassion, but not just compassion. Also, comprehension. 'Did you know what he was, Chanoch? Did you know? I thought once that you were warning me…'

'Am I to assume your husband has not honoured his marriage vows?'

Adah nodded.

'I had a suspicion. Something about Lamech sat uneasily with me. I have never trusted Methushael, and it has been my observation that each generation builds on the sins of their fathers. But I had no real cause to accuse him. When Lamech stood up for you against Methushael, I thought he might be different, and I decided not to say anything to your father. I have come to regret that.'

She allowed a moment for the words to sink into her soul. Did she wish Chanoch had said something? Perhaps. Would it have made a difference? She wasn't sure. If Abba had withdrawn his support for the marriage, she would have been distraught. She had desired Lamech as much as he had desired her. Perhaps they would have both been willing to go against their parents' wishes. That eventuality didn't bear consideration. But something else did.

'You said to me that day "Yahweh has plans." What did you mean by that? Why would the Creator allow this to happen? Why should my womb be empty when others are not? What have I done that He would so afflict me and refuse to answer my prayers?'

Chanoch squeezed her hand tighter. 'I don't know Yahweh's plans. I don't think there has been a person since Havel able to discern those.' The name *Havel* sounded familiar, but Adah couldn't place it. Chanoch was still talking. 'But I do know this. He does not allow affliction without cause. And everything that happens to us, He purposes for our good.'

'Is it my sin that caused it? I don't know what I have done.'

'Oh no, dear. I don't think so. Not your sin. Though for sure, you have sinned. We all have. If truth be told, there is little difference between Lamech, yourself and me. Though it is hard to believe that right now, I am sure. But my parents maintain that we are all guilty before Yahweh. On that, they are very clear. I grew up having to repent daily – it was quite a chore, I tell you. So many times I rolled my eyes at my abba saying, "What again?" And he would say, "Yes, Chanoch. If we do not constantly examine our hearts, then we soon fall into the trap of believing we are right, and Elohim is wrong."'

'Your abba is The Wanderer, isn't he?'

'Hmm? Yes, that is what they call him.' Chanoch chuckled gently. 'To me, he is just Abba.'

I wonder if they look similar. Adah examined Chanoch's features. *No, Chanoch is too short, surely. Also, his abba sounds very different from the gruff man Eliana described.*

'Now. What are we going to do about your Lamech? What do you *want* to do?'

Pulled back to the present, Adah didn't know how she felt. She would rather sit here and hear stories about The Wanderer than deal with her situation and the ache in her womb.

Chanoch tilted his head, observing her. 'I expect it is far too early to know.'

Yes, that was it exactly. The dual longing and disgust of the previous night still sat on the cusp of her heart, ready to do battle.

'Have you seen Lamech since you found out?' Chanoch asked.

'No. I mean, after I found him, he didn't speak to me. He just left. Then I lost the child during the night.'

Chanoch took a sharp breath. 'This all happened yesterday? You found him?'

As tears threatened again, she could only nod.

'Oh, dear. So many things you have been dealt. May Yahweh have mercy.' He looked deep in thought for a moment. 'Is it painful for you to be here? Would you like to go to your abba's? Or mine?'

'Your house would be better. Abba has—'

'Your little brother. Of course, that would be difficult. We would be glad to welcome you. You know that my wife is not well, but perhaps someone could come to assist you. Your housekeeper?'

'I'm not sure what Lamech would make of that. He would probably be angrier to lose her than me. She cooks his food.'

Chanoch laughed, then tried to apologise.

'Don't apologise. I meant it to be amusing, even though it's probably true.' She thought about asking for her maid, but decided she'd rather have another. 'I would like Mela to come if it could be arranged?'

'Mela?'

'My friend Eliana's daughter. Though her mother constantly needs her, she is a comfort to me.'

'I will arrange something then. Is Eliana the weaver's wife?'

Adah confirmed she was.

Lamech didn't return home before she left with Chanoch later that day. Adah was glad. She had no idea what she would say to him. Perhaps he was out telling Methushael that he'd been right, that she would never bear a son. But that couldn't be, for he still didn't know she'd lost the child… He was hiding then.

It was a slow walk to the other side of the city with Shua holding one of her arms and Leah the other. Adah had little strength in her legs and kept having to stop and discretely adjust her linens, for she was still bleeding heavily. She was grateful for the women by her side, supporting her and shielding her from prying eyes, but she'd send them home once she reached Chanoch's, for she wanted as few reminders of her husband as possible.

When they arrived, Chanoch showed her to a simple straw mattress in a room adjacent to the only other chamber. She collapsed exhausted, not even drawing the privacy curtain.

CHAPTER 18

'Peace to you, Noa,' Chanoch said to the woman at the entrance to his home.

'Where is she?' Noa strode in, looking about her.

Chanoch raised his eyebrows. Adah had been with them for a week. He was pleased she had been allowed that time of recovery but was not surprised to see Lamech's mother at his door. His surprise was at her lack of greeting. 'She is abed. Please take a seat and I will make you some tea.'

'Don't you have a servant to do that?'

'No. Why would I?'

Noa pulled a face, inspected the humble wicker chair by the fire pit and lowered herself tentatively onto it. 'How is Adah?'

So, she did care. 'She is better now than when she came, but still in shock.'

Noa nodded and relaxed slightly. 'And your wife, Shiphrah? Is she well?'

She'd found her manners. 'Shiphrah is much the same as usual, thank you. But we manage.'

In truth, Chanoch felt exhausted. He'd traded his wife's companion for Mela, so that Eliana's daughter could be free to look after Adah. The past week, he'd cared for Shiphrah himself. He didn't begrudge it, in fact, he'd enjoyed the additional time with his wife. But doing most of the household duties was taking its toll and he'd had little time for anything else. Mela was a good girl though and had helped, as well as benefitting Adah immensely. Chanoch's duties as elder could wait.

Mela entered the room just then, coming from Adah's chamber. 'Ah, Mela. This is Adah's mother, Noa, come to see how she is.'

Mela looked Noa up and down with brows drawn together, scrutinising everything from the expensive, colourful turban to the immaculately polished toenails. 'You must mean Lamech's mother. Adah has no mother,' Mela said.

Noa raised an eyebrow, then chuckled. 'I see you have Eliana's tongue. I like that in a woman. Though not in a girl. Come closer so I can examine you the way you did me.'

Mela flushed and tiptoed forward a few steps. Noa stood, lifted the girl's chin with her hand and rotated her head.

'Pretty little thing. You will do well if you don't scare off all your potential suitors.'

'I have just turned thirteen!'

'Indeed? My daughter was betrothed when she was twelve.'

Mela gasped. Chanoch knew of Dinah's unfortunate marriage and how little choice she'd had. He had disapproved and had tried to speak sense to Methushael, but as usual, had been ignored. Well, not entirely. Methushael had agreed to hold off matrimony for several years but had not annulled the engagement. Chanoch had seen Dinah recently in the marketplace, visiting her family without her husband or children. When she barely acknowledged him, he'd moved on.

'Don't fear, Mela. I'm sure your abba has no designs for you to marry just yet. Besides, you're indispensable to your mother as I understand it,' Chanoch commented.

'I am.'

'And I am Adah's mother now,' Noa said. 'When a woman gets married, she joins her husband's family. Adah became a daughter to me the day she married my Lamech. I love her as my own.'

As Chanoch thought on this, it didn't seem right. Not the part about Noa being Adah's mother – that he agreed with. It was the part about the woman leaving her family, for he remembered it the other way round. *'A man will leave his father and his mother and hold fast to his wife, and they will become one flesh.'* That's what his parents had taught.

He supposed they hadn't followed that pattern themselves. As Kayin was a fugitive, his mother had abandoned her family to join him in Nod. But when she'd reluctantly escorted Chanoch to his

Uncle Set, to find a wife in the land between the rivers, Chanoch had asked her why he must go.

'I may be taking it too far,' she'd confessed. 'But I believe it's wise for you to leave us. If a man always joins a woman's family, he takes her name and cannot establish one for himself. Then he's more likely to marry for the right reasons – to love, honour and protect his wife, rather than for his own increase. But if a woman must join a man's family, he might be tempted to choose a wife based on her material value instead of her spiritual value – so she increases his estate. Then she becomes little more than a possession, and he honours only himself. It is always Yahweh's name we should hold high, Chanoch. Never our own.'

When Shiphrah had insisted on returning to Nod with Chanoch, despite his intention to stay between the two rivers, the pattern had been abandoned again. Then over several centuries, its wisdom faded, culminating in Methushael selling his daughter, Dinah, to Barsabas. Methushael cared nothing for Yahweh's name. And he, Chanoch, the patriarch of the city – responsible for all its inhabitants – had allowed innocent Adah to marry into Methushael's family.

'So, may I see my daughter?' Noa asked, breaking into Chanoch's wandering thoughts. He had no idea what Noa had been saying to Mela for the last few moments.

Mela sent him a questioning glance.

Chanoch could hardly refuse Noa. 'Of course. Follow me.'

When he entered the chamber, Adah was sitting up with more colour in her cheeks than she'd had that morning. The healer's recommendations, of plentiful water and green vegetables, were certainly helping.

'Noa. I thought I heard your voice.' Adah smiled.

'Adah, dearest.' Noa strolled towards her, brushing some dirt away with her foot before crouching next to Adah's mat. 'I have been so worried, but I didn't want to set you back by visiting before you were healed.'

'You are most welcome here. I'm pleased to see you.'

Noa took Adah's face in her hands and inspected it, much as she had done with Mela. 'Does he know everything?' She tilted her head in Chanoch's direction.

'Of course. That's why I am here,' Adah replied.

'Hmm. Lamech came to stay with us that night and told me what you had seen. We heard about the child from Shua afterwards. He wanted to come here himself, but I forbade him. I insisted you needed rest.'

'Thank you.'

'But you cannot stay here.'

Adah's eyes welled with tears. She glanced Chanoch's way. He wanted to offer for her to stay as long as she liked, but he didn't want to contradict Noa. Making an enemy of her would achieve nothing. He smiled encouragingly at Adah, hoping she would catch his meaning. *Let Noa continue.*

'I am disgusted at my son, Adah. He has acted shamelessly. Carrying on with your own friend, in your own home. How could he be so careless?'

Was carelessness her primary concern? Not immorality?

'You should come with me, my dear. I will arrange for you to be properly looked after. When you are ready to see Lamech again, I will be by your side.'

Panic flashed in Adah's eyes.

'Do you intend to take Adah to your home, Noa, or hers?' he asked.

'Whichever she prefers.'

Adah took a deep breath. 'With all due respect, Ima, I don't think I can cope with Methushael right now. But the memories in my own home—'

'I understand. But you do need to fortify yourself, daughter. Those memories will not subside unless you face them head-on. My son has been a fool. He was driven mad by abstinence. But he loves you. You *will* forgive him.'

Noa's tone allowed no argument, and Chanoch's heart went out to Adah – it was too early to make such a demand. Chanoch didn't like the idea of Adah going back to Lamech at all, but he was her husband, and he knew that she loved him. 'Perhaps Adah can remain here a few more days while she considers what you have said. Why don't you come back the day after Shabbat?'

Though her piercing gaze never left Adah, Noa rose with a sigh. 'Very well. Let us do as Chanoch suggests.' She kissed her hand and placed it on Adah's forehead. 'I will see you soon.'

Noa rose and strode past, straight to the outer doorway. She stopped on the threshold and peered back over her shoulder. 'I will be back in three days, Chanoch. Make sure she is ready. If she is not, Methushael may get involved. And he will not be as understanding.'

Then she was gone, as quickly as she had arrived, leaving the tea Chanoch had made sitting by the wicker chair.

CHAPTER 19

'Are you ready?' Chanoch's hand was on the curtain that surrounded Adah's mat. He waited for her permission before drawing it back.

Adah checked her tunic fully covered her. 'Yes.'

He drew the curtain back and considered her, his eyes full of concern. 'I wish you didn't need to leave so early. It feels to me like you've only just begun to recover.'

Adah's heart concurred with his words. 'I have. The bleeding only ceased yesterday. Yet, Noa will be here any moment, and I have nothing to contradict her with. Chanoch, I want to thank you for your kindness. I enjoyed yesterday so much.'

Shabbat with Chanoch, Shiphrah and Mela had been wonderful. A simple meal accompanied by worship of Yahweh. Though Adah hadn't understood much of what they'd sung, she wanted to know more. 'I have so many things still to ask you.'

'Ask away.' Chanoch said, taking a seat.

'I didn't pray for this babe,' Adah said, stroking her empty midriff. 'The first one I prayed for over and over; I desperately wanted him to be what Lamech wanted. And, well, he was a boy. But he died. This time, I felt like I couldn't pray. Yahweh had let me down before, what good would it do to ask again?'

Chanoch nodded slowly. 'I understand.'

'This babe…' Adah sniffed. Her words caught on her tongue. 'This babe… I thought this one would live. It felt different. I suppose I bought into the lie that if Lamech left me alone, he would be healthy. Even so—'

'Your tragedy is incomprehensible, Adah. Yet, this isn't your fault. The child didn't die because you didn't pray.'

'I suppose I know that. But fear... Ima always said Yahweh's name holds protection.'

'Did she now?' Chanoch's eyebrow raised.

'She talked more about Him than Abba does. Yet, I'm coming to see she knew little. The way you and Shiphrah sang of Yahweh yesterday – that He is your joy, your salvation. To me, the Creator is distant and now, He feels harsh. I'm sorry, I shouldn't say such things.'

'Do not fret. It's always better to be honest. I don't believe Yahweh is harsh, Adah. Yet, He is holy. And He is not some token we can use to command favour. You know, I have seen many things in my long years. There are some who've rejected Yahweh, choosing to worship created things rather than the Creator. They believe the host of heaven dwell in the sun, moon and the stars. They believe that by worshipping these they can command favour – good weather, a bountiful harvest – that sort of thing. They make images and bow to them, using them like charms against evil. Yahweh cannot be used like that. He is sovereign. Yet, He does care for you, Adah. He does want to know you.'

'What should I do?'

'You can start by repenting. Tell Him you are sorry for treating Him that way and ask for strength to endure.'

'Chanoch. Adah. Are you here?' Noa's call rang shrill from the other room.

'Ah.' Chanoch smiled. 'Your mother awaits.'

No, not yet. Just a few more moments. Adah's fingers trembled.

Her benefactor saw and laid his hand over hers. 'Yahweh Elohim, forgive Adah's sin. Give her strength to do what is right, and courage to withstand all suffering.'

WHEN ADAH FIRST ENTERED her bedchamber, the images came straight back. She paused on the threshold. Noa linked her arm and walked her forwards to the bed.

'Come now. Let's sit. The best way to forget the old memories is to make happy new ones.'

Noa tucked her into bed and ordered Shua to make a healthy broth and some tea. By the time Adah had eaten, she was exhausted again.

'So, when do you want to see Lamech?'

Adah's eyelids had been drooping before Noa asked the question, and she'd been almost asleep. She forced them open. Noa's eyes – so similar to Lamech's – brought on a longing for her husband. How could she cope with his touch? She didn't know, but she had to. There was no point in delaying the inevitable.

'Send him tomorrow.'

'Good girl.' Noa kissed her forehead and tucked the sheet in around her legs. 'I'll see you then.'

Adah had a mild panic the next morning. Her eyes shot open as she remembered where she was, and she cried out for her housekeeper. 'Shua, you must make me respectable. Lamech cannot see me like this.'

Shua filled the large wooden bathing barrel with warm water and helped Adah into it. Then Shua washed her, using gentle hands to massage her head and body. When Adah was out and dry, Shua rubbed olive oil into her skin, but when she brought out the thyme for under her arms, Adah refused.

'I shall never use thyme again. Find something else.'

As the scent caught in her nostrils, a memory flashed into her mind. The day Eliana found out about her pregnancy, when she'd returned to find Lamech home early, the room had smelt of thyme. She had assumed it was left over from her own bathing, for Lamech preferred to use only salt. But what if it had been Nasya? Nasya had left her children at her neighbours that day. Had the affair begun before Lamech even knew about the baby?

Adah shivered as she was rubbed down.

'Apologies, mistress, I will dress you now. I didn't mean to take so long that you got cold.'

'It's not you. It is just my thoughts.' It was a warm day. There was no reason she should be cold, and it certainly wasn't Shua's fault.

Adah had almost finished her broth when Lamech arrived and spoke her name. He couldn't meet her eyes but hovered on the threshold of the living room, where Adah reclined next to a low table, bowl in hand.

She looked for Noa, but Lamech's mother was not there. *She abandons me already?*

Her husband crept into the room and knelt before her. Taking her hand in his, he bowed his head over it and kissed it. Soon her fingers were wet with his tears. 'Adah. Forgive me.'

The chill in her body subsided as she gazed at her husband's sun-freckled neck. Closing her eyes, all she could feel was his warmth, seeping into her soul once again. The heaviness of betrayal began to lift and float as he humbled himself. When she opened her eyes again, he was still bowed over her lap. She squeezed his hand and his tear-streaked face slowly lifted.

'I love you so much, Adah. I have been such a fool. You are the best thing in my life, and I have taken you for granted.'

Adah stroked the side of his face, running her fingers through the soft stubble on his cheek, gazing into eyes red from weeping. Those dependable eyes had proved deceptive. Could they be redeemed?

'It will not be easy, Lamech.'

'I know.'

'You must promise to talk to me. You must tell me if you are struggling. Let me help you.'

He shifted onto his knees until their faces were level. 'I have been taught to be strong, Adah. To never show my emotion. You have broken down so many barriers in me. It started the first day I met you, when we instantly connected. I knew I would never be the same again. I wanted to fight for you; I needed you. I still need you. But my instinct when something is hard is to harden myself. Do you understand?'

Adah nodded and trailed her fingers over his soft lips. Oh, how she loved him! The longing was heightening, and the disgust in his actions had almost faded to nothing. She knew the disgust would return. She would think of what she'd seen many times again, like she still thought of her mother's last moments. Some experiences never leave. *Yet he has suffered under Methushael's despotic temperament.*

Pity triumphed over pain. 'I forgive you.'

Lamech sighed long and deep, his body relaxing as he reached up and touched her face.

'But Lamech.'

'Yes?'

'I require something from you.'

'Name it.'

'You must allow me to see my friend Eliana again. You can't claim she had anything to do with us losing a child now.'

Lamech stiffened. Conflict raged in his face. He clearly didn't want to concede, but to claim Eliana caused the death of their first child was to admit he had caused the death of the second. Which would be a step too far for her husband.

'Alright. You may see her. But please do not bring her here.'

Adah could live with that compromise.

Resuming normality after the affair was not easy, yet in time they settled, each trying to move on and keep the peace. Rather than blaming Lamech for the loss of their child, Adah more readily blamed herself.

I know it's my fault, Yahweh. I treated You as a token, just like Chanoch said. I repent of trying to tell You how to do Your job. I also treated Lamech with indifference. I neglected him. I disobeyed him. If I satisfy him better, then he will be happy. She prayed as she knelt by the bed each morning, trying to make sure she didn't anger the Creator or her husband again. Invariably though, her prayers turned into sobs for her lost children, which no amount of reasoning or prayer could quell.

What am I saying? Lamech will never be happy while I have no child. And can I – can I ever be happy again? Must my womb ache forever? Yet, I must try. Perhaps if I am good enough, repentant enough, Yahweh will change His mind and bless me.

Setting out to prove she could fulfil her husband's appetites, Adah both encouraged him in the bedchamber and joined him more often at his workplace, blocking her conscience from commenting on the things she saw there. *I will repent for us both, Yahweh. Lamech doesn't mean ill; he is just trying to be a good businessman. Besides, if he didn't provide for the slaves, they'd have nothing.*

Sedating her conscience was more achievable at the vineyard where Lamech employed no slaves – only the most skilful workers were allowed near his precious grapes. Pleased with Adah's enthusiasm, Lamech decided they would go there together on the same day each week. He guided her through the process of tending the vines and seemed surprised when she took to it naturally.

Adah laughed. 'I am a farmer's daughter, Lamech. You took me away from honest work when you placed me in that big house with the servants.'

Her words seemed to hit home. As Adah filled her days with visits to her friends, work with Lamech and care for her goats, her husband allowed her more freedom to do as she pleased, noticing that she was happier when occupied. With his permission granted, she could rest easy at night, not fearing she would be found sneaking behind her husband's back.

However, despite the relative happiness, Adah did not conceive. And the issue hung between them, unvocalised but ever-present.

CHAPTER 20

Adah gazed across Methushael's oppressive dining hall at the newcomer chatting with Noa. She hadn't seen this woman before, and she was intrigued. Lamech was watching the animated conversation between the women too, though he was pretending not to. Adah kept talking to her husband, but their eyes didn't quite meet. It was three years since the affair and, though most of the time they lived in harmony, distracted, guilt-laden glances were common on both sides. Particularly when they were with Lamech's parents.

Midway through their meal, Lamech kissed Adah's cheek, then got up to sit near Bekhor. Adah sighed in relief, then anticipation, as Noa approached with her intriguing guest. She still panicked when Lamech was near attractive women and would enjoy talking to this one without her husband's presence.

'Dearest, you must meet my friend, Tzillah. She is the daughter of one of my cousins and is visiting the area. Naturally, we welcomed her into our home.'

This didn't seem very natural. Of late, Methushael had been increasingly insular, and visitors rarely joined them on Shabbat. Not that Noa stopped preparing for them, ensuring every Shabbat meal was a spectacular array.

Putting her thoughts aside, Adah enjoyed the opportunity to inspect Tzillah. She was captivating. Her eyes sparkled with mischief and her petite nose was slightly scrunched up, as if she was inwardly chuckling at everything she saw. Rather than tying them back, she allowed her bronze curls to cascade around her face and neck, each one adding to the impression of an independent spirit. Adah liked her instantly.

'I will leave you two to chat while I inspect the next course,' Noa declared, departing in a flounce of fabric.

'So, what really brings you here?' Adah asked as Tzillah sat by her.

Tzillah laughed. 'Oh good, you say things straight. By all they said about you, I was worried you wouldn't speak to me.'

'What can you mean? What did they say?' Adah suddenly felt enormously self-conscious, dreading anything that Methushael might have disclosed. She turned her back to her husband's family, encouraging Tzillah to do the same.

'Oh, just that you are a private person and don't join in with the family,' Tzillah crooned.

Adah was sure that wasn't all, but Tzillah was clearly tactful. 'I don't join in because they have never accepted me. I haven't had the chance.'

Tzillah grabbed Adah's hand and kissed it, inclining towards her ear. 'Then I both pity you and envy you.'

Adah chuckled. 'Although everyone seems to think I am worthy of envy, I do not often feel it.'

'Oh, so serious. My darling, you have clearly been married too long. I should take you out to the hills and let you run free.'

'I would love that. Forgive me; I must sound like a selfish fool. Being married to Lamech is a privilege, I know it. And I adore him. I am a self-pitying monster.'

'There you go again – being serious. Be careful or I will drag you out of here before Noa has a chance to serve us so many sweet things that we want to be sick.'

'You have only been here a few days, but you clearly know Noa well.'

'I am an excellent judge of character. Which is why I like you so much already.'

Adah smiled. 'So why are you here? You didn't answer me.'

'Ha! Quick as well. I am… scouting out a business opportunity for my father.'

'That's unusual. Many men in this city won't deal with women. Though I don't know when they decided not to. My abba says women used to be treated equally. His mother was a respected seamstress and had her own business. His father's farm provided the food for the family, but my sava was often out at meetings in the city. She helped determine some of the practices that ensure fair trades for goods.'

'Is that so? How marvellous. With such a heritage, no wonder you feel trapped.'

'Oh, that sort of thing isn't for me. I'm far happier rearing goats than arguing with men.'

A contagious grin lit up Tzillah's features. 'Ah yes, I've heard about your goats.'

'You have?'

Her companion briefly paused, bit her lip, then winked. 'Noa mentioned them eating your garden.'

'Oh, yes. Noa is almost as precious about my garden as she is about hers. In truth, although the flower garden is beautiful, I would rather be up the watchtower looking out over the hills than staring at a decorated wall. When the goats escape and cause a riot, I secretly find it amusing, though I must act outraged in front of Noa, of course.'

Tzillah's peel of laughter flew around the room, and several looked up from their conversations, eyebrows raised.

'They are probably wondering what you have to laugh about. I don't think any of them have ever laughed at a word I've said,' Adah muttered.

'Oh, this is splendid. I can't wait to meet your goats.'

'Are you staying for long?'

'Yes, quite possibly. It depends on the outcome of the negotiations.'

'Then you must come for tea. I will invite some friends. I just know you and Eliana will get on superbly—' Adah paused. She had so far respected Lamech's wishes and not invited Eliana to her home. Perhaps she'd have to restrict it to other women in the first instance. She could arrange for Tzillah to meet Eliana another time.

'That would be wonderful,' Tzillah replied. 'I can't wait.'

'I AM GOING AWAY for a while.' Lamech was sitting on a stool in the antechamber while Shua stood over him, cutting his hair with a sharp stone.

'Oh. Why is that?' Adah asked. She was reclining in the comfier, padded seat near the fire. She had some sewing in her lap, but really, she'd been daydreaming about having her new friend for tea while she watched her husband.

'I have some business to conduct in the north. I've been putting it off, but it's become urgent. When I spoke to Abba and Bekhor yesterday, we decided I must go.'

The north. There was a lot of north. Where exactly did he mean? 'How long will you be gone?'

'A few weeks, I would think,' Lamech replied, tilting his head towards the ceiling so Shua could get to his beard.

'And who will look after the business here?'

'I've put Azurak in charge.'

A shiver of anxiety rippled through her. There was something about Azurak that made her uncomfortable. Not just the way he treated the workers, but also the way he looked at her. Still, Lamech trusted him. And Azurak certainly wouldn't let anything get out of hand while his master was gone.

'I will miss you.' She crossed the room to stand behind Lamech, massaging his shoulders as Shua brushed down his face. 'Can I make a request in return?'

'Of course,' he said, appreciating the massage.

'I'd like some friends to come for a meal. May I include Eliana in my invitation?'

She felt his shoulders stiffen beneath her fingers before he released a long sigh. 'Very well. Just this once.'

'Thank you,' she replied, as relief washed through her. 'When are you leaving?'

'Tomorrow, at first light.'

Adah arranged for her friends and their children to come the following day, then sent word to Tzillah at Methushael's.

Her messenger soon returned. 'The mistress says that Tzillah is no longer there.'

'She has gone already? But it's only been a few days, and I promised her.'

The boy scrunched his nose and held out his palm.

'Thank you anyway,' Adah sighed, giving him bread and figs as payment.

Knowing Tzillah couldn't come, Adah went about the preparations with less enthusiasm, though it did occur to her that there was one benefit to Lamech being away.

'I will serve my guests myself,' she said to Shua. 'Once everything is ready, you must eat with us. Leah and Avram the gatekeeper too.'

'Oh no, mistress; we could not possibly eat with you.'

'Nonsense. You are part of my household. I insist.'

In the event, Shua gave in, and those who would never have dared sit near Lamech to eat joined the families in the courtyard garden.

It softened the occasion for Adah, having people that belonged to her there. She treated the servants almost like they were her children – serving, chastising and encouraging them to conversation. Of course, Eliana would never treat servants differently from anyone else, and the others always followed Eliana's lead. So, the sting of Adah's childlessness didn't dominate the day spent with her friends and their multiple offspring. All enjoyed it as equals.

When Adah went to bed that night, exhausted and content, she imagined Lamech joining such a gathering. For the briefest moment, she saw him in her mind's eye, lounging with his arm around her shoulders, laughing at something Eliana said. She remembered the way he'd greeted her other friends, when he'd found them all in the garden the first time he'd met Nasya. Had she wronged him by assuming he wasn't hospitable?

Then Nasya's alternative image flew into her head, along with the guilt she always carried for letting that woman into her home. She pulled the covers over her face, trying to block it and return to the Lamech she'd imagined moments before.

'THE MASTER IS HOME.'

Adah jumped up from the ground, almost tripping over her new favourite goat. She'd been cleaning out the pen but had suddenly come across tired, so she'd rested a moment, leaning her head against the hand-reared male goat whom Lamech called 'useless', but she loved.

'Oh no,' she said. 'He's here now? I must stink.'

'I'll help you, mistress.'

Adah followed Shua to the kitchen courtyard where a jar of fresh water and hanging herbs were a welcome sight. Quickly, she freshened up and flung on the clean tunic Shua pulled off the line.

'I know I often say I don't need servants, but really, I don't know what I'd do without you, my friend,' Adah said, kissing Shua on the cheek.

'Now, don't let us be too familiar in front of the master. The previous few weeks have been a delight, mistress, but he won't like it.'

'I know, and I'm sorry for it.'

'Mistress?'

'Yes, Shua.'

'Lamech has someone else with him. A woman. I thought you should know before you enter.'

'Oh, that's strange. Do you know who she is?'

'No, mistress.'

'Alright. Thank you, Shua. I better get inside before he comes looking for me.'

When Adah stumbled into the hallway, Lamech was a welcome sight. He looked so well – sun-kissed and carefree. She ran to him and embraced him warmly. He felt just as wonderful as he wrapped his muscular arms around her and pulled her into his chest.

As she drew away, stepping out of the shadows, came a familiar figure.

'Tzillah! You're back.' Thrilled to see her again, Adah hugged her also, but Tzillah's return squeeze seemed reluctant.

'Come in, come in.' She tugged on Tzillah's hand. 'Let me get you some refreshment. I'm so pleased Lamech has brought you here.'

'Adah.' Lamech's voice pulled her away from Tzillah, who still hadn't met her eye. 'There's something you need to know.'

Why did he look so serious?

'I'm sure it can wait. Come and rest your legs, both of you. You must be exhausted from your journey, especially if you returned via your parents' house.' Adah laughed and pushed a stool towards her husband.

Lamech didn't smile or move. 'I did not return via my parents' house.'

'Then how did you meet Tzillah?'

'Woman, stop fussing and sit down!'

Lamech's words bit hard after his warm embrace. Adah stared at her husband as he strode to the padded wicker chair they'd obtained for nursing babies which were never born, and lowered himself onto it. What was going on? Tzillah shuffled behind him. He didn't speak again until Adah had obediently perched herself on the stool.

'Adah,' Lamech said. 'Tzillah and I are wed.'

CHAPTER 21

Adah almost laughed. Surely this was some kind of joke? Perhaps Tzillah had put him up to it. But when she looked at the woman who had been so vivacious the day they'd met, Tzillah was chewing her bottom lip and staring at the floor.

'What can you mean? What—'

'I wanted to tell you before. But Ima forbade it. She said I would never go through with it if I told you and saw your reaction. Adah...' Lamech pulled himself off the chair and began to pace. 'This was the only way.'

'What are you talking about?'

'Abba wanted me to throw you out! He was ready to come here and remove you himself. To send you back to Shimiel in shame, or... or worse! We came up with this plan – Ima and me. But even then, I insisted you meet Tzillah first. I needed to know that you would get along. I couldn't stand the thought that you would be unhappy in your own home. Adah, please say you understand. You like Tzillah don't you?'

His words were coming too fast. They made no sense. How could he have married Tzillah? No one had two wives. One flesh, they were. *One flesh.* The betrayal with Nasya had been enough, but that was something temporary, the passions of the moment. This was... this was *planned.* Permanent.

'Adah.' Lamech was at her side. 'Tell me you understand.'

Understand? No, she did not. Was this her husband truly before her or had she stepped into some dream?

'I love you, Adah. I couldn't bear you being taken from me. I could not bear it.' Lamech rubbed his beard.

He wasn't joking. He wasn't lying. Somehow – she didn't know how – he'd actually married Tzillah. He expected to have them *both*. She choked.

'I did this for you, Adah.'

'For me?' No. That wasn't possible. What did he mean, her being taken... taken back to her abba's? Was that even an option? Could it be? Why didn't he stand up to his despotic father – did he fear Methushael so much? 'This wasn't for me, or you would have asked my opinion,' she spat. 'What if I would rather go there than... than... live with this? Shouldn't I be allowed to choose? Is this just because Methushael hates me, for he won't hate me less if I remain.'

'I knew you would have an opinion; that is why we couldn't tell you! Because I can't lose you, whether Abba likes you or not. Even so, your womb is useless, Adah. Whereas Tzillah is certain to provide me with an heir. She has eleven siblings, many of them boys. And her family needed the money. We arranged everything, so everyone would be happy and...'

Through the venom, his meaning came into sharp focus. 'You *bought* her?'

'No. No. Not like a slave. We just gave them a generous bride price, ensuring that her father's debts were paid off. He gets freedom, she gets a good home and I get an heir. Everyone benefits.'

Everyone except me. Adah's eyes flew to Tzillah, who still wouldn't meet her gaze. Calm and clarity descended on Adah's soul. This was who her husband truly was. She had always known it but had been living in naïve optimism their entire marriage. He gave the appearance of strength but was as much a slave to his father's whims as Dinah. He wasn't dependable. He was weak. Their entire relationship had been on borrowed time from the beginning.

'So, during your time away, you were with her? *She* was your business transaction?'

Lamech nodded, finally looking shameful.

'And can I assume you have consummated this marriage?' All the previous disgust at Lamech's affair reared its ugly head as she spoke the words.

Lamech's nose twitched. 'We have.'

No images of Nasya entered Adah's mind this time. She would not allow them to. Her nostrils widened as fury mounted. Yet it wasn't jealous fury, it was disenchantment. Repulsion. She'd wasted half her lifetime on a false dream.

Without a further word, Adah got up and left.

Tzillah followed her out, catching her arm just as Adah passed the gatekeeper and entered the street. 'Adah, wait!'

'What do you want?'

'I didn't know, Adah.'

'What?'

'I knew I had come here to marry one of Noa's sons, but I didn't know which one. When Lamech came to fetch me, I was shocked. I almost refused to accompany him, knowing he was yours.'

A neighbour stopped to watch them, so Adah pulled Tzillah closer and lowered her voice. 'But you did not refuse.'

Tzillah chewed her lip again. 'My abba is from a good family, but he gambled away everything he earned and then started trading household items to settle his debts. He left my ima with no way of feeding my younger siblings. If it weren't for the generosity of friends, we would have starved. I was on the verge of selling—' She paused, swallowing hard, as if choking on the thought of what might have been, before continuing.

'A few full moons ago, this man turned up to demand payment for a huge debt. There was no way we could pay. He was tying rope around Abba's wrists when his eyes alighted on me. He paused. "Is she betrothed?" he asked. Ima replied negatively. "I have reason to believe my master would take her as payment instead of your husband. If you would prefer it," he said. Ima was distraught, as was I. "Not as a slave," he clarified, seeing our reaction. "As a wife. I'll return in three days for your answer."

'He posted a guard at our door to prevent us escaping. Those days were full of tears and wails. Poor Ima, she was beside herself with grief that things had come to this. But if Abba was taken, she would have nothing. It had to be me.

'On the allotted day, Noa appeared on our doorstep. It was such a shock to see a wealthy woman, that we let her in immediately. She confirmed her son was in want of a wife and that there were reasons why he could not procure one in the usual way. They asked me to leave the room. By the time I returned, the matter was settled. I was to go with Noa that very day and, as well as his debts being absolved, my parents would receive regular, generous provisions. Ima looked so guilty as she said goodbye, but I assumed she was just sad I couldn't choose my own husband. I didn't know they had agreed I would be a second wife.

'After bringing me back to the city – for I lived over a day's walk away in a small village – Noa took me shopping. She bought me fine clothes and jewellery and treated me with such kindness that I trusted her. I assumed that her son was an invalid or had some other impediment to finding a wife. She refused to tell me anything, saying she would like me to judge him for myself. The day we met, I had already been with her for several days and was feeling more at ease. Noa told me my future husband was in the room, and I should be sure to charm everyone, but she would not tell me who he was. I thought it might be Erad, because he was painfully shy and refused to meet my gaze.'

As she concluded her speech, Tzillah clasped Adah's hands. 'Believe me, Adah. I would never have agreed had I known. But I had no choice. The contract was sealed.'

Though several women had taken note now, watching their hushed conversation with interest, Adah doubted her neighbours had heard anything. Even so, the news would soon be all over the city. To think Lamech had used the excuse about preventing her shame, as if moving back with her father was less shameful than being usurped by a second wife! Her hatred for him deepened.

Nevertheless, Adah believed Tzillah's story. Everything she had said sounded exactly like something Noa would do. And when she looked at her rival, instead of the strong woman she had admired a few weeks before, she saw another victim of Methushael's evil. Tzillah could put on the charm, for sure, but she had just been playing her part in the game.

'Did you really like me, or was that for show as well?' Adah asked.

'Of course I liked you! I thought we would be sisters. I didn't imagine we'd be sharing the same husband.'

Adah nodded. 'Did Lamech... Did Lamech treat you well?'

'Yes.' Tzillah's eyes glistened with tears, and knowing how charming Lamech could be, Adah didn't doubt that he'd endeared himself to her.

Adah wasn't sure why, but she felt the compulsion to hug this woman in front of her neighbours. She wasn't sure she would ever return to this house, but they didn't need to know that Tzillah was paid for, rather than willing, nor that Adah knew nothing of it. Let Lamech bear the shame. Tzillah should not.

'Where will you go?' Tzillah murmured, snuggling into Adah's shoulder.

'I expect to my abba's. If nothing else, it will be a kick in the teeth to my husband.' *No, our husband. How strange that sounded.*

'You are so gracious, Adah. If I was in your position, I would have pulled his eyes out. And mine.'

'It would achieve nothing. Farewell.'

As she walked towards the city gates, Adah realised she hadn't said goodbye to Shua. In Tzillah's presence, she had been calm and diplomatic, but now that no one was present to check her emotions, Adah spun and leaned against a wall, holding her head in her hands as she panted in fury. What had Lamech done? For it was not just him she would lose, it was also her servants.

As she released her self-control, imaginings of what had transpired in the last month began to crowd in. Now she saw Lamech in Tzillah's arms. She recalled how well he'd looked moments earlier. He hadn't felt guilty until he'd been forced to justify himself. He'd been delighted with his two wives, pleased with his successful subterfuge. They must be laughing about her misfortune: Lamech and Noa.

She had to get out of there – had to escape the city before Lamech followed. If he'd gone to these lengths to keep her, he wouldn't just let her walk free. Lost in her tempest of thoughts, Adah hurried so quickly down the street that she didn't see Chanoch until she crashed into him.

'Adah. What are you doing here?'

Pulled back to reality, she realised she had knocked Chanoch over and sent a basket of food flying all over the path. 'Oh, I'm sorry. Let me help you.'

She knelt and crawled to retrieve the various scattered oranges, figs and pistachios, but stopped when her hands wrapped around a pomegranate.

Lamech's image at the pomegranate tree on the day they met flashed before her eyes. Overcome, Adah sat up, cradling the fruit to her chest, and let out a sharp, piercing cry.

CHAPTER 22

When Chanoch witnessed Adah's breakdown, he wasted no time abandoning the search for fruit and rushed to her side. It was only a few steps to his home, so he helped Adah inside as she began wailing uncontrollably. Unusually, Shiphrah was out of bed, so his wife held Adah's hand and made comforting sounds while Chanoch boiled water for chamomile tea. He couldn't imagine the cause of Adah's current distress, but he silently thanked Yahweh for their unexpected encounter.

Once she had sipped her tea and partially recovered, Adah released a few sentences between sobs, disclosing the depths of Lamech's new depravity.

Chanoch was astounded. 'It's not unheard of for men to abandon their wives, and far too many seek pleasure in taverns, but openly having two wives at the same time is unprecedented.' He repeated his thoughts aloud several times, muttering under his breath as he paced his one-roomed living area, wondering what on earth he could do to help Adah.

'I should call the company of elders!' he finally said, stopping and standing resolutely. 'I shall inform them what has happened. Of late we have been rather lax at meeting together, it is true, but I know they will be outraged by this behaviour. Just imagine if every man took two wives. Where would that leave us? It is unconscionable!'

Adah took another sip while Shiphrah raised her eyebrows at him. 'I haven't seen you this rattled for many moons, my dear. It is quite unlike you.'

'But I'm right, am I not? We can't allow it to pass without condemnation. It sets a precedent that cannot be continued.'

'I agree with you. Entirely. But you will be setting yourself against powerful men, my dear. Who knows how many of the elders Methushael has in his pocket?'

'This evil was not Methushael's idea, for a change. This is Noa and Lamech's doing,' he replied.

Shiphrah stroked Adah's back. 'But we both know Methushael's capabilities. He would use his wealth and influence to bribe every man in the city if it meant protecting his family name. And if trade-offs fail, I have little doubt he would stoop to more violent measures.'

Chanoch stopped pacing. Shiphrah was right. It was a dangerous game. But Chanoch had completed many centuries of life. He had witnessed the decline of morality and Yahweh-worship in the city. Out of fear, he had done little. If he did not stand up now, he would never forgive himself.

'I am going to do it anyway. Even if I must carry you from the city and flee to join my parents, I cannot stand by and do nothing.'

'What about Tzillah?' Adah asked.

Chanoch stopped pacing.

'If you parade the matter before the city, Tzillah will be disgraced. Her family, dishonoured.'

'But it isn't Tzillah's fault,' he said.

Adah shook her head. 'That doesn't matter. They have consummated the marriage. If she is sent away, she is ruined. And if it gets out that her parents sold her to pay a debt, what then?'

Oh, Adah. What other woman whose husband had just been stolen would be worrying about the thief? Yahweh must be working in Adah's heart. Dare I send her back to Lamech, the unbeliever? For a moment, Chanoch forced himself to think about the people involved, rather than the principle.

Adah would be publicly shamed. Tzillah as well. What would their lives be like if he intervened – if the elders annulled the marriage? Adah would return to a husband who would likely hate her. Tzillah would be abandoned, her family impoverished, or – he suspected – removed.

'How did this even take place? No one in this city would perform such a ceremony, surely?' he thought aloud.

'All I know is they went north,' Adah replied.

'Ah. It must have been Barsabas' people. Dinah's husband is a law unto himself. He cares for nothing but the acquisition of land and power. He wouldn't think twice about doing such a thing.'

Chanoch poured some more tea. He needed further fortification to think. Handing Adah a refilled cup, he realised he had no idea what she wanted. How selfish of him. He took a seat near her. 'Now that you have processed somewhat, what are your feelings regarding your husband?'

Adah rubbed her eyes and took a deep breath. 'I think I finally see him for what he is. All this time, I've been trying to convince myself he might change. He's always been volatile, and, as you know, this isn't the first time he's taken another woman. But I loved him still! I forgave him. Now... Now it feels quite different. My blindness has lifted. I don't want to live in fear or guilt. I don't want to constantly feel like I'm not enough. I don't think... I don't think I want him anymore.'

Sorrow filled Chanoch's heart as Adah's red-rimmed eyes pleaded for understanding. Though it would make things easier to let Adah leave, it was always sad to see a marriage fail. 'So, if we were to leave things – leave Lamech with Tzillah – how would you feel?'

'Dejected, undoubtedly. But perhaps it's for the best.'

'And what would you do?'

'I suppose I can go back to my abba and work on the farm. I would be content doing that. Perhaps I can build my own home, so I'm not in Rivkah's way.'

'What if Lamech pursues you?' he asked. 'The whole reason he did this was to prevent you being taken from him. He could mount a challenge before the elders, insisting you return home.'

'Do you think he would succeed, given that he's taken two wives?'

'As Shiphrah said, we don't know how far Methushael might go...'

'But Methushael hates me. I don't think he would support Lamech in this. My husband assumed I wouldn't leave voluntarily. I have caught him off-guard.'

Adah was speaking sensibly, though he doubted her conclusion. 'Doesn't Lamech have finance enough of his own to mount a defensive?' He could likely bribe people as effectively as Methushael.

'Probably. But he looked so happy when he returned... I suspect Tzillah will provide his needs, and he will soon forget about me. She's better suited to him than I ever was.'

Chanoch thought for a moment. He was not convinced, for Lamech was extremely stubborn and determined. Also, Adah would surely long for a husband again one day. But she was young, beautiful and unencumbered by offspring. There may be a good man who would gladly take her in. A widower perhaps, who wouldn't care about having more children. In the meantime, he would do what he could to support her.

'If you're right, then I suppose we could let matters rest. At least if we do, I shouldn't end up with the city believing it's acceptable for Lamech to have two wives. I think I will still hold a private meeting with the elders I trust, to inform them of what has happened. It would be good to be on our guard. But I don't want to burden you further, Adah. You shouldn't be forced to return to a husband who has treated you so shamefully.'

'It is now dark,' Shiphrah said. 'You must stay the night with us. Then in the morning, Chanoch will accompany you to your father's home.'

Adah nodded. 'Thank you.'

When they had all retired to bed, Adah taking the place she'd occupied before in the spare chamber, Chanoch spoke again with his wife. 'I still don't like it, Shiphrah. Though there is a slim chance, I very much doubt this will end well. And it tells Methushael's people that they can do whatever they please and get away with it. What will it be next?'

'I agree with you, dearest. But that poor girl has been through enough. I wouldn't go back to such a man, given the choice.'

Chanoch kissed Shiphrah on the head. 'How are you feeling after all that exertion?'

'Physically, exhausted. Though I did little more than hold her hand. But spiritually, I feel alive. I so rarely get to help people these days. I'm pleased Yahweh allowed me that privilege today.'

'Rest then. Goodnight, my love.'

As Shiphrah snuggled in closer to his side, Chanoch thanked Yahweh for her. He might never know why they had been burdened with her illness, but he wouldn't change his wife for anything. Once more, the thought of what Lamech had done, merely because Adah hadn't provided an heir, disgusted him. He would try to find a way to right this wrong without making the girl suffer.

CHAPTER 23

When Adah trundled up the hill towards her old home the following day, she was surprised to find that her family were not alone. Sitting outside around a crackling fire were not just her abba, Rivkah and their seven-year-old son, Levi, but also Ruhamah, Eliana's brother.

'Adah, my love. Chanoch too. Welcome! To what do I owe the company of my two favourite people?' As Abba jumped up and shuffled things around to make room for them, Levi hopped over and gave Adah a quick squeeze before settling next to Ruhamah, who'd only briefly glanced up before continuing his demonstration of stone sharpening. He held a stone formed into a curve, suitable for digging worms from sheep hooves.

Adah hesitated, not ready to explain the intricacies of her situation in front of a guest, even one who had been her childhood friend. That was a long time ago. Fortunately, Chanoch's gentleness discerned her need, and he sat next to her abba and launched into a story about a neighbouring farmer that distracted him for some time.

The space left was on Ruhamah's other side. Adah hadn't seen him since his wife had asked her not to visit. He looked older, of course, but maturity had chiselled his features into a finer version of the familiar. He was so different to Lamech – petite and scruffy, with no hint of pride or refinement in his clothing. She wondered if his wife would mind her being there, and why he was.

'How are you, Ruhamah? What are you doing this far west?' she asked, kneeling into the gap.

'Adah, it's good to see you.' Ruhamah smiled warmly, his dimples revealing her old friend and putting her almost at ease. *Good, I was worried by his brief glance that he didn't want to see me.*

'I'm surprised Shimiel hasn't told you,' Ruhamah continued. 'We decided to combine our flocks. He has so few, it isn't worth him taking them to the further pastures, but I'm quite happy to care for them in return for some of his other produce. We came to our agreement last winter. There aren't many others we trust.'

'I have barely seen Abba of late. Do you go far now, then?'

'The grass around the city is no longer sufficient for the greater number of shepherds. I prefer to travel into the hills rather than argue.'

'You always were a peacekeeper.' She was remembering the multiple times Ruhamah had gotten Eliana out of scrapes caused by her friend's active tongue.

'It is good to see you,' he said, grinding the stone again.

'You said that.' She grinned. 'But how is your wife? Is she not here?'

Ruhamah passed the stone to Levi to continue what he'd demonstrated, then gazed into his sweaty palms. Had she said something amiss? 'Haven't you seen my sister either? Surely, Eliana would have told you...'

'I saw her last week, but she didn't mention you.'

'Nadia died three years ago, Adah.'

Her hand flew to her mouth. *No!* How could Nadia die? She was so young and healthy. Why had Eliana not told her? She racked her mind... three years ago... That was when Adah had lost her second baby, when Lamech had the affair with Nasya.

She exhaled. 'I think Eliana didn't tell me because I had my own grief to bear. Then perhaps it slipped her mind afterwards.'

'She didn't tell me of your grief either...' Ruhamah said, his brows drawn together in concern.

Adah instinctively reached for her old friend's hand. 'I am sorry for it all, though I dare say Eliana was right at the time. Oh, your loss, Ruhamah. Your poor heart!'

Their eyes locked and in his she saw new depths. He wasn't a carefree boy anymore. Suffering had changed him, as it had changed her. She released his hand, suddenly aware of what she'd done. 'My apologies.'

His mouth twitched. 'Adah, how many times did we hold hands as children?'

'Yes, but it is different now.'

'It is. It is.' Ruhamah stared into the fire and gradually all chatter around them ceased. Chanoch's story was finished, Abba's questions satisfied, and Rivkah's eyes were closed as she reclined on the only chair, the fold of her clothing no longer concealing the roundness of another child in her womb. The only noise was the squawking of blackbirds, for Levi had got bored of grinding, and was throwing stones behind the hut.

Chanoch rose from the ground – he'd refused to take Rivkah's chair. 'I'd better return to my wife. I will leave Adah in your most capable hands, my friend. Do come by or send a messenger – perhaps this young man here – should you need anything whatsoever. Anything at all.'

Abba tilted his head, puzzled at being left with his daughter, but Adah knew he would never question his elder. As Chanoch descended the hill, Ruhamah's eyes flicked between the remaining persons. Then he made an excuse about checking on the flock and took Levi with him, leaving Adah alone with Abba and his wife.

'Well, my love. It is a pleasure to have you, for sure. But I must confess I'm not sure why you have come accompanied by Chanoch. Perhaps you could enlighten us?'

Rivkah had sat up, and she was now alert, waiting for the explanation also. Adah glanced at her and forced herself to recall the woman who had fed her raisin cakes as a child, rather than the woman who carried another healthy baby for her abba.

'I need to ask you a favour. I can't live with Lamech anymore. Will you take me in until I can find another solution?'

Abba's eyes narrowed, and his cheeks reddened. 'What has that man done to you?'

'Abba?' As far as she knew, her father still liked Lamech. What was this change?

He jumped up. 'You have been unhappy, I know, but you would not leave without severe provocation. You are too loyal for that.'

'That is true.' Severe provocation it was indeed, but where could she start in explaining it?

Abba paced before the fire, his jittering speech and movement amplified by distress. 'Oh, for years I have regretted marrying you to that man. Why did I fall for his charm? Why did I allow you to? When I went to Chanoch's to ask him to recommend a husband for you, I jumped at Lamech's presence as a sign. I didn't even ask Chanoch the question. I should have pulled you out of Lamech's clutches the moment I saw Methushael's face. I should have walked you right out of that abominable house, back home to safety. Never... Never have I made such a terrible mistake! Your dear ima would be so angry with me...'

'Oh, Abba!' She stood and stepped in front of him, stopping his tracks. 'You must not blame yourself.'

'Who can I blame but myself? Your mother left me with one task – one task! To find you a good husband who would treasure you and treat you as you deserve. And... and look what I did.'

She flung herself into his chest, squeezing him tightly as she'd done when she was a little girl. 'I do not blame you, Abba. Don't blame yourself.'

'You are too good, my sweet daughter.' His shoulders racked with sobs, and his tears dampened her shoulders. 'I miss her so much. Oh, I miss her. One task she gave me. One task.'

Adah peeked at Rivkah. The woman must be made of stone not to be upset by her husband crying over his dead wife. But Rivkah's face held only compassion. Pulling an arm out from under Abba, she extended it to Rivkah, who shifted reluctantly.

Come, she mouthed.

So, Rivkah did. As the three of them held each other, unsteady walls began crumbling, until the walls ceased to exist. They were just a man, his daughter and his wife. And they loved each other.

RIVKAH REARRANGED THINGS in the home so Adah could fit in, but it wasn't really big enough for four, especially when one of them was heavily pregnant and the chickens came in for the night. Adah found herself tucked in a corner with Levi's wriggly feet kicking her sides whenever he had an exciting dream.

She gradually explained to her abba all that had happened in her years of marriage, most of which she hadn't revealed to a soul.

Several times during the revelations, he rose as if he would storm to Lamech's house at once and call him out, but he did not.

When she got to the part about Tzillah, he was firm. 'You are never going back to that man. If he can take another wife, then you can have another husband.'

'I'm not looking for another husband, Abba.'

He didn't respond but looked about their cramped home and nodded. Of course, she couldn't stay with them forever, but as she'd suggested previously, she could build her own home nearby, still under his protection.

'I'm not sure about that,' Ruhamah said one day when they were walking together. She often strolled in the hills, revelling in the freedom she'd craved for so long, and came across him. 'It is no longer safe to live alone, even for a man. It's another reason I moved this way, within eyesight of my parents' home and Shimiel's. Even if you were within our triangle, Adah, we'd all worry about you.'

'I'm sure we'll find a solution.'

She enjoyed working on the farm again, getting her fingers into the soil and taking her grief out on the weeds. With the sheep and goats in Ruhamah's care, she started spending time with her old friend frequently, helping him check for worms in hooves and ticks in coats.

Ruhamah barely talked about his wife or what had happened to her, and she did not talk about Lamech. It was easier that way, pretending that half their lives hadn't happened.

One day, Lamech came to the house. Adah was feeling sick that morning, so she was still in bed, which was unusual, but providential.

'Where is Adah? I know she is here.'

She stiffened at Lamech's voice, then pulled the bedsheet higher, trying to squeeze into the corner as far as possible.

'Adah is not receiving visitors.' Abba's voice. Not Rivkah's. Praise Yahweh for that. Perhaps Lamech would listen to him.

'I am not a visitor. I am her husband.'

'As I said, she is not receiving visitors.'

'Get out of my way, you insolent fool.'

Adah heard a scuffle.

'I will not get out of your way. You lost all rights over my daughter when you took another woman, forcing her out of your home.'

'I did no such thing. She left me!'

'So, you deny having another wife?'

'Of course not. I deny forcing Adah from her home. She belongs with me.'

'My daughter belongs with no man who treats her with such contempt.'

'Shimiel, be reasonable! I have been gracious, allowing Adah time to process what happened. Now she must return with me.'

'She will do no such thing.'

'I didn't want to do this, Shimiel. Adah forced my hand. If she had just given me a child—'

'You should hear yourself! Did Adah ever deny you, Lamech?'

'No.'

'Then none of this is her fault, and you know it. Don't you dare blame her again. You knew what the risks were when you married her. If you cared so much for producing a son, you should have listened to your vile father.'

Abba's defence stung, but it was effective. There was a pause. Adah held her breath, waiting for Lamech's softening.

'Please, my friend. I see I have upset you. Truly, I am sorry for it. But I love your daughter. I just want to bring her home. Please, let me see my wife.'

Lamech *was* predictable. Why had she not noticed it before?

'I will not allow you to see her, for she is unwell. But I will tell her you called, and if she wants to speak to you – and only if – I will send a messenger.'

Lamech's sigh was so loud, it penetrated the walls. Then came his thumping, irritated gait, getting softer as he departed.

Moments later, Abba was kneeling at her side. 'You heard that?'

She nodded. 'Thank you.'

As he stroked her forehead, his own crinkled. 'You are warm. Here, have some more of Rivkah's broth.'

But the broth turned her stomach, and she couldn't take it. 'Just let me sleep, Abba. I'm sure I will be fine by morning.'

'Very well.' After kissing her, he left. But Adah's mind would not rest. Lamech's voice had stirred the disquiet within.

CHAPTER 24

'This one needs trimming, and a good clean. Do you have a poultice for it?' Adah was holding one of the goat's legs, inspecting its rotten hoof. She'd spied the limp soon after she'd joined Ruhamah that morning.

'Yes, back at my hut. Here.' Ruhamah threw her a rope, and she tied it around the goat's neck so they could escort it back.

As Adah straightened, she felt a tightening in her back and winced.

'Are you alright?' Ruhamah joined her, placing a hand on the small of her back.

'Yes, yes. It just twinged, that's all.'

'That's the third time today.'

'Have you been watching me?'

Ruhamah blushed.

'I'm joking. I appreciate your concern. But I'm fine really. I'm finding it hard to sleep comfortably, that's all. I'm afraid my back has been pampered for the past fifteen years and isn't used to a hard floor.'

'I can help. Let me make you a bed.'

'Thank you, but there is no room.'

Ruhamah's fingers lingered on her back, seemingly reluctant to relinquish his concern. 'Adah, may I ask you something?'

'Of course.'

He removed his hand and lifted the injured goat onto his shoulders. 'Your husband. Is he... Is it final? You've left him?' he asked as they began walking towards his home.

She must choose her words carefully. Four full moons had passed since she'd arrived, and she had sensed for some time that Ruhamah's old feelings may be resurfacing. 'He took a second wife. There's no sign of him changing his mind.'

Ruhamah's breath caught. 'Another wife? When you were still in his home? How—'

'He does as he pleases, Ruhamah. He always has.'

Her friend ran his free hand through his walnut-brown hair. 'I meant how could anyone want someone else if they had you? It's incomprehensible.'

Adah chuckled. 'You act like I'm some kind of perfect woman. I am not, I assure you.'

'Nothing could warrant being treated like that.'

'With that, I must agree.'

His hand descended to his short but unruly beard, and he stopped walking, stroking it as his eyes flickered from hers to the ground repeatedly. 'So, you don't intend to go back?'

Adah regarded the scenery: the hill country in the distance, the stream they walked alongside, the smell of the animals and crops catching on the breeze. This had been her happy childhood home, and the past season, her sanctuary. Sometimes at night her heart still ached for her husband's companionship, but when it did, reminding herself what he'd done soon cured the longing. 'I do not.'

'And do you think he has any right to claim you back?'

'Chanoch seems confident he won't try. He has rallied the elders to my defence, just in case.' Chanoch had visited the previous week to update them on his progress and had been optimistic. 'Lamech tried to claim me once, when I'd been here two weeks, but Abba scared him off.'

'Shimiel?' Ruhamah's mouth twitched into a half-smile.

'I know.' She grinned. 'But he hasn't returned.'

Ruhamah nodded his head thoughtfully and stroked his beard again. 'Nadia died in childbirth. I lost my wife and daughter in one day.'

'Oh! Oh, Ruhamah. How terrible.' Unconsciously, her hand was on his arm.

His fingers covered it. 'It still pains me, even though it was so long ago.'

Adah understood. She continued to mourn for her lost children, and her mother.

'But I don't believe things must stay this way,' Ruhamah said. 'Hurt and hardship are not Yahweh's design. I didn't understand that at first, of course. I blamed Him for taking them away. I lost my faith in Yahweh's goodness for a while.'

'You did?'

Ruhamah had always been strong in faith. His parents had been far more consistent in their instruction than hers. Although hers had acknowledged Yahweh and kept Shabbat, they had not been devoted; they had not prayed as Ruhamah's family had done, committing every detail of their lives to the Creator.

When the goat bleated its disapproval, Ruhamah continued walking. 'My parents were always adamant that Yahweh Elohim created us for good, that He watches over us and answers our prayers. They claim nothing happens outside His will. That is hard to stomach when things happen that seem nonsensical, or when prayers go unanswered.'

'Yes.' Adah thought of her own prayers. Then about Lamech's faith, or lack of it. Had he ever had any? He'd shown no inclination to pray since they lost their first child. Did sin prevent him – did he ever feel guilty? He claimed to after Nasya, but had it all been an act to win her back? Had he ever repented as she did, night after night? Perhaps it was because Lamech sinned that she'd not conceived again. Either way, she had no child to show for her efforts. No evidence that Yahweh cared for her, except in the kindness of His people.

'What are you thinking about?' Ruhamah asked.

She didn't want to admit she'd been thinking of Lamech. 'Of how little I know the Creator. I don't feel my prayers have been answered either. However, I always supposed it was my fault; that I did something wrong. What stopped you blaming Elohim?'

They'd reached Ruhamah's home. He shifted the goat from his shoulders and sighed. 'Hope. Hope that the future held answers to earlier prayers, and those utterances I never thought, or dared, to vocalise.'

After a pause, during which she didn't know how to respond, he tied the goat to a post then took her hands. 'Is there hope, Adah?'

His eyes, surrounded by waves of tousled hair, were pools of implication. She had no doubt what he meant. For him, it had been nearly four years. For her, just four full moons. But he was considerate, he was safe, and he was good. A tiny spark ignited in her heart again. 'Yes. Though it is too soon right now.'

'I understand.' He placed a simple kiss on her hands then released them and went to find the poultice.

As Adah watched him walk away, something else flickered inside her. Barely discernible, she didn't know what it meant. Only later would she comprehend.

THE FOLLOWING MORNING, Adah was lying awake, head too heavy to start the day. Levi had kept her up with a particularly invigorating dream. Rivkah's newborn child had also been restless and had woken her several times. Everything ached, from her shoulders to her knees. She thought immediately of Ruhamah's offer. He would make her a proper bed. And there was space in his hut.

'I must not think of it. It is too soon,' she told herself. She wondered if Tzillah was expecting a child yet. If she had conceived while Lamech was away, she could already be halfway through her time. She could be feeling movement inside her right now as she lay in bed. Lamech would no doubt surround her in cushions and refuse to let her move a finger.

Perhaps that was why he hadn't come. He had no need of her anymore. He was content with his new wife and promised heir. But would he manage to control himself? Perhaps Lamech had such confidence in Tzillah's abilities that he continued satisfying his passions in her bedchamber. If not, could desire for Adah flare up due to abstinence from his new wife? Might he appear to claim her soon?

As Adah considered the possibility, Ruhamah suddenly became a more favourable prospect. Why should she refrain from someone new, when Lamech had never done so? She was not the one who had been unfaithful. What chance was there of her finding another man who would not consider her purity sullied and her womb useless? Ruhamah didn't seem to care. He had loved her when she was a girl, and he loved her still. Yet, he had no child of his own. Perhaps he'd later resent her, as Lamech had.

As she thought of her womb, Adah moved a hand to it. She stroked the place that had once contained her children. She remembered the tightening. The agony. The blood.

When was the last time she had bled? She took a sharp intake of breath – she had not. She hadn't bled since she had been in her Abba's house. How had it not occurred to her before now?

No, it wasn't possible. It couldn't be. Women often missed their bleeds when life was particularly stressful; she had been told that many times. Sometimes even because they wished so much for a child, their body was fooled into thinking it had one. It could not be the case. It could not be so…

Then she felt it again – the tiniest flicker, like someone gently tapping her insides.

It was a voice crying out, 'I'm here. I am alive!'

CHAPTER 25

'Adah, a word.'

Eliana had come to visit and now she stood, hand on hip with determination set into the purse of her lips. Her children were scattered about the farm and Levi was having the time of his life with his friends. Mela sat outside the hut, holding Rivkah's baby cradled in one arm and Eliana's youngest on her opposite knee, singing them both a rhyming song. The noonday sun was cheerfully bright and just the right temperature. All should be well with the world, but by Eliana's face, she knew Adah's secret.

Her friend marched her away until they were outside everyone's earshot. 'You are with child.'

Adah looked down at her loose tunic, a meagre attempt to hide her gently swelling stomach. 'I knew you would guess immediately.'

'Does anyone else know?'

'I only realised two weeks ago.'

'What? How is that even possible? You must be what...' Eliana counted back, 'over halfway now?'

'Presumably.'

'If it's Lamech's.'

'Of course!'

'Sorry. So, no one knows?'

'I think Rivkah has been too preoccupied to notice. Goodness, I was too preoccupied to notice! The men wouldn't even suspect. But it will be obvious soon.'

'It's obvious to me now.'

'Yes, but you are *you*.'

'Oh, Adah! What are you going to do?'

'I don't know. That's why I haven't said anything. Oh, Eliana, why did this have to happen now? Why not years ago when we were happy? I don't understand.'

Adah's head found her hands and she buried it there, fighting to hold back the tears that had been threatening her constantly for the last two weeks. She'd barely been able to look Ruhamah in the eye.

Eliana grasped them and pulled them away from her face. 'Adah, look at me.'

As she did, relief began to filter in. Her best friend knew. Someone knew. Now Eliana would take control, tell her what to do, and it needn't plague her any longer.

Eliana's hands moved to Adah's middle, where she placed them either side of the growing babe. 'The most important thing is the safety of this child – *Yahweh may you keep this little one secure in your hands and bring it to full term in health and vigour* – but we have to face the fact that you have not carried to term before.'

'This is the first time I have felt my child move inside me.'

'Praise Yahweh! That is wonderful. Still, we must not be rash. There is no need to rush into anything.'

'What do you mean? What might I rush into?'

'Telling Lamech for starters.'

'But the babe is his. If he found out I had kept this from him—'

'Adah, Tzillah is with child. Lamech parades her around the marketplace like a piece of expensive jewellery, showing off her rounded stomach to anyone who will allow him. Everyone wonders what happened to his first wife, but no one dares ask. Imagine what would happen if— No! Lamech is content with Tzillah. We must make the most of his temporary memory loss.'

Adah could well imagine everything Eliana said. She could see her husband doing just that, displaying his sin with such effrontery that no one would dare question it. It was exactly his style. Chanoch must be furious.

'But what if my condition becomes known? He will be up here immediately, dragging me home. He would never let me stay.'

'You must remain hidden. History suggests Lamech's very presence would endanger this child, Adah. If he finds out and drags you home, you might lose it again. After it is born healthy, then we can decide what to do. If anyone questions your absence, I will set about a rumour that you have moved away.'

'You must not lie on my account.'

'Then don't give me cause to.'

Adah made circles on her stomach. The little one responded spiritedly. 'I love him already so much. Now I know what it feels like – although it is still so faint – I feel him all the time, kicking away, telling me he's going to make it. Then I feel such sorrow. Sorrow that I must choose between what is best for me, and what is best for him.'

'Which is?'

'To be with his father.'

'Why do you think being with Lamech will be good for him?'

'Lamech may not be ideal, but he would love his child. You cannot deny that.'

'I think you are still blinded. If I were you, I would escape to a different city and bring up the child as far away from that man as possible.'

'I don't think I can do that. Besides, where would I go? All I know is here.'

'What about your mother's kin; in the land between the rivers?'

'I never met them.' Her eyes were still fixed on her abdomen.

Eliana tilted Adah's chin until she had her gaze. 'Just promise me you'll think about it. And say nothing to Lamech.'

Adah nodded. 'I promise.'

When they arrived back to the hut, Ruhamah had appeared with a little lamb under his arm. Several children were running around him, jumping up and down to try and see the lamb.

'Steady, steady,' he laughed. 'She is only half a day old. You may all have a turn in due course.'

Adah smiled as Ruhamah sat on the ground, withdrew a bladder-pouch filled with milk and passed it to the eldest of the children surrounding him.

'You don't need to squeeze it; the lamb will suckle well enough. Gently now.'

'Triplets?' Adah asked, drawing near. Eliana had wandered off to relieve Mela of the babies.

'Yes. What a blessing they all survived. But the mother won't be able to feed them all.'

'I should think not.'

Ruhamah looked up and grinned. 'What were you gossiping with my sister about?'

'Oh. Um...'

'It's fine, I don't need to know. I am quite happy being ignorant of the vast majority of things Eliana knows.'

'And I.' Adah laughed.

'Pass it along to Levi now. Slowly, so the lamb doesn't lose her hold... Are you well? At one point Eliana looked serious, though I couldn't see your face.'

Might Ruhamah have seen them stroking her stomach? Should she tell him? The thought brought her more sorrow. He had opened his heart to her again, only to have it torn away. Look at him now, surrounded by these children. He would make such a good father. He deserved a faithful wife and many children of his own.

His eyebrows drew together. 'Adah?'

She had to tell him. The longer she delayed, the harder it would be. 'Are you staying for dinner?'

'Oh yes, I have my sister's orders. She and Rivkah seem to have planned quite a feast.'

'Then perhaps we might take a walk afterwards.' *Before I lose my nerve.*

'I would like that.' The bladder was passed to the next child, who grabbed it too hastily and spilt it over Ruhamah's lap. The next few moments were taken up with sorting out the mess. Ruhamah laughed, Levi scolded, the child who'd dropped the pouch cried and the lamb bleated hungrily.

'Give it to me,' Adah interjected, removing the tiny lamb from Ruhamah so he could stand. As she did so, their hands brushed, and they both looked up. His eyes had flecks of green in them – she hadn't noticed that before.

'Is it my turn yet?' another child asked. How long had Ruhamah's eyes distracted her?

'Yes, of course.' She sat down and the pouch was hastily shoved into the lamb's mouth by the impatient child. Then she felt Ruhamah's hand on her shoulder.

His thumb rubbed her neck. 'If you're comfortable managing the tribe, I'll go change my tunic.'

'Of course.'

He paused, mid stroke. She heard his ragged breathing. Then with a slight squeeze of her shoulder, he was gone.

Dinner hadn't been exaggerated. Eliana had brought baskets of food with her, all carried up the hill by her brood. Eliana's husband, Manon, joined them after work and the feast lasted well into the evening. Around the fire they ate, laughed and chatted. The children were thrilled with staying up late and were soon playing games in the semi-dark, hiding, running and squealing. Abba was in high spirits too. He sang songs from the stories of old. It had been so long since Adah had heard her abba sing, she had forgotten how rich his voice was.

When Mela was pulled away from the fire by the younger children and forced to join in the games, Adah found herself next to Ruhamah. He smiled and scooted a little closer. Across from them, Eliana was sitting on Manon's lap, their expressions shielded by the firelight dancing in Adah's eyes.

As Shimiel commenced an old love song between The Wanderer and his wife, Rivkah joined him to duet.

> *Long we have travelled, and long we have roamed,*
> *Never finding a permanent place to call home.*
> *With you by my side, I don't travel alone.*
> *You're flesh of my flesh, and bone of my bones.*
>
> *So sing now – don't settle or travel alone,*
> *But wander, oh wander, with the bone of your bones.*
>
> *Once I did travel, did travel alone,*
> *'Til she found me and mercy, oh mercy, was shown.*
> *My heart was a tangle of thorns and of stone,*
> *'Til she loved me and showed me the one on the throne.*
>
> *So sing now – don't settle or travel alone,*
> *But wander, oh wander, with the bone of your bones.*
>
> *Long we have waited for seasons to pass,*
> *To glean what we can from the trees and the grass.*
> *With you by my side, I will labour at last,*
> *With the flesh of my flesh, and the fire of my heart.*

*So sing now – don't settle or travel alone,
But wander, oh wander, with the bone of your bones.*

During the song, Ruhamah's fingers reached for Adah's. Ripples of nervousness moved up her arms and through her chest, like sparks from the fire tickling her skin.

'It's getting late. Do you still want that walk?' he whispered.

Adah turned her head. He was close, closer than she'd realised. She started back.

He removed his hand. 'Forgive me. I should not…'

'Perhaps now is not the best time. We will set off Eliana's tongue, for sure.' Yet her fingers missed his.

Ruhamah chuckled. 'That is very true. So far, she seems ignorant, but she could be playing us.'

A smile tugged at her lips. That wouldn't surprise her. But would Eliana really want a match between them when she knew the truth of Adah's condition? Surely she wouldn't want her brother mixed up in the mess.

'You have that look on your face again. Won't you tell me what's troubling you?' Ruhamah said.

'I will.' Adah glanced again across the fire. Eliana and Manon showed no signs of leaving, and all their attention was on each other. 'Alright, let's go. No doubt she'll give us her opinion soon enough.'

CHAPTER 26

'I'm sorry I held your hand. I shouldn't have done that,' Ruhamah said, slowing his stride.

They were walking uphill, following their usual route to the outer grazing land through the trees. No one seemed to have noticed them leave. The children continued to play around the hut, but their squeals sounded far enough away that there was no danger of their conversation being overheard.

'It's alright.'

'I thought we shared a moment, earlier on. If I was wrong…'

'You weren't wrong.'

'I know you said you aren't ready. If I'm rushing you, tell me and I'll stay away. Because when I'm near you—'

Adah stopped walking. 'I said you weren't wrong.'

Ruhamah stopped too. He was close enough that she could hear his breath, yet darkness concealed all but the outlines of his face. She didn't need to see it. Though he had aged since their late teens, she knew every contour. The cut of his jaw line, the dimple that appeared when he smiled, the unruly wisp of hair that hung around his ears, needing constantly tucking back. That was why she'd been so shocked to see that fleck in his eyes for the first time. Was it recently acquired, or had she not paid him enough attention to notice?

He cradled her cheek in his hand. His palms were warm and calloused, and his fingers long and delicate – unlike Lamech's broad ones. But his touch was most different. With every movement he sought her permission, showing her tenderness and respect. She nestled into his hand and closed her eyes.

'I love you, Adah.'

How many times had she heard those words? But never like this.

He stroked her cheek. 'I see you changing. Yet you carry hurt and fear like a heavy shroud. Is that all that holds you back, or do you still yearn for Lamech?'

Did she? For so long Lamech had been her world. She had loved him as fiercely as he had loved her. Yet, he wasn't the man she married, the man he'd promised to be. He wasn't safe or secure, or anything she needed. 'A piece of me still belongs to Lamech, I cannot deny it. I still think of him constantly. Everywhere I walk, I expect to see him there. Whatever I do, I say to myself, "What would Lamech think of this? Would he approve?" Yet recently, the only exception to that is being with you. You have brought me freedom, Ruhamah. Freedom to breathe without needing permission.'

Both hands cradled her face. 'Then marry me. Leave Shimiel's crowded home and join mine. I will protect you. We can go to Chanoch – ask the elders' approval. They are already on your side; they will see it as a satisfactory solution. I'm sure Shimiel will support us. He knows I would never hurt you—'

'I am carrying Lamech's child.' The words were out before she'd realised she was speaking.

Silence. His hands moved away, and the chill of the evening struck her face.

'I see.' The two words were laboured and slow, like they had been dragged through a deep bog.

'He doesn't know. Eliana was the first to find out, just this afternoon.'

'And you – how long have you known?'

'A couple of weeks.'

Ruhamah sniffed and her heart ripped. 'I didn't know how to tell you, Ruhamah! I knew it would change everything, and I wasn't ready for things to change.'

He walked ahead. 'I assumed you couldn't have children.'

'So did I. Wait—' She caught up with him. 'You assumed this, and you still wanted to marry me?'

'Yes.'

'That is what Lamech thought before the reality hit.'

'I am not Lamech.' This time he sounded like she'd slapped him in the face. She supposed she had.

'Forgive me. I didn't mean it that way. I have just been through too much to make the same mistake twice. Not that it matters now.'

'Why would you say that?'

'Because we cannot marry.'

'You mean to go back then. Be one of two wives?'

'Eliana doesn't think I should. She says I should hide or run away, ensuring Lamech never finds out about the child. After all, we don't even know that it will survive.'

Ruhamah paused. 'What gives you cause to think that?'

'You have experience of this yourself. You know the risks.'

'I know them well...' His voice broke.

She hated to cause him pain. Suddenly she wanted to escape far away from Ruhamah, leave him so that he had nothing to do with her or her pregnancy, so his heart was never again at risk of being torn as it had been before.

'...however, it is not common,' he continued. 'Most women do not die in childbirth. Most children survive.'

'Mine have not.'

'Adah, you have told me nothing of this.'

'There was no cause to before, but now you know. I have been with child twice. Both times they have died.'

Though the night masked his tears, she knew they were there. He rubbed his face with his arm.

'I will return home. I don't want to cause you further pain,' she said.

'No. Adah, this doesn't change how I feel. My tears are not for myself but for you.' He reached forward. 'I still want to marry you.'

He could not mean it. Why would he want to marry her now?

'If the babe lives, I will take it as my own. Love it as my own. No one need ever know.'

Adah's mind raced. Was it possible? Could he really love a child that belonged to another man? Could Lamech be fooled? What if the child looked like his father?

They had meandered away from the trees now and the moonlight highlighted the ground enough to see the familiar path. She picked up the pace, as her feet followed her racing mind. 'We would still have to go away. If Lamech sees me—'

'Then we go away! We take the flock to the meadows near the hill country. We live off the land for a few years until it has been long enough that no one will question it. The Wanderer has lived in the wild his entire life. It must be possible. We could even find out from Chanoch where he lives, go to him and ask for his help.'

'You're not afraid?'

'No. He fears Yahweh. Why should we fear him?'

'But we'll be leaving everyone we know. Your parents, Eliana, Abba…'

'… will survive without us.'

'And if the child looks like Lamech? He will surely realise.'

Ruhamah touched her waist, and she stopped short. 'May I hold you?' he asked.

She nodded.

He drew her into his arms, wrapping them gently around her and tucking her head into his chest. Adah inhaled the familiar smell of sheep, finding it comforting rather than repulsive.

Ruhamah tilted his face to the skies. 'Yahweh Elohim, we praise You for the child growing inside Adah. We praise You for the gift of life. We both know what it is to lose this precious gift, and we do not take it for granted. Though our circumstances have changed, we praise You still. Though the seasons change, Your love remains. Help us to trust in this.

'Yahweh, we pray for Your hand of strength to be on Adah. I confess that when I consider her giving birth, I tremble. I fear. But I will trust in Your unfailing love. I will praise You for bringing us back together after all this time and for the opportunity You have given us to love again.

'Yahweh Elohim, You are truth. You are righteousness. You are justice. Removing Adah from Lamech – it feels like a wise thing to do. Yet concealing the truth from him… it does not sit well with us. It holds much risk. Would you help us, Yahweh? Help us to do what is good and right? Show us Your way.'

An unfamiliar peace descended on Adah's soul. This was a man who could teach her the ways of Yahweh. And what he did not know, he was willing to ask.

Her fingers tightened around his clothing. The babe within her kicked its approval and Ruhamah kissed the top of her head.

There was no question left in her mind. 'I will marry you.'

WHEN SHIMIEL FOUND OUT about their plans to wed, and the pregnancy, he approved. 'Lamech lost all rights to my daughter when he traded her for another woman,' he said. 'I don't see why he deserves any rights over this child. You should go to Chanoch immediately and have your engagement approved.'

'What would we tell him about the baby?' Adah asked.

Shimiel scratched his chin. 'There is no need to complicate matters at this stage. Chanoch has an overactive conscience. Let's not burden it until the child is safely delivered.'

The decision did not sit well with Ruhamah. 'I would prefer honesty. We have asked Yahweh to protect us, and we should assume He will.'

However, Adah would not contradict her father, primarily because she feared Lamech finding out. So, when they went to Chanoch and told him of their intentions the following day, her pregnancy wasn't mentioned.

Despite her anxiety, the babe inside Adah seemed determined to prove its vitality. The movements grew stronger daily, and her tunic began to bulge. By the time Chanoch sent word that the elders had approved the engagement several weeks later, there was no hiding the pregnancy.

'It looks like we will have to hide you instead,' Shimiel joked.

It was no joke. The elders had also requested a formal notification from Lamech that he would relinquish his claims on Adah. Only once he gave his consent would Ruhamah be free to marry her.

When another week had passed and Lamech had not complied, Adah dreaded what he would do. Eliana's assurances that he was still exhibiting Tzillah on the city streets did little to alleviate her fear. If he wouldn't let her go, might he suddenly reappear at the farm and find her swollen with his child? When she was far out in the fields with Ruhamah, she could almost think herself free, but any time she neared the hut, she expected to see her husband waiting for her.

Her dreams didn't allow her rest either. In them, Lamech dragged her to his home, threw her into bed and tied her in place so she could not escape. Other dreams placed him there during her labour, looming over her, waiting to snatch his heir. He salivated as she screamed in agony, then he fought with Ruhamah, each holding one arm of the child, ripping it to pieces.

CHAPTER 27

'I can't bear it any longer,' Adah declared. She was sitting on a boulder at the top of the hill. Ruhamah was on the ground next to her, pulling the dirt from some fleece he'd collected in the thorns. He stopped, put the fleece down and rested his hands on her enormous stomach.

'Are you restless, little one?' he asked. His voice and touch set the baby kicking, and he tickled the spot, chuckling. 'Are you giving your ima trouble?'

'It is not him,' Adah said. They'd always referred to the babe as a boy, ever since she'd told Ruhamah of her pregnancy. 'Of course I can bear him. It is Lamech.'

'Have you heard something?'

'No, but he must have done! If he hasn't given his permission for us to wed, why hasn't he come up here?'

'Did you expect him to?'

'I know him, Ruhamah. He will not let me go so easily. It doesn't matter if he thinks Tzillah bears an heir. He wants me too. I know it. It makes no sense that he hasn't come.'

'Perhaps Methushael has convinced him not to.'

Adah shook her head. 'Methushael is ruthless.'

'But he is less impulsive than Lamech. At least, that's what I have gathered. I can't say I know either of them personally.'

'It is true that Methushael's hatred of me was my greatest hope of freedom. The irony stings somewhat.'

'Adah, do you want to leave?' The wind picked up and blew the hair from Ruhamah's face. Was it telling them to flee?

Adah fiddled with her tunic. 'I know that isn't what you want. You want to do things properly – have us married before we disappear.'

'Little about this situation is straightforward or proper, my love.'

'But you are uneasy about the deceit.'

'Of course. So are you.'

Her lip trembled. 'It terrifies me.'

'How about we give it another week? If Lamech hasn't responded, we will go. We've always said the most important thing is the safety of this little one.'

'Alright. One more week.'

Three days later, Adah was once again seated on a boulder, watching over the flock as Ruhamah climbed the hill behind her, looking for a lost sheep.

Suddenly she heard a shriek. Turning around, Adah watched with horror as Ruhamah's head slipped out of sight. A ravine was beyond that ridge!

'Ruhamah!' She scrambled as fast as she dared towards where he'd disappeared, her swollen abdomen scraping the stony ground as she sank to all fours near the top of the ridge. 'Ruhamah!' As she tilted over the edge, her scream echoed into the valley where he had landed, some twenty strides below.

She could see his back near a tree, his face in the dirt, his hair splayed around still shoulders. It seemed like forever before he raised his head. At last, relief flooded through her. 'Are you safe?' she shouted.

As he tried to reply, a cry of pain came first. No, he was not. What could she do? Adah looked about her for help. There was no one, just their flock grazing below. The rope Ruhamah had been carrying for the lost sheep lay in a tangled mass halfway down the slope.

'I'll try to get the rope,' Adah shouted, sitting on her bottom and considering how best she could slide to it.

Ruhamah managed to turn his head towards her. His eyes were wide and his voice firm. 'No, Adah. You must not. I think my leg is broken, but I can move my arms, and by some miracle I haven't banged my head. Don't endanger yourself and our boy.'

'I must reach you. You cannot stay there.'

'Nor can we risk you falling. You must go to get help.'

'I don't want to leave you.' A salty tear touched her lips.
'Adah. Please.'

As his face implored her, she nodded, sending further tears dripping into the grass below. Committing every detail of the location to memory, she stood again and began clambering as fast as she dared back down the hill. Once on the safety of the flat plain, she tried to pick up her pace, holding beneath her stomach. But she could do no more than a fast walk. Each time she tried to run, her stomach tightened.

'No Yahweh, not again! This is not the answer we sought. Please, Yahweh,' she begged as she pushed her body towards home.

When she arrived, no one was there. She remembered that Abba was going to the city that day to sell some wares. What should she do? Another rope. She hunted for something longer, but nothing would reach the distance Ruhamah had fallen, and she could barely hope to pull him up.

She would have to go further. But which way? She could go to his parents' home at the end of the long track, but they were the last on that run, with no other neighbours. If they were at market too, she'd have to retrace her steps.

Her eyes alighted on the water jar. What about the well? No, it was midday, no one would be there. Her best option was to head towards the city where she should meet plenty of people on the way. Hopefully people she didn't know, who wouldn't ask questions. *Please, Yahweh, let it be that.*

Adah grabbed a cup of water from the house and drank her fill. Then she wrapped a long scarf around her neck, covering her abdomen as well as she could.

'Here goes.' She set out again, imploring her lower legs to keep going. They were tensing with every stride and her ankles felt swollen to twice their original size. As she passed the few homes outside the city gates, they were void of people except one old woman, who raised an eyebrow at Adah's flustered entry into her home.

'Are there no men here?' Adah asked, panting.

'It's harvest. Everyone is in the fields,' the woman said.

'Will you help me then?'

The woman shoved a leg out in front and pointed at it. Toes curled under her sole so far, it looked like the end of a gnarled trunk. 'I'm a cripple, dear, or I'd be out there with them.'

THE WANDERER'S LEGACY

Fearful that Ruhamah would soon be crippled just as badly, Adah nodded condolences and pushed on. Soon, the north gate came into view. Though her abba's home stood north-west of the city, using the western gate was out of the question – Chanoch lived near it. Covering her face with the scarf, she avoided the gaze of the elders watching the entrance as she passed through and veered off down a side passageway towards Eliana's neighbourhood. Small clay and straw homes cluttered the street, but they were better built than the new ones that sprang up between the gaps, barely more than shelters, really.

She couldn't recall when she'd last walked down this particular street, but something about it felt familiar. She was rounding a corner, just approaching the spot where the ground veered upwards towards Eliana's home atop the hill, when she heard a voice.

'Adah? I thought it was you. What are you doing here?' The words came from behind – a familiar voice that caused uncomfortable sensations in her chest. *Ignore it, push on.*

Fifty strides of steep climb ahead, she saw Eliana at the grinding stone with a toddler by her feet. Walking out from under the woven entrance was Eliana's husband – he was home. He would help! *Thank you, Yahweh.*

'Adah. I know it's you. Lamech! Adah is here.' Realisation dawned. The voice was Nasya's. Nasya lived here? Was Lamech with her?

Adah ran, forcing her swollen feet into submission, clutching her belly. She would make it to Eliana's door; she would hide in the safety of her friend's home.

Seeing her panicked approach, Eliana stood. She sprinted downhill, grabbed her hand and pulled her the remaining way.

'He's behind you. Hide!' Eliana pushed Adah through the doorway.

Adah didn't need the command. She flew behind the loom as Eliana and her husband blocked the entrance. Squeezing into the corner, she closed her eyes tightly shut. Her womb protested the run, her stomach muscles contracted harder than stone and the babe within flailed and kicked. She hugged her legs. *Breathe. Breathe.*

'Where is she?' Lamech's voice boomed.

'Why do you want to know?' Eliana's husband was defending her.

'She is my wife.'

'Not last I heard,' Manon said.

'Let me in.'

A scuffle. The sound of bone on bone.

Eliana shrieked. 'You swine! You would attack a man in his own home?'

'Get out of my way.'

The crash of a jar breaking. A trip and clunk as a body hit a wall, then a child crying. Her friend, her dear friend…

Footsteps came closer. 'Adah.'

Lamech's voice was close, commanding her to look up. She squeezed her eyes tighter.

He grabbed her arm and hauled her to her feet.

'Aah!' she shrieked, her stomach betrayed, her back indignant. Still, she refused to open her eyes. Perhaps if she couldn't see him, he would not see her.

'I knew it,' he sneered. 'I knew it the moment I saw you run. You are with child.'

CHAPTER 28

'Lamech, please. Let me explain.'

She had expected him to drag her through the street like a harlot, but instead he stood there before her – too calmly – staring at her midriff. He wasn't in a full state of dress himself: his tunic was crumpled and unfastened. To accuse her of adultery at this point would be the height of hypocrisy. It seemed he knew it.

Behind him stood Eliana and her black-eyed husband, clenching each other, with the toddler inside their protective embrace. The pieces of shattered jar lay scattered over the floor.

'I have never seen you this size. You must be what – eight moon cycles in?' Lamech said.

'Not quite. This child seems unusually large.'

'But it is mine?'

'Of course it's yours.'

'And you didn't think I should know. Instead, you appealed to the elders to marry another man?'

Adah hung her head.

'Look at me, woman.' Spit hit the floor.

She forced her eyes upwards to meet her husband's. *Dependable eyes.* How had she ever thought it?

Lamech's fury began transforming. His lip twitched to one side. 'I always thought you a paragon of virtue. My little wife who could do no wrong.' He sneered. 'Now, it seems we are not so different after all.'

As Lamech took a step forward, his fingers wrapped around her chin, tilting it upwards. His face descended, his lips onto hers. Despite the slight brush of his teeth, the kiss was far too soft. He was enjoying this too much. 'You will return with me, Adah. You will raise my child in my home.'

She gritted her teeth. 'I will not.'

He stiffened. His grip tightened. He paused, thinking. 'Fine. I will give you a choice. You can raise the child in my home as my wife, or I will remove him and raise him without you.'

Gasps met his announcement. It was just as she'd dreamt. The shaking that had begun in her legs, still exhausted from her panicked quest, grew to something uncontrollable.

Lamech caught her as she fell. He lifted her and carried her to a bed. Then he felt her stomach, still tight. 'Are you well?' He was suddenly tender. 'Is my child?'

'I don't know.'

He turned swiftly. 'Fetch a healer. Now.' Eliana nodded and ran from the hut.

'Adah.' He stroked her hair as he spoke. 'I don't want to do this. No mother should be forced from her child. But you leave me no choice. I cannot allow another man to raise him. You know that.'

She nodded. She knew it. This was exactly what she expected of him. He kissed her again, like he was forcing her to swallow a spear. 'Despite what you have done to me, I still love you, Adah. I will gladly take you back. I will care for you and treat you well, as I always have, with no hard feelings. You can raise our child in happiness, becoming the mother you always wanted to be.'

I never wanted to be a mother as much as I longed for you to accept me. It was all about you, Lamech. Until I saw through you.

The healer returned with Eliana. She gave Adah a thorough examination, but her abdomen had already loosened, and no pains or blood had come. The little one was still kicking away inside.

'Everything seems fine.' The healer smiled. 'You've had a bit of a scare. You must rest now; take to your bed for a few days. And no more running.'

'Thank you,' Lamech said with all his charm turned on. 'I will send you the trade as soon as we are home.'

'Wait!' Adah cried as the healer turned to leave. 'I must ask your help.' With her own child well, all Adah's thoughts returned to Ruhamah, still trapped in the ravine in the hills, no doubt in unbearable pain. 'Please go with Manon to the hills. My friend is trapped in a ravine; he has broken his leg. It's why I ran to the city.'

'Adah, I'm sure the healer is far too busy to trek up into the hills...' Lamech's expression revealed that he knew exactly who her 'friend' was.

'Please, Lamech.' She grasped his hand, appealing to the goodness that must still be inside him somewhere.

He did not relent. 'Send the healer away. I'm sure Adah's friend will be fine.'

'No, he might die. No one knows he is there!'

Eliana must have clocked whom she was talking about, for Manon pushed his way to the bed. 'Where is Ruhamah? Tell me and I will go immediately.'

'You'll need several men to rescue him. And he'll need treatment.'

Lamech fixed her with a pointed stare. 'If Adah agrees to come home with me, I will instruct the healer and my men to help, and I'll pay all their expenses.'

'No. He is our family. We will go and we will pay,' Manon argued.

Tears pricked at Adah's eyes and her lip quivered. She knew that for all Manon's good intentions, he couldn't afford the treatment. Nor could he afford to make an enemy of her husband. Lamech's eyebrow lifted, waiting for her decision. He knew it too and was using it to his advantage. The man she had married was gone. The goodness had departed.

Sending all hope for her future to join Lamech's departed virtue, she made her decision. 'Fine. I will return and be your wife. Just save Ruhamah.'

Lamech called his men. Three of them went with Manon and the healer to find Ruhamah, and two of them carried Adah to Lamech's home on a suspended straw mat.

'Send me word as soon as you have Ruhamah,' Adah said to Eliana as they departed.

'Of course. I will call on you tomorrow.'

'I'm sorry about Manon's face.'

'Think nothing of it. He'll be bragging about it for weeks.'

Despite herself, Adah smiled. She had never been more grateful for good friends.

They carried Adah past Nasya's house. The traitor stood at the door waving, with a smirk lining her face. How had Adah forgotten where she lived? Still, she couldn't have anticipated Lamech would be there – not when he had Tzillah now. She should not blame herself. Yet she did.

Might things have been different if she had just confessed to Lamech weeks ago? No. He would have found a way to get what he wanted. He always did. The only way to avoid this had been leaving with Ruhamah immediately. And Ruhamah was too noble for that. He had trusted the Elohim he prayed to too much.

The only positive as they entered Adah's old home was the sight of Shua. At least Lamech hadn't replaced Shua.

'Mistress. You're back,' the housekeeper exclaimed.

Adah alighted cautiously from her peculiar transport. She stood still as Shua inspected her. With Lamech's back turned, Shua mouthed, *'What happened?'* but Lamech turned before Adah could answer.

He led her to her old bed. It didn't look like Tzillah was using it. Inwardly, Adah scoffed. Lamech had clearly been confident he'd get her to return eventually. Just too preoccupied to fetch her from her father's house, she supposed.

'I'm returning to work,' Lamech said while tucking the sheet so tight around her that she couldn't move.

Work. So that was what you were doing at Nasya's, was it? she wanted to say, but she held her tongue.

'Try to stay out of trouble until I return.'

Adah refused to acknowledge him as he bent to kiss her goodbye. His touch felt like a bee sting upon her cheek. Hatred penetrated her bones like a sickening fever. Then when he was gone, the fury morphed into pain. By the time Shua entered with some food, Adah's clothing was wet with tears.

'Mistress. Here, drink this. It will help to calm you.' Shua gave her watered wine and Adah glugged it thirstily. Her housekeeper sat on the bed and loosened the sheets.

'I almost escaped, Shua. I was days away. Now I am bound to Lamech forever. And my Ruhamah is gone. Oh, I wish I'd joined him in that ravine! At least then I could die in his arms instead of in Lamech's prison.'

'Oh, mistress. Things aren't that bad. Drink some more. Eat. You will feel better about it soon. I'm glad to have you back, at least. And glad to see your enlarged womb.'

Adah briefly considered the foolishness of her words, speaking, as she was, to an older woman who was unmarried and working as a servant. But her grief triumphed. The sudden wrenching of hope tugged deep and she could not see beyond her misery.

As she lay back on the cushions and closed her eyes – exhaustion piling heaviness on her body – Shua continued to murmur, stroking her head.

'You are going to have a child. This is good. Though I don't know what happened with this Ruhamah fellow, I remember how you loved Lamech once. He may be unfaithful, but he is not the worst husband. Think of dear Dinah, married to that terrible man, Barsabas. And all those poor people sold into slavery... Lamech at least loves you and provides for you.'

Perhaps Shua was right. But it didn't prevent Adah slipping into the fitful, restless sleep that despair specialises in.

When she woke later that evening, Adah immediately sensed someone nearby. Fearing it was Lamech, she resisted opening her eyes. When she eventually did, Tzillah lay next to her, face to face.

'Sorry, I didn't mean to wake you,' Tzillah said.

'How long have you been there?'

'Just a few moments. Shua has gone to bed. I thought you might not want to be alone when you woke.'

'Thank you. Is this your bed?'

'No. I'm in the room further down the hall. Lamech insisted on keeping this for you. He sometimes sleeps here alone.'

'Really?' *Alone or with someone else? Did Tzillah know?* The images that Adah associated with this bed flew back into her mind, but they didn't hold the same venom. Adah loved someone else. Someone of more humble circumstance, but infinitely better.

Her heart suddenly felt hollow. 'Has there been any news from Eliana?'

Tzillah raised an eyebrow. She wouldn't know who Eliana was. 'I've heard nothing. But I've been with Noa and only just got back.' She reached forward and took Adah's hand. They were close to each other, their rounded bellies almost touching. 'Lamech was riled the other night about your engagement to another man. Is that who you're worried about? Are you in love, Adah?'

Adah nodded.

'Then I'm sorry you're here, for your sake. Though I'm glad for my own.'

'Why? Surely sharing your husband holds no appeal?'

'I share him anyway; as I'm sure you're aware. I'd rather share him with you than the other women. You're the only friend I have here.'

'Have you not met anyone else in two seasons? I heard Lamech was taking you to parties and parading you proudly around.'

'Yes. Parading is right. He drags me from one person to the next, never allowing me a moment to have a decent conversation. The only person I get to be alone with is his mother. He trusts no one else.'

'I'm sorry for that. I would be pleased to introduce you to my friends.'

'You mean that?'

'Of course.'

'I was afraid you would hate me.'

Adah considered Tzillah's abdomen, considerably smaller than her own. She hadn't put on any additional weight, but her face looked tired, and her vivacity had dimmed somewhat. 'Tzillah, I don't hate you. Lamech on the other hand…'

Tzillah chortled, then paused. 'May I ask you something?'

'Yes.'

Tzillah took some of Adah's hair in her fingers and began to braid it. 'Do you mind if I don't hate him?'

Despite her heartache, Adah smiled. 'Has our wayward husband charmed you into submission, Tzillah?'

'I do quite like him. Oh, I see why he drives you crazy, I absolutely do. And if I'd had your expectations – *one flesh for life*, that sort of thing – I imagine I would feel as you do. But I knew what I'd married. I enjoy the attention and the luxuries, and I'm pleased I'm carrying his child. He makes me laugh! Is that terrible?'

Compassion swelled in Adah's heart again. 'I expect not.'

'Also, I suppose, if at least one of us likes him, we might stand a chance of keeping him at home once our bodies are more… amenable.'

Adah baulked at the thought of allowing Lamech into her bed again. Everything in her screamed that sleeping with Lamech betrayed Ruhamah to the highest degree. But it was likely part of the agreement. She would have to accept it if she lived as his wife.

It was certainly better for her if he preferred Tzillah's company. 'You hereby have my permission to charm our husband magnificently and – preferably – to keep his charms to yourself as far as possible,' Adah concluded.

At this, Tzillah let out a full-blown roar of laughter, then kissed her cheek. Perhaps living with Tzillah wasn't going to be so bad.

CHAPTER 29

'We should build a hall like my father's. No— bigger! To celebrate the birth of my children. I will speak to Azurak about the arrangements today. There's little chance we'll get it done before they all arrive, but if we pull some slaves off the job on the west tower and add in some of the workers at Uriah's house, I think we'll get it finished within a few seasons. What do you say?'

Lamech was looking at his two wives expectantly. Adah's mind was elsewhere, focused on the new tapestry that adorned the wall in their living room, but Tzillah replied, 'It's a wonderful idea. Exactly the thing to celebrate.'

'You would love to have a hall, wouldn't you, Adah? You could invite your friends over then.'

Adah supposed she'd better reply, though the thought of living through more of Lamech's projects, and having a house surrounded by workers when her baby was born, was less than appealing. 'I can invite them over already. And I always prefer eating outside.'

'Oh, Adah. Eating outside is what our ancestors did. We live in a new era now. One of progress and importance. Tzillah understands, don't you?'

Tzillah grinned. 'I understand that you'd like to better your abba's house so you can show him up and prove he has no hold on you.'

'Well, you cheeky little—'

Tzillah squealed as Lamech pulled her into his lap, feigning offence by punishing her with a pounding of tickles and kisses. Adah sighed, turned away and allowed her mind to wander to where it had been fighting to get back to all evening – the day's events.

The morning had begun with a welcome visit from Eliana. Relief had washed over her as Eliana confirmed Ruhamah was safe. Despite Adah's directions, it had taken the search party some time to find him, and he'd already caught a fever before they'd returned to Eliana's home. He would be bed-bound for the time being, but Eliana would force him to stay with them and be 'fed up'. Lamech had done as promised, giving the healer a generous amount of wine from the vineyard in return for looking after Ruhamah until he was well. For that, Adah must at least be thankful.

Adah blocked out her husband's voice to dwell on the man she'd almost escaped with. His soft, unruly hair, little dimple and gentle touch. The lilt of his voice when he was excited about something, the stillness and calm when they sat together on the hillside watching nothing in particular.

She wondered how Ruhamah was feeling now, knowing that she was gone and trapped in Lamech's possession. She, the second woman he'd loved and lost. The second unborn child he'd lost too. Every fibre of her being ached for him and for his pain. Yahweh Elohim had betrayed him once again.

'What would you like, Adah? How about steps all around a central floor. We could hold dances! And room for a fire; that's necessary for the colder evenings.'

'I know,' Tzillah interjected, 'We could sit up on a raised area, in front of everyone. Us and our children. Then you can show us off to everyone.'

Adah recognised the tease in Tzillah's voice, but Lamech didn't register it. 'Of course! You are a marvel, my love. I might just have to employ you...'

Adah gave a grunt, quietly enough that Lamech didn't hear. She switched off again, grateful that Tzillah could play to Lamech's vanity and sustain the conversation without her.

It didn't surprise her that Lamech would love the idea of them all on a raised platform. He'd lost no time announcing to all their acquaintances that she was expecting a child. He and Tzillah had done the rounds that morning while Adah had been mourning over Ruhamah. From what she understood, Lamech had suggested that Adah had never left, but had been absent from society due to her delicate pregnancy.

Humiliation warmed Adah's face as she recalled an early consequence of Lamech's storytelling. While Lamech and Tzillah were still about town, Chanoch had visited.

When Shua had informed her that Chanoch was waiting in the ornamental garden, Adah had hastily washed the tear stains from her face and put on a clean dress of Tzillah's. None of her old clothes, tucked away in a chest, would fit over her swollen abdomen, and what she had been wearing was saturated in tears and perspiration.

She shuffled out to the garden to see her benefactor, barely taking her eyes off the ground. Chanoch watched her silently as she eased herself onto the bench opposite the wall where he perched among the violet and mauve flowering vines.

She wondered if he would wait for her to speak first. Finally, he asked how she was, his voice soft but constrained.

'Do you need to ask?' she replied.

'Adah…'

She sniffed in the prickles of disgrace that threatened to ruin her newly cleaned face.

'Adah, why didn't you come to me? Why didn't you tell me the truth? I promised to help you.'

She gripped the bench, not wanting to relinquish her defence. 'I didn't know the child would survive. It still may not.'

'It looks to me like it is thriving. I knew there was something strange in your request to marry so soon, but I put it down to the lack of space in Shimiel's house. I never imagined you would deceive me.'

'We thought about telling you, but Abba said not to.'

'Shimiel, I might expect this from. But when have I given you cause to distrust me? And as for Ruhamah— I thought he was a follower of Yahweh. I am shocked he would consider this. You – all of you – have made me into a fool.'

'Oh no, Chanoch. That was never the intention…'

'I vouched for you in front of the elders, Adah. I defended you! I told them Lamech was to blame, and you were an innocent victim. I asked them to leave Lamech be, at your request, then to allow you to remarry so you might not be put to shame. I told them Ruhamah was a good man, a trustworthy man. Yet now they know you were both deceiving them.'

'They know? They all know?'

'Lamech has been spreading the story that you've been confined to your bed – and none would dare challenge him. But the elders know the truth. Can you imagine how that makes me look?'

'I'm sorry.' Her fingers trembled. 'I didn't consider how it might affect you if the news got out. Please believe me. I didn't intend to deceive. I didn't know for some time that I was with child. I was distraught that something I'd desired for so long would come at such a time.'

'Yet, you knew it when you requested your engagement.'

As shame crept through her swollen belly like beetles through a crack in the wall, Adah was unable to do anything but nod.

'I thought so. The worst part is, if you had just told me the truth, perhaps I could have helped you. But it is far too late for that now. Now, Lamech must keep his two wives – which will have a detrimental impact on the morality of the entire city – and there is nothing I can do about it.'

'How could you have helped? We could see no solution except leaving and staying away until the child was older, when no one would realise he wasn't Ruhamah's.'

'You mean *never* telling Lamech? You would have kept this from him forever?' Chanoch sank forwards and buried his face in his hands. 'Oh, Adah.'

'He would have taken my son away, Chanoch! I know he would have. He has threatened it already. It's the only reason I'm here.'

Chanoch looked up. 'He's threatened to?'

Adah nodded as her tears gathered, ready to spill. 'He said if I didn't stay, he would take my baby... he wouldn't let me—'

Though her sight was obscured, Adah felt Chanoch draw near and sit beside her. 'Oh, my dear girl. I am so sorry. I knew he was ambitious and stubborn, but I didn't know he could be so ruthless.'

'Yet, strangely, it didn't surprise me. It was precisely what I expected. So, you understand why we did what we did?'

Chanoch sighed. 'I understand. He has treated you abominably, and I don't blame you for fearing him. However, it is still Lamech's child. He has a right to know his child. Perhaps, if you'd told us, we could have gathered you together and negotiated a solution. We could have put safeguards in place to ensure you were protected. It wouldn't have been perfect, but it would have been truthful...'

There was no holding back the tears after that. Adah had not just lost her love and her hope, she had alienated her principal ally and advocate, a man who had shown her nothing but compassion and kindness. 'I know Ruhamah thought it was wrong to withhold the truth, but I thought only of self-preservation. I was so happy with him. After years of living in misery, I was free at last. I couldn't bear the thought of returning—'

She choked on her last words, so Chanoch spoke again. 'Has your life been so bad? I know marriage to Lamech hasn't been what you expected, but I thought you liked him. Otherwise, you wouldn't have been so upset by his betrayal.'

'I did like him. I loved him. So very much. Yet now I realise that the life I had was controlled by fear. Fear that I would lose him, fear that I would dissatisfy him, fear that I could never be whom he, or Methushael, wanted me to be. I didn't even have the courage to ask him to let me do chores around the home. I did them in secret to waylay my boredom. I saw my friends in secret too.'

Chanoch shook his head. 'I had no idea…'

'No one did.'

'Have you ever taken your fears before Yahweh and asked Him to help you?'

'Yahweh? Yahweh!' She would have stood if her legs weren't so weak. 'The times I prayed to Him, He allowed my babies to die. He did the same for Ruhamah's wife and child – though they never did a thing wrong. Then, as I fell in love with that sweet man on those hillsides, Yahweh dangled hope before our eyes, only to snatch it away again. No, I am done with Yahweh, Chanoch! I see no evidence that He cares in the slightest.'

'Oh, Adah. Dearest girl. I am so sorry for your pain. I understand what it is to live with unanswered prayer, and to lose a child. Such things are hard to comprehend and even harder to bear. The consequences of my grandparents' rejection in the Garden have been grave indeed, and we all suffer for it. Yet, I do believe there is design behind all Yahweh allows, though I daresay that doesn't provide much comfort in the moment. Perhaps the opposite.'

Chanoch took her trembling hand. 'If there's one thing I've learnt from my parents and their story, it's that we must trust Yahweh to be good, even when everything points to the contrary. Through every situation life throws at us, He will be working for the good of those who are willing to trust Him. It may take a very long time for us to perceive what He sees through His eternal vision, but if we will rest content in His care, I believe in the end we will look back and we will understand.'

Her nostrils burned. 'But I don't want to look back and understand. I want to look forward and have hope.'

'Yes. Yes. You are young, with your whole life ahead of you. The temptation to run away and start again must have been strong indeed. I see that. Even so, I wish you'd come to me. If nothing else, I could have assured you that Yahweh loves you and considers you precious. We could have sought His guidance together.'

Though Chanoch's hands had steadied hers, her lip quivered now instead, as sadness once again replaced anger. 'I'm not sure I believe He loves me. And, though you will hate me for saying it, I would rather be living in sin with Ruhamah than be a second wife to Lamech.'

Chanoch nodded and stood to leave. 'As I said, I don't expect this to make any sense to you now. I am sorry for your suffering. I will call in on Ruhamah and see how he fares, and I shall pray for you both. If things get worse with Lamech, promise you'll tell me?'

She nodded as he paused at the archway leading into the courtyard and turned back. 'Adah, before I go, I must ask your forgiveness for my part in this.'

'Your part?'

'I told you once that I regretted not speaking out when Lamech proposed to you. I'm afraid my guilt runs deeper than that. The truth is, I think Yahweh wanted me to intervene. I fear my disobedience has led to your suffering, and it weighs heavily on me.'

'What do you mean?'

'It is hard to explain. It felt something like... like a compelling word speaking into my heart. It was this kind of word that sent my ima over the mountains to find Abba in these lands. I fear I am not so obedient as she.'

'I have never heard of this. You said it's from Yahweh?'

'Yes.'

'What does it sound like?'

'Oh well, I think that varies. But it always bears the Creator's character. My abba heard Yahweh's voice audibly, and very loudly. He speaks of it with trembling. Yet, that was at the sacrifice, you know. It is not the most common way. Most commonly, Yahweh speaks not in thunder, lightning, or miraculous signs, but in a still, small voice. You must listen carefully to hear it. I never hear it out loud.'

While Chanoch's words mystified her, they produced a strange longing to hear this voice he referred to – as she longed to hear anything more about his father, The Wanderer.

Chanoch stepped closer again and gazed earnestly into her eyes. 'The point is, I failed you. Whilst chastising you for withholding the truth, I bear the greater sin. Will you forgive me?'

'I don't quite understand what I am to forgive. But yes, I forgive you. And please, Chanoch, forgive me also? I am truly sorry for not trusting you and for bringing you to such trouble.'

Chanoch had patted her cheek and given her a brief smile. 'Think no more of it.' Then he had left.

'So, it is settled then. I will speak to Azurak tomorrow.' Lamech sauntered to Adah's side and tilted her chin. 'Where have you been, my wife?'

Pulled back to the present, Adah felt her cheeks warm. She had been wondering what her life would have been like if Chanoch had obeyed that still, small voice. If she and Lamech had never married.

'What do you mean?' she deflected. 'I've been here all day.'

'You haven't said a word throughout that entire conversation. I hope our plans don't displease you. Isn't that Tzillah's dress?'

'Yes. I have none that fit,' she replied, glad she didn't have to answer his previous question.

'Well, we will have to remedy that immediately. I will send word to the seamstress.'

'I can make my own clothes, Lamech. I'll go and get some fabric…'

'Nonsense. You just rest, my sweet. We will soon have you tidied up and back to your former glory.'

ADAH'S LABOUR COMMENCED on the night of the full moon, six weeks after she'd been dragged back to Lamech's home. She had not delivered the child before the builders came at dawn, in their tens and twenties, hauling around stone, clay and straw, adding to the foundations laid in the previous weeks. Her screams rang through the house as the workers pounded on, and the healer delivered first one boy, and then another.

Lamech barged in soon after Adah stopped screaming. 'Is it over? Do I have a son?'

The first to be born – the darker skinned one – was suckling at Adah's breast, soothing the distress of labour away with every little grunt of milk-filled satisfaction. Caught up in wonder, she breathed in the scent of his soft, downy hair, cherishing the unique, delicate fragrance. Everything in her body hurt, but her son was the most wonderful thing she'd ever beheld.

The boy just born was in the healer's arms, being wiped clean with a strip of linen. Adah ached to nurse him as well, but the healer held him out proudly towards her benefactor. 'You have two sons, my lord.'

'Two? Two sons! Oh, Adah.' Lamech took the offered child then hastened towards her. She looked up, and through tear-blurred eyes saw him – the man who had given her such wonder. She smiled.

Lamech kneeled at the bedside, reached forward his spare hand and stroked the cheek of the suckling infant. 'You did it, Adah. I always knew you could.' He planted a kiss on the foreheads of both babies. 'Two sons. Two boys to fill their mother's heart and continue their father's name. Just what we prayed for.'

PART TWO

CHAPTER 30

City of Chanoch, 750th year of Wandering

'You there. Woman!'

Adah squeezes her eyes tight, takes a deep breath then continues her saunter down the alley, faster now.

'Woman. I called you.'

Don't stop. Don't stop.

'Come now, don't make me run. A woman with your figure is just what I need to improve my evening. I'll pay you well.'

The thought churns Adah's stomach. She quickens her pace through the shadows looming over stone and mud, determined not to let Azurak's husky tones threaten her escape. *Let him find another. It will not be me.*

There's a scuffle behind her as he knocks into a feed bin. Then another shout. He is getting angrier. She glances at every passageway she passes, inspecting the doorways. Does she know anyone here? Might some afford an opportunity to lose the furious foreman, or are they all dead ends? What will happen if he catches her, spins her around, sees who she is?

Azurak is gaining ground. Adah rises to her toes and jogs. She must go faster - even if it runs the risk of recognition. This is her only opportunity for escape. There might never be another...

A door opens ahead. A silhouette steps out. The figure, surrounded by the orange glow of lamplight, is familiar. Is he friend or foe? She barely has time to consider, for as she approaches, he grabs her arm, pulling her towards him into the recess of the doorway.

Then he speaks. 'It *is* you. Now, what are you doing here?'

As Adah stops running, panting takes over, and she fails to answer the question. Though she doesn't know how he will react, being caught by this man is infinitely preferable to being attacked by the one she's running from.

Azurak shouts from behind. 'Hey. That woman is mine.'

'I'm sorry, my friend. I reserved her earlier. She was on her way here. I'm sure that's why she didn't stop for you.' The speaker puts his arm around Adah and pulls her close to his shoulder. His familiar scent bathes her trembling extremities in safety. He whispers into her ear. 'Tuck your face in so he cannot see you.'

'Juval? Is that you?' Azurak calls.

'Ah, Azurak. I see you now. It looks like you've had a good night.' Juval chuckles.

'On the contrary. Your suggestion didn't pay off, Juval. Why are you hiring a woman this side of town? That's not your house.'

'No, no. I'm at a party. Fancy joining us?'

'Thank you, but no. I'd better get back to the complex and check on your mother. I've already stayed away long enough.'

Juval nods. 'Loyal as always. You do Abba proud.'

'I aim to please.' Adah hears Azurak turn, then stop. 'Juval?'

'Yes?'

'Any women in your party unspoken for?'

'No women of the night, I'm afraid. Perhaps at the tavern?'

'Yes. Well, enjoy yours.'

'Oh, I will. I will.'

Azurak's crunching footsteps retreat. Adah stays, breathing deeply until she is sure her enemy has rounded a corner. Then Juval pulls her inside. In the rooms down the corridor, she can hear the telltale noises of one of his parties - lyres, pipes, singing, giggles and grunts. She knows better than to ask about them.

He pierces her with a stare. 'Why are you this side of the city? You told me you were going to Eliana's.'

'I had to adjust course. Azurak was in the way, for Naamah's husband refused him entry.'

'Did he? This is an interesting development... But why come this way? Have you any idea how dangerous it is in these parts? If I hadn't been here, if Azurak had caught you–'

Adah gazes into Juval's concerned face. Love for him rushes through her, love that no amount of wrongdoing on his part can ever extinguish - a mother's unconditional love. She regrets not telling her son the truth before; not trusting him. 'I wasn't just visiting Eliana. She was arranging my escape. I am leaving,' she says.

'Leaving?'

'Leaving the city. Leaving your abba. I have been a prisoner since The Wanderer told his story. Lamech grows more suspicious every day and I can no longer bear it.'

Deep hurt manifests in her son's eyes. 'You would leave without saying goodbye?'

'Oh, my darling!' Adah throws her arms around him, trying to pour the tenderness and regret of a lifetime into this embrace. When will she see him again? 'I wanted to tell you when I called by yesterday. Yet with Shadow and your friends there, I couldn't get you alone. I'm sorry.'

Juval's brow furrows in thought, before the deep voice of his host commands his attention for a moment. 'Juval? Is that you? I thought you'd gone.'

'Yes, I'm going again now. I forgot something.' Juval turns back to Adah and lowers his voice. 'How can I help?'

'Help? You can't. It's too dangerous. If your abba finds out…'

'I can handle Abba.'

'No. You don't know what he's capable of.'

'Ima,' Juval takes her face in his hands. 'I do. I've been working for him for years, and I've seen more than you have. Your safety is more important right now. Let me help.'

Adah's heart swells, then tightens in conflict. She cannot put him in danger. Yet, she needs him. 'Perhaps accompany me to Chanoch's house?'

'Chanoch. He's involved?'

'No. But I trust no one else, and like you said, I've gone in the wrong direction for Eliana's.'

'Very well. It looks like you will be playing my woman for a little longer. We must cross the worst part of the city to reach Chanoch's. Let's go.'

CHAPTER 31

City of Chanoch, 720th year of Wandering

Adah chose the name Juval for her younger son, the one who settled every time she sang him a lullaby. She hoped naming him after the brook carrying the water of life into their courtyard would signify hope for the future. Little did she realise that his easy temperament would provide the greater challenge. For he favoured his father in almost everything, from his dark-rimmed eyes to the russet hair with its tiny waves at the tips. Except he was more delicately proportioned than Lamech.

Lamech decided the eldest boy, who favoured Adah in appearance, should be named Yaval. 'Because brooks follow streams,' he chortled. 'Besides, it'll be amusing.'

'You think it amusing to have sons named Yaval and Juval? It sounds anything but amusing.'

'Oh Adah, where's your sense of fun?'

'I won't let him name my child,' Tzillah whispered. 'I have a store of options ready, just in case he suggests anything terrible.'

Adah considered Tzillah's bump. 'Do you think it's a boy or a girl?'

'How should I know?' Tzillah replied. 'Besides, it doesn't matter now you've provided Lamech with an heir, does it?'

When Tzillah gave birth to a girl eight weeks later, the irony wasn't lost on Adah. All those years they'd waited for a son, then they got two. Whereas Tzillah, brought in to supply Adah's deficiency, bore a daughter.

'You can name her,' Lamech announced. 'I care not.'

Tzillah was delighted at Lamech's indifference. 'She will be called Naamah. For to me at least, she is perfectly lovely.'

Adah had to agree. Little Naamah was a treasure. She loved her alongside the boys who claimed her heart so immediately and profoundly. And so, the three children grew up together, with their two mothers sharing everything from their food and clothing to their husband and their tears.

Yaval, the eldest, was an adventurer. As soon as he could walk, he climbed. One day, Adah couldn't find him anywhere.

'I last saw him in the garden,' Shua said, as Adah tore through the kitchen courtyard, frantically searching.

'I've looked there.'

'Did you check the walls?'

'You don't think he can get over them already?'

'I wouldn't put anything past him.'

'Ima.' Five-year-old Juval tugged at her sleeve.

'Yes, my love?'

Juval pointed. His twin was beyond the courtyard, standing on top of the wall that separated Adah's goats from the ornamental garden.

Adah's heart stopped. 'Yaval! Get down this instant.'

Yaval's expression mirrored the goat's. They'd both enjoyed the climb up the wall but had no idea how to get down. Confusion answered Adah's plea as he stood, steeling himself against the breeze, which ruffled his tunic but not his black, tightly curled hair.

'Wait there. Don't move!' She ran through the garden, grabbed the bench and dragged it to the wall. After clambering onto it, she held out her arms. He was still a stride from her reach. 'Jump. I'll catch you.'

Yaval pointed at the goat. 'Dotty first.'

Really? She was sure the goat would figure out the way soon enough.

Yaval crossed his arms. 'I'm not going 'til Dotty is safe.'

'But I can't reach her.'

'Jump, Dotty,' Yaval said.

Dotty looked at her young master quizzically. She chewed whatever cud was in her mouth and moved to nudge him.

'No!' Adah screamed, terrified that Dotty would send Yaval off the edge.

'What is going on?'

Adah spun to see Lamech striding into view. 'Praise Yahweh, you're back!'

'He had nothing to do with it,' Lamech muttered as he crossed the garden in a few long strides, climbed the bench and held out his arms. 'Yaval. Down now.'

'Dotty first.'

'Don't be ridiculous. It's a goat.'

'Dotty first!'

'You first, or I shall give your backside a beating the moment you touch the ground.'

Yaval humphed then reluctantly stepped forward. With his extra height, Lamech was able to grab him with no jump needed.

Once he was on the ground, Adah pulled Yaval into her chest. 'Don't you do that again; do you hear me?'

'Dotty started it.' Yaval stuck out his bottom lip, a move that always melted Adah's heart. Soon the goat had clambered down by itself and was next to them.

Lamech joined in. 'Dotty is a very naughty girl. It is not wise to follow goats everywhere they go.'

Adah suppressed a smile. 'Exactly so. Naughty Dotty. She will go back to her pen for the day.'

'But—'

'No buts. You're fortunate we're not banning you from the pen,' Lamech said.

'So, I can go there with her?' Yaval's brown eyes lit up.

Lamech's fierce expression broke before Adah's. He ruffled Yaval's hair. 'You are far too much like your ima.' He turned, strode towards the gate and called out to Avram's son who was a few years older than Yaval. After instructing the older lad to keep an eye on his unruly child, he dismissed them both.

Taking that as permission to stay with the goats, Yaval grabbed hold of Dotty's leather band and dragged her through the gateway that led to the pen beyond, with Avram's son skittering behind.

Putting his arm around Adah's waist, Lamech pulled her to his side. 'It's a good thing I love you both. How did the boy get up there?'

'I have no idea.'

'I will have to inspect the wall on the other side and chip off any footholds. Adah?'

'Yes?' She glanced up at her husband, grateful that their son had prevented the build-up of his anger. His face was calm, though a question lined his brows.

'Do we need to hire someone to care for the children?'

A pit opened in Adah's stomach and her words flew out. 'No! Oh, please don't, Lamech. I've finally found my purpose and joy. Don't take that from me.'

Concern flitted across Lamech's eyes. He raised his hand and traced the side of her face. Then he bent and kissed her. 'As you wish, my love. If you change your mind though...'

'I won't.'

'Alright. I'll agree, so long as I don't find my boy on the roof next time. He is... he is precious to me.'

'I know.' She did know. For Yaval wasn't just Lamech's heir; he did love him. Indeed, he loved them all. Though Lamech might not admit to having bonded with his daughter, Naamah could often be found sitting on her abba's knee playing with his beard while he told the boys about his day.

Adah was wondering where Juval and Naamah might be when Lamech threaded his fingers through hers and led her to the other side of the garden. Then she spotted her son, happily playing in the corner with Naamah, behind the wicker trellis separating the children's area from theirs. Lamech couldn't stand the children's mess being on view in the ornamental garden.

Her husband pulled her into an embrace and kissed her again. 'I'm glad the children have brought you joy. I always knew you'd be a good mother.'

She allowed him to continue his caress. She'd grown used to it over the past few years, and it didn't cause immediate revulsion anymore. When she closed her eyes, she would imagine he was the man she truly wanted. Or, if she was in a good mood, she might take herself back to their early years, to her first love in its excitement and promise, shutting out other unpleasant, encroaching images. This was her life now; she had to make the most of it.

'Abba?' Juval tugged at his father's sleeve, drawing Lamech away.

'Yes, my son.' Lamech's face was flushed with passion, but fortunately, he didn't look annoyed at the intrusion.

'Come see what we built.' Juval led the way to his creation. A miniature city of sticks, stones and mud filled the space next to Naamah, who was sat cross-legged on the ground, her beautiful copper hair covering the full length of her back.

'What is this?' Lamech knelt and examined the design.

'We are going to build houses like you, Abba,' Juval said proudly.

'Both of you?' Lamech looked to his daughter.

She beamed at him. 'Yes, Abba. It was my idea.'

'Of course it was. And these houses, will they be as little as this, or as big as ours?'

'Bigger than ours. Bigger than Sav Methushael's!'

'Bigger than that? Well, that is big. Your city is missing something though: the most important part.'

'What's that, Abba?' Naamah asked, wide-eyed.

'A wall. A city is no city without a wall. It's what keeps us safe.' He started to gather Juval's mud and craft it around the houses.

Unconsciously, Adah moved towards Lamech and massaged his shoulders. When he was like this, she could almost forget the other Lamech existed.

'Did you know, children, that our wall was built by The Wanderer himself?' she said.

'Who is The Wanderer?' Naamah asked.

'He's the cursed man!' Juval giggled.

Naamah looked confused. 'What's a curse?'

Her brother shrugged. 'I don't know. But some say he is half beast...'

Adah's heart felt squeezed like a sponge. 'Now where did you hear that?'

'The boys in the courtyard.'

'What boys?' Lamech asked.

Rubbing her husband's neck again, Adah answered, 'They play with the gatekeeper's children.'

With his eyes closed in contentment, Lamech raised his eyebrows. 'I see. Juval, you mustn't listen to all the nonsense people say. You are my son; you are better than that. The Wanderer is the first ancestor of all who live in the land of Nod.'

'I thought that was Chanoch,' Naamah muttered.

Adah shook her head. 'Chanoch is the father of our city, but there are many more cities. Many more peoples.'

'Where does The Wanderer live then?' Naamah asked.

'Think about it,' Lamech said.

Juval pursed his lips, then whispered in Naamah's ear. She nodded. 'Juval says he has no home.'

Lamech opened his eyes and smiled. 'That's right. He was cursed to be a fugitive. He cannot settle in one city but moves from place to place.'

Naamah looked puzzled. 'Why? What did he do?'

Lamech opened his mouth, then closed it again. 'That's a story for when you're older,' he said at last.

The children seemed discontent with this conclusion but knew not to argue with their father. Lamech groaned as Adah found a knot in his shoulder and dug her thumb into it.

'What brought you home early today?' she asked.

'Tzillah and I are going out this evening to Bekhor's party. It is his birthday.'

'Oh yes, of course. Tzillah isn't here.'

'I gathered that. Her tongue has its own timekeeping. Get her in a room full of women and she'll never realise the day has passed. Will you come with me, Adah?'

Adah had been quite content to let Tzillah take charge of all social necessities while she stayed with the children. It had been some time since Lamech had requested her presence. Still, he was in a pleasant mood. 'Will Methushael be there?'

'No. He and Bekhor have fallen out.'

'Again?'

'You know Abba.'

'Can I come to the party?' Juval asked. 'I haven't seen my cousins for ages.'

'It's an adult party, Juval. It will last past your bedtime.'

'Oh, please, Abba!'

Adah crouched next to Lamech and snatched Juval into a cuddle. 'Perhaps I will come. I can bring the children, let them wish their uncle a Happy Birthday and play with their cousins for a while, before bringing them home.'

'I don't want you to leave early. I want you by my side. We used to always be together, Adah.'

'Yes, Lamech. But that was before—' She stopped herself and released Juval back to Naamah.

As she stood, Lamech pulled her away from the children and lowered his voice. 'Have you not let that go? You tell me you are happy. You come here and massage me like you used to. I haven't touched another woman for a long time…'

'Except Tzillah,' she muttered.

'Of course, Tzillah; but that's different. I can't undo the past, Adah. I can only make the best of the future. Don't pretend you haven't thought of your sheepherder. I know you have.'

'I haven't spoken to him since I returned.'

'I know.'

Adah's brows drew together. *How would you know? I might have done so secretly.*

'But you have thought of him,' Lamech finished.

She hesitated. Juval and Naamah were both silent, shuffling in discomfort at their parent's hushed conversation.

Lamech didn't waver. 'Stay, Adah. Stay by my side.'

Adah sighed, stepped closer to the children and kissed Juval on the cheek. 'Very well. I'll ask Shua to collect them at dusk.'

CHAPTER 32

Bekhor's home was bedecked in finery. Everything portrayed his profession – from the ceiling to the floors, wooden carvings dominated, adorned by carpets. The tables were ornate too and populated with beautifully turned serving dishes, holding fruits of every shape and size, clay goblets filled with wine for every guest and copper plates of leavened bread.

Bekhor's six oldest children were singing in one corner, harmonising their voices in a most practised way. His bashful wife stood behind them, holding a baby and whispering instructions. The youngsters ran around playing games, while their father sat at the top table, already intoxicated. Next to him was Barsabas, Dinah's husband.

'I didn't know Barsabas was in the city,' Adah whispered, as her children zoomed off to join in their cousins' game.

Lamech shrugged. 'Nor did I. We better greet them.'

Adah scanned the room again. In the far corner, behind the top table, several men with weapons stood guard. Lamech saw them too. To their left was the back of Dinah's head. Just then, Dinah's companion turned. It was Tzillah.

'So, this is where Tzillah's been,' Lamech said. 'She was meant to come home first and arrive with me.'

'Perhaps she and Dinah have a mutual friend?'

Lamech grunted, grabbed Adah's hand, and led her to the top table. Adah had only met Barsabas once, and after that meeting, she'd had no desire to meet him again. He had the kind of eyes that held superiority and malice in equal measure, much like Methushael's. But where Methushael was broad and domineering, Barsabas was scrawny and wily. He had pale skin and black hair, which accentuated the pits under his eyes and the blueness of his irises.

None of that would be a problem if he hadn't the same malice in his tongue.

'Barsabas, good to see you again.' Lamech's greeting was stilted. But Barsabas stood up, almost stumbled in his inebriated state, and pulled Lamech into a bear hug.

'Lamech! Just the man I wanted to see. Dinah found your pretty little wife in the marketplace and brought her back here. And now, I see, your original adornment is here as well.'

Not for the first time, Adah hated the meaning of her name. Her parents had meant it as a compliment, she knew that, but the way Barsabas' eyes roamed made her feel sick. Ruhamah had told her she was a human made in the image of the Creator, not an object intended to embellish a man.

'I see you've brought your army,' Lamech said, ignoring Barsabas' comment and nodding towards the weaponed men. That was strange. He usually claimed her swiftly any time there was competition.

'Those five guards?' Barsabas laughed. A snively kind of laugh that made the stomach churn. 'Hardly. I have five hundred at home.'

Lamech narrowed his eyes and turned to Bekhor. 'Happy birthday, brother.' As Lamech and Bekhor talked, Barsabas continued to drink Adah in. A leer formed on his face, and he ran his tongue over his teeth.

Adah tapped Lamech's arm. 'I'm going to sit with Tzillah.' He nodded and she picked her way across the floor to safety.

'Adah. What are you doing here?' Tzillah almost jumped, a flush creeping into her cheeks, though Adah couldn't think why.

'You didn't come home, so Lamech dragged me into it.'

'Only you would describe visiting family as being dragged, Adah,' Dinah responded.

'Hello, Dinah. I didn't know you'd be here, otherwise I would have been pleased to come.'

Dinah rolled her eyes, not buying her insincere apology for a moment.

Adah plonked herself next to Tzillah. 'So, what have you been up to all day?'

'Oh well, Dinah and I met in the marketplace and got chatting. She invited me back and, we just kept chatting. I had no idea it was so late.'

'Naamah is over there.' Adah gestured with her head, just as Naamah spotted Tzillah and gave her a wave. Then Juval tapped her shoulder before squeezing into her lap. 'What is it, my love?' There were tears in his eyes.

'I don't want to play their game anymore. I just want to listen to the singing.'

'Oh, what a shame. You were desperate to see your cousins.' Adah wrapped her arms around him, breathing in his sweet scent as he relaxed into her hold.

'Not anymore.' Juval snuggled his face into her chest and closed his eyes.

'What's wrong with your child?' Dinah asked.

Rescuing her from the jab at her heart, Tzillah defended him. 'Nothing. He's just a quiet one. He has a particular affinity with music. Every time Adah sings at night he goes straight off to sleep. He probably felt tired the moment he walked through the door.'

'Not like the other two,' Adah said. 'Yaval is full of energy and never stops wriggling and Naamah's head is too busy. They both take forever to get to sleep. What about yours?' At least they had something to talk about now they all had children.

Dinah gave a dramatic sigh. 'Oh, I don't deal with bedtime. My househelp does it. Bedtime for the younger ones is always at that time of night when I need dressing before going out. Luckily, most of them are older now. They do their own thing.'

'Don't you ever sing them songs or tell them stories? Even Lamech does that.'

Dinah looked disgusted. 'Tell them stories? What about, Adah? About how wonderful my life is, married to a tyrant who has a new enemy every week? My job is keeping them away from their abba as best I can, so they stand a chance of staying safe and avoiding his fate. My best hope of doing that is keeping Barsabas entertained and the children well out of the way.'

Dinah's explanation took her aback. Her role was keeping her children safe from their father? How awful. She must want to spend time with them, though. 'You could tell them tales about other people or make things up,' Adah suggested.

'I haven't that sort of imagination.'

'Don't you worry they'll feel unloved?'

'Oh, they are loved well enough. They dote on their old nursemaid. I kept her on so they'd be happy. I'm not a terrible person, Adah.'

'I never said you were.'

'But you think it. You've always looked down on me.'

Adah glanced at Tzillah, appealing for help.

'Of course she hasn't, sister. Adah is harmless. Besides, she's had her own difficult husband. Perhaps if you both pulled your walls down you might get along.'

Dinah's lip turned up. 'Lamech is an angel compared to Barsabas.'

Tzillah poured Dinah another goblet of wine. 'Drink up, Dinah. Relax. We women have a lot more chance of staying sane if we stick together.'

Dinah sighed and downed the entire goblet of wine. 'You're right. Sorry, Adah.'

Adah's heart warmed. She reached across the table. 'I'm sorry for criticising your parenting. I'm sure I don't know how hard it is for you.'

Tzillah poured all three of them another drink. 'To solidarity!' she said, lifting her goblet high. Adah chuckled. Then Dinah's lips twitched, and Adah witnessed something she'd not seen before – Dinah smiled.

THE FOLLOWING MORNING, Adah woke to the sound of retching. She turned over and saw Lamech's bare back. Of course. He'd spent the night with her instead of Tzillah. Who was throwing up then?

After hauling herself out of bed, she tiptoed wearily towards the noise. Her head was heavy with last night's wine. She could hear the children playing quietly down the hall; Shua must be with them. Shua was wonderful.

Creeping into the next bedroom, she found Tzillah leaning over her chamber pot.

'Tzillah, dearest. Are you alright?' Tzillah sat up and smeared her hair from her face. It was pale and blotchy, and she stank of vomit. 'Oh dear. Did you have too much drink?'

'It's not that,' Tzillah croaked. Adah mentally counted the weeks. 'You bled before me last month. Now you haven't. You're with child.'

Tzillah nodded. 'Clearly wine and pregnancy don't go well together.'

'They certainly don't. I'll fetch you some water.'

She tiptoed back down the passageway, concentrating on the swish of her nightdress to stop herself wobbling. After spending the night with her husband, her loins ached as much as her head.

When she entered the living area, Yaval jumped up and ran to hug her. 'Ima!'

Adah put a finger to her lips. 'Your abba is still sleeping. Well done for playing quietly.'

Shua was sitting in the corner, sewing. The room was dotted with cushions, a couple of chairs, rugs, woven tapestries and a large, low table. Apertures let in the daylight, highlighting all but the deepest crevices.

'Is everything well, mistress?'

'Tzillah is sick. I'm fetching some water.' She poured some from a pitcher on the table, then picked a few mint leaves from the trough in the courtyard outside.

'Is there anything I can do?' Shua asked when she returned.

'Boiling a pot for the tub would be helpful.'

After kissing the children, she returned to Tzillah.

'Thanks.' Tzillah took the cup. 'I was feeling fine until this morning.'

'Shua is boiling some water. You'll feel better after we've cleaned you up.'

Tzillah drank, removed the mint leaves to chew on, then flopped back on the bed and sighed. 'I'm glad you're getting on better with Lamech.'

'Me too, surprisingly. Fatherhood has redeemed him somewhat.'

'I hope you can keep him content throughout my pregnancy. I don't want him going to someone else.'

Having Lamech in her bed occasionally was tolerable. The thought of having him constantly caused a shooting pain in her aching body.

She swallowed and focused on Tzillah's pleading expression. 'Would it hurt you if he went elsewhere?'

Tzillah nodded and tears slid down her cheeks. 'I love him, Adah. At first, I just enjoyed the attention. But now... I can cope with him being with you. I'll hate it, but you have the prior claim. The thought of him going off with the tavern girls, or going back to that woman, Nasya—'

'I understand.' She knew exactly what it felt like to be betrayed by Lamech. She pulled her sleeve down and wiped Tzillah's tears with it. 'I will do my best.'

'Thank you.'

CHAPTER 33

'Barsabas is coming tomorrow,' Tzillah announced. 'We have to tidy up, apparently.'

'Not Barsabas... Why?' Adah looked around at the children's things strewn all over the floor. They'd been building dens in Lamech's new hall. Why he needed to entertain a family member in this enormous room she didn't know, least of all Barsabas, who had been in the city for more than a season and hadn't set foot in their home yet.

'Lamech invited him,' Tzillah said. Tzillah was two-thirds into her pregnancy and her bump was more pronounced this time. She staggered as she struggled to pick a cushion up.

Adah fetched it for her. 'But Lamech dislikes Barsabas.'

'What makes you say that?'

'He told me so. When I first met Dinah, he said Barsabas was a fool.' She began untying some of the fabrics from the pillars.

'Well, Lamech seemed to like him well enough when I met him.'

'When was that?'

Tzillah stopped mid-bend for another cushion. 'Oh. I wasn't supposed to say. You mustn't tell Lamech I told you.'

'I won't. Go on.'

'It was Barsabas we stayed with when we got married. In the north, near the sea. The sea is wonderful, Adah – you should go sometime. One of Barsabas' people did the ceremony.'

'That explains why you're so friendly with Dinah. I did wonder. Help me fold this?' Adah held out two corners of the fabric. 'What do you mean by *one of his people*?'

Tzillah shook the sheet straight then walked the corners back towards her. 'This strange little man that hangs around Barsabas' household. He calls himself Kohen of the elohim.'

'Priest of the gods?'

'I thought it was odd too. But when Lamech turned up with a second wife to marry, Barsabas' people were incredibly pleased to see us. They dressed me in all this finery and gave me a copper armlet that coiled around my arm like a nachash.'

'Like Dinah's snake ring?'

'Exactly. Though it had several heads. Apparently, it's a representation of Leviathan – the huge sea serpent. Dinah told me she's never seen a beast with three heads, but that they signify something... I can't remember what. Anyway, there was this peculiar ceremony where we had to join our blood. We each cut our palms and the blood mingled in a dish. Then we had to dip our hands in and suck it off.'

'How vile.' Adah tucked the sheet over her arm for the final fold, then started on the next one.

'I assumed it was some northern custom, a way of expressing the joining of flesh. But now I look back on it, when the kohen chanted over us, his eyes looked peculiar, as if he wasn't quite present. They kind of rolled into the back of his head. My family used to sing to the elohim of the stars, but I'd never seen anything like this. Then Barsabas threw us this enormous feast, with seats of honour. The kohen gave a speech about how pleased El-Nachash would be that Lamech was following his path. All the people were ecstatic – strangely so, considering they didn't even know us.'

Adah fumbled with a particularly tight knot. 'El-Nachash? The nachash is no god, Tzillah. Have you not heard the stories about the Deceiver in the Garden?'

'What stories?'

'Our ancestors, the first man and woman, walked with the Creator, Yahweh Elohim, in the Garden. It was in Eden, from where the rivers flow. The Deceiver came to our ancestors as a serpent and tricked them into disobeying Yahweh.'

'Oh, I think I recall something about this story, but my parents told it very differently.'

'How so?'

'They said Yahweh Elohim tricked the first people into believing he was the only elohim, and the nachash revealed to them the truth – that there are many. So, we've always worshipped the whole host of heaven – the sun, moon and stars, as he revealed.'

'I've never seen you worship anything.'

A straw brush that had been a prop clattered to the floor. Tzillah retrieved it and started sweeping. 'When I said *we*, I meant *they*. It clearly did my abba no good, so I haven't continued his customs. What happened afterwards, in your story?'

'Yahweh banished our ancestors from the Garden.'

'Banished?'

'Yes, they couldn't walk with Him. They had to leave Eden and go east. Eventually, they ended up between the twin rivers, west of here, beyond the mountains.'

Tzillah's brow furrowed, and she stopped sweeping.

'You know – where The Wanderer came from,' Adah clarified.

'Oh,' Tzillah said, continuing. 'I've heard of him.'

'My parents didn't follow Yahweh closely either, but they still told me these stories. The one about the banishment was a useful threat. "Be a good girl and don't disobey us" always followed it.'

A groan escaped as Tzillah massaged her lower back. 'I must say, it sounds a bit harsh. What did the ancestors do to disobey? Was it murder, like The Wanderer? He was banished too, wasn't he?'

'Yes, banished further east. That's why he roams the whole area this side of the mountains. But that was separate. The first parents ate a forbidden fruit.'

'A fruit. That's all?'

'I think so.' Having gathered all the sheets, Adah placed them in the corner of the room.

'This Yahweh doesn't sound very fair. I've done a lot worse than eat fruit and He hasn't banished me.'

'Not yet.' Adah grinned. 'Chanoch talks about Yahweh a lot, and always maintains He is good. I know He's also powerful. You can ask Him for things and sometimes He gives them. But Chanoch says you must also repent. I don't understand it all, but Ruhamah honoured Yahweh too. It's part of the reason I'm here…'

Adah realised the smile had dropped from her lips when Tzillah raised an eyebrow. 'My prayers weren't answered the way I intended, but I'm not sure I'm ready to abandon the Creator for the created just yet.'

'So, you think this Yahweh made the host of heaven? It does seem strange to worship them in that case. Though, I know fear drove my abba to do what he did. He used to say, "better to worship too many things than not enough."'

Adah wasn't sure the logic held. She retrieved some toys scattered over the floor. Most, the boys had made themselves, but one was a figurine, a little like a woman in appearance, but roughly carved from wood.

'That was from the market,' Tzillah said, pointing at it. 'Naamah liked it, so I purchased it for her, but the trader said something about it bringing good fortune.'

'How peculiar,' she replied, running her fingers over the voluptuous carving. 'Tell me more about this kohen.'

'The kohen was asking the gods for things as part of the ceremony. A lot was in a strange tongue, but some parts I caught. He called on them to bless our union, speaking of Leviathan with awe, as if he holds some related great power, and referring to the sea as *The Realm of Leviathan*. Oh. Perhaps that's it? Yahweh reigns over the land, but El-Nachash rules the sea and sky? He may have told the first parents to disobey because he's at war with Yahweh Elohim?'

'Perhaps. Though, why would my parents call him the Deceiver if he was good? If he is a rival to Yahweh, and Yahweh is good as Chanoch claims, surely El-Nachash must be bad.' A chill suddenly ran through Adah's neck. 'Tzillah, what if you have been married by a servant of the Deceiver?'

Tzillah laughed. 'Adah, you're so dramatic. It's likely just a load of old stories. We didn't even know what was going on in the ceremony, and our marriage has been fruitful so far, so something must have worked.' She stroked her expanding belly.

Tzillah's fruitfulness after her own struggles stabbed Adah's heart, and she suddenly needed to change the subject. 'I'm surprised Barsabas and Dinah are still here. Don't they have matters to address at home?'

'Dinah says things got a little hot there. They needed to leave for a while.'

'Is the climate different in the north?'

Another chortle escaped Tzillah's mouth. 'No, Adah. She means they have been tense – perhaps dangerous.'

'Oh. Is it Barsabas' enemies? If he stays away, could they lose their land?'

'No, he has paid guards all over it. He'd rather put their lives at risk and get his family out of the way.'

That sounded like Barsabas. Adah dropped everything she'd collected into a wooden box. 'I wonder what Lamech wants to speak with him about?' Getting involved with someone like Barsabas could surely not be wise.

Tzillah threw her another toy. 'I don't know, and I don't care. I just want to put my feet up and have a massage.'

Trust Tzillah to be so carefree; Adah longed for her disposition. 'This is the last thing.' She pushed the box into one corner, stacked the linens on top, then pulled a small table in front of it. 'Will that do?'

'Perfect,' Tzillah said. 'I can't wait for Shua to get back from her sick ima's. Leah can't keep up and the hired cook isn't the same. I don't mean to be selfish, but I can't imagine how other women do everything. Cleaning, cooking, children, pregnancy. Ah!'

'Yes, we have it easy, Tzillah.' Adah chuckled. 'No one would believe you used to live in poverty.'

'I know. Terrible, isn't it? It's been scarcely six years and I'm completely useless now.'

'You're hardly useless. It takes a lot of effort to keep Lamech out of trouble.'

'And Yaval.'

'Ha! Yes, indeed.'

As if to prove the point, at that moment, Yaval scampered into the hall followed by Dotty the goat.

'Not again! Yaval, you must shut the gate!' Adah ran forwards and grabbed Dotty by her collar.

'She wanted to come inside. Why can't she live inside with us, Ima?'

'You know, I once had a goat who lived inside. I reared her by hand, like you did with Dotty. But when she was old enough, she went out to join the others.'

'That's not fair. I wasn't allowed Dotty in my room. Even after I sneaked her under my covers.'

Adah suppressed a chuckle. 'No, your abba doesn't approve of such things.'

Yaval pouted and crossed his arms. 'I want to live with Sav Shimiel. Levi and the others have way more fun than we do. When can we go, Ima? It's been ages!'

Adah sighed. Though she missed her abba, she rarely visited. Lamech hadn't expressly forbidden it, but the danger of bumping into Ruhamah kept her away. She had seen him from afar once, and her heart had almost cracked in her chest; it had taken every part of her strength not to turn and run away.

She'd asked her abba about him afterwards. 'How is Ruhamah?'

He had looked at her, solemnly. 'He's as you would expect of someone who lives alone and has lost a wife and unborn child twice over.'

'It's that bad?' She had often thought of sending a messenger directly to her love but had never found the courage.

Abba had continued. 'The flock keeps him sane. Though I don't think it does him any good being in the fields alone for such lengths of time. Rivkah wants to find him another wife, but he refuses to let her and shuns everyone she invites over. He rarely eats with us now, but Eliana visits him as often as she can.'

The thought of Ruhamah marrying someone else tightened Adah's chest. She knew it was selfish, but she was glad he'd refused. As long as he was alone, she could pretend he still belonged to her. Even if she hadn't the courage to be near him.

Yaval was shifting impatiently from one foot to the other. She made a decision. 'Let's go now. We're all tidied up here.' *And it's the middle of the day; Ruhamah should be in the farthest field right now.*

'Yes!' Yaval skipped and turned.

'But you're not staying there. We are just visiting.'

'I know.' Yaval's face dropped slightly, but soon brightened again. 'I'll go tell the others.' And he scampered off, leaving Dotty behind.

'I'll take your goat and put her away then,' Adah mumbled, rolling her eyes.

A chuckle escaped Tzillah, who'd swept the dust, threads and crumbs into a pile and was staring at it, hoping it'd pick itself up.

'Would you like to come?' Adah asked.

'To the goat pen or your abba's?'

'Abba's of course.'

'Oh no. I don't fancy the hike. Like I said, feet up; massage.'

'Alright. I'll ask Leah to clear that pile and see if she can spare you a rub.'

'You're wonderful. Do say hello to everyone from me.'

The first time Tzillah had accompanied Adah to her abba's home for dinner it had felt strange indeed. However, Shimiel and Rivkah had graciously, if rather awkwardly, welcomed her, and before long, Tzillah had charmed her way into their affections the way only Tzillah could.

'I see why you liked her, despite the circumstances,' Abba had said when they were walking the grounds together.

'Nothing puts Tzillah out of sorts. She is permanently optimistic. If I had to choose anyone to share a husband with, I would choose her.'

'Still, don't expect it to always be easy. Like tensions between siblings, you're bound to clash eventually, and I can't imagine sharing a husband is easier than sharing parents.'

'I know.' Adah had scanned the familiar landscape, breathing in the scent of the hillsides. 'My boys have given me a reason to live, and to keep peace with Lamech. I made the right choice not giving them up, but I still long for the life I lost.'

'I expect you always will,' he said. Abba had also apologised for his part in Adah's ordeal, but she didn't blame him for it. In truth, it couldn't have turned out differently, whatever Chanoch claimed. Lamech would always get his way.

CHAPTER 34

Adah never found out why Barsabas had been invited that day, but Lamech left shortly afterwards, accompanying Dinah and her husband on their journey north. He didn't take either wife with him.

'I wish he'd taken you,' Tzillah said at breakfast, several weeks later.

Adah wiped Juval's face and sent him off to play. He was always the last to finish eating. 'I suspect he knows I'd disapprove of their customs.'

'You do lecture him sometimes.'

'Only when necessary.'

Tzillah rolled her eyes. 'Still, I can't help wondering what woman Barsabas will provide for him.'

'What do you mean?'

She paused. 'Several women are in the service of Barsabas' kohen.'

Adah still didn't understand. She raised an eyebrow as she stacked the plates.

'You know. In service, like the tavern women.'

Adah's eyes widened. 'What could that have to do with their rituals?'

'I'm not exactly sure, but they certainly sleep with many men. Often, I think, as part of the rituals.'

'No. Really?'

'I only noticed it shortly before we left. Before that, I thought they were just ordinary servants, dressed provocatively for Barsabas' pleasure. However, on the final night's banquet, there was definitely more going on. It was unnerving. Fortunately, Lamech's attention was fixed firmly on me. Of course, I didn't love him then, but I would have still hated him going off like the other men.'

'Does Barsabas *go off like other men?*'

'Of course.'

A chill shot through Adah's bones. She sipped a cup of warm grape juice that Naamah had left unfinished, but it barely helped. 'How could Methushael have given his daughter to that man – has he no heart at all?'

'I think you know the answer to that.'

'You're alright, Methushael likes you. He still hates me, even though I bore two sons.'

Tzillah's nose wrinkled. 'Actually, I think Methushael feels the shame of Lamech having two wives. Have you noticed he no longer pays Noa the same respect? Going behind his back with Lamech was a step too far, I think.'

'Strange that he hasn't taken that out on you.'

'I flirt with him, Adah. You should try it sometime.'

'Ugh.' The thought made her sick.

Shua walked into the room. 'Mistress, you needn't tidy the breakfast. Leave it to me.'

'I don't mind.'

'There was a message for you from Eliana. She's asked everyone to lunch.'

'Oh, I'd love that. Please, accept.'

Tzillah decided to accompany them but moaned all the way to Eliana's. 'Of course I like your friend, Adah, but I wish she didn't live so far away.'

'It's only the other side of the city. Not as far as Abba's.' They passed through most of the north-eastern streets to get there, which became more densely packed the closer they got, with laundry hanging everywhere and rubbish strewn in the streets. Goats were the primary clean-up team and had to be dodged all the way. At one point, Naamah had a near-miss with a billy goat.

'It's still too far.' Tzillah said, as they reached the foot of Eliana's hill. 'And now, we have to climb that.'

Adah started up it, holding her gift basket with one arm and Juval with the other. Fortunately, the other two children walked by themselves. When Tzillah continued to moan, Adah quipped, 'When I was far more pregnant than you, I ran all the way to the city from the hills.'

'Yes. And look where that got you.'

The words stabbed her heart.

'Sorry. That was thoughtless,' Tzillah said, and chewed her lip.

'You're forgiven.'

'Mela!' Yaval ran ahead, having seen his favourite person halfway up the hill. Mela was now a lovely young woman, fiercely protected by her abba who refused to see her engaged, which suited Eliana fine, as she was still producing babies and needed constant help. Mela picked Yaval up and swung him around.

Tzillah continued her rant. 'In all seriousness though, Adah, why would you do it? Leave Ruhamah in the hills and run down?'

'Because he was injured and in danger. Anyone would have done so.'

'Not me. I would have saved myself.'

'Nonsense. You gave up your happiness for the sake of your family once. Don't pretend you're selfish.'

Tzillah turned and stopped three doors down from Eliana's. She regarded Adah squarely. 'I am. Purely so. And you should have left that man in the ravine.'

A figure emerged from Eliana's house. Adah's heart palpitated and her throat tightened. She loosened her hold on Juval, who slid to the floor but continued to cling to her arm. The man at the top of the hill studied Yaval, then turned their way.

Oblivious, Tzillah continued, walking backwards past the adjacent houses with hands aloft. 'If you'd never run to the city, you'd still be free…'

'And I would likely be dead,' the man said.

Tzillah spun on her heel, her eyes widening at the person standing a few strides from her. Her gaze flicked to Adah, then back again. 'He's… this is…'

'Ruhamah.' One side of his mouth turned slightly up. He stepped forward and bowed his head. 'You must be Tzillah. I'm pleased to meet you.'

Ruhamah didn't meet Adah's eye. His attention was fixed on Tzillah, and amusement still tugged at his lips.

Adah gulped. Her mouth felt dry. She should say something, but she'd forgotten how to speak. An apologetic glance from Mela passed her way.

Tzillah whistled. 'I'm sorry. It seems I'm full of idiocy today. My big mouth—'

'Don't worry. I'm used to my sister.' Ruhamah smiled, and Adah wanted to steal his smile for herself. All these years avoiding him, and now, she wanted nothing more than to dissolve in his gaze forever.

Yaval tugged at Mela's arm, pointing towards the side of the house where Adah knew she kept poultry, but Juval and Naamah remained by Adah's legs. The gaze of the man she loved wavered between her sons, but he still didn't meet her eye, returning instead to Tzillah.

Tzillah scratched her belly. 'Well, I'm going to find a drink and a seat. You two can… well, do whatever you need to do. Naamah, Juval – come.'

Then Tzillah was gone. Naamah too. But Juval clung insistently to Adah's thigh. Finally, Ruhamah tilted his head her way, and then she saw his sorrow break through. The horrors of his loss, that had ceased haunting him when he'd been with her on the hills, had returned to his eyes.

Her lip quivered. They hadn't spoken since she'd abandoned him, since they'd been ready to run away together, since before her children were born. The children that were almost his.

'Hello, Adah.'

Words still failed her. Instead, tears pricked at her eyes.

'Ima. Who is that man?' Juval whispered.

Her son brought her out of her trance. She must say something. 'This is Eliana's brother, and my good friend, Ruhamah.'

Ruhamah approached and bent on one knee. 'I have been looking forward to meeting you for a long time, Juval.'

A gulp emitted from Juval's throat. 'Really? Why haven't I met you before?'

'My work keeps me in the hills. I am a shepherd.'

'Oh. Well then you should talk to Yaval, my brother. He is the one who loves animals.'

'I would like that. Are you staying for lunch, Juval?'

'Yes. Ima promised there would be raisin cakes.'

'There certainly will. They are my favourite too.'

Her son's eyes lit up and his grip on her leg loosened.

'Why don't you go inside and see if Eliana has any ready?' Ruhamah said.

'But Ima says we cannot eat them before lunch.'

'She is quite right. But if you get in there first, you can choose the biggest one for yourself, and the next biggest for me, and put them aside.'

Juval grinned, then he let go and bounded into the house.

Slowly, Ruhamah stood up. 'The other boy favours you. But that one looks just like Lamech.'

'He does.' She could hear his unsteady breathing and feel the warmth emanating from his body.

Ruhamah fixed her gaze. 'He would never have passed for my child.'

The tear that had been threatening to come rolled down her cheek. Ruhamah lifted his finger and wiped it, sending shivers through her. She nestled into his palm and closed her eyes. 'Can you ever forgive me?'

'Adah, there is nothing to forgive.'

'Oh, but there is. I should never have dragged you into my mess.' More tears escaped.

'You didn't drag me. I entered willingly.' He stroked her cheek with his thumb, the rest of him hovering. 'Oh, I wish I could hold you now, but the world is watching.'

'How can you say so? I never even came to see you, nor sent word.'

'I knew Lamech wouldn't let you. If I was in his position, I wouldn't have.'

'It's true, he watched me closely at first. It was a long time before he'd let me visit Abba. But I've had freedom recently, for I've earnt his trust again. Though he knows I think of you.'

'You do?'

'Always.'

Ruhamah sighed. 'And I you. Yet it cannot be. You are Lamech's wife. We must put it behind us. Though, thanks to my scheming sister, we have met again.'

'What are you saying about me?' Eliana walked out, laden with a huge earthenware pot. 'Ruhamah, make yourself useful and take this – it weighs as much as a behemoth.'

The intensity broken, Ruhamah grinned and grabbed the pot from his sister's arms.

'I had to get you two together,' Eliana continued, fetching bowls from a cubby-hole in the wall. 'You were driving me crazy. Every time I mention Adah, you look like I've punched you, and every time I mention you to her, she goes all wistful and teary. It's been years!'

Having put the pot down, Ruhamah grabbed her in a bear hug. 'I'm sorry. Forgive me?'

Eliana pushed him away. 'Oh, get off me, I'm too busy for that. Go inside and bring out the bread before this stew goes cold. And shout for everyone to gather.'

Soon they were all seated on the ground outside Eliana's home, forming a circle around the pot; nearly twenty of them. Adah and Ruhamah had been separated as multiple children squeezed between them.

'How do you feed this many children?' Tzillah asked in disbelief. 'Or know where they all are at one time?'

'Oh, I rarely know where they all are. But they know when it's mealtime and gather like vultures beforehand.' Eliana waved her serving spoon in the air.

This produced a chuckle from Tzillah. 'I have one child, and even then, Adah does most of the work.'

A correction was necessary. 'No, Shua does,' Adah smirked.

'But we like it when Ima plays with us best,' Yaval said, grasping her hand. 'Plus, she knows how to look after the goats.'

From opposite her, Ruhamah joined in. 'She is very good with goats. Have you hand-reared any?'

'Yes – Dotty. Her ima rejected her. We traded her after. Nasty goat.'

Ruhamah scratched his beard and laughed. 'I agree. What sort of ima would leave her children?' He paused and caught Adah's eye. 'Mothers put their babies first. That's how Elohim designed it.'

Everything else faded as Adah submerged into the pool of Ruhamah's gaze. Conversations continued without them as children grew preoccupied with ensuring they got their fair share of food. In silence, Ruhamah communicated what needed to be said. Though she hadn't told him, he knew of Lamech's ultimatum. He understood, and he didn't judge her.

Tzillah snaked their arms together. Adah sniffed, wiped her nose and leaned on Tzillah's shoulder.

'He is giving you permission to forgive yourself; to close this door and walk on,' Tzillah whispered, kissing her forehead.

As tears clouded her vision of the man she loved, Adah blinked them away and nodded. Ruhamah nodded back, put two fingers to his lips and kissed them away.

CHAPTER 35

Tzillah's son was born towards the end of winter. Apparently, food had been scarce in the city all season. Shua complained of the trade deals in the marketplace, saying far more wine was needed than usual to acquire grain. Yet Lamech didn't mention it. Rather, he increased the number of banquets they held. With Tzillah out of action, Adah and Shua managed these together.

'I'm pleased the master is being generous, sharing our food and fire with those less fortunate,' Shua said, as they were setting up for the baby's naming celebration in the banquet hall.

'Have you seen our guests? They may be slightly less fortunate, but they are hardly slaves. Lamech wants to show off his third son, that is all.' Adah arranged some flowers in a stoneware vase. She'd been out that morning collecting from the fields and hedgerows nearby.

'Several of the city elders are coming, and they are not all wealthy,' Shua insisted.

'Yes, but he's desperate to get them on-side. There are some that still refuse to speak to him since he married Tzillah.'

'Are we expecting Methushael?' The cushions reserved for Lamech's abba needed freshening, so Shua beat them against the pillars.

'Yes, the whole family are coming. Bekhor and Methushael still aren't talking – we better put Bekhor at the foot of Methushael's table rather than on his right.'

'Those two. Will they ever get along?'

'Not until Bekhor joins Methushael in business, which he refuses to do. Shouldn't Lamech sit on his father's right then?'

'No, Lamech wants our family on the raised platform.'

'Up there?' Shua motioned to the stage taking up the opposite end of the hall to the entrance. Though Tzillah had meant the idea as a joke, Lamech's workmen had installed it the previous month. It consisted of a suspended wooden floor, large enough for several tables and performers, with wooden steps leading down to the main hall. Bekhor had carved floral designs into the panelling that breached the gap between the two floors.

'I told you. It's all for show. He built this hall for his previous children. He builds the platform for the next one. Something about a legacy. I can't make sense of it.'

Shua muttered under her breath as together they shifted a table up the steps and onto the platform.

'I assume he'll finally announce the boy's name tomorrow?'

'I believe so. Though he and Tzillah are still arguing about it. Tzillah wishes she'd had another girl so she could have chosen alone.'

'I've got it!' Lamech strode into the hall, grabbed Adah by the waist and roughly kissed her. He stank of blood and his tunic was filthy.

'Where have you been?'

'Hunting. I've left you a deer in the courtyard.'

'Hunting? You don't hunt.'

'I do now. Azurak took me to these brilliant woods, due west. It was terrific fun, Adah. He showed me how to wield a spear and knife.'

'Didn't you have work to do?'

'Oh, it's all under control, don't worry.' Picking up the tallest vase of flowers, he moved it to the top table. 'We have lots of mouths to feed though. And there's plenty of food in the woods. I don't know why I didn't think of it before. We're going to train some of the workers to hunt, then we can send them out to catch food for the community. Less grain to purchase. The women can go too and gather fruit. It's perfect.'

She should be pleased Lamech was thinking of how to feed others, except the only reason he had to was that they were all his slaves.

'So, what is it you've *got*? The deer?' she asked.

'Oh no. A name! We found this brook in the woods. Azurak said it flows all the way from the mountains and in the summer, the flow is far more powerful, for the snow melts on the tips and joins it. He called it a *tuval*, Adah. Just imagine! It's perfect. I shall have a Yaval, Juval, and Tuval. Three courses of water demonstrating my prosperity to the city.'

Adah grimaced as Lamech jumped down the steps and embraced her again. She knew exactly what Tzillah would make of Lamech's idea and didn't want to be there for the argument. It was bad enough getting her two sons muddled up, never mind a third.

Lamech didn't notice. He was too pleased with himself. 'I'm going to tell Tzillah the good news. Take care of that deer, will you? Let's eat it tomorrow.'

As he left, Shua's mouth dropped open. 'Does he not know?'

'That a deer must hang? I don't think he's ever had to consider it,' Adah said.

'It's a good thing he knows his way around a vineyard, or I would be worried.'

Adah chuckled. Shua was so much more confident now. She wouldn't have dared speak so about her master years ago. She still wouldn't in his presence, of course. No one would.

'I'll have to see if I can find a carcass at the meat vendors.' Shua tutted. 'Can I leave you to finish setting up here while I *take care of it.*'

As Shua rolled her eyes, another laugh escaped Adah's mouth 'Of course. Though if Tzillah goes into a temper and starts throwing things around later, I'll be joining you in the courtyard.'

A COMPANY OF SOME fifty people gathered in the hall the following evening. Bekhor's little family choir had been outdone by the singers Lamech hired. Apparently, Azurak had scouted a man whose four daughters performed for payment. They sang well, but the accompanying movements made Adah's cheeks warm. After she pointed out the obvious disapproval of some elders, Lamech quietly had a word, and the dancing ceased.

It felt peculiar sitting on the raised platform with her family. She'd far rather have been serving with Shua, Leah and those Lamech had hired for the night. Yet he'd specifically instructed his wives to stay by his side, his stern face permitting no argument.

The twins hated it too. All they wanted to do was play behind the pillar, not have everyone's eyes on them. Adah had stashed a few wooden blocks in the shadows. Fortunately, Naamah looked pretty as a picture, reclining quietly at the end of the table, and most of the onlookers were more interested in Tzillah's newborn bundle anyway.

When Lamech stood halfway through the meal, the room quietened. 'Friends, family, and fellow workers. I have gathered you tonight to celebrate the birth of my third son and heir.' Lamech removed the bundle from Tzillah and held him up for all to see. 'I present to you: Tuval-Kayin.'

Adah's heart skipped. She stared at Lamech, then at Tzillah. Tzillah's petite nose crinkled, and she winked. Though Adah had goaded her, she had refused to divulge what name she and Lamech had settled on, claiming it was a surprise.

It took ages for the cheers to cease and Lamech to move out of the way. As he paraded the hall with his son, Adah claimed his seat next to Tzillah. 'What is the meaning of this?'

Tzillah grinned. 'I did it for you. A little nod to your obsession.'

'Why?'

'I could hardly call him *The Wanderer*, could I?'

'And Lamech allowed it?'

'I don't think he grasped the reference. He just thought it brilliant he was *acquiring*[1] another *stream*!'

'Oh, Tzillah; you are clever. Does this mean we can call him Kayin, or will Lamech insist on confusing us all with Tuval?'

'Lamech can call him Tuval if he wants. I'm sure we'll come up with little nicknames to differentiate them, as we have with the others.'

'I hope we don't have any more boys. What will be next – Nahar[2]?'

'Perhaps Agam[3].'

Adah burst into giggles. 'Oh, Tzillah! That's awful.'

---

[1] Kayin means acquired.

[2] Nahar means river.

[3] Agam means lake.

Tzillah cupped her hand round her mouth. 'It might not be just our sons. I can quite imagine Lamech naming a daughter Mayim[4].'

'He would. It would fit perfectly with his view of women.'

Tzillah's resulting peel of laughter was so loud that Lamech turned and frowned at her. Tzillah pursed her lips. 'We'd better control ourselves, or he'll take it out on you tonight.'

'Oh, don't. I can't wait until you're healed.'

'Neither can I. It's been a long time.'

'Whereas I wish to be with child again just so he'll leave me alone.'

Tzillah tilted her head. 'Oh, Adah, you are naughty.'

'Not as naughty as you.'

'Ha. I can't disagree with that.' A wide yawn escaped Tzillah's mouth. 'All this amusement has worn me out. Mini-Kayin had me up most of last night. He's a hungry little beast. Why Lamech insists on dining so late, I don't know.'

'It's so he doesn't have to serve as much wine.' She shuffled closer to Tzillah. 'He told Shua to water it down four to one after dark.'

'No. Really?'

'No one notices when they're tired.'

Another yawn escaped. 'Do you think he'll notice if I go to bed?'

'I'm certain he'll notice.' Adah glanced over at their husband. His posture indicated that he was trying to listen to his wives' conversation while speaking with Chanoch. *Chanoch... I haven't seen him in a long time.*

Tzillah followed her gaze. 'That's your friend, isn't it?'

'Yes. He has been good to me.'

'Go join them. While you've got their attention, I can sneak out.'

'Leaving me to entertain Lamech? And what about Mini-Kayin?'

'Bring him to my bed when he starts screaming.'

'Alright. But only because I love you and the bags under your eyes look like overripe figs.'

'Charming. I love you too.'

Adah kissed Tzillah on the cheek and gave her a shove. 'Go on. To bed. I'll distract Lamech as long as I can.'

---

[4] Mayim means water, from the root word for chaos.

She would have to turn on her charm to keep Lamech from spotting Tzillah's escape. She sidled to her husband and threaded her arm around his waist, bending to inspect Tuval-Kayin, who was still happily dozing in Lamech's arms.

Chanoch studied her face. 'How are you, Adah?'

Her adoring looks at her husband must seem strange to Chanoch. Still, she must play the game for Tzillah's sake. 'I am well, thank you.'

'I knew motherhood would suit Adah. She's never been happier than she is with my sons,' Lamech interjected. 'She's pleased she came home. Aren't you?'

Adah forced a smile. 'Of course. And how is Shiphrah?'

Chanoch raised an eyebrow, then lowered it. 'No better, no worse. We miss you. You must call over sometime soon. Bring your children to meet Shiphrah. Are they here?'

'They're behind the pillar with some toys.'

Lamech stiffened. 'You must get them out from there, *dearest*. They should be meeting our guests.'

'They dislike crowds, Lamech.'

'Nonsense.' He dropped Tuval-Kayin into her arm like a sack. 'If you cannot control them, I shall do it myself.' After turning on his heel, he strode towards the platform.

He would see Tzillah missing. Adah sped after him, grasping his arm with her spare hand before he reached the top.

'What are you doing?' Lamech hissed.

Only one excuse would work. She lifted onto her toes and kissed him on the lips, lingering long enough to ensure a response.

Lamech's arm encircled her waist. 'Public affection. This isn't like you.'

She ran her fingers through his hair and smiled.

'Hmmm,' he mused. 'Much as I would love to carry you away right now, I must see to our guests. And children.'

'The twins won't come out if they think you are angry. It might cause a scene. Let me coax them, my love.'

Lamech's eyes narrowed. 'Do you promise to continue this later?'

She swallowed the lump in her throat and twiddled his lock of hair. 'I promise.'

Tuval-Kayin stirred, turning his face towards her breast.

'Tuval is hungry. Where is Tzillah?' Lamech turned his head, loosening her hold. She flattened her hand on his cheek and pulled him back.

'He's not hungry. Tzillah nursed him before we came in. She...' Adah lowered her voice to a whisper. '...had to relieve herself. I'm sure she'll be back directly.'

Lamech grunted. He hated all talk of bodily functions, thinking it primitive.

'Why don't you show Tuval-Kayin to your grandfather while I get the boys? He won't root against your chest. I'll bring them to you in just a moment.' Not waiting for an answer, she passed the baby back.

Lamech's nose twitched, then he relented. 'Don't be long. Tonight, we are a united family for all to see.'

CHAPTER 36

The sight of sixty or so men lined up in the field beyond the vineyard was quite extraordinary. Adah had helped the three eldest children climb up the watchtower to see their abba and Azurak preparing workers to hunt collectively in the woods. She'd expected the boys to enjoy watching the training, but hadn't anticipated that first, the hunters must make their weapons.

Lamech had previously sent several men on a trip to the mountains near the sea, where they collected flint and obsidian needed for spear heads. Now the men sat hunched over, flaking the stones by hitting them repeatedly with a sharpening tool.

'When are they going to go hunting?' Yaval asked, shifting from one foot to another.

'I'm bored,' Juval complained, hitting his brother with a stick.

'Stop that.' Adah removed the stick and threw it over the side of the tower.

'Ima! That was my stick.' Juval stuck out his bottom lip and stamped his foot. Naamah giggled.

Adah was unmoved, unlike the watchtower's wooden floor which wobbled. 'It ceased to be your stick when you turned it into a weapon,' she said.

Yaval stuck his tongue out and this time, Juval stamped his foot onto his brother's toe.

'Right, that's enough. You can come back once they've made the spears. Down the ladder. Go.'

Yaval groaned. 'But I want to stay up here. I can see the mountains from here. I might see some new animals.'

'You couldn't even see a behemoth from this distance. How about we go for a walk?'

Now it was Juval's turn to groan. 'I hate walks, Ima. They hurt my legs.'

'Don't be so lazy.'

'Ima Tzillah also hates walks. You don't call her lazy.'

'Ima Tzillah has a baby to nurse. Now come along.'

Adah lifted Naamah onto the ladder and watched, heart in mouth, as the girl descended. Lamech had made it as safe as possible, but she still imagined them all falling to their deaths. Once all three children were safely on the ground, she descended herself.

A few days later, they went up again. Now the men held weapons, sharpened stones at one end, bound with leather cord to straight branches. Azurak's commanding voice rang out across the field, reaching them in the tower.

He called out a number, demonstrated a corresponding movement, then repeated it. Once the men had copied him, he called the next number and demonstrated the next movement. Then he put the two together.

Over and over, they practiced until each could seamlessly raise the spear, step back and launch it. Then they formed a long row and started throwing.

Lamech was watching with strong arms crossed over a bare chest and hair tied roughly back, revealing eyebrows drawn in concentration. The sight might have quickened Adah's heart again, if not for the fear coursing through her gut. People had hunted individually since the banishment, but training a host of hunters? It felt vastly different. How long before the hunters became an army, like Barsabas'?

The boys leaned against the railings of the watchtower, faces squeezed in the gaps, enraptured by the sight.

'When I grow up, I want to be like Azurak,' Juval said. 'Everyone does as he says.'

Adah flinched. *Please, no.* 'Well, Azurak is under your abba's command.'

'You mean all these men are doing what Abba wants?'

'Yes.' *Perhaps.* She sometimes wondered who really controlled who.

'What are they going to hunt?' Yaval asked.

'Wild animals of course,' Naamah whispered. She was always softly spoken.

Yaval drew back. 'Really? Why animals? What have they ever done to us?'

Adah squeezed his shoulder. 'Food is scarce, my love. Your abba is trying to ensure we all have enough.'

The whites of Yaval's eyes swelled. 'Then I will give them my food.'

Adah's heart could have burst, and she pulled her boy into an embrace. 'That is very kind, but I don't think it will feed so many men and their families.'

'There can't be enough wild animals for all those people. It will be a bloodbath.'

Her mouth fell open. 'Now, where did you hear that phrase?'

'I overheard Abba talking about a fight at the tavern the other night. He said several men were injured – it was *a bloodbath*.'

The tone of his voice was so full of innocence that Adah swallowed down her indignation. Lamech's indiscretion wasn't Yaval's fault. She must not show the fear raging inside that her boys would be exposed to such horrors. Better to brush it away. 'Your abba seems to think there are plenty of animals. There's no need to worry.'

Yaval sat and dipped his head into his crossed legs. 'I don't want to watch anymore. Can we go now?'

The floor wobbled again as Juval stamped his foot. 'No. I want to stay.'

Juval's fascination was intriguing. He was the more timid of her sons, the quieter one who didn't like the boisterous games of his cousins but would rather cuddle up or sit in a quiet corner. Yet this hinted of being his father's son after all. It was like the boys had swapped places.

'Just a little while longer, then we'd better get back for supper,' she said.

Naamah squeezed into the spot vacated by Yaval, and Adah followed the direction of the little girl's eyes. They were focused on Lamech, her face a picture of awe.

When they returned home, Tzillah was asleep in the wicker chair with a chunky baby on her shoulder. He was being weaned but still screamed regularly for his ima's milk.

Adah put a finger to her lips, but too late. Juval ran into the living room, brandishing a stick and hollering. The baby started and began to cry.

Tzillah sighed and opened one eye. 'You know, hunters must be absolutely silent, otherwise they catch nothing.'

'Is that true?' Juval approached Tzillah and gave his baby brother a sloppy kiss. The infant blinked, then his face stretched into a smile. 'Can I hold him?' Juval asked.

'Of course.' Tzillah vacated her seat and placed her heavy load on Juval's lap. Mini-Kayin (the nickname had stuck) immediately started crying again. Tzillah gave a big sigh and rolled her eyes. 'Won't he ever leave me be?'

'Oh, you'll miss it when he stops caring,' Adah said, putting a pot on to boil. Shua always kept a small fire alight, even in summer.

'I have an idea!' Juval announced, plonking his brother on the floor and running off to his room.

Tzillah raised her eyebrows. 'So, what was the training like today? Did they do anything?'

'Oh yes. They are quite a sight, in long rows, throwing their spears. Most of them were getting the hang of it before we left and hitting the mark.'

'Lamech will have to take them to the forest in smaller groups than that. They'll scare everything off.'

'I think he means to divide them into companies and send one group each day.'

Tzillah nodded. 'Azurak mentioned more areas to explore too.'

'Wouldn't that be wandering onto land owned by others?' Adah asked.

'I don't know,' Tzillah shrugged.

As Adah poured hot water over the herbs, an ethereal tune, like a whispered song, carried from the other side of the room. Almost dropping the pot, she spun around.

Juval was holding a piece of bone and blowing into it. As his fingers moved over the top, bottom and end, he varied the volume and tone, producing something like a funeral lament, yet without words.

Mini-Kayin stopped crying and looked up. Everyone in the room stared as the brilliance continued, finishing on a long, warbling tone. Silence followed. Adah could barely breathe; she had never heard anything so hauntingly beautiful.

Juval glanced around and shuffled his feet. His eyes caught hers, pleading. 'Was it really bad?' he asked.

Adah tiptoed towards him then drew him into her chest. Tears slid down her cheeks as she cradled him and kissed the top of his head. 'You made that?'

'Yes. I've been making it since I heard the girls singing at Uncle's party and practicing in secret.'

'I have never heard anything like it. How did you carve the holes?'

'I took a sharp stone from the kitchen. Am I in trouble?'

'No, my love! It was wonderful. I never imagined such a sound could exist.'

Below them, Mini-Kayin smacked his lips and gurgled.

Tzillah smiled. 'You better not put that away, Juval. From now on, you are chief babysitter.'

'IT WAS INCREDIBLE,' Adah said to Lamech in bed that night.

Lamech smiled and kissed her neck. 'I can't wait to hear it.'

'Have you ever heard anyone create music with something other than their voice?'

'I've heard whistling, plenty of drums, and rhythms shaken with pots of rice.'

'Yes, but a tune, Lamech! And he's only seen seven winters. How is it possible he should have such a gift?'

He caressed her midriff. 'He's always had an ear for music. You said that when he was a baby. Besides, I don't know why you're so shocked. He's our child, Adah. You and me. We were meant to produce greatness.'

She ran her hands into his hair, matted from being tied back. Her finger got stuck, so she twirled it until it loosened. When he looked up, she saw the reflection of her son – her gifted son. Warmth penetrated her heart once more. She remembered Lamech's pose earlier in the field, the one that had attracted her.

Lamech's mouth twitched into a half-smile. 'I haven't seen you look at me like that in a long time.'

She lifted her other hand up and threaded her fingers together behind his head. Then she eased him forward, kissing him willingly for the first time since her return.

'Oh, I've missed you,' Lamech sighed once they'd pulled away. She'd never admit it, but a small part of her had missed him too.

She kissed him again, then, before thinking it through, asked, 'Do you ever regret it?'

'What?'

'Marrying Tzillah.'

Lamech's body stiffened. 'How can you ask me that?'

Her eyes pleaded for understanding. 'Because it's important. You claim to love me; you claim we are destined for each other...'

Lamech sat up and stroked his beard. 'Asking me that is like asking me if I regret my children. I could never do so. Tuval-Kayin and Naamah mean so much to me.'

'And Tzillah?'

He sniffed. 'Tzillah is tremendous fun. She suits me and acts her part perfectly.'

'You argue a lot.'

'Not about anything serious.' He turned back to her. 'Adah, you are the passion of my heart. You know that. But you are always serious.'

Her heart sank. Was it true? She had fun when she was with her friends; He just affected her differently. 'So, you don't regret it?'

His hand reached for her side again and his fingers swept up her skin. 'No, I don't. Though I hope for a brighter future.' Then his other hand cradled her jaw, thumb stroking her cheek as he delved into her eyes. 'Whether or not we have one is up to you.'

CHAPTER 37

'Have you seen Mini-Kayin?' Tzillah stormed into the kitchen courtyard, looking furious.

Adah glanced up from her dough. 'No. Have you seen Yaval?'

Tzillah stamped her foot. 'Those boys. I wish your son would not constantly lead mine astray, Adah!'

'My son?'

'Yes, your son. He is always disappearing into the hills, looking for something or other, and mine looks up to him, copying everything he does. Now, it is Mini-Kayin's sixth birthday, and he is nowhere to be found.'

'I'm sure they're fine. Don't worry.'

'How can I not be worried? People will be arriving for his party at the high point of the sun.'

Adah continued to pound the dough. 'I am well aware. That's why I'm so busy cooking.'

'Ugh. Adah, why do you think we have servants? You have one job to do – look after the children – and you can't even manage that.' Tzillah turned about and stomped back into the house.

Shua let out a whistle. 'What's got into her? Last I checked, Mini-Kayin was her son.'

'I don't know,' Adah muttered. *Though I have my suspicions.* Tzillah had become increasingly envious since Adah had renewed her affection for Lamech. 'Leah, would you finish this for me?'

Leah nodded and started kneading while Adah washed her hands. Then she strolled to see their gatekeeper.

'Have Yaval and Tuval-Kayin been this way?' she asked Avram, ever loyal, staring out on an almost-empty street.

'Yes, mistress. They left shortly after dawn.'

'Unaccompanied?'

'Of course not, mistress. I sent my son with them. One of the young men from down the way was showing them a mining site. They said you knew.'

Adah rolled her eyes. 'Thank you. What would we do without you?'

Avram grinned. They'd built an unlikely friendship since the day she invited him to dine with her friends years before, accelerated by Yaval's frequent disappearances. Her sons were reaching the teen years and had grown in height but not responsibility. Adah ascertained their young guide's name and set off to find his parents.

She found the father at his booth in the marketplace, surrounded by cuts of meat and hanging rabbits. 'Ah, yes. They were going on a metal hunt. I did tell them they must be back before midday, on account of the younger one's celebrations.'

'Thank you, but Yaval is notorious for losing track of the sun.'

She was just deciding which of the boys hovering around the stall would make the best tracker when Yaval ran into view, followed by his younger brother and a very lanky twenty-something who must be their guide.

'Ima. What are you doing here? Look what we found.' Yaval shoved a large rock into her arms. It was heavier than expected.

'You carried this all the way back?'

'No. He carried it.' Adah followed Yaval's pointing finger towards the gatekeeper's son, who was dragging behind, looking exhausted. Yaval had one of those faces you couldn't refuse. She should know. She failed every time.

'But I found it,' Tuval-Kayin piped up. Mini-Kayin, as they always called him unless he was in trouble, was the image of his robust abba – except Tzillah's bronze curls fell about his face. His chubby cheeks, now red from exertion, sat beneath eyes proud and gleeful.

Adah turned the rock in her hands. It gleamed. 'Is there copper in it?' she asked.

'Yes, but also look…' The guide's hand reached over, pointing at the dark grey shiny areas. 'Something else.'

'What?'

'Another metal. We're still trying to figure out how to purify both metals without losing either, but this one is softer. See, I can pick at it.' He demonstrated with another sharpened stone.

'Fascinating. If it's softer though, it won't be much use. We need something tougher for tools, don't we?'

'They have started making tools from copper, Ima Adah,' Tuval-Kayin said.

'Is that so. How?'

'We've been experimenting with heating them underground,' the guide replied.

'Underground?'

'Yes, you can make a fire hotter underground.'

'I want to be a metal-hunter when I grow up,' Mini-Kayin pronounced.

'Just like your namesake,' Adah replied. 'I'm sure you will be an exceptionally good one. However, speaking of growing up, we are late for your birthday party. Your ima is frantic. Come along, we must get you all cleaned up.'

They said farewell to their guide then started walking back.

Yaval continued talking. 'Guess what else we saw near the caves, Ima?'

The eyes of the oldest boy widened – Avram's son didn't want her to know.

'A tannin,' Yaval pronounced.

Adah stopped. 'A tannin?'

'Yes, one as big as me with huge, sharp teeth and claws. It was tremendous.' Yaval had recently had a growth spurt and overtaken her.

Instinctively, she grabbed Yaval's arm. 'Where? How close was it?'

'At the top of the hill. We saw it from the cave, but it didn't come closer.'

'Is this a frequent occurrence?' she asked Avram's boy.

'Worryingly, yes. Giant lizards have come down from the mountains. Abba said there are plans to reinforce the city walls. The main part of it hasn't changed since The Wanderer laid the foundation.'

'What about the safety of those living outside the city?'

'They are being encouraged to move closer.'

'But they can't. They have farmland to tend. How did I miss all of this?'

'It was discussed at the recent city meeting, mistress.'

Oh. She hadn't been to one of those for years.

'Did Master Lamech not tell you? They want him overseeing the building work.'

That stood to reason. No doubt Lamech's slaves would be tasked with the work but receive none of the benefits, for they lived in poorly constructed huts in one of Lamech's fields outside the city.

'I'm sure it just slipped his mind.' *Or he kept it from me to avoid my condemnation.* Her thoughts turned to her own father, vulnerable near the hills. 'I should call on Abba and make sure he's safe.'

'But my party, Ima Adah!' Mini-Kayin's eyes filled with tears.

'I didn't mean at this moment, dearest.' She pulled him into a cuddle. 'Of course, your party is most important.'

When they arrived home, the hall looked splendid. Tzillah had outdone herself with the design, though she'd acquired extra staff to help execute her plans. Decorations hung from the pillars, and food in every colour – purple, green, orange, yellow and red – filled platters on as many tables as they could squeeze around the perimeter of the hall. The centre remained bare for party games.

Guests from every major family in the city were streaming in, some stopping, lifting their eyes to the ceiling and floral arrangements, expressing admiration for how impressive it all was. Noa flitted about, commanding the servants she'd brought as reinforcements. Though Noa and Tzillah got on superbly, Adah had barely spoken to Lamech's mother since she was betrayed. Lamech stood atop the platform with Methushael, who had claimed his son's favourite seat.

Tzillah caught sight of Adah and her face visibly relaxed. She pushed her way through the crowds to her son's side. 'Where was he?'

'Metal hunting,' Adah replied.

Tzillah huffed, grabbed Mini-Kayin's arm and pulled him around. 'You look clean, at least.'

'I smartened him up for you.'

'Good.' Sharp, stony eyes accompanied Tzillah's curt voice.

Then Lamech noticed them. He bowed slightly to his father then crossed the room. 'Tzillah. Get Tuval-Kayin onto the platform for all his friends to see.' His eyes swept over Yaval. 'You are a troublemaker, my boy.'

'Sorry, Abba.'

The edge of Lamech's lip twitched as Yaval looked at the floor. Lamech began chortling, then pulled his eldest son into his shoulder and ruffled his hair. 'No harm done. Just choose your timing more carefully next time unless you want Tzillah to blame you for every future mishap.'

Yaval's sparkle returned. 'May I leave now?'

'No. You may work the room; make yourself useful and entertain this ridiculous number of children.'

Just then, music floated from the far corner. 'Ah, good. Your brother is ready,' Lamech said.

The sound of Juval's flute soothed Adah's soul and was shortly joined by Naamah's voice. Adah peered through the crowds until she could see them, her handsome young son standing next to his sister, who was also blossoming.

Lamech shuffled behind her. His arms encircled her waist, and he rested his chin on her shoulder, his beard tickling her neck as he spoke. 'Now that everyone is happy, perhaps we could escape. I've had enough of this party already.'

'That's only because you're not the centre of attention,' she chuckled, watching Tzillah rounding up the children for some games. Yaval ran around behind them, encouraging each to join the large circle forming in the middle. Several little ones looked up at him with wide eyes, grasped his arms or smiled bashfully.

'You cheeky woman. I don't always want to be seen. Sometimes I want to be with you in private,' Lamech said.

'Even so…'

'We can return before anyone notices.'

'I think you'll find Tzillah already has.' Tzillah sent spears their way, then tilted her head, motioning for Lamech to join her.

He exhaled a large sigh. 'We'll continue this later.'

With relief, Adah spotted Shua replacing jugs of watered wine and made her way to her, acknowledging several guests as she went, but not stopping to hold conversation.

She reached her housekeeper. 'How's it going?'

Shua's eyes flickered to Noa, then she rolled them.

'I see.' Adah chuckled. Noa didn't know how to respect someone else's command.

'I organised everything in accordance with mistress Tzillah's wishes, then that woman came and turned it all upside down,' Shua whispered.

'Would you like me to go and distract her?'

Shua's eyes pleaded affirmative.

Adah found Noa standing behind Methushael's imposing figure, brandishing an empty platter. A terrified servant was trying to clean mess off the floor while cowering at Noa's raised arm.

'Is everything alright?' Adah asked. Methushael didn't acknowledge her, but his heavy, meat-infused breath sent a snake slithering down her neck.

'This ridiculous girl gave my husband deer,' Noa spat.

'Oh?'

'She should know that he hates it. She has been with us for several seasons.' Noa ran her fingers over Methushael's shoulder. He turned slightly and caught Adah's eye for the briefest moment. A tiny sneer crept from his mouth to his nose. Adah shivered. Methushael must have once been handsome, but malevolence had destroyed his looks, never mind his spirit.

Noa continued. 'He couldn't help but spit it out. She's lucky he didn't throw up all over the table.'

'So, this mess?'

'Naturally he threw the meat back at her.'

Adah gulped. *Naturally.*

'Now I will have to find another servant. He won't bear her presence again. Oh, the trials of getting decent servants these days...'

Adah felt a warmth press against her lower leg. Now beetles crawled up her inner thigh, though the sticky hand did not move. Instead, fingernails pressed tightly into her skin. She flicked her gaze towards their owner. Methushael's sneer remained in place, his eyes aimed at his wife who was still talking, entirely oblivious.

Adah tried to move her leg, but the nail pushed deeper. Then the hand stroked up and down.

'Abba. Let me replace that for you.' Lamech appeared before her with a fresh platter. The hand slid from her calf and retreated. Lamech leaned over and placed a plate of boar and berries before his father, then claimed her palm as he returned to full height.

'Excuse me a moment. Adah and I must discuss the wine.' He tugged her towards the door, narrowly avoiding the servant retreating with hands full of dirty cast-offs.

Once in the hallway, he pushed her against the wall, flattening their arms together above her head. Then he kissed her roughly, biting her bottom lip. She winced.

'Did my abba touch you?' Lamech growled. The hallway was dark, but she could see the flicker of rage in the whites of his eyes.

'How did you know?'

'Your face. You looked like a stunned deer. Has he done it before?'

'No.'

'Oh, how I hate him. How dare he touch my property.'

Her heart was beating quickly, but at Lamech's words, the heavy stone of anguish crushed it. Now his hands released her arms and roamed over *his property*, tugging at her tunic.

'Lamech. Not here. Not now.'

'I can do what I like in my house.'

'We must return to the party. Tzillah will be most upset.'

'I don't care.' He drew back, then grasped her again. The servant girl walked into her vision, then stopped, gasping.

Lamech spun around. 'Get out!'

The girl stammered. 'I-I… need to get to the hall.'

Lamech slammed his hand against the wall, catching some of Adah's hair. She recoiled, and he noticed.

'Fine.' Lamech released her. 'We will finish this later.' Then he thundered back to the party.

The girl, too young to be serving really, approached and tenderly touched her arm. 'Are you well, mistress?'

Adah closed her eyes and exhaled, long and slow. 'I'll be fine. You may leave.'

As the patter of footsteps grew quieter, Adah breathed deeply. She squeezed her eyelids tight, determined to escape to the hills. Gradually, clattering dishes, drunken laughter and wandering fingers exchanged places with the soft bleating of sheep and a gentle breeze. Yet she wandered alone, seeking the sheepherder who would bring her safety.

CHAPTER 38

Lamech growled in frustration. He needed more men. The work on the wall was progressing, but it had already been four years since they commenced and the workers kept getting slower, like the motivation was draining out of them more each day. Despite the success of the hunting parties, most of the men were thin. But what else could he do? He didn't have enough food and housing for them all and their numerous offspring. How did these weak men produce so many children, when his two wives had just four between them?

He ground his teeth. His abba had been taunting him again. He always had a comment, a snide remark, a lift of the eyebrow. Lamech had worked so hard to build up his legacy. A thriving business with hundreds of workers, the best vineyard in the valley – which he hardly ever got to spend time in – and the most beautiful woman in the city as his wife. A woman he knew his father desired.

Bile rose in his throat. All of this and three sons. It still wasn't enough for Methushael. It would never be enough. Bekhor at least understood. He had twelve children and a submissive woman who stayed out of the way. Still, Methushael fought with him, despising Bekhor's pacifist ways, wanting his eldest son to follow in Barsabas' footsteps by claiming additional territories, which Bekhor refused to do. He was content creating things in his workshop and had no interest in managing or expanding his father's already extensive farmlands. The only interest they shared was the woodlands.

Barsabas should have been born to Methushael. His rage-red blood and ruthless ambition suited Methushael perfectly. Neither Lamech nor Bekhor could compete with Dinah's husband, who took what he wanted and extended his power at every opportunity. Yet Barsabas was bold where Methushael was subversive, and

Methushael was careful not to associate himself with Barsabas' more dubious dealings. He would never openly defy the elders and had been furious when Lamech had taken Tzillah for a wife.

'Why couldn't you have slept with the maids and claimed the children were Adah's?' Methushael had shouted. 'You must have borne children through women at the tavern. What about that harlot, Nasya? Are none of her boys yours?'

Lamech didn't think so. He'd studied them and could see no likeness. Besides, her husband was one of Lamech's business partners. An expert in roof thatch. He couldn't claim a child of Nasya's without causing serious complications. Moreover, Lamech hadn't partaken of nearly as many women as his father supposed. He'd not been to a tavern woman since Adah had let him back in her bed. He would choose his first wife over any other, so long as she let him.

He just wished she'd stop thinking so much. He'd noticed how her ears pricked every time the name *Yahweh* was mentioned. Particularly if Chanoch was speaking. That meddler. He still invited Chanoch to their social events out of deference for his position in the city, but he knew Chanoch had not forgiven him for marrying Tzillah, even after all these years.

At the thought of Yahweh, Lamech sighed. The Elohim had given him what he'd asked for eventually, but it hadn't solved any of his problems. What use was revering the Creator if it didn't lead to prosperity? He'd hoped the birth of Adah's twins would open her womb permanently. It hadn't. Barsabas was having far more success, at least success as defined by his abba. He had no qualms in claiming sons born to his many mistresses. And Barsabas worshipped the serpent. Perhaps there were ways he could learn from his errant brother-by-marriage.

Azurak entered. Here was a man who resembled Barsabas in so many ways, except Azurak's figure was strong and powerful. He was a fighter rather than a leader, yet his intelligence declared him capable of so much more. Lamech knew Azurak was a weapon to be mobilised.

'I have secured more workers for the eastern wall,' Azurak said. 'We will have to pay them a fair wage, but it will get everything moving again. Also, the third hunting party have returned from the northern coast with great success. Not only did they slaughter a herd of cattle, but they also found fields of wheat ripe for harvesting and have brought the grain home.'

'Ripe for harvesting? Were they not tended by anyone?'

'Yes. They belonged to an old man. But he had just two sons, and they were no match for our hunters, who pinned them inside their hut while they took what they pleased.'

Lamech swallowed. 'Will the family have enough?'

Annoyance crossed Azurak's face as his brow furrowed beneath his black hair. 'You either want to feed your workers, or you do not, master. There is no room for pity in successful business.'

It was fortunate Adah wasn't hearing this. Lamech was careful to keep his business dealings as far away from her as possible. Oh, how he longed to return to those early years where they walked together through the vineyard hand in hand, the early evening sun trickling through the trees, highlighting their joy.

Azurak was waiting for him to say something. 'How about purchasing the land from that family.'

'Master?'

'I want you to conduct a survey. Take a team of people into the surrounding countryside, assess the status of all the farmland – who owns it, the size and productivity of their land, and the health of their sons. Also consider the movement of the tanninim. They threaten our borders, let's use this to our advantage.'

Azurak's lip twitched. 'You mean, providing protection in return for a share of the harvest?'

'Yes. Though some may wish to go further. We could purchase the land, but they could keep control of it, acting as stewards on our behalf. Still living on their father's soil, but not bearing the burden of it.'

Pleasure replaced the annoyance in Azurak's eyes. 'Many are scared by the encroachment of predators. This could be a highly effective method of enlarging your territory.'

'Far better than attacking people at will as Barsabas does. Or as those starving men did today.'

'Indeed.'

Lamech turned from his second-in-command and lifted two skins of wine from a hook on the wall, then passed one to Azurak. 'To our new venture.'

Lamech returned home later with blood full of wine. He and Azurak had spent the afternoon planning the details and he was optimistic about his brilliant new idea. He checked the status of his family at the gate.

'Has anyone been anywhere today?' he asked the gatekeeper.

'Mistress Adah visited her abba but returned some time ago. Your usual man followed her, keeping his distance. Yaval and Tuval-Kayin have been metal-hunting again. I sent my son with them. I haven't seen Juval and Naamah today but sounds of music have floated on the wind.'

'And Tzillah?'

'She had a visit from her favourite dressmaker. That is all.'

Lamech pondered. 'Find out who that dressmaker is, would you, Avram? The visits seem rather frequent.'

'Certainly, master. I will do some digging and let you know tomorrow.'

'Good night.'

Lamech strolled through the newly refurbished courtyard with its fine pillars – several spans taller than his abba's – then turned to the right, towards the side entrance. The hall had been built in front of the house, but they only used it for entertaining. He passed Shua, washing up in the kitchen courtyard near Adah's garden, then entered the main house and strolled through the antechamber into the principal living space.

Adah was seated on a cushion before the table. Next to her, eleven-year-old Tuval-Kayin chipped away at a stone while Juval was carving a hoof-shaped piece of wood. Behind them, Naamah weaved. As usual, Yaval wasn't anywhere to be seen. He was probably with the goats.

Adah looked up and the light from the central fire flickered over her features. *Still beautiful.*

'Ima Adah, look what I've done.' Tuval-Kayin held up a chipping for Adah to inspect. Her gaze fell from Lamech's as her attention turned to his son. He looked around for Tzillah. She was in the wicker chair in the corner, eyes closed. Something wasn't right with her.

'Tzillah.' Lamech touched his second wife's leg. She stirred and her eyes flickered open. Alarm turned to recognition, followed by something else. Lamech ran his hand further up her leg. Tzillah smiled gently and kissed him, but when he withdrew and studied her again, the *something else* in her eyes intensified. It was guilt.

'Are you with child?' he whispered.

Tzillah's eyebrows raised. She shook her head, then her eyes lowered.

He put his hand under her chin, raising her sight again. 'I've noticed you are ordering new clothing, and you're tired.'

Fear flickered this time. Guilt and fear. What was going on if she wasn't pregnant? 'Tzillah?'

She gulped. Her gaze swept past him to Adah and their children. She felt his neglect, he knew that. But that wasn't all. Was it possible she had another man? Surely not. She adored him.

Tzillah returned a stubborn look. 'I just got tired of the old clothes. Shouldn't I be allowed something new?'

'Tzillah. Times are hard for the city. There isn't enough food—'

'We have plenty.'

'Of course. And by all appearances, we are generous with it. But if you go around with a new dress every day, tongues will start wagging. Be prudent, my love.'

'So others may notice me, but my husband does not.'

'Stop complaining. You get plenty of attention.'

She scoffed. 'Your eyes are reserved for your first wife.'

Her spittle might have reached him, had he not recoiled at her words. Yet the bitterness wasn't accompanied by passion. Had her vibrancy retreated?

He would rekindle her fire. He flattened his palms against the sides of her face, forcing her to keep his gaze. It was a struggle, for alcohol blurred his vision. She tried to look away. *No Tzillah. You are mine.* He kissed her as passionately as he could manage.

'Lamech, stop. I don't want to.'

'Since when?'

'Since now.'

She was being insolent. He offered her himself. What more did she want?

'Come.' He pulled her up.

She fought him, tugging her arms away. 'Lamech, I'm tired.'

'Yet, you've given no explanation why.'

'Just leave me alone.'

He wanted to wrestle her into submission, to teach her a lesson – she deserved it. But just then, Yaval careened into the room.

'Look what I found!' Yaval held a gaggle of goslings, and had a distressed goose at his feet, honking at the theft of her babies.

Lamech groaned at the cacophony. 'What are you doing?'

Yaval jumped. 'Abba!'

He clearly hadn't expected his father's presence. Did Yaval always get away with things like this when he wasn't around to control his eldest, wayward son?

'Get those creatures out of my house.'

Yaval's eyes opened wide. 'But they are babies. They need a—'

'They need a lake, which no doubt you have snatched them from. Get out!'

'But Abba...'

Adah stood and shuffled towards Yaval with outstretched arms. She was far too soft. Anger tugged at his chest. His second wife refused to bed him. His son refused to obey him. Now his love crossed him like he didn't exist.

The goslings squawked. The honking mother flapped her wings and ran around the room, causing Naamah to shriek and jump on the table.

Lamech spied a clay cup near Tzillah. He reached for it, lifted it, then smashed it to the floor. 'OUT!'

Yaval leapt then ran from the room, followed by the goose. Silence. Precious silence.

Lamech's head was pounding. He strode to Adah and grasped her arm, pulling her round. That boy was meant to be his heir. He was a disgrace. 'As you are incapable of keeping your son under control, from now on he comes to work with me.'

'But he is only seventeen.' Adah's eyes were hollows of fear.

'I started working far younger than that. He has been spoilt.'

Adah's lip quivered.

He sighed. Why was he so powerless against her? It was infuriating. 'He can start in the vineyard.'

Her flushed cheeks dimpled, and her eyes softened. 'Thank you. Just please...'

He lifted an eyebrow. She still had the audacity to argue?

Then her hand brushed his face, settling his furious heart somewhat. 'Please promise me he won't do building work. He must have nothing to do with the slaves.'

The hairs on his skin prickled. What use was an heir if the boy's mother wouldn't let him continue their business? Yet inside, he knew Yaval was completely unsuited to it. He could try to train him, but his unreliable nature would remain. They were bound to become as unsuccessful a partnership as Methushael and Bekhor.

Moreover, despite building model cities as a child and a brief flirtation with hunting, Yaval's twin was now obsessed with his instruments. Juval's name was becoming well known though. As he played in the marketplace and at parties, everyone praised him, and Lamech liked that. But Juval wouldn't be joining the construction business any time soon either.

Must all his hopes for a legacy pin on Tuval-Kayin?

He glanced at his youngest child, still chipping away at the stone, oblivious to the tension gripping the room. A boy with singular focus. A metal-worker. Yes, he would do nicely. But was it enough?

'You win. Yaval stays in the vineyard.' His heart suddenly surged as he imagined his boy walking among the vines. 'In fact, I might train him myself. No one knows the vineyard better than me, and I miss it.'

Adah's mouth broadened into a smile that lit up her face. 'That would be wonderful. You are never happier than when you are in the vineyard. And it will do you good to spend time with Yaval. He is a dear.'

Dearly troublesome, he thought, but kept it to himself. If Adah was happy, at least one of his wives might give him attention tonight.

Beyond Tuval-Kayin, Naamah gingerly stepped down from the table. Her copper hair fell in front of her face and her chest wobbled as she descended. She was a young woman now. He'd barely noticed before.

He tore his eyes from Naamah back to his wife, then tugged Adah into an embrace, needing to feel her against his skin. In Adah's arms, he suddenly noticed the grime and dust of the day clinging to his pores. Wine and sweat wafted up his nose. He kissed her then drew away and turned towards the exit, intending to find a washing bucket.

Tzillah was staring at him, blades of envy aimed his way. See, she did love him. She'd never go to anyone else. Perhaps he should try again?

No. She had refused him. Let her face the consequences.

CHAPTER 39

'Not like that!' Lamech shouted.

Adah was watching Yaval pruning vines under his abba's direction. He wasn't picking it up quickly.

'Sorry, Abba.' Yaval's focus shifted to the ground as he tightly gripped the sharp stone in his hand.

'Don't look at your toes. Look at me.' Lamech grabbed the stone, then swore when it cut him. 'Now see what you've done.'

That was unfair. It was Lamech's impatience which led to the streaming blood, not Yaval's.

'Here.' Adah ripped a piece from the sleeve of her tunic and tended Lamech's wound.

'Your son is useless,' Lamech murmured as she bound it.

'He just needs time, my love. Who was it that taught you to tend vines?'

Lamech paused and his gaze moved wistfully beyond her. 'My abba's old servant, Lemuel. He was always there as a child – around when abba was not. As soon as I took an interest in tending the vines, he took me under his wing.'

'What happened to Lemuel?'

Lamech ran his uninjured hand through his beard. 'I don't know exactly. Just that one day he displeased Abba, and then he was gone.'

'Did you ever seek him out?'

'No.' Lamech's eyes looked softer than they had done in many years.

Compassion swelled in Adah's heart. Though he'd revealed little, it seemed this man had been more of a father to Lamech than Methushael. She reached out and touched his cheek.

Lamech pulled his gaze from the mountains and met hers, coming back to the present. 'It's of no consequence.'

She stroked his cheek. 'If you say so. Still, I get the impression Lemuel wasn't short with you as Methushael is.'

'He was not. Ever.' Lamech glanced at his injured hand, then at his son who was standing nearby, unsure what to say or do. 'I'm sorry, Yaval. I will try to be a better teacher.' Lamech wrapped the cloth around his hand two more times, tucked it in, then picked up the sharp stone from the floor.

Adah watched as he turned back to the vine, pointing to the stem that Yaval should have cut, then demonstrating the correct angle and length. She allowed herself a small smile. 'Thank you, Yahweh,' she whispered. Then she picked up a tool herself and moved to the next row, remembering the times she and Lamech had worked together so many years ago.

As she reached the end of the row, she caught a snippet of the conversation between her husband and son.

'You know, Yaval, rumour has reached me that beyond the mountains, people are training animals as mounts.'

'Mounts?' Yaval took a vine between his finger and studied it.

'They are sitting on them.'

'To what purpose?' Yaval folded the vine over the stone to cut it.

'No – here.' Lamech corrected his position. 'To get around quicker. Families there are more spread out, I believe. They haven't constructed cities like us, so as each generation expands, they must move further apart so they don't overcrowd the land.'

'Who gave you this information?'

Lamech smiled. 'I have scouts who travel far and wide. You might know this if you took an interest in my dealings.'

Adah inwardly groaned. *Don't start another argument.*

Fortunately, Yaval ignored the remark. 'Tell me about these animals.'

'They are something like large goats, I think. A flat, cloven-toed creature with a long neck covered in a thick mane. Lazy enough to be caught but nervous enough to be persuaded to run fast at the threat of a whip. I've ordered some brought here.'

'Truly?' Yaval said. 'Why?'

'Will you never see beyond the limits of your years? Think of their potential, boy.'

'I do think about potential. But I don't like the idea of whipping something into submission.'

Lamech scoffed. 'Yahweh Elohim commanded people to subdue the earth. Even I know that. We are meant to control things.'

Yaval chewed his lip as he wrapped an errant vine around its support. Adah thought the notion strange too. Did cruelty really come under the responsibility to subdue? Wasn't it more about what Yaval was doing to the vine – training and nurturing?

'So, will you help me with them?' Lamech asked.

'With the mounts?'

'Yes. I thought we could inspect them together.'

At this, Yaval smiled gratefully. 'I'd love to see them. Thank you, Abba.'

The afternoon wasn't complete before Azurak stood at the entrance to the vineyard, his black hair loose and blowing in the breeze that caught the top of the hill. Adah's heart sank when she spied him.

Below her, Lamech and Yaval were oblivious, still working together on the vines. Lamech clutched his left hand. Now too sore to continue with the stone, he was content to instruct Yaval, who was doing much better at following his father's instructions.

Adah picked up the basket of cuttings she had collected and ascended the hill. 'Azurak. Is it urgent?'

'Good afternoon, mistress. Yes. One of the survey parties has returned. Lamech will wish to see them immediately.'

'He is enjoying the time with Yaval. Surely it can—'

'Azurak!' Lamech had seen him and was striding up. 'See how well my son is doing.'

'Excellent, master. I thought you'd want to know that the third scouting party has returned.'

Lamech's eyebrows drew together. He considered Yaval, still pruning below. 'Perhaps I'll see them tomorrow. They must be weary and longing to return to their families.'

'They are gathered in your hall waiting for you, master. Tzillah has mustered refreshment for them.'

Lamech's nose crinkled, and his jaw stiffened.

'Why not ask the keeper to continue working with Yaval now?' Azurak suggested.

Adah glanced to where Lamech's principal vineyard-keeper was tending vines halfway across the wide field. Further than that, several workers carried water in skins from the nearby stream. As her husband sniffed, Adah turned back and caught his eye.

'I'd better go, but I will return directly,' Lamech said.

'Of course.' She nodded her reassurance, knowing he would not return. Still, Yaval needn't be without a parent. She could help him herself. It had been so long since she'd been out here in the vineyard, she was rather enjoying it. 'With your permission, I'll stay. It sounds like Tzillah has everything under control at home.'

'Of course. Thank you.'

Azurak spun on his heel and headed back towards the house. Lamech hesitated until Adah smiled, giving him permission to leave. He glanced at her one final time before following his foreman.

'What is this?' Adah asked as she entered the house later. She could hear laughter from the hall, and music. Yaval had gone straight to the goats, not entering with her.

Tzillah was holding two pitchers and balancing a basket of bread between them.

'Finally, you're back. Grab some, will you?' Tzillah motioned to the wine on the side. Beyond them, Shua was filling more baskets with flat bread, straight from the oven outside.

Adah grabbed a jug and a basket. 'Are the scouts still here?'

'Yes. Some light refreshment turned into a full-on party. Lamech seems especially pleased about something. I have no idea what. Our courtyard has several braces of hare and two dead boar in it.'

'I noticed that,' she said, entering the passageway to the hall.

'Just the trimmings off the side of a bountiful hunting trip, apparently.'

'I thought they were scouting. Though I didn't know what that meant.'

'He's been sending parties out to survey the neighbouring lands and see what we can do to help the farmers.'

'How do you know that?'

'I have my methods of finding things out. Besides, he talks to me. Doesn't he talk to you?'

'Not much.'

Tzillah laughed bitterly. 'Perhaps that's why he keeps me. He needs to offload to someone who'll listen.'

Indignation rose in Adah's stomach. 'I would listen.'

'No, you wouldn't. You would judge.' Tzillah pushed the skin on the entrance aside with her bottom and backed into the banquet hall. Adah followed.

It was heaving. Atop his platform, Lamech sat on a luxurious pile of cushions, next to Azurak on a stool and some other foremen she vaguely recognised.

'More wine?' Tzillah asked, ascending the steps and placing her offering in front of her husband. Lamech was flushed red.

He roared with pleasure, 'Now there's a good woman.' Lamech pulled her roughly towards him, then fell back into the cushions, with Tzillah toppling into his lap. Peels of laughter rose from them both. Several of the men with Lamech cheered and encouraged the caressing of his wife, but Azurak sat silently, stroking his chin.

Adah slowly lowered the jug and basket onto a table nearby and followed Azurak's gaze. He always unsettled her, but something about his eyes tonight carved the pit in her stomach deeper. He was looking neither at Lamech, nor her, but to the other side of the stage, where Naamah sang with Juval.

Juval had shared his instruments tonight. Two of his friends sat with him on woven, three-legged stools, one playing a stringed instrument and the other shaking a rice container, while Juval maintained the tune on the flute, blending it expertly with Naamah's voice. The song concluded and those who noticed applauded.

Naamah bowed graciously, then turned to Juval, who embraced her and stroked her arm. As they whispered together, Adah noticed Azurak's response. He shuffled in his seat, then bent forward, clutching his chin with his hands. His eyes narrowed, not wavering from his master's daughter.

Juval started the next tune and Azurak relaxed slightly as Naamah sang again and walked a few paces from her half-brother.

A voice from behind claimed Adah's attention and she was distracted by the request for more meat. As she exited to supply the request, she glanced back at the stage once more. Azurak was gone.

CHAPTER 40

Adah felt the clench of Naamah's hand as Eliana's young children hid between her legs and under their skirts. Before them, between the poplar trees, four cloven-hooved mounts were constrained by two travellers, who had brought them from the west at Lamech's request. All around, people lined the Elders' square, squeezing between sheaves of straw and chairs, and craning to see the sight.

Adah looked for Eliana, knowing she was somewhere nearby, but lost in the crowd. Perhaps she'd found Tzillah, who rarely joined them now. She always seemed to be 'engaged', and Adah was fearful of the consequences should Lamech discover the truth. Noa appeared on the other side of the city square, much to Adah's annoyance. She'd sent a messenger to Noa earlier, asking if she'd like to join them, but Noa had said she was too busy.

The boldest of Eliana's children pushed to the front of the crowd and sat, chins on hands, in awe of the creatures dominating the square. Adah shouted at them to be careful, fearful that they might get trampled. For the beasts looked terrified – wide-eyed and tossing their heads up and down at the commotion and noise. Their expressions reminded Adah of her old flock encountering a predator.

Lamech had presented them to Yaval as promised, but instead of doing it in private, in typical Lamech fashion, he'd chosen the most public place possible, hoping to impress the entire city in the process. Now Yaval and Lamech were having a heated discussion in front of everyone, and Adah's gut rippled with worry.

'Well?' Lamech said.

'They are certainly impressive, but I don't know what you expect me to do, Abba.'

'Take them. Train them to carry these men.' Lamech motioned to a group behind. Juval was there, along with Eliana's eldest son and others who worked as lookouts, patrolling the borderlands and reporting approaching danger to the hunters.

'I can't train them like this. I've never encountered these creatures before. I need to get to know them and see them in their natural habitat. In their herd.'

Lamech's face was growing red at his son's refusal.

'Does he really expect people to ride those things?' Naamah whispered. Adah glanced at her. Naamah's gaze was fixed beyond Yaval at the group of men behind the animals. Her concern for her favourite brother was unmistakeable. As Adah imagined Juval riding one of the wild creatures, she felt it too.

Meanwhile, Lamech took a step towards Yaval, biting down his fury for the sake of those watching. 'Then let us take them to a walled field and set them loose. You can observe their behaviour and train them from there. But I want them ready by the next full moon.'

Yaval threw his hands up. 'That's three weeks away.'

'The tanninim could attack again any moment. We need the advantage they will give us.'

One of the handlers stepped forward, trying to drag a reluctant beast with him. When it stood firm and refused to come, he whipped its legs until it moved. 'Excuse me, but two have been ridden already. We rode them part-way here and guided the others. We will gladly stay for a week with the young master and aid him – if compensated for our time.'

Lamech opened his arms wide and fixed Yaval with a stare. 'There, you have help. Will that suffice, or will you throw further objections my way?'

Adah could read Yaval's expression clearly. He had hoped this was something he could do with his abba, but it had turned into another Lamech superiority parade. Still, he conceded. 'I'll do my best.'

His father turned back to the handler. 'Before we complete the trade, I require a demonstration. Mount and ride to the field, following my son.'

The handler bowed. 'Yes, master.' He tugged his animal to one of the straw bales and, after stepping up onto it, swung a leg over the creature's back. At the end of its long neck, the animal's ears flattened, and it straightened its long snout and uttered a high-pitched whinny, protesting the weight. The whip came straight back out, thrashing the rump beneath until it submitted and walked on calmly. Yaval grimaced.

As they ambled past, another animal followed with its lead rope attached to the tail of the one being ridden. The whip slashed back and forth between the two beasts of burden, keeping them steadily compliant.

'Why are they beating it?' Eliana's little daughter, Keziah, asked, clinging to Adah's skirt as she called for the older children to come back.

'Because it needs to learn that we are the masters,' one of the boys replied, as he approached with a glint of blood lust in his eye.

Adah bit her tongue then finally spied Eliana and waved her over – Yaval was leading the way towards the city gates.

'Can we follow them?' Naamah asked, craning her neck to catch sight of Juval.

It seemed that most of the city wanted to see what happened next. As Adah replied in the affirmative and the remaining handler mounted, everyone started filing through the streets. Noise and commotion filled every corner, frightening the animals further. At one point, the middle creature grew skittish and took back its head, careening into a market stall and unsettling baskets of fruit and vegetables, narrowly missing a child before it was brought back under control.

'I don't like this,' Naamah said, still clutching Adah's hand tightly. 'They are too dangerous.'

Adah gripped Keziah with her other hand, desperate not to lose the little girl as she did a head count of the children. Eliana was pushing her way through the crowd, but several families were still between them.

'They are not predators,' Adah replied to Naamah. 'They're simply scared. If anyone can settle them, it's Yaval.' She didn't feel the confidence she was trying to convey. This latest scheme of Lamech's was madness.

After the riders had entered the field, Lamech ordered a gate to be pulled into the wall's opening. Slaves stood against it, terror lining their faces. Yaval approached the penned creatures as their riders dismounted. He unhooked their harnesses and immediately they bucked, jumped and skittered away. Yaval stood firm and silent, watching.

'What did you do that for?' Lamech shouted from outside the pen. 'You'll never catch them again.'

Yaval didn't dignify his father with a glance. 'You asked me to do it; I do it my way. Everyone can leave.'

As the creatures began to graze, steadily settling and drawing closer to each other like a herd, bemusement spread through the crowd at the anti-climax.

'What's happening?' Keziah asked.

'Nothing. Yaval wants everyone to go.' Despite the disappointment dominating the atmosphere, amusement tickled her. Yaval had never cared for anyone's opinion, and here he was, with almost the entire city watching, refusing to perform. Pride swelled in her bosom.

Lamech was the first to depart. 'I have better things to do with my time,' he muttered. He stomped past, pushing several hopeful onlookers out of the way.

Gradually the crowd dispersed. Yaval sat on a boulder, surveying the animals with his hand on his chin. As Adah lifted a tired Keziah into her arms she spied Mela, Eliana's eldest daughter, climbing over the stony wall with a pouch slung on her back. Mela approached Yaval silently, withdrew fig bread from her pouch and after handing it to Yaval, sat herself on the boulder beside him.

'Can I go to Mela?' Keziah asked, straining to look over her shoulder.

Adah shook her head. 'No, no; we must find your ima.'

'Should I join Yaval too?' Naamah asked.

'I'd leave them be. They will be content like that until dark.'

'May I come back to yours, Adah?' Keziah said.

'Of course, my love; let's have supper together. I just need to find...'

Eliana appeared, the dispersed crowd finally enabling her to reach them. 'Have I missed the whole thing?' she asked.

Once they'd rounded everyone up, the friends and young ones wandered back through the city towards Lamech's sprawling complex, which dwarfed all the other houses nearby, taking up a whole street. They'd drawn near Lamech's newly fortified gates before anyone spoke again.

'I see your husband is taking measures to protect you all. Some of us are not so fortunate. I'm scared for the hunters going to fight the tanninim. What if we lose them all?' Eliana said.

Adah felt Eliana's pain like a stab to her heart. One of Eliana's older sons was keen to go, as was Juval, and fear for their lives haunted her. She placed a wriggling Keziah down and watched as the children all ran past the gate Avram slid open for them.

'Lamech told me the giant lizards have been spied on the northern border, but they are still several days' walk from here. Perhaps the danger will pass, and we shall never see it?'

'Oh no,' Eliana said. 'My parents say they are certainly coming. They have discovered our flocks are an easy target. All the farmers who live furthest from the city are terrified. Though I don't relish violence, I agree with your husband. We must be prepared.'

Adah noticed Naamah trembling. She slid a hand into hers again and squeezed it. 'We must pray for Yahweh's protection over our loved ones.'

'Do you really think that will work?'

Eliana was ready to back her up. 'The Creator's name is powerful. He can protect them.'

'What proof do you have?' Naamah asked, being uncharacteristically bold. 'Juval says many think Yahweh has abandoned our people.'

Doubt flickered through Adah's heart. She didn't know many believers, and Juval had more contact with the general population than her. Still, she wouldn't show that to Naamah. 'Chanoch promised me Yahweh was good.'

'He is good,' Eliana said. 'While there are still some faithful in the city, He will not leave us.'

This encouraged Adah, and she sided with Eliana. 'I would rather align myself with the Creator too. If I keep doing what is right, then He will look out for me.'

Naamah removed her hand and tightened her lips. 'I fear we will be disappointed. Danger is coming. Juval speaks of little else than joining the fighters.'

As Naamah shook her copper hair in front of her face and followed the children into the garden, Adah held back. Distantly, she heard the effort of Avram closing the gate, the gentle footsteps of someone else tucking into an alcove and the chatter of the children as they met Shua and gave her their food orders.

She had lost so many loved ones already – must she lose more? She held on to what Chanoch had told her, but the suspicion that Naamah was right tugged deep down. She had caught rumours about the way the city had abandoned the faith of its ancestors. She knew that worse things went on than Lamech admitted, things she dared not think about.

She had lost her mother, her babies, her Ruhamah. What if Juval got hurt? She remembered the day he'd first watched the hunters with fascination. Now he was desperate to go out with his father. A part of her even worried about losing Lamech – what would happen to them all if he died?

'Are you well, mistress?' Avram's gentle voice was at her shoulder.

Adah tucked her fear away. She must be strong. Everyone depended on her. She would try harder – that must be the answer. Try harder to be strong, supporting those in her care and tending to those less fortunate than herself. If she did, hopefully Yahweh would still see them – the flames of goodness flickering in the darkness.

CHAPTER 41

Adah woke as Lamech shuffled into bed beside her, stretching his arm out and pulling her into his side. It must be the middle of the night. She stayed unresponsive – best he didn't know he'd woken her. Soon he was snoring, and tavern smells carried on his heavy breath. Wine mixed with sweat, smoke and various perfumes.

One dominated. It wasn't Nasya's. This one had hints of lavender and rosemary. She'd noticed it a few times recently, usually when he crept in before dawn. She'd also noticed the way he left her alone on those nights.

Tzillah still assumed Lamech's presence in Adah's bed meant he was deriving all his pleasure from her. Adah knew differently. For two years he'd feigned loyalty, when the reality was, he'd resumed his evening wanderings soon after the banquet celebrating his success with the farmers.

Lamech shuffled forward again until his body was flat against her back. He still wanted her comforting presence, but someone else was supplying his other needs. Someone who perfumed herself with lavender and rosemary. She should find out more. For Tzillah's sake, if nothing else. *Not now though*, she thought as she fell back into sleep.

She woke to the sensation of her stomach being stroked and opened her eyes to find Lamech watching her. Dawn was just breaking into the bedroom.

'Morning greetings. Did you have a good night?' she asked.

'Yes. It was excellent.' Lamech didn't lean forward to kiss her. Instead, he spoke again. 'Adah?'

'Umm?'

'Do you think you'll ever have another child? There has been plenty of opportunity.'

Adah placed her hand over his. 'It doesn't seem likely. The twins are twenty now, and I haven't conceived once. I'm sorry to disappoint you.'

He threaded their fingers together. 'It is disappointing.'

'Do you really need anyone else? Our family feels complete to me. Soon, one of the children might fall in love and give you grandchildren.' The thought of one of her boys leaving created an abrupt cavern in her stomach.

'On that subject,' Lamech replied. 'I think it's time I introduced them to some suitable candidates. However, I would like to take them to the tavern first.'

'The tavern. Why?'

'My abba took me when I was their age. To educate me about women.'

A lump formed in her throat. He couldn't mean… Her hand reached to grasp his face. 'Lamech. Please don't.'

'Why not? It is an important part of—'

'No, it isn't! I knew nothing when I married you, and I was fine.'

'That's different. You're a woman. I don't mean to take Naamah.'

'I should think not. Please, Lamech. I don't want the boys to go. It's important to me that they don't…'

'Don't what?' Lamech's eyes narrowed and hardened.

Adah swallowed, then spoke slowly. 'Do you really want them to be like you?'

He pursed his lips. 'What is wrong with me?'

'Your desires. Your appetites. Even now, you stray.'

Lamech's face turned red, with fury or embarrassment, she wasn't sure. 'I am not straying,' he said through gritted teeth.

'Don't take me for a fool. I know the signs well enough.'

'It is a business transaction. I am trying to produce another son.'

She covered her mouth. 'What?'

'Neither you nor Tzillah will give me another child. I need sons, Adah.'

'You have sons!'

'Only one that's any use. I am training Tuval-Kayin, but he is not sufficient. I have hundreds of workers, I have won the respect of most of the elders, I have multiple contracts across the city and many farmlands under my control. I am more prosperous than ever before –

perhaps even than my father. Yet my own family? My family is a failure. An embarrassment!'

His words bit like teeth into her heart. She had served him, given him two sons, stayed with him, borne his mood swings and infidelity. Even tried to love him. It was not enough. It would never be enough. When Yaval and Juval married and left, she would be back to where she was years ago – heartbroken, empty and purposeless.

Still, disparagement of herself she could bear; what she could not bear was his derogatory opinion of her sons.

Adah pulled herself up and rested her back against the wall. 'Yaval is successfully training those kavash for your hunters and working in your vineyard. Why, he delivered you two fully trained beasts yesterday, with no hint of a whip! And Juval is incredibly talented at his music. What can you mean, they are no use?'

'For my business. My legacy. Not… not in general. I don't mean that.'

Adah breathed deeply though her nose, trying to calm herself. Getting upset only made Lamech angry. 'So, what is your plan with this woman?'

Lamech sat up next to her. 'When she has a son, I will adopt him into our household.'

'And how will you convince people he is ours? Do you intend to confine Tzillah or me for a season, then claim he came from one of us?'

'Don't be ridiculous.'

'I'm not being ridiculous. I'm thinking practically.'

'You're acting insane.'

'No, Lamech. You are the one out of your mind.'

The force of his slap threw her into the wall. The pain ran from the back of her head all the way to her eyes. Why had she opened her mouth? She should have learnt by now.

'You insolent woman. I *should* tie you up for such disrespect.'

'Do it,' Adah murmured. 'What difference will it make? You already have me followed.'

The crash of a vase smashing and scattering across the floor announced Lamech's fury as he stormed from the room. Adah slipped down into the bed and pulled her blanket back over her, closing her eyes against the throbbing ache. Dizziness swamped her senses and soon all was black.

When Adah forced her eyes open again, the room was in full daylight.

Yaval sat on her bed. 'Ima. Are you alright?' He reached forward and touched her cheek.

Pain penetrated to her bone, and she winced.

'Sorry,' Yaval said. 'Where is Shua? Does she know?'

'I haven't seen her. I've been sleeping.'

'I shouldn't have woken you. I'll see if I can find a poultice.'

As Yaval left, Adah tried to sit up. Her head was full of stones. What had happened? She looked about the room. Lamech's bedclothes lay discarded on the floor. Memories started returning.

'I can't find Shua. She must have gone to market. Is this the right one?' Yaval held up a clay jar with plant etchings in the side. In his other hand was a cup of water.

'Yes.'

Yaval was as gentle as could be, applying the herbs that might reduce the swelling, but she had to tell him about the back of her head, for he couldn't see it beneath her hair.

'This was no accident, was it?' he commented.

She didn't want him to know what his father was capable of. She wanted to protect him. But his eyes held understanding – he already knew.

Fear punctuated that realisation. 'Has he mistreated you in the vineyard?' she asked.

'He's barely there. I work with the vineyard-keeper now. I must confess, I still find it boring. I'd far rather be with the kavash or scaling the hills. Tuval-Kayin still gets to go metal-hunting.'

'Yes, but he does have a gift, that one. Have you noticed how well he already works the furnace? I find it fascinating to watch him.'

'He's turning into Abba though.'

'How so?'

'His attitude. He always thinks he is right, even though he's still a child. It gets annoying.'

Compassion swelled in her heart for her eldest boy. Tuval-Kayin was Lamech's favourite, Juval and Naamah had each other. Yaval was so often alone, except for the animals. 'How are my goats this morning?'

His face lit up. 'Ezza is pregnant. Have you noticed? It means we'll have more milk soon, for Nona is starting to run dry. Also, Shua loves my geese now. She's quite forgiven me for bringing them home. We're getting several eggs a day.'

'And do the geese get on well with the goats?'

'Of course. It might be a little cramped, but they're happy with their pond.' Pride crossed Yaval's face. He had dug that pond himself, filling it from the same brook that fed their household water supply, the one Juval was named after. 'Ima? Did you hear about the tannin attack?'

'Another one. When?'

'It was last week. They went for Eliana's parents.'

'No!'

'Yes, the sharp-tooth churned up the farm, destroying half the crop. Fortunately, they managed to hide in a cave, so no one was hurt. They're moving to Eliana's home inside the city.'

'Oh no; they will despise that. They've had that farm for generations. It's all they know. Where was Ruhamah? Could he not protect them?'

'You've not heard that either? Ruhamah moved west.'

The cavern from early that morning opened again. 'When?'

'Honestly, Ima. When was the last time you left the house?'

'I go to Sav Shimiel's fairly often. I haven't visited Eliana in a long time though. Her side of the city displeases me.'

'That explains why you haven't heard. Ruhamah left several weeks ago. He was also displeased with the city and fed up with the fights among the other herders. He was hoping to reach the land between the rivers before winter.'

'Oh.' Sorrow joined desolation in her cavern. There was only one reason people from the east went to the land between the rivers – to find faithful wives or husbands. No matter what Yaval had heard, Ruhamah would soon marry someone else. *As he deserves. Oh, how can I cope without the hope of you?*

She sniffed back the sorrow which threatened to pull her into despair and concentrated on practical matters. 'I must invite your Sav to come and live with us. At least until the tanninim move on. We'll have to make room.'

'There's no need, Ima.' Yaval wiped his fingers on a cloth. 'Abba has been tasked with setting up a perimeter of fighters outside the city to protect the farmers. We can't abandon them all. There would be no food.'

'Your abba is at the forefront of this?'

'Of course. He trained the hunters. They are under his command.'

Like an army. Just as I feared.

Yaval reached forward and held her hand. 'Sav and Rivkah will be fine, Ima. They'll keep them safe.'

Of course, she was worried about that. But why did the army worry her more? Had she so little trust in her own husband? *Better to ask Abba's family here, just in case.*

'How do you know all this anyway? Have you been attending the elders' meetings?' she asked.

Yaval shook his head. 'Mela told me. She hears everything through her mother.'

'Mela?'

Yaval flushed. 'Yes. We still see each other often.'

Adah raised an eyebrow. 'Indeed? And has Mela found herself a young man yet?'

Yaval withdrew his hand slowly and clenched his fist. 'No. Why would she?'

'She's well past marriageable age.'

'She doesn't need a husband. She is exceptional and can look after herself. Besides, she still helps her ima.'

'Eliana doesn't need Mela's help. She has plenty of other grown-up children. And several of Mela's younger siblings have already married.'

'I know. We witnessed their vows, remember. Why are you so full of questions?'

Adah hesitated. She knew Mela was still the light in Yaval's life. But she should not tease. Mela was almost twice his age and she had held him as a baby.

'Your abba wants to take you to the tavern.'

Yaval startled. 'What?'

Adah nodded.

'No, Ima! I shall not go.'

'He thinks you need *educating*.'

Yaval shook his head and stared at the linens on the bed. 'I know exactly what men do at the tavern. And it's not just drinking.'

'How exactly?'

'They all talk about it. Boasting. Sneering. Joking. It makes me sick. Treating women like possessions.'

As indignation lit her son's features, warmth filled Adah's cavern, spreading from her heart to her stomach.

'Good,' she said.

Yaval looked up. 'So, I don't have to go?'

'Believe me, I don't want you to go. But your abba—'

'That's why he hit you!' Yaval stood up and paced. 'You had a fight. He hit you because you refused. Ima! You need to leave him.'

'I can't do that, my love.'

'Why? You don't love him.'

'What makes you say that?'

'I'm not a fool. You stay with him for us. Well, you don't need to do that anymore. We are grown men…'

'… who still need my guidance and protection. You cannot set up on your own against your abba. He's too powerful. And I worry for Juval.'

'He won't go to the tavern. Out of respect for Naamah, you and Tzillah. He won't.'

Adah pursed her lips. She wasn't so sure. Juval rather enjoyed Lamech's parties now, despite disliking large gatherings as a child. Since he began playing music, he had grown accustomed to the noise and could block it out, focusing on making melodies with his sister.

'I'll do my best to protect you both,' she confirmed.

'I know you will, Ima. That's exactly the problem.'

Tzillah was getting dressed when Adah walked into her chamber later that morning.

'You better cover that up,' she said, poking Tzillah's shoulder blade.

'I'm surprised to see you,' Tzillah said. 'Lamech sounded furious earlier; I thought he might have tied you to the bed.'

'Not yet. But he will tie you up if he catches you with that.' Adah picked up a shawl and slung it over Tzillah's shoulders.

'What is it?'

'A mark from your lover.'

'Oh. I tell him to be careful, but he gets a bit carried away.'

'Tzillah, you need to stop.'

Tzillah turned around to retort but checked herself and narrowed her eyes. 'You look awful. What did he do to you?'

Instinctively, Adah touched her cheek. 'Nothing.' Before, she might have confided in Tzillah about Lamech's behaviour, but their relationship was different now.

Tzillah shrugged. 'Fine, don't tell me. But don't try to rule over me either, Adah. What's wrong with me seeking love elsewhere when I am so neglected?'

Adah grasped her hands. 'It's too dangerous. What if Lamech finds out? He might kill—'

'Don't be ridiculous. Lamech isn't as bad as that.'

Was Tzillah being purposefully obtuse? Did she not know Lamech at all? Adah shook her head. 'You need to win back our husband.'

'Why? He's happy with you.'

'He isn't. He's taken another woman.'

'What?'

'I know you love him, Tzillah. I know seeing him with me eats you inside.'

Tzillah's nose crinkled, and she ground her teeth.

'You once said you'd rather it was me than someone else. Now it is someone else. It's because he wants another boy. You must give him one, or we might lose him forever.'

Tzillah pouted. 'He doesn't want me.'

'Yes, he does. He adores you. Stop being so stubborn and charm him back.'

'The only time he gives me attention is in public when others are watching – then it's all happy families. As soon as everyone leaves, he runs back to you.'

'Well, he's now running to a woman he has hired – hired to have a son whom he will force us to adopt.'

Tzillah's eyes widened. Then she spat on the floor. 'Fine. Don't let him go out tonight. I will serve him the evening meal and give him plenty of wine.'

'That usually works.'

Tzillah nodded, then paused. 'Thank you, Adah.'

'What for?'

'For not telling him about my exploits. I know he doesn't give you the freedom he gives me. At any point, you could have told him what I was doing and been rid of me.'

Adah couldn't help herself. She drew her rival into an embrace. 'I would never do that. We are family, you and me. We face this together.'

Tzillah snuggled into her shoulder. The movement sent the pain shooting back up Adah's neck to her head, and she drew in a sharp breath.

Tzillah drew back. 'He did hurt you. I knew it.'

Tears sprung to Adah's eyes, and she nodded slowly, swallowing down the pain.

Tzillah's hand cupped her face. 'What can I do to help?'

'Keep him happy. And be careful.

CHAPTER 42

Adah sat before her broth, unmoving. Meat and vegetables turned stodgy and cold as her mind wandered elsewhere. Lamech hadn't returned home. Shua and Leah were elbow-high in laundry outside; all the children – who were no longer children – were out, and Tzillah was visiting a friend. As her future loomed before her, silent and uncertain, her thoughts escaped into familiar fantasies.

She wandered the high places. Not the mountains in the west that Ruhamah would have crossed by now, but the hills in the north. As she approached a peak, the sea appeared before her, stretching to the boundaries of the earth, mingling with the heavens that kissed its surface, so that one couldn't tell where the sky began, and the sea ended.

Adah had never seen the sea, but she'd heard the tales. Now Leviathan reared his three enormous heads above the surface, rising up until his scaled belly came level with her face, then crashing back, creating a wave so fierce it enveloped the other sea swimmers that had been playing together nearby, singing songs as they bowed over the surface.

'Stunning, isn't he?' said a voice at her shoulder.

Adah turned to see The Wanderer, a man so often in her dreams, though his face was always hazy. She trembled, the cold tingling her arms as tiny hairs lifted on them.

The Wanderer touched her at the elbow. 'Don't be afraid.'

The monster of the deep leapt high again, and his waves smashed the rocks below. 'How can I not be?' she said.

'Leviathan thrashes about, asserting his dominance over every creature, destroying at will and growing more powerful with every season, but he cannot harm you in here.' The Wanderer touched his hand to his chest.

Ah, it is a different Leviathan you speak of. 'He has done before. Many times.'

'You are used to him now. He doesn't have your soul in his clutches the way he did previously. Your expectations have been shattered. At least that means things can improve.'

'I'm not so sure. There is plenty of evil left. Like the water, it gathers momentum as it nears the sand.'

'I know how that feels,' The Wanderer said. 'I was there once, remember? What started as a raindrop in the sea became a flood of envy, discontent and bitterness. I thought there was no way back. But with Yahweh, there is always hope.'

'Good afternoon, Ima.'

Yaval pulled her from her daydream, and from the longing to hear more about Yahweh. She used to associate The Wanderer with excitement and adventure. Now, after hearing Chanoch speak about his father, she knew it was his deep-seated faith and incredible walk to redemption that made him special. Why hadn't she been to see Chanoch recently? She so easily hid herself away, hoping that life and its problems would cease if she ignored them.

The thought of being with Chanoch still made her edgy since her reprimand years ago, but whenever she entered his home, her circumstances seemed lighter. How could that be so – when Yahweh was so strict and exacting? Why did repentance and submission to something mysteriously greater than oneself produce the kind of peace she felt among Chanoch's household, while the freedom Lamech espoused – freedom to do as one liked – produced devastation?

'Are you going to eat that, Ima?' Yaval was looking longingly at her broth.

'No, you have it.' She pushed the bowl toward him and rose.

She hadn't reached the other side of the room before Lamech entered and clapped Yaval on the back, making him choke on his broth.

'Has your ima told you? Tonight, I am taking you to the tavern,' Lamech declared, sending a stern look Adah's way which said, *Don't you dare contradict me.* 'Tonight, my boys become men.'

So, this was Lamech's tactic: tell the boys in front of her and get them excited so she couldn't argue. At least she'd spoken to Yaval already.

'Ima told me,' Yaval said. 'I'm not going.'

Lamech's face reddened. 'You must not listen to your ima's concerns, Yaval. She is a woman; she doesn't understand.'

'Ima didn't need to express any concerns. I decided myself from the outset.'

'You are just being bashful. There's nothing to be afraid of. We will go out, have a drink, and I will introduce you to my associates. Men with whom you need to build relationships in order to succeed in our city. It is an important part of our business, Yaval. You are my heir. You will come.'

'And after that? What do you expect me to do after that?'

Lamech's eyes narrowed. 'I have no expectations.'

'Good. Then let's host a meal here. We have plenty of wine. Invite your associates, business partners and foremen. Let me meet them all in the comfort of our home with fewer… distractions.'

Lamech's jaw stiffened. He clearly hadn't expected such an intelligent retort. 'You don't understand. Joining the culture of the tavern is an important part of how things run around here, son. We can certainly do what you wish. But you must also come with me. The tavern is a great leveller. All mix together – young and old, successful and servant. There we establish our status, Yaval.'

'I do not deny that important relationships are built up in the place. But I think there's a better way.'

Lamech's fingers curled into fists. 'And what do you know? You are too young. You need me to teach you the way of the world.'

At that moment, Juval and Naamah entered.

'Abba said he is taking us to the tavern tonight, Yaval. Our first time. Are you excited?' Juval said.

'I'm not going,' Yaval stated, glancing at Naamah.

Adah also noticed her particularly low-cut tunic and the necklace that dropped into her cleavage. Where had such items been made? Did Tzillah know?

Lamech had raised his hand to Yaval, but seeing Naamah, he checked himself, uncurled his fist and embraced his daughter. Surprised, Naamah flushed and bowed her head.

Her father put his hands on her shoulders and looked her up and down. 'I see you have been to the seamstress I recommended. Very nice indeed. I'm glad two of my children are excited about growing up.'

Adah had so far held her tongue, but this was beyond what she could bear. Naamah was not a plaything to be dressed according to her father's despicable whims. With Tzillah absent, she must defend her. 'What is the meaning of this?'

Lamech spun. 'What is your problem now?' The look in his eye made her cheek throb, but continue, she must.

'Why are you dressing Naamah like Dinah?'

Lamech laughed, though his eyes held a contradicting anger. 'Are you blind? Naamah is a young woman. You cannot keep her a child forever, Adah.'

'There is only one reason why you would encourage her to dress this way.'

The vein on Lamech's forehead bulged. The eyes of his children flitted between Adah and their father, as if trying to discern what they were fighting about, and who was going to win. Adah stood unmoving. *Do what you like to me. I didn't back down about Yaval and neither will I about Naamah.*

Lamech broke the standoff first. 'Why not pursue a match for her? I'm having to hold off proposals on a weekly basis.'

'What?' Juval stepped forward. 'Proposals for Naamah's hand? You're not going to choose Naamah a husband, are you, Abba? She must choose for herself.'

Lamech's face reddened once more. He slammed his fist against a side table. 'Is there anyone in my household willing to show me due respect? How dare you all talk to me like this?' His fist slammed down again. 'I am in charge. I provide for you all. I decide what happens to you.'

Naamah, who had cowered at the noise, backed into the corner of the room. Juval followed her, holding her and checking she was alright.

This seemed to anger Lamech more. 'I am not going to sell my daughter off as my abba did to Dinah! But I do need her to dress appropriately for her position. What is wrong with that?' He turned towards Adah and fixed her with a stare. 'You are not even her mother. What right have you to question me?'

Sticking her chin out, Adah persisted. 'Tzillah knows, then? Knows you are encouraging her daughter to dress like a harlot. I doubt that. You speak of respect! What respect will you get when people see your only daughter walking the streets looking like that?'

Adah motioned to Naamah. 'I know what it feels like to receive lustful glances everywhere you go, and to be considered a prize. I shall not have it for Naamah. My abba protected me – at least, he tried. It is your job to do the same for her.'

Lamech's control broke. He came at her with full force, shoving her into the wall. Adah shielded her already injured face.

'No, Abba!' Yaval pulled at his father's arms but wasn't strong enough. One blow pounded her shoulder, and she fell to the floor before Juval grasped Lamech's middle and pulled him away. Naamah wailed as both boys restrained their abba.

Then Lamech broke free, seized Yaval's empty bowl and smashed it across his eldest son's head.

Yaval stumbled back, tripped on the table leg and fell. With a sharp shard of pottery in hand, Lamech lurched forward again, slicing Yaval's forehead above the right eye.

Adah screamed as blood splattered the walls. Then Lamech's eyes opened wide, and he stepped back, dropping the shard to the floor. She crawled through the shattered pottery to her son, throwing herself around him like a shield.

No more blows came. After a moment of silence, furious footsteps stomped away. Then Juval and Naamah were at her side, forming a tearful huddle around Yaval. Juval stripped his tunic off and held it against his brother's head.

'I'm fine,' Yaval murmured. 'It's only a scratch.' But his eyelids drooped.

'Mistress?' Shua entered and, seeing the chaos, rushed back out before returning with a skin of water and clean linen. Adah cleaned and wrapped Yaval's head as Shua brushed up the shards of pottery. Juval remained at his brother's side, hugging Naamah close to his chest.

'What are we going to do?' Yaval croaked once his eyes had refocused.

Adah considered the three young people she loved. None of them deserved this. Should they all leave? Was it even possible? What about Tzillah and Mini-Kayin?

Naamah's small voice broke the silence. 'Abba will never let us go. Besides, I don't want to.'

'He will marry you to one of his business partners,' Juval exclaimed.

'We don't know that. And I love him; I love pleasing him.'

Adah reached forward and cupped Naamah's cheek, thinking of all the times the girl had been ignored in favour of her brothers. Perhaps there was a better way. 'Of course you do, my love. And he has promised he won't sell you off. Is there anyone you like among your father's associates – anyone who has been kind to you?'

Naamah bit her lip. 'Recently, Azurak has been showing me particular favour. But I'm not sure I like it.'

'You're not marrying Azurak.' Juval grabbed her hand. 'He's far too old for you.'

'I don't think your abba would allow that, anyway. Azurak is his servant, not his equal or his better. What about among the leading families?'

'All the men I love live in this house.'

'Well, you can't marry any of them.' Adah smiled gently. 'Why don't I do some research? I can ask Chanoch about kind, eligible men. If we can find you someone who will treat you well and whose company you enjoy before your abba makes his choice, we may be able to secure you a good future.'

Naamah nodded.

Juval's eyebrows were still knitted. 'I don't see why we should compromise. Naamah deserves someone she loves.'

'We will do our best. I'll speak to Tzillah about it. Perhaps she'll be able to influence your abba to give us more time.'

Now Juval nodded his submission. 'I suppose I'm not going to the tavern tonight?'

Disappointment tugged at Adah's heart. 'Who knows what time your abba will cool down and come home? Though, I'd rather you didn't go at all.'

Juval glanced at his brother, whose blood had begun seeping through the bandage. 'I don't want to anger Abba further by refusing. If I go, he might be happy enough to leave Naamah and Yaval alone.'

His sentiment sounded like self-sacrifice, but Adah could see the flicker of hope in Juval's eyes. He wanted to go to the tavern – had been excited about going. Even after seeing Lamech's abuse of his twin and his sister, he still longed for his father's company and the pleasures it promised. She sighed. Juval was a man now. She had done her best to train him, but she had to let him make his own mistakes.

She leaned forward and kissed his forehead. 'You do what you think is best.'

CHAPTER 43

City of Chanoch, 750th year of Wandering

Adah grasps her son's hand as they scurry through the streets. They have come across a couple of groups outside, spilling from or walking between houses, but Juval, with his in-depth knowledge of the city and its uninhibited nightlife, has skilfully steered her to safety each time. Perhaps there is one benefit to him spending so much time in the city's embrace.

'This way,' her son murmurs, tugging her sideways and into a tight alleyway. The walls feel like they're closing in around her, but it's no time at all before he's led her out the other side into a wider street. She realises they have avoided the tavern, where Azurak could have gone seeking a woman. Though it's most likely he returned straight to the complex as intended, looking for her. How long do they have? How long before he finds her missing and sounds the alarm?

'We've crossed the worst area,' Juval says softly, and his pace slows slightly. As they shuffle through the next few streets, silence reigns over most abodes, but behind the doors of some are unwelcome noises. Adah blocks her ears, as Juval's eyes flicker over her.

'We're on the western side now,' he whispers. 'Elders' houses abound here. The noises should cease soon.'

Although Adah has no doubt that such activities take place in elders' houses too, they are at least subtle about it. Unfortunately, many of them are under her husband's control. Which means they are not free from danger yet.

Her heart leaps into her throat as something slaps her face. A squeal, sharp and piercing, cuts through the stillness, echoing eerily through the deserted streets. As the assaulting creature, a soft, almost weightless thing, flutters back towards the dark recesses of some eaves, leaving behind a faint scent of decaying leaves, Adah realises the squeal was her own.

Juval drops her hand and tucks his arm around her waist instead. 'Alright, Ima?'

She nods. It was just a bat. *I've endured far worse.*

He considers the next intersection, pausing. 'Come. We'll go the longer way, in case someone heard your squeal.'

Someone? Someone like who? The memory of a conversation with her shadowy pursuer sends a shiver through her, freezing her legs in place. She glances about, trying to make out which house is the most rundown on this street. It is too dark and impossible to tell.

Juval nudges her forward. 'Faster, Ima.' They continue their hurried walk as, behind them, a door opens. There is no corresponding flicker of light. Could the opener of the door possibly see them with no light? Juval seems to believe so, for his footsteps break into a jog.

Her heart beats faster as he guides her sharply to the left, pulling her into a space between two houses and putting a finger to his lips.

They wait, listening.

Silence.

Juval releases a withheld breath and kisses her forehead. How curious that her wayward son should be her shield now, when for so long she's protected him - or tried to. She hasn't time now to think about all the ways she's failed to prevent his immoral lifestyle. *At least he still loves his ima.* It is her only hope now that Yaval has left her.

As they round the next left-hand bend, the western gate finally comes into view. The moon shines above it - a full moon, glittering high in the sky. There is no chance of escape through the fortified gate, though. In the previous year, Lamech has doubled the guard. Yet, the gate means Chanoch's house is close.

One more corner and she sees it. The street is empty. Just a few more steps...

Juval stops suddenly, and she bumps into his broad back.

'What is it?' she whispers.

He points across the way. Standing beside the entrance to Chanoch's home, with a spear in hand, is a guard.

CHAPTER 44

City of Chanoch, 737th year of Wandering

'What is this?' Adah held up Juval's arm. He still smelt of the campfire as he lay draped sideways across his bed in only his loin cloth.

'Everyone has them,' Juval slurred, scrunching up his eyes against the unwelcome dawn.

Everyone had them? Adah examined the black ink, running her finger over the surface of her son's forearm, the tip of it following the coil of the serpent displayed there, from its three heads to its arrowed tail.

'Do you know what this means?' she asked. The image filled her with foreboding.

'No, Ima. And I don't care. Barsabas' men gave it to me last night. We were just having some fun. Please let me sleep.'

Barsabas' men? An organised army under the command of Dinah's husband had arrived at the city gates two seasons ago. They were there to help drive out the tanninim – at least, that's what they claimed. Certainly, there had been multiple joint hunting parties regularly dispatched, but the bulk of the army seemed to do more drinking and wheedling than anything else, and Adah was less than thrilled when Juval joined in with them.

Her son pulled his arm away, rolled over and sighed into the bed. His upper body looked so different now – toned and tanned. He was physically strong. Was he strong in other ways?

'How did they do it?' she asked.

Juval groaned and mumbled into the bed. 'They pierced my skin with a thorn then rubbed soot into it. Now will you leave me alone?'

'Didn't that hurt?'

Juval rolled over again and stared at her. 'Of course it hurt. But I was drunk. I barely remember.'

How could he treat this so nonchalantly? Had he no concept what that mark meant – did he know nothing of the rival elohim? Or perhaps he did know. She wasn't sure which was worse.

There were other practices Barsabas' men celebrated. 'Did you sleep with a woman last night too?'

Her son rolled his eyes. 'No, Ima. I was with the men in the camp.'

Those two things were not exclusive. The soldiers often hired or cajoled women to join them in the camps. Adah couldn't wait for Barsabas to finish his task and leave their city in peace. Tanninim attacks were preferable to the moral corruption the northerners brought with them.

Lamech would be telling her to leave her son alone now – that he was a man, and she couldn't control him forever. Still, she must protect him. And herself. What if he'd opened the way for spiritual forces of evil in their home?

'There's a cup of water for you on the floor,' Adah said, then left her son to sleep off his headache, passing by his collection of instruments on the way out. At least he hadn't abandoned playing since joining the fighters, often taking an instrument with him when he went to camp. Lamech told her Juval's songs helped their morale and he was well liked. In fact, her husband had been thrilled when Juval had announced his intention to join the *city protectors* shortly after his trips to the tavern commenced.

By contrast, Adah had been terrified. 'I don't want my son battling tanninim! He could die, or worse.'

'What could be worse?' Lamech said, raising an eyebrow.

'I can't imagine.' Though images of her precious boy in the jaws of a giant predator flooded her mind.

'He'll be fine,' Lamech said. 'He showed great promise when we trained him to be a hunter. And he's a good rider too. Azurak will be most disappointed if he gives it up.'

'I don't care about Azurak's feelings. I care about my boy.'

'He's not a boy anymore, Adah. You must let him grow up sometime.'

'You've seen to his *growing up* with great efficiency,' Adah replied bitterly. Indeed, the only benefit of Juval's degenerating behaviour was that Lamech seemed to have temporarily forgotten about his other children – he'd backed off both Yaval and Naamah – though he likely still schemed in the background.

Her comment about Juval had angered Lamech, whose eyes flared as he backed her into a corner of the room. 'Hold your tongue, woman. It grows looser every day.'

No. Your grip just grows tighter. You used to enjoy banter. Now you take everything as an assault on your dominance.

When Adah didn't reply, Lamech sneered and kissed her roughly. 'That's better. Stay in the corner and keep your thoughts to yourself. You look most attractive when they wage war behind your eyes, my little adornment.'

He had taken to calling her that often recently, knowing how much she hated it. With every conversation he tested her, goading her to argue back so he could release his rage, pent up inside. To everyone outside their home, he was the picture of self-control and charm – people constantly complimented him to her. Behind these walls, though, his household knew the truth.

Fortunately, Tzillah had taken Adah's earlier advice and ended her affair, so she now kept Lamech occupied in the bedroom – mostly. The relief meant Adah slept much better, so could cope with Lamech's tirade in the daytime which had become worse since he'd favoured his second wife again. However, Tzillah had done nothing to find Naamah a suitable husband. She seemed to trust Lamech with the decision.

I certainly don't.

Having passed through and out of the house, Adah sighed as she slumped to the floor of the goat pen and dropped her head into her hands. She faced a daily choice. Either she pretended to love Lamech, kept quiet and endured his unwanted affection, or she continued protecting her children and bore his daily fury.

'I must settle for the latter,' she said, sinking her fingers into Ezza's rough, short hair. 'This is my job now. Advocating for them whatever the cost. I remember Dinah once confessing her role was to keep her children safe from their father. How ironic that I should take on the same, when I thought it so strange at the time. Yes, Ezza. This is how it must be. Tzillah is far better than I at keeping Lamech happy. She can switch off from his evil, whereas I can't help but comment. Therefore, she must prioritise him, and I must prioritise them.'

The goat nudged at Adah's elbow, then her kid came bounding up for milk. Lamech had arranged a dinner the following night for his business associates. Adah suspected it meant the grace period was over. This was a test. Would Yaval do as he had suggested and make his connections at this dinner? Would Naamah secure the affection of any of these important men?

After a quick suckle, the kid scampered off. Adah chuckled at Ezza's expression. 'Hard being a mother, isn't it, my dear? The dinner is tomorrow, which means I must talk to Chanoch about Naamah today. When I called weeks ago, he was absent, and he's not visited since.'

Ezza snorted.

'Yes, I know. I'd better get going.'

Adah pulled herself off the floor, gave Ezza one last stroke and departed, barely taking note of her ornamental garden as she passed it with thoughts consumed by the upcoming dinner party. If Yaval was allowed to shine, his refusal to go to the tavern might be vindicated. And if she could just point Naamah in the right direction…

'Please, Yahweh; I don't know if I should pray like this – I don't know if I have repented enough to earn your favour – but please, let Chanoch be home,' she whispered to the sky as she approached the gateway. 'I need his guidance to find Naamah a good husband. Perhaps Chanoch can speak to You about it? He might get one of those prompt things. Whereas I have no idea where to start.'

The man who always followed when she left the complex slipped out of the shadows. Adah pretended not to notice him. She'd long given up on secrecy, for Lamech knew her every movement.

There were so many people in the streets. Men, women and children filled every available space outside cramped dwelling places. Although a few sections of wall had been extended when Lamech fortified the city, most of the perimeter stayed the same, forcing smaller homes to fill in the spaces between what was already there, while tiny huts cropped up on street corners, and the next generation made use of existing rooftops, erecting canopies above the stone. As most roofs were thatched, only the richest families could support their relatives this way. Many slept on mats in the open air, having fled their farmlands with few possessions.

Adah never failed to feel guilty when she went out. If it was up to her, her huge home would be divided among the poor and she'd return to a hut like her abba's. Maybe a little bigger – there were nine people in permanent residence in their complex, plus the day servants and nightwatchmen. Avram lived with his family next door. Coping without Shua would be hard; she'd never have time for little outings if Shua wasn't around. *But I don't need her; she's still a luxury.*

Adah passed a narrow alleyway, and something compelled her to peer into it. Several people sat huddled together. Seeing her, they spread arms out, begging for food. Behind them, street children played in the mud and refuse.

Cursing herself for forgetting to bring a basket of bread, she made her way to the nearest vendor, gave Lamech's name and took as much food as she could carry. On returning to the beggars, she tried to divide the food equally.

A groan came from around a corner. She turned into a smaller passage, used only for disposing of waste. An old man sat hunched next to a pile of it, emaciated and filthy. He was alone, but he looked up at her, eyes glazed and hopeless.

As she reached towards the old man with the remainder of her food, someone else grabbed her shoulders. Nails dug into her as she was pulled backwards. Adah slipped and squealed, but a hand muffled it. Another person grasped her arm, hauling her back to standing. The food dropped into the dirt. Fingers tightened around her midriff, then sweaty, stinking breath warmed her neck.

The street children scrambled for the fallen food, kicking and biting. They were all Adah could see as she fought to escape, shoving her weight one way then another, while her attackers remained behind her back, twisting her arms tight until they immobilised her.

'Alright, feisty,' said the man who'd caught her, as he stuffed her mouth with a cloth. Hopelessness joined it. They were too strong for her.

'She's the rich man's wife,' a raspy voice added. 'What do you think he'd give us for her?'

As the first speaker chuckled, the noise dropped into her stomach. 'A fair amount I reckon.' Teeth smacked upon lips. 'Though she's a pretty one. We could have some fun with her first.' The stench of urine penetrated her nostrils. The breath on her neck grew hotter, burning like fire behind her ear.

Adah struggled again and tried to spit out the cloth, but the second man stuffed it back in. 'We'd have to be careful. If we spoil her, he might not pay so well.'

'He pays well enough for his harlots.' A chill shivered the length of her body. 'Why, he has one set up in a house far better than the one I share with ten others.'

'That's true.' New spindly fingers ran over her chest. 'How do you fancy a bit of fun with us then, girl, before we hand you back to your revolting husband?'

Adah bit down on the cloth, trying not to cry. The street children had all gone. She stared towards the old beggar she'd tried to feed, pleading for help. He shuffled sideways, hungrily chomping on the little bread he'd acquired. The constricted passageway was otherwise empty. No one wanted to witness the trouble they knew was coming.

The man holding her snickered. The other fumbled at her clothing. Then suddenly, his chin hit her neck. The impact made her jump, and the cloth fell from her mouth. A different head slammed between her shoulder blades, then both slid down her back until she heard the thump of bodies hitting the ground.

Adah spun and cried out at the two figures slumped in the soil, which pooled with blood. Standing above them was a man she had only seen from a distance, but his stature made him recognisable. She'd secretly nicknamed him 'Shadow', and despite his slight and nimble appearance, his forearms showed his true strength.

Her follower bowed his head. 'Mistress.' Scarlet dripped from the narrow, sharpened stone in his hand.

'They're... they're dead.'

'Yes, mistress.'

'You killed them.'

'They were attacking you, mistress.'

She should be relieved, but her chest felt hollow, and shock stole over her, clouding her head. 'What do we do now?' She blinked rapidly and glanced from side to side. Apart from the old beggar, they were alone.

The beggar had turned back and stared at her. He took another slow bite of bread. 'I saw nothing,' he mumbled as he chewed, mouth open.

Adah concentrated on staying upright as Shadow picked up the arms of one attacker and dragged him backwards towards a heap of rubbish where a goat stood atop, contentedly consuming scraps. Dumping the body near the mound, he returned for the other. Then he shifted the mound with his foot, covering the bodies as best he could as the goat bleated and jumped off.

Children's faces peered around the corner.

'Let's go.' Shadow grabbed her arm. She flinched, memories of the vice-like grip of her attacker rooting her feet to the spot. 'Sorry, mistress, but we must leave. Now.'

As he pulled her away, her feet found their purpose and soon she was jostling behind him as he expertly navigated the alleyways between the houses, taking routes Adah would never have known until eventually, she was before her own gate.

As Avram rushed forward to help, her follower slipped away.

She called after him. 'Where are you going?'

'To report to the master.'

'Come with me, mistress,' Avram said. He beckoned his son. 'Guard the gate while I help Adah inside.'

As soon as she was in the courtyard, her knees buckled. Avram scooped her up and carried her to the house, calling for Shua before laying her gently on her bed.

After Shua had brought her a warm drink and laid softened cabbage leaves over her bruised arms, Adah slipped into a fretful sleep. Fingers gripped, voices rasped, and bodies thumped repeatedly to the ground.

She woke at sundown to find Lamech sitting beside her. As she tried to sit up, he peeled the leaves from her arms and threw them to the floor. Then he pulled her into his chest, and she sank her face into him, allowing her tears to trickle down his torso. Kisses caressed her forehead as his familiar, stony, salty scent provided a measure of comfort.

'He killed them,' she croaked, seeing the bloody, lifeless bodies slumped at her feet once more, and the dripping slaughter stone.

'Don't worry, Adah. It's all been taken care of.'

'What do you mean?' She tilted her head to catch her husband's dependable eyes through her haze of tears.

'The bodies have been properly seen to and burnt. There were no witnesses.'

'There was the old man—'

'No, Adah.'

She sat up a little more and rubbed her eyes to see him clearly. His eyes were not dependable. Of course they weren't. They held a strange mixture of compassion and resistance.

He cupped her chin and gave her a prolonged, penetrating look. 'There *are* no witnesses, Adah. It has all been taken care of.'

Understanding dawned. Her fingers trembled against Lamech's chest. It was not just the bodies he had disposed of, but the old beggar too.

Lamech kissed her lips. 'You are safe now, my love.' Then he pulled her head back to his chest.

She studied the linens gathered in untidy swirls beneath her husband's strong legs. She blinked several times, but the trembling would not stop as it spread from her hands throughout her body. She was safe from her attackers. Safe from association with their deaths. *Safe in the arms of a murderer.*

Lamech hushed her, but her quaking continued. He shifted, laid her down and got up. 'I'll leave you to rest.'

Then he was gone.

CHAPTER 45

Adah stood at the entrance to the vineyard, watching Yaval atop the watchtower. He hadn't noticed her; his eyes were fixed firmly on the hills beyond.

She reached forward. Her hands trembled again. She slapped one on top of the other. *Stop it. There is no one here but your son. Stop worrying.*

Breathing in deeply, she clasped the first handhold then climbed up, holding on to the branches wedged between the rocks until she clutched the platform.

Yaval turned as he heard her and smiled. 'Hello, Ima.'

Her hand still trembled as she tried to pull herself up. 'What are you doing up here, love?'

Her son put an arm around her. She appreciated his steadying; the watchtower had been neglected and needed some repairs, and she wasn't really in any state to climb it.

Yaval helped her up to standing. 'How are you, Ima? I didn't see you this morning. Abba said you were resting.'

'Yes.' She had slept for a long time after the attack, though she'd woken several times in a panic and had to fight the shadows with Yahweh's name to get back to sleep.

She followed Yaval's gaze to a herd of large cattle grazing on a far hillside due south. She could barely make out more than brown lumps, but she knew her son had better eyes than her.

'Those creatures have begun entering our lands as the tanninim leave,' Yaval said. 'They must consider it safer here than their old home.'

Must they? I wish I did.

Silence reigned for a few moments as they watched the barely perceptible movement of the far-off animals. 'They have exceedingly long horns. I expect they would put up a good fight if I tried to train them.'

'Why would you?' she asked.

Yaval didn't answer, but his gaze betrayed his longing. He would make a wonderful sheepherder, but she didn't think training longhorns was a good idea.

The thought of sheepherders stung her heart and subconsciously, she turned her gaze to the western mountains. Might she ever see Ruhamah walking this way again?

Yaval squeezed her shoulders. 'You're thinking about Eliana's brother again, aren't you?'

A gentle smile tugged at her lips. 'Am I that obvious?'

'I know you loved him.'

She gasped. How could he know? She had barely mentioned Ruhamah.

'I understand the look in your eyes, Ima. I feel the same way about Mela. And she does about me.'

This was a surprising development. 'But she is so much older than you.'

'Now she is. But when we're six hundred, who will care?'

Adah chuckled. 'I suppose that's true. What is your plan, then?'

'Stay out of Abba's way and hope he forgets I exist.'

'Not tonight, you won't. I've come to fetch you so you can get ready for the banquet. You must impress your abba or he will insist you go to the tavern for business.'

'I can't, Ima. I can't bear the thought of being thrown in the way of other women. I love Mela!'

'Surely you can go to the tavern without encountering them?'

'No, Ima. You don't know what it's like. I've heard the stories, especially from Juval.'

She lifted her hands and put them on either side of his face. 'Then do what you need to do. Though so little like him, you are still your abba's son. Pull out your charm. Make connections this evening. Impress him. If you help to grow his business, he will be pleased with you.'

Yaval sighed. 'I'd rather be out on the hills with those cattle.'

'I know you would.'

'I don't want to live my whole life in his shade as you do, Ima, never getting what I want.'

She dropped her hands. Oh, the torture of being young and having ideals. 'I used to dream of something better for my life, Yaval. It was that dream that convinced me to marry your abba in the first place, though I'd have been more suited to staying on the farm. Caution and patience – they are better than chasing after what you think you want.'

Yaval ran his hand through his beard, reminding her that he was a grown man now. He still needed protecting, just like Juval did.

'Will you help me?' he asked. 'I don't know where to start in making *business connections.*'

Adah was pleased to find Tzillah in the kitchen courtyard when they returned, laying out trays of smoked meat and flat bread.

'Tzillah. We need your help. You know Lamech's associates better than anyone else. You must teach Yaval how to charm them,' Adah said.

Tzillah stopped and laughed. 'I'll try. Though it might be rather tricky given what Yaval lacks.'

'What is that?'

'Long eyelashes and large breasts.' Tzillah grinned.

Fortunately, Yaval saw the funny side. 'I may lack breasts, but I have hair as wonderful as yours, Ima Tzillah.' He pulled his long, curly black hair out of its twine and shook it out, then twirled it through his slender, mahogany fingers. Imitating Tzillah, he skittered over to Leah and grabbed her waist.

The elderly maid kissed Yaval's cheek. 'A fine-looking young man, for sure, though a little forward for my tastes.' Leah chuckled, continuing to chop the salad.

'Come now, Tzillah,' Adah interjected through her laughter. 'You know these men. You've listened to their conversations for years. You must know what their interests are beyond admiring your figure.'

'Alright,' Tzillah said. 'It's Kenan your abba is most concerned with impressing at present. He is Chanoch's grandson, by marriage. You'll know him for he'll be the eldest in the room, though he was late to have children and some of them are little older than you. Kenan owns the stone quarry to the east of the city, and Lamech is seeking better trade terms with him. Talk to him about his daughter, Dania. She is the sunshine in his gloom.'

Tzillah proceeded to recall several more people of note, quizzing Yaval about the information to ensure he'd got siblings and children the right way round, and businesses and interests tied to the right names.

'I don't know why Lamech hasn't told you all this himself,' she finished.

'Because he wants me to fail,' Yaval said.

'Nonsense. He's desperate for his eldest son to inherit his business. It's more likely you haven't asked.'

Yaval chewed his fingernail. 'It's true, I haven't. But what if I do well – will he be angry? My last injury has only just healed.'

Tzillah lifted a hand and stroked the scar above Yaval's right eye. Adah watched with pleasure as her rival showed affection to one of their children. It was rare.

'If you win over Kenan, he will love you for it. And I feel that you may be just the person for the task. Kenan has a distrust of Lamech inherited from Chanoch. You lack your abba's arrogance. Show Kenan that the next generation will honour the traditions of the elders and be fair to the poor, and he'll give us his business.'

Adah was speechless. She'd always known Tzillah was far more intelligent than she let on, but she hadn't expected such in-depth knowledge. If only she'd paid more attention to Lamech's associates, she might have been able to help her son as Tzillah was doing now. Instead, she'd hidden herself away from parties as far as possible, proving herself useless. *Useless and too terrified to achieve anything.*

Yaval glanced at her. 'Do you agree, Ima?'

She pulled herself away from unhelpful thoughts. 'Of course, my love. Do whatever Tzillah says.'

CHAPTER 46

From his new watchtower near the city gate, Lamech gazed over Barsabas' army camped outside the city walls, where they'd been living under constructions of long branches and animal skins. He needed Barsabas out of his city. It had been several seasons since his sister's husband had interfered in his business and brought his troops here, and he showed no signs of leaving.

Before the elders, Lamech had spun a story about needing the extra men to rid the city of tanninim, but the truth was, Barsabas had imposed, and Lamech hadn't known how to refuse.

It had been Methushael's arrangement, which made Lamech even angrier. He'd had things as he wanted them – his building projects were appreciated, his fortification of the city was needed and his moral discrepancies, all but forgotten. He commanded the fighting men that provided the barrier against attacks on their lands, many of which Lamech now owned or controlled. The harvest fed his slaves who in turn, built his business.

Yet, when one of Methushael's friends had lost a relative to a tannin attack, his father sent word to Barsabas – behind his back – that they needed more men.

When Azurak had first reported the oversized army marching on the city, Lamech had been compelled to think fast. He must make the elders believe it was his idea. He'd figure out how to get rid of Barsabas later. So, he'd appeared before the council – something his underhand abba would never do – and had convinced them that Barsabas was present at his invitation, rather than Methushael's, and that Barsabas owed him a favour, meaning his army would stay at no cost to the city.

It had achieved its aim. They had slaughtered countless tanninim and wild beasts, frightening the rest from the lands. The people were safe, and slowly, farmers were returning to their fields, planting greater areas of land. The famine was easing. The herders had returned to the hills, meaning the city smelt less constantly of dung. The elders attributed the success of the venture to Lamech. As such, his plan had worked.

Yet the decision had cost Lamech dearly. Perhaps he should have let the elders throw Barsabas out instead. Then he wouldn't have needed to feed hundreds of extra men for so long from his own supplies. For he should have guessed it would come to this. It was like when Barsabas agreed to facilitate his wedding to Tzillah. Afterwards, he'd called in favour after favour, even forcing Lamech to travel north to advise him on how to fortify his city defences, leaving his wives when Tzillah was pregnant with Tuval-Kayin. Barsabas never did anything without expecting something in return, and he always outstayed his welcome.

Now he needed Barsabas gone, before his father's loyalty was forever wedded to his vagrant son-by-marriage instead of his real son. Before the balance of power shifted. Before he ran out of food. But how could he achieve it? Barsabas was enjoying the luxury of Methushael's hospitality. Dinah was revelling in being home among her old friends...

Perhaps an agreement of sorts. Barsabas' exit in exchange for something he desired. What did Lamech have to barter with?

His mind immediately flew to his only daughter, whom he had been keeping close until the opportune moment came to make the most of her beauty. Barsabas and Dinah had a son of marriageable age – Anak. The young man was impressive – dwarfing his father in height – and they had already expressed interest in a match between the cousins. Would they take Naamah as payment to leave, dressed up as gratitude for their services?

Conflict raged within. He had despised his abba for selling off Dinah; had pitied his sister and vowed not to do the same to his own daughter. Could Naamah be happy in northern Nod, amongst Barsabas' people? She seemed to get on well enough with her cousin. Their marriage could be a happy one...

Yet, Adah had sheltered the girl. Despite his efforts to introduce her to the wider community, she would no doubt find the north shocking. He loved Naamah. He didn't want to cause her distress. Still, she hadn't produced another suitable candidate for marriage, and neither had either of his wives. Naamah still seemed more attached to Juval than anyone else.

Lamech smiled as he thought about his second son. Juval was doing brilliantly. He'd far exceeded expectations since joining him at the tavern. Juval was handsome, successful, popular among all strata of society and had women fighting over him. Yet he only ever messed around with them. He hadn't yet fallen in love.

He's just like me before I met Adah. I spent all my days working hard and all my nights in the company of liquor, friends, and women. Adah changed everything. The moment I met her she consumed my every thought. I had to have her, or I would die. Look where that got me. I slipped back into my previous lifestyle anyway and made her miserable. Do I want that kind of love for my children? Has it worked out well for me?

A thought suddenly struck him. Here he was conflicted about Naamah and her future. Yet why put his daughter in the centre of something he could likely create without her? There was nothing Barsabas loved better than a conflict. Lamech felt sure Barsabas would return north at the merest hint of disquiet in his lands.

'Azurak.' Lamech called to his foreman below, where he was inspecting the camp. Azurak looked up and Lamech beckoned. Then his man scaled the watchtower walls with ease, his strong arms and legs flying over the handholds. A moment later, Azurak stood before him.

'I need your help,' Lamech said softly. 'It's time we created a little chaos.'

Later, having spent some time discussing his thoughts with Azurak, Lamech visited his youngest son at the furnace near the caves outside the city.

'Abba,' Tuval-Kayin emerged from a pit, climbing up to see him. Joy radiated from his face.

'You look like you're having a good day.'

'I am. Look at this this.' Tuval-Kayin led him towards a large stone that looked like a millstone, on top of which were two smaller sandstone pieces, hollowed out into the inverse shape of a very thin knife. He picked up a knife sitting nearby and placed it in Lamech's hand.

Lamech turned it over, feeling the weight of it. 'You made this from that?' he asked, pointing to the hollowed stones.

'Yes. Not by hammering. Well, we worked it afterwards a little. But the shape was formed by pouring molten metal into the stone.'

'And what is the benefit?'

'Push the knife against the stone.'

Lamech aimed the point of the knife. Its bright reddish-orange glinted in the sunlight. It was far smoother than the hammered copper that made up their jewellery and small receptacles. He knew what he expected to happen – against the strength of the stone, the knife tip would bend. He pushed.

It didn't yield. He drew his eyebrows together, then lifted one at his son. Tuval-Kayin grinned and held out a sugarcane. 'Try it.'

Lamech ran the knife through the cane. Straight through it, with ease. He inspected the knife – no wear. It looked just the same. Tuval-Kayin grinned again and passed him one half of the cane. They chewed them as they spoke.

'I knew some of the men had been successful in strengthening copper by heating it in a pit. But this is something else, isn't it?' Lamech asked.

'Yes. I've smelted the rocks that contain more than one metal. Initially, it didn't work, Abba. They would come out impure. A mess, really. All I succeeded in doing was ruining the copper. The other men even grew angry with me.

'Then I had the idea to use a receptacle. I crush the stones repeatedly, into as fine pieces as I can. Then I crush the charcoal also, mixing it together inside the clay jar. Putting this into the ground, with more charcoal all around, and blowing air into it from below, creates heat inside the jar, but keeps it separate. The metal is able to melt completely and detach from its rock. It took me many attempts, for the grey, shiny pieces seem to melt more readily than the copper.'

'But I thought the grey metals were softer? How then can they combine with the copper to make something hard?'

'I hardly know! But the pieces from the jar were so much tougher to work with than copper. I soon realised we could never hope to hammer them into shape consistently. It was then I thought of creating a mould, like this one.'

'It must have taken you a long time to carve those out.'

Tuval-Kayin laughed. 'Oh, I didn't do it. Carving sandstone with flint is tough, but I found a boy happy to trade for his labour.'

'This is incredible, son. With this stronger metal, we could make life much easier for the farmers.'

'Yes, I've already thought of that. I've been experimenting with different shapes and watching how Sav Shimiel cuts the crops.'

'You've spent time with Shimiel?'

'Yes. We get along well.'

'How is he? I haven't seen him for an age.' The truth was, they had barely spoken since their argument outside Shimiel's home when Adah was hiding somewhere inside. Lamech couldn't meet eyes with Adah's father without remembering all the emotions that day pulled up and needing to repress them heavily. She was better with him. Better with their sons. He would not allow himself to think otherwise.

'He's well,' Tuval-Kayin said. 'Glad to be free from the fear of tanninim.'

Shimiel had never left his farm, refusing to come into the city even when Adah had offered his family room in their home. Lamech had been very relieved when they'd refused the offer, made without his consent. To placate Adah, he'd set up an extra guard around her abba's farm, happy to sacrifice one of his hunters if it kept Shimiel from their home and stopped Adah's constant worry. She nagged an awful lot when she was worried.

'Good,' he replied. He could relocate his hunter to somewhere more useful.

'As I was saying, Abba, I've watched the way Sav harvests, and I think it would be far more efficient if he could use a pre-curved blade, like this.' Tuval-Kayin pulled up a piece of grass and bent it into a half-moon. 'You can cut several stalks at once with this, see?'

'I'm sure I've seen farmers using curved tools already. What is new?'

'At present, Sav uses a curved wooden or bone handle, in which several indentations have been made, and sharpened stone pieces fixed inside with resin. He saws at a clump like this...' Tuval-Kayin demonstrated. 'It's better than the old system of a single stone on stalk for sure, but imagine if you had a sharp, curved blade, so that the whole clump could be cut in one swoop. A metal blade.'

As Tuval-Kayin pretended to cut a clump of grass with the other blade in his hand, Lamech's mind wandered. If his son was right, they could increase the yield of the farms further. Farmers would trade well for tools that made their work easier. They wouldn't be able to glean these tools from the land or make them themselves, as they could with stone. They would need his son. The demand could be very lucrative.

'Have you explained this idea to anyone else?' he asked.

'No, Abba.'

'Good. Make me one of these tools. Demonstrate it to me.'

'Of course. The new metal requires a lot of rock though. And it must be a specific rock to produce the hardened form. Each piece will take many metal-hunters several trips. It will be some time before we can produce enough to help everyone.'

Lamech turned over the knife in his hand again. 'I can provide you with more men. Your metal-hunters can train them. Have you tried this knife on flesh?'

'Yes, it is excellent. But Abba—'

Lamech looked up. Tuval-Kayin's glee had diminished somewhat. 'Yes?'

'We might need to send the metal-hunters into other territories. I'm not sure there's enough of the right rock around here.'

'Where is best to go?'

'Mountainous regions, and the coast. It is rather too flat and dry here, though there are metal deposits in some of the riverbeds, they're not the sort I want. Areas north of here, more affected by water, seem to produce metal-containing rocks more readily.'

Lamech felt his mouth twitch upwards. His son needed northern rocks. He needed Barsabas occupied. He stood and patted his son on the shoulder. 'Leave it with me, Tuval. I'll send you some more men tomorrow. Can I keep this?' He held up the knife.

'Of course, Abba.'

Lamech stood. 'Oh, Tuval. You better start finishing up. Remember we have a banquet at dusk. I expect you there, collecting the crumbs your brother drops.'

CHAPTER 47

The noise in the room was unbearable. It beat in Adah's ears like a drum, though there was nothing steady about it. Closing in around her, each sound mingled into a pulsating hum. She closed her eyes against it, focusing on the breathing she could control, though the smoke from the fire filled her nostrils with each intake, drying the back of her throat.

'Mistress?'

The soft voice jolted her back to the business dinner, her body jumping in an involuntary spasm. The smell of the fire intensified as Azurak calmly knelt beside her. He always brought that smell with him.

'I trust you are recovered from yesterday's mishap,' he said. He trusted wrong. Shouldn't her trembling tell him that? 'It was fortunate your protector was there.'

Adah forced herself to turn her head slightly, so that Azurak's black hair caught her peripheral vision. 'My protector?' *More like my captor.*

'Of course, mistress. Your safety is the master's primary concern.'

'What do you want, Azurak? It's not like you to approach me directly.' She had no head space for pointless conversation. She was present for her children, but the sooner she could leave and return to bed, the better. The thought gave her uncommon boldness with this man who had always set her on edge.

'I want to talk about Naamah,' he replied.

Adah sighed. Her eyes scanned the room for her almost-daughter. As usual, she was near Juval over the far side. 'There's no use you approaching me about Naamah. She is not my daughter.'

'It's my impression that you are invested in her, perhaps more than her mother is.'

'It is still not my decision whom she marries, though I would advise you to stay away.'

'Me? You misunderstand. I would never touch something that belongs to my master.'

'Naamah is not something. She is someone.'

'Of course. I did not mean to—'

Courage escaped her lips. Naamah was worth it. 'Do you have designs on her or not?'

Azurak paused. He was a man of few words and always chose them carefully. 'I am not blind, mistress. I am also not stupid. I know my station. Instead of assuming my intention, if you open your eyes and look, you might see what I see.'

Adah blinked. She had turned to face him during his speech, and now Azurak's darkest-brown eyes penetrated hers. He was being particularly audacious. She wasn't sure which she preferred – secretive, brooding Azurak or this new, bold one. She held his gaze a moment before scanning the room again. On the other side, Lamech was conversing with Barsabas. Anak – Barsabas' son – stood next to his father. He was much taller than Barsabas but had a combination of his parents' features. Not unhandsome, but not soft either. At something Lamech said, Anak's eyes flitted towards his copper-haired cousin and remained there. Anak licked his top lip.

What was Lamech's game?

'My master's mind is weighing several options,' Azurak said. Lamech's hand rested on the small of Tzillah's back, and she looked radiant as she laughed with Dinah about something.

'His pressing needs may push him into deciding something foolish... whereas Kenan's family is a good match.'

'Kenan's?'

'Look again.'

Adah turned her attention back to Naamah. Despite her earlier assumption, Naamah's focus wasn't on Juval. Next to her reclined another young man, leaning back on his elbow, chatting enthusiastically. He was likely below average height, but his arms expressed much as he flung them about before him, animating every word. Naamah was inclined forward, twirling her loose hair between her fingers. Her cheeks were almost the colour of her hair, and her eyes shone.

'That young man is Gomer, the fifth son of Kenan,' Azurak said.

Ah, she remembered. Kenan was the one Yaval was to impress. This was good, wasn't it? Kenan was a respectable man. Adah glanced back at Juval. His gaze hadn't wavered from his sister and her admirer, despite the pretty young woman seeking his attention on his other side. Was he jealous? Naamah's interest must be significant if Juval was jealous.

'I feel I must warn you, mistress, that by all accounts, Gomer lacks ambition.'

Gomer lacks ambition… is that bad?

Azurak continued. 'I doubt Lamech would be satisfied with the match. He may well refuse. However, at the end of the table – also staring at your daughter – is Kenan's second eldest son, the one likely to inherit most of his father's business.'

'Why?'

'Unlike his brother, Eber drives forward Kenan's trade, making himself indispensable to his father, and a worthy business ally. This man, Lamech would consider.'

Adah waved a hand. 'Why are you telling me this, and not Lamech?'

'You know how quickly young girls fall in love, and you have access to Naamah's heart, do you not?'

'So does her abba.'

'She may suspect some ulterior motive from him. Not so from you. You may struggle to influence your husband, but you can influence Naamah to favour Kenan's elder son.'

'Why would I do that?' Naamah was clearly besotted by the younger brother.

'Because it will be good for business and Lamech will be pleased with you for forming the alliance. Additionally, it will save Naamah from someone she would soon tire of – Gomer is too simple for her – and from Barsabas.'

'From Barsabas?' Adah's eyes widened.

Azurak coughed. 'I meant Barsabas' son.'

Was that a purposeful slip to heighten her fear? She believed him that Lamech was considering Naamah's cousin. It could not be. She must do everything she could to keep Naamah from Barsabas' household. Sending her precious girl into the lion's den was unthinkable.

Azurak continued. 'Contrary to what everyone thinks, I do have feelings, mistress. For Naamah, at least, I want the best.'

Could it be true, or was Azurak playing some game? She had not imagined his own lustful glances towards Naamah. He clearly didn't want her moving to the north, and neither did he want her married to someone she loved. Perhaps he thought he could comfort his way into her bed if she entered a loveless marriage with Eber.

'Thank you for the information, Azurak. I will consider what you have said.'

Azurak bowed slightly then left her. The pressure in her head had abated somewhat as she'd concentrated on the conversation and her duty to Naamah. She needed to find out more about Kenan's sons. Was Chanoch here to speak with? She'd been so overwhelmed by panic previously that she hadn't registered any individuals.

Her eyes took in the remaining people in the hall, a quarter of the number they usually had. Why had it seemed like so many moments ago? *Just business,* Lamech had said. So, no social acquaintances then. Chanoch wouldn't be present. Of course, Tzillah had said Kenan would be the eldest. How was Yaval doing at making his acquaintance? She couldn't see him.

'Ima.'

'Oh!' For the second time that evening, she'd been snuck up on. 'Yaval, I was just wondering how you were.'

'I have been following Tzillah's instructions. It is going well, I think.'

'Oh good. Your abba certainly seems to be having a good evening.'

Yaval rolled his eyes. 'He's showing off Tuval-Kayin as usual. He's not even noticed me.'

'Nonsense.'

'It isn't.'

He was right. Poor Yaval. He would really have to impress tonight if Lamech was to forgive him for not going to the tavern, and his abba had no intention of helping him along.

'My love, do you know Naamah's companion?' she asked.

Yaval followed the tilt of her head. 'Gomer? A little. We are a similar age, but he was always quiet.'

'He doesn't seem quiet presently. And his brother? The stern one.'

'Oh, yes. Eber is older. He used to pick on my friends as children. He particularly didn't like *the gatekeeper's son* joining our games. We got along apart from that.'

'They both seem enamoured with your sister.'

'Everyone is. Juval is quite put out. Though, this is the first time I've seen her respond. She looks... different.'

She did. 'Would you do something for me?'

'Of course.'

'As you move around the room tonight, try to find out more about those young men. Particularly, find out if they go to the tavern.'

'Yes, Ima. Now will you do something for me?'

'Name it, dearest.'

Yaval stood, then leaned down and kissed her forehead. 'Take yourself to bed. You look exhausted.'

'I will. Soon.' Now that she had Naamah's future in mind again, she doubted she would fall into that exhausted sleep her body craved. She stood and collected some of the empty dishes, watching Yaval as he approached Eber and made some joke to begin a conversation. Across the table, Juval had risen and retrieved his lyre ready to play the next tune. Naamah hadn't even realised she was required to sing – Gomer still held all her attention.

The tune was beautiful, even without Naamah. As Juval played, Adah's eyes flitted across to her husband. He had joined Tuval-Kayin, and they were speaking with the thatcher – Nasya's husband, if she wasn't mistaken. Afterwards, he turned and considered his older children. As his gaze fell on Naamah, his brow furrowed in concentration.

When the music finished, Tzillah approached. 'What did Azurak want? I've never seen him hold such a lengthy conversation with a woman before.'

A chuckle escaped. 'He was concerned about Naamah's admirer.'

Tzillah's eyes flitted to her daughter. 'Kenan's son. Why the concern?'

'What do you know of him?'

'He keeps himself to himself. Though he works for his abba, he doesn't do more than basic labour. I'm surprised he's here.'

'Perhaps he came to see Naamah.'

'That's exactly why he came.' Yaval had returned. He fixed his eyes on Adah. 'Ima, you are very disobedient. You promised me you'd go to bed ages ago.'

'Never mind that, what do you mean, that's why he's here?'

'According to Eber, his brother has been infatuated with Naamah for years, but he is *exceptionally boring*, lacking motivation to do anything but delicately carve pictures from the rocks they are meant to be quarrying, and has *never even been* to the tavern.'

The corners of Adah's mouth twitched as Yaval's eyebrows rose with each sarcastic comment.

She nudged Tzillah. 'He sounds ideal, don't you think?'

Tzillah planted a hand on her hip and pouted.

Yaval grinned. 'What do you have in mind, Ima?'

'Exactly what we originally planned. You charm his father into a supply covenant. Then, we might stand a chance of securing your abba's blessing for Naamah's attachment.'

Yaval nodded. 'Eber seems to know all about the business.'

'What is your impression of him?'

'His attitude has altered little since childhood. I like his father better.'

'Still, Azurak insists the future lies with Eber...'

Yaval stroked his chin, looking once again at his sister. 'Naamah's future is most important. But creating rivalry in the family will benefit no one.'

'Rivalry is a horrible thing,' Tzillah said. 'Do you think Eber is also attached to Naamah?'

'Yes, for sure. Though I suspect his attachment is more fickle.'

'We must tread carefully,' Tzillah said.

Yaval nodded. 'Then I will continue my quest. Excuse me.'

Once Yaval was out of earshot, Adah gripped Tzillah's arm. 'Do you think it's wrong, discussing Naamah's fate like this?'

'No,' Tzillah replied. 'It's necessary. I confess, I have been content to let Lamech handle it. But tonight, I've been listening to the men with new ears. When she sang earlier, I noticed all the remarks, the sneers, the comments. I also noticed Anak's expression.' Tzillah shivered. 'Seeing Naamah with Gomer – her innocent, besotted, impressionable little face, it brings up all these feelings in me. I want to—'

'Protect her?'

'Yes. Any of these men could offer for her. If they act this way in our home, how might they act in theirs, or in the tavern, or in a darkened alley, or... Adah – are you alright?'

Adah's legs had started to shake.

Tzillah's grip tightened as they gave way. She caught Adah and lowered her onto her mat. 'What's wrong?'

The room closed in again, and Adah's clothing bound her arms as Tzillah's words transformed into a grasping sneer.

'Adah!'

She blinked. *It's not those men. It's just Tzillah. It's not them.*

'I'm taking you to bed.'

The corridor passed in a blur. She struggled against the involuntary removal, but soon felt the mattress soft beneath her back. This was no hard, unyielding ground. There was no thump of fallen bodies.

As Tzillah wiped her brow with cool water, one of her curls danced above Adah's eyes, like a butterfly in a meadow. *Butterfly in a meadow. Think on that.* The ceiling slowly came back into focus, followed by Tzillah's concerned features.

Adah took a deep breath, filling her lungs, then exhaling through her nose, as she had done during labour. She caught Tzillah's hand. 'Naamah must not marry Lamech.'

'Lamech? Adah, you're not making sense.'

Adah nodded. It was clear in her mind.

Tzillah's eyes narrowed. 'Adah, you married for love. You married Lamech. Do you mean you don't want Naamah to do the same?'

No. That wasn't it. She shook her head. 'Lamech. Barsabas. Azurak. Eber. They are all the same, Tzillah.'

Adah scrambled to sit up. She had to make Tzillah see. Placing her hands on Tzillah's shoulders, she fixed her in sight. 'Do not let them have your daughter.'

Tzillah nodded. 'What do you want me to do?'

Her throat felt dry. She fumbled for the bowl of water. Tzillah placed it in her hand, and she drank. As the cool liquid slid down her throat, her thoughts clarified. She took another deep breath, then spoke again. 'Choose someone good, Tzillah. Not someone good for business. Someone *good*.'

'You mean someone like Gomer.'
Adah closed her eyes, allowing the bed to envelop her. 'Find out.'

CHAPTER 48

'You've been interfering again.'

Adah peeled her eyes open. The light hit her like a punch. She groaned and closed them again.

Lamech shuffled on the bed. 'Tzillah made her request last night, when I was in far too good a mood to refuse her. I know you put her up to it.'

'I don't know what you mean.' Had she hit her head again? The throbbing was intense behind her eyes and across her forehead. She didn't remember hitting her head at the banquet. Was that last night, or had more time passed?

'Fortunately for you, Yaval has done surprisingly well. He's made progress with Kenan regarding a supply covenant I've sought for some time – I almost fell off my chair when he told me. To secure the deal, I may just speak to Kenan about Naamah and his son. But you'd better hope this doesn't come back to bite you, Adah.'

She fumbled for his arm and grabbed it. 'Which son?'

'What?'

'Which son will you speak to Kenan about?'

His weight shifted until she felt his breath in front of her face. She forced her eyes open again to see Lamech's face before her.

'What is wrong with you, Adah? It's not like you to take so much wine.'

'I didn't. I think it's the attack... it visits me.'

Lamech rolled his eyes. 'You've always been overdramatic. Now, I must leave. Get up and go for a walk. I expect you to be well again by tonight.'

Tonight?

It was a further three days before Adah felt well enough to leave her room. Fortunately, Lamech was barely at home, so she didn't face his annoyance. In that time, Yaval secured the trade terms with Kenan.

'We are having a dinner to celebrate in two weeks' time,' Yaval told her at breakfast. 'Will you be well, Ima?'

She felt much better now, but the thought of many bodies crowding into the hall again was less than appealing. Couldn't she stay in the living room? No, she must do it for Yaval. 'Of course, my love.'

Naamah looked up. 'Will Gomer be there?'

'Yes, everyone from Kenan's family and business are invited,' Yaval replied.

'What terms have you agreed, Yaval?' Adah asked.

Yaval explained the various details: how he had worked out terms that would benefit both parties, and how he'd keep Lamech's slaves – Kenan's principal objection – away from Kenan's sites.

The agreement sounded ideal. Yaval clearly had a better head for business than he or Lamech had realised. Pride swelled in Adah's chest. Her son was doing exactly what was right. But could Lamech be pleased with these terms?

Tzillah was thinking along the same lines. 'We have hundreds of slave mouths to feed. How do we do that if they are not allowed on site?'

'Abba is seeking to expand the business into other territories. Repairs on the wall use considerable resources, and there are many other families who have abandoned construction in favour of using Abba's men. Not to mention the hunters and protectors.'

'We're also expanding the forge,' Tuval-Kayin said. He'd been quiet thus far, and Adah had barely noticed his presence. 'Abba has given me slaves to work there.'

'I had no idea the business had grown so large,' Adah murmured. 'It feels unfair. Especially for our cousins whose lives are at risk. Many of these slaves are relatives—'

'It's progress, Adah,' Tzillah said. 'You still go on about Yahweh's will. Didn't He command people to multiply and spread over the earth? If every woman had as many children as your friend Eliana, that wouldn't take long. We must build. We must protect.'

'I suppose.' The idea still caused a tightening in her stomach, the same feeling she'd experienced when she'd first seen the slaves, and the army.

Yaval reached for her hand. 'I can't say the business excites me, Ima, but at least I'm doing something good, enabling one part to become more ethical again.'

'Well, I want to know more about Gomer,' Juval said. He'd also been silent until that point. Now he pierced Naamah with a stare. Had they had a disagreement?

Naamah blushed red and scrutinised her lap. Tzillah stood up and moved behind her daughter, putting her hands proudly on her shoulders. 'Lamech has agreed that Naamah may have her choice of Kenan's sons, subject to their father's approval. The joining of our family names will provide extra security for the covenant.'

Juval bit down on his lip, staring Naamah out, but she refused to meet his gaze. 'I suppose I should be grateful she's not going north,' he said at last.

'What?' Naamah glanced up, her eyes flashing in fear.

'Abba was considering marrying you to our cousin, Anak.'

Naamah's eyes widened.

'Where did you hear that?' Tzillah asked.

'I hear loads of gossip in the camps,' Juval replied. 'They often speculate about Naamah. 'Lamech's only daughter' is quite a prospect. I've fought several fights defending her honour. The men tend to shut up when I come near now. Anak was the only suggestion I took seriously, because it seemed like just the thing Abba might do.'

'Your sister is not an object to be traded,' Tzillah said.

Juval slammed his hands down. 'Why do you think I have fought for her? Someone has to!' Daggers shot Tzillah's way. 'I just wished she'd come to me if she liked Gomer, instead of making me a fool the other night.'

'How did I?' Naamah exclaimed, tears springing to her eyes.

'You spent the whole evening fawning over him. You barely spoke to a single other soul. I didn't even know you liked him! We have always been a team, Naamah. Now you will leave me.'

'You left me first!' The tears flowed down Naamah's cheeks, dripping onto her tunic. 'You left me to join the army camp, where you knew I could not go. Who knows how many women you've had, Juval? Treating them like objects. How do you think their brothers and mothers feel? Why should my honour be anything different to theirs? You are just the same as Abba. You make me so... so angry!'

Brother and sister glared at each other across the table. What was happening to her little family? Adah had tried so hard to keep them all together, but it wasn't possible. Naamah had to leave, and Juval had to let her go.

A vein on Juval's forehead bulged, just like Lamech's. He was holding his tongue, desperate to let something else pour out, but he did not. Instead, he turned about, left the room and moments later, could be heard pouring his woes into a dirge on the flute. Naamah wiped her tears and followed him.

Adah counted to twenty, then tiptoed from the room and peered around the doorway of Juval's chamber. Naamah had her head on his lap and was singing softly to his tune. She exhaled. For now, at least, they had made peace.

When she returned to the living area, the others were gone and Shua was clearing up. 'Where did Tzillah go?' Adah asked.

'I think she's shopping with Dinah today. You might catch up with them if you're quick.'

Adah almost picked up the shawl hanging in the doorway. Shopping might be just the distraction she needed, and she wanted to ask Tzillah what she'd discovered about Gomer. Yet, as her foot touched the threshold, the opening seemed to grow tighter and the minor movements Shua was making magnified.

'Mistress, do you need anything?' Shua asked.

'No.' She backed up a few steps. 'May I help you instead?' Adah asked.

Pity crept into her housekeeper's eyes and she smiled. 'I'm sure I can find you something to do.'

THE DAY OF THE celebratory banquet arrived. The house was once again a flurry of activity with extra staff bustling about, which was fine so long as Adah could stick close to those she knew well. She kept having to push the thought of more people arriving out of her mind.

'Keep breathing through it,' Shua said, putting a hand on her arm. 'I'll be by your side as much as I can be.'

Yaval entered the kitchen courtyard. 'Have you made provision for the goat in the colonnade?'

'Yes, it's all seen to,' Shua answered. A flicker of sadness crossed Yaval's features, but he smiled it away and nodded. 'Good. I'll get her ready.'

At dusk, people started streaming into the compound. Lamech had recently built eight imposing columns in two colonnades indicating the way from the gatekeeper's lodge to the banquet hall on the left side of their compound. The first part of the covenant ceremony was taking place between the colonnades. The two families lined up on either side, among the flowering honeysuckle that climbed the pillars and draped down between them.

Lamech's family looked small compared to Kenan's. Though he included Bekhor, who had a small stake in his business, neither Methushael, Lamech's younger brothers, nor Barsabas had been invited. Azurak was immediately on Bekhor's right. Adah supposed she should be central too, but she stood in her husband's shadow instead, quivering from the cold until Juval appeared and slipped his arm around her shoulders. As she leaned into her son's chest, her feet found their strength.

When Kenan's collection of guests was almost complete, with fifty to sixty persons opposite, a commotion occurred at the gate. Barsabas entered with Dinah, resplendent in a red tunic, and several of their adult children, including Anak who stood out for his height. About ten soldiers followed them through the gateway, holding spears. Naamah whispered to Tzillah about the colour Dinah wore, wondering where she got the dye.

'It's probably blood,' Juval joked in Adah's ear.

I wouldn't be surprised.

'You may wish to hire a new messenger, Brother,' Barsabas declared, walking forward with hands held up. His family stayed back, but the soldiers followed several paces behind until Barsabas stood between the two families, his shorter stature doing nothing to diminish his countenance of superiority. 'Yours failed to deliver my invitation.'

Lamech's attention turned to Azurak, and they held a hushed but animated conversation. Across the gap, Kenan did the same with Eber. Knowing his predilection for moral business dealings, Adah assumed Kenan had no wish to enter any kind of covenant where Barsabas was involved.

Then Azurak and Eber caught each other's gaze and nodded. After a moment, Lamech and Kenan walked forward, joining Barsabas in the centre. Behind them all, not far from the gate where he'd been welcoming the party, Yaval hovered, watching the circumstances outside his control.

As the three powerful men in the centre silently considered each other, the tension was sliceable.

'This covenant doesn't concern you, Barsabas,' Lamech finally said. 'There was no need for you to be involved.'

'On the contrary,' the smaller man countered. 'Since you have decided to seal it with a marriage bond, it certainly does concern me. For we had an understanding, did we not?'

They did? Surely Lamech hadn't promised Naamah to Anak... Could Barsabas be so bold as to claim what wasn't true?

'Lamech?' Kenan was clearly thinking the same thing, for he fixed Lamech with a stare and tilted his head.

'We had no such understanding,' Lamech muttered through gritted teeth. 'A conversation does not constitute an understanding.'

Yaval pushed through the crowd, almost tumbling in front of his abba. 'The marriage isn't the bond anyway. I have already prepared that. I am giving one of my goats. She is tied up over there—'

Barsabas took one step back and his eyes flickered to the goat. 'A sacrifice? So Naamah is not betrothed?'

The crowd began to murmur, wondering how this would play out, as Lamech shifted almost imperceptibly on his feet.

'Lamech?' Kenan repeated.

Tzillah had confessed earlier that the betrothal between Naamah and Gomer was arranged, and the intention was to announce it formally tonight after the covenant was sealed. As far as she knew, the two were bound together. Kenan clearly thought the same thing.

'I decided to give my daughter a choice,' Lamech finally said, straightening his neck. 'She will declare it tonight. If you care for her at all, you will respect her wishes.'

Barsabas' eyes narrowed. He raised a fist – some sort of signal to the soldiers? – then thought better of it and put his arm back down. 'What is your custom regarding this sacrifice? I would be pleased to give my guidance.'

'We have our own customs, Barsabas,' Kenan said. 'We do not need your northern ways. That said…' Kenan fixed Barsabas with a firm stare, 'we would welcome your involvement as a witness to this agreement, historic as it is.'

Barsabas, who'd been ready to interrupt before Kenan gave the concession, closed his mouth and nodded. A smirk crept over his features. 'As you wish, Elder. My family and I will wait and watch.'

Lamech's shoulders relaxed, and he put a hand on Yaval's. 'Prepare the goat, son.'

Barsabas moved back, standing in the space between the gatehouse and the colonnade. Yaval fetched the goat and tied it in the centre space, where a small stone platform had been erected with a wooden pole at one end. Then he secured its back legs with rope.

'The terms of our covenant are thus,' Yaval began. He took his time recounting those things he had explained to Adah a few days previously, ensuring every person involved could hear. Then Lamech, Kenan and Eber walked forward, and they each placed their hands on the back of the goat.

As senior, Kenan began. 'By the name of Yahweh Elohim, I do solemnly vow to uphold the terms of this covenant, in order that both our families may prosper, for the good of our descendants, the whole people of the city of Chanoch, and the glory of Yahweh. I declare that if I fail to uphold this covenant, may what is done to this creature be done to me and my family, that the name of Yahweh may not be dishonoured by my vow made here today.'

Lamech repeated the same words. Then Barsabas approached the goat's neck and spoke. 'I hereby declare that I have witnessed this covenant ceremony, and that this life is given to secure it. You may cut the covenant.'

While the three younger men held the goat in position, Kenan slit its neck with one swift movement. With tears in his eyes, Yaval lifted the back legs by the rope, hooking them high over a wooden post and allowing the blood to spill liberally over the platform until it pooled beneath the feet of the men standing there. They all watched as the animal involuntarily twitched – feeling nothing, for it had lost consciousness instantly – but disturbing, nonetheless. It brought home the words they had spoken. If any of them broke the covenant, such a fate would be theirs.

'Will none of the blood be collected?' Barsabas said, breaking the silence.

Kenan's head turned sharply, and he fixed Barsabas with a glare. 'Rituals with the blood are not our way. The covenant is sealed.'

A grin spread over Lamech's face, and he raised his arms. 'Now to the feast!'

Just like that, the tension broke, and the families abandoned the goat to hurry towards the hall. Adah gripped Juval's hand as they moved with the crowd, through the remaining courtyard, up the steps and down the corridor. Juval must have noticed the breath being squeezed from her lungs, for he pulled her into the kitchen courtyard, then carried her past the storehouses to the rear of the hall. Before she could comprehend what was happening, he had deposited her safely on the stage.

Shua spotted her, and within moments, was at her side. Then Tzillah approached from the front of the hall, ascended the wooden steps onto the platform and shuffled in on her left, followed by Naamah, Yaval and Tuval-Kayin.

Soon Lamech, having taken his time at the rear of the crowd, was striding up the steps with Kenan by his side. 'I apologise for the misunderstanding with Barsabas. I assure you my commitment to you is unwavering. You must sit with us in pride of place. Your sons too. How many are here?'

'Six, my friend.'

'Six sons. You have been blessed indeed.' Lamech made eyes at Shua to fetch another rug.

Kenan smiled. 'I have eight. The eldest left thirty years ago to marry into my kin in the west, and the young surprise is at home with his ima. I have five wonderful daughters as well.'

Lamech raised his eyebrows as a woman of slight figure and plain face ascended the platform with Kenan's six sons.

'Speaking of which, meet my daughter, Dania, who has an exceptional business head. She oversees the supervisors at the quarry – they are all terrified of her.' Kenan chuckled.

When there was no space around the low table, Juval rose to give Dania his seat.

Lamech put out a hand. 'Juval, you are my son. You need not leave. We'll make room.'

'Abba, I have little to do with the business. Please, let Dania take my space. I'd rather sit with my instruments anyway.' Juval flashed Dania a marvellous smile that seemed to set everyone at ease, then hastened to the other side of the stage. Once everyone was settled, Lamech asked if Kenan would bless Yahweh Elohim for the food.

Tzillah nudged Adah in the ribs and whispered. 'Since when do we say prayers?'

Adah bit her lip and followed everyone else, lifting her hands and eyes high.

When Tzillah got up to join the dancing after dinner, Azurak slipped into her vacated space. Adah's body tensed from neck to toe. With the aid of several cups of wine, she had managed not to slip into a panic. As the night advanced, even Kenan had relaxed enough to clap and sing along to the music. Yet Naamah's announcement still hadn't been made. What were they waiting for?

Adah listened with interest to Lamech and Kenan's conversation as they continued discussing their children.

'Of course, she is my only daughter,' Lamech said. 'A father's prize possession, as you well know, my friend.'

'Don't worry, Lamech. Gomer will treat her well. He has an excellent character – the best of his brothers.'

'Her happiness is all I desire, though she is of significant value to me.'

Kenan laughed. 'I'm aware, and I have been more than generous with my terms. Of course, we would both rather she wed Eber…'

'There can be little chance of that.' Lamech motioned to the couple at the other end of the table, aware of no one in the room but each other as Naamah tried to convince Gomer to dance.

Azurak had evidently been listening too. He edged closer to Adah. 'I thought we had an agreement.'

She gulped down another mouthful of liquor. 'I agreed to consider what you said, no more.'

'Then why are they speaking of Gomer?'

'Because Naamah loves him.'

Azurak tensed his fist beneath the table, but Adah saw it. 'Love is not the only consideration.'

'It is an important consideration.' Adah took a mouthful of food, trying to keep her hand steady.

'He is not good for her.'

'And who are you to decide on the goodness of a person?'

'I suggest you keep your tongue harnessed, mistress. I know Lamech lets you get away with speaking your mind, but you have no idea what I am capable of. Make an enemy of me, and you will regret it.'

'I thought you said you would never lay a hand on your master's property?' *Whereas Lamech has laid hands on me, many times.*

'Oh, I don't need to lay a hand on you to ruin your life.' The corner of Azurak's mouth twitched.

'My life is already ruined. My task now is to protect my children.'

'*I* am trying to protect your children. They are my future too. Trust me when I say that Eber is the right choice for Naamah. We need him in our camp.'

'He already is. Did you not witness the ceremony? He and Yaval made a bond, as sure as Lamech and Kenan did.'

'Such ceremonies are not as useful as a marriage. If Naamah marries Eber, she gains us influence. Influence we will never have if she is palmed off to Gomer and allowed to live in obscurity.'

'Lamech agreed she was not part of his game. We all agreed. This was not my decision.'

'Don't pretend you had nothing to do with it. I know you have far more influence than you let on. It is why I came to you.'

'Then you made a mistake. You should have gone straight to Tzillah.'

'Do you really want to make an enemy of me, Adah, when we could have been allies?'

'I will do whatever I need to do. Lamech is my husband, Azurak. If what you say is true, then I am indispensable to him, whereas you are not.'

Azurak laughed under his breath. 'Ah, mistress. Now that is where you are wrong. You will soon see just how powerful and indispensable I am.'

He rose and left, settling in a spot in the shadows behind Juval, where he had an unobstructed view of Naamah dancing but couldn't be seen by anyone except those who already knew he was there.

Adah breathed in through her nose and out through her mouth. She would not be scared into submission, no matter what Azurak threatened. If she could cope with Lamech, she could cope with him. Though, it was certainly worth trying to get her husband back on her side.

She was just considering how she might when a messenger burst into the room. He ran towards Barsabas, lounging on the far side of the hall with one of the serving girls pressed into his lap.

'Master Barsabas. Attacks in the north!'

Barsabas stood up, stumbling from his liquor. The girl fell to the floor, then shuffled behind him, humiliated.

'What attacks? Speak man.'

'There are rumours that northwestern armies are amassing against your lands. The Iradites return to reclaim them.'

'Rumours? I have no interest in rumours. Where is your evidence?'

The messenger opened his leather pouch and withdrew a copper armband – the figure of a serpent, crushed flat.

Barsabas snatched it. 'This belonged to my son.'

'Yes, my lord. He was murdered while out hunting.'

Adah gasped. She looked at Dinah, but Dinah's face was stone. How? Hadn't her child just been killed? Tzillah must have thought the same, for she wound her way to Dinah's side and enveloped her in an embrace.

Dinah brushed Tzillah off and stood tall. 'That belongs to Keber. Keber is not my son.' Then Dinah poked Barsabas in the arm. 'I told you trouble would come from installing your illegitimate son in the western province! You fool.'

Barsabas spun and slapped Dinah with such force that she almost toppled. The room gave a collective gasp. 'Anak, we are leaving.'

Anak stepped forward to meet his father, ignoring his mother.

'Join us if you wish.' Barsabas spat at Dinah. 'I care not.'

As Barsabas, Anak and the messenger made a hasty exit, something compelled Adah to glance in Azurak's direction. He lifted a hand at her and waved slightly, a smirk dominating his features. Was it possible this was his doing? Surely not. Yet the hollow opening in her gut told her that it was.

CHAPTER 49

Barsabas' armies were hastily packing up their camp, leaving behind them a mass of dead grass, burnt out campfires and pregnant women. Lamech was on his way to a consultation with the elders.

'We should go with Barsabas' men,' Juval said, running behind him.

'Out of the question,' Lamech replied.

'But they came to our aid. Isn't it right that we go to theirs?'

Lamech shook his head. *Foolish boy.* 'We have no idea what the situation is. We cannot move our hunters based on rumours brought by one messenger.'

'But Barsabas' dead son!'

Lamech halted and placed a hand on Juval's shoulder. 'Barsabas' *illegitimate* son. Dinah was right, and she is my sister. I am loyal to her before Barsabas. You know what that feels like, Juval. You are the same way with Naamah.'

Juval pursed his lips and nodded. 'It is true. If someone treated Naamah that way, I would kill them.'

'So you see, I am being gracious by allowing Barsabas to go freely. I have no intention and no obligation to help him.'

'Yes, Abba. I see.'

'Good boy.' Lamech strode between the eight poplar trees that formed the borders of the city square, into the company of elders – some forty men and women sat in a semi-circle on bushels of straw and wicker stools. They were selected to represent all the families in the city. Many were Chanoch's direct descendants, some, like Kenan, were not. All had seen at least four hundred summers and brought their collective wisdom to the proceedings. All except him.

He nodded at Kenan, who was looking slightly worse for wear next to Chanoch. Perhaps he had partied the old man a little hard the night before. It had been a good one. When Barsabas' entourage had left and the crowd had begun to stumble in confusion, Lamech had pulled out his final flourish, parading his benevolence as Naamah publicly chose Gomer for her husband. As they distributed the celebratory wine, the crowd had warmed again. Now everyone knew he was not like his father – he gave his daughter choice.

He must not smile. The elders' meeting was about Barsabas, and Lamech must temporarily forget about his triumph. Though he had given Azurak no specific instructions, to reveal any part in Barsabas' exit would be reckless indeed. He must keep to the same story he had just given Juval. *Distressed, Lamech. You are distressed.*

His grandfather spoke first. 'Lamech, thank you for coming. What is the news?'

'Barsabas' army will be ready to leave by sunset. They will travel through the night.'

'Have you discovered more about the cause of the trouble? Is there any threat to our lands?' another elder asked.

'Not that I am aware of. At present, the attack seems isolated to the western edge of Barsabas' land, far from his central city. His son was ambushed, and the entire hunting party slaughtered, except for one whom they released to carry the message to his master. He was told that if Barsabas did not surrender, the rest of his family would be next.'

'It doesn't sound like something my father's people would do.' Lamech's grandfather, Mehujael, was the youngest of the elders, having only recently joined them, and Lamech hadn't seen him so vocal in years. He was always quiet in their home. Lamech had almost forgotten he was related to the northern tribes.

'Indeed,' Chanoch added. 'The last I heard, my eldest son was still faithful to Yahweh, who requires a reckoning for the spilling of blood.'

'You know how quickly people can change, Abba,' Chanoch's daughter, Selah, said. She was the oldest woman in the assembly, and often Lamech's most vocal opponent. 'Barsabas forcibly took their lands. They must have regrouped, reinforced and returned to reclaim them.'

Chanoch stroked his chin and shook his head.

Lamech decided to change tactics. 'My sister Dinah is naturally distraught. I am going to my abba's house immediately after this council to see to her welfare. I believe we should make it a priority to support those the delinquent army are leaving behind.'

'Indeed,' Chanoch said. 'This was my principal fear when Barsabas arrived. His people have been catastrophic to the morality of the city.'

'Something I would appreciate your help in rectifying,' Lamech said. 'My son, Juval, is particularly concerned for the welfare of women.'

Next to him, Juval stood up straight, though Lamech noticed that Chanoch's eyes narrowed. Did he know of Juval's exploits?

He continued. 'I suggest setting up a group to identify those who need our help. Juval may coordinate it, and I will supply its needs. It's my deepest regret that innocents have been caught up in this when the reason we invited Barsabas was to protect them. I tried many times to get his troops under control, but alas, I have failed.'

Lamech hung his head, feigning shame, willing his son not to contradict his sincerity and ruin the ruse. Fortunately, Juval kept silent. Presumably he knew that to confess the lie was to incriminate himself.

Kenan spoke up. 'This sounds like an excellent idea. I will task Gomer with helping you, Juval. It would be good for you to work together, as you are going to be brothers. Any other volunteers?'

The elders talked amongst themselves for a moment, several putting forward someone who might be willing to help. Lamech dreaded to think what this idea was going to cost him, but he would find a way to make it beneficial. The most important thing at present was maintaining the elders' trust.

'That is settled then,' Kenan said at last. 'Please give our sympathies to your sister and let us know as soon as you have more news.'

'Of course. I have already sent riders to our borders to keep an eye out. At the first hint of trouble, I will know.'

Yet, there would be no trouble. For although Barsabas' son was certainly dead, there was no army of Iradites. If all went according to plan, by the time anyone realised it, Lamech's story would be so solidified that no one would doubt him.

'Thank you, Lamech. You may go. Now, on to this business with the plague…'

Lamech bowed his head and led Juval back through the poplar trees.

Once out of the elders' earshot, Juval spoke again. 'Abba, how are we to do this thing – looking after the women?'

'Firstly, you must ascertain which women have been left behind by the army. That should be easy with your experience and connections. Then set up a reward for any man who would take one as his wife – say, four seasons' worth of grain.'

'That's very generous, Abba.'

'On the contrary. The sooner we can get them off our hands, the better. Otherwise, we could end up with many more mouths to feed, and I do not want anyone accusing me of taking them as slaves. That would not do. Thanks to our recent acquisition of extra land in return for protective services, we have plenty of grain. Just don't tell anyone I said so.'

'Who do you think will marry the women, knowing they will birth another man's child?'

'It doesn't matter. Old men, young men, those already married… I care not.'

'What if the others object – those I must work with? They might insist on the husbands being reputable or single.'

'My son, have you learnt nothing? You don't need to explain everything. Tell people what they *want* to hear, nothing more. Appearances are everything, boy. Besides, it's better for a woman to be a second wife than to be left on the streets. Just look at Tzillah, she has an excellent life.'

'Yes, but she married you, Abba. Those women may not be so fortunate.'

Lamech smiled. 'I wish your mothers appreciated me as you do. From them, I get nothing but grief.'

As Juval left to begin his investigations, Lamech trudged on to his abba's house. He avoided the place as much as possible. Noa occasionally came to visit Tzillah, but they ceased joining her Shabbat celebrations the day Methushael touched Adah.

'Welcome, young master. It has been some time,' the gatekeeper said as he approached.

'Is my father in?'

'Yes.'

Any hopes that Methushael would be engaged in business vanished as Lamech entered the house to find his parents, his sister and his youngest unmarried brother sitting together inside. Dinah's two eldest daughters were in the far corner of the room, embroidering a large piece of cloth.

Methushael looked up as he entered. 'Lamech. I hope you come with good news.'

He nodded his head towards Dinah. 'Your husband has gone north with Anak. They left immediately after giving orders for the camp to pack up, with a small accompanying guard. The rest of the soldiers will be gone by tonight.'

Dinah, looking dishevelled for the first time in years, nodded and sniffed.

He lowered himself to sit next to her. 'What are your intentions?'

She opened her mouth to speak, then closed it again. Her hand, laid before her on the arm of her chair, was quivering. Lamech reached out and placed his fingers over hers, but she withdrew them.

Methushael spoke for her. 'Your sister is in distress. She has been publicly humiliated at your house. If I find out you had anything to do with this—'

Anger coursed through Lamech's veins, and he answered through clenched teeth. 'You will not find that out, because I did not.'

His abba leaned forward, fixing him with a stare. 'Dinah is my daughter. But Barsabas is like a son to me. I do not want to lose my son.'

Lamech's nostrils flared. 'Your son? *I am* your son! I am swiftly becoming the most powerful man in the city, with the elders now on my side. Will nothing I do ever be good enough for you, Abba?'

'Now, dearest. That isn't what your abba meant.' Noa widened her eyes at her husband.

Methushael grunted and shifted in his seat. 'You shame me, Lamech. Because of you, I shall forever be known as the man whose son was the first to take two wives.'

That was what this was all about? Barsabas had multiple concubines, had installed his illegitimate son over his lands, had slapped his daughter in front of one of the most important families in the city. And he still preferred that abomination to his own son?

Lamech stood, unable to take his father's presence any longer. 'I was not the first to take two wives, Abba. I was just the first to admit it.'

He made for the exit, ignoring his mother's calls. 'Lamech. Please, Lamech, come back.'

He would not go back. If he could help it, he would never return again.

CHAPTER 50

'Dinah has moved to Bekhor's house,' Tzillah said, several weeks after the covenant ceremony. Tzillah was trying on new tunics in her chamber and forcing Adah to watch and give her opinion. 'She's also asked Lamech to build her a permanent home.'

'Why Bekhor's?'

'Why do you think? She much prefers it there. She only stays with Methushael when Barsabas is with her because he insists. But her abba has always been harsh with her, using her only for his own gains.'

'Poor Dinah. We have more space than Bekhor. Couldn't she stay here?'

Tzillah raised an eyebrow. 'Really? You really think that would work out well?'

No. Although she and Dinah had made their peace, they shouldn't live together. 'Perhaps we could house her daughters? Wait – what is happening to Dinah's other children? She has five more in the north.'

'Yes, but don't judge Dinah by your standards, Adah. No doubt they will stay with their father. Whether she'll see them again I suppose depends on whether she and Barsabas ever reunite. In any case, Noa is on a mission to find husbands for the girls here. No doubt she'll have matched them up before the next full moon, whether she has permission from Barsabas or not.'

Adah sighed. 'That may be for the best. What a mess it all is.'

'Ima. Are you here?' It was Juval's voice, calling from the living quarters.

Adah stood up. 'I prefer the first one. This reveals too much flesh,' she said, pointing at Tzillah's tunic, then leaving the room.

Juval had thrown himself onto their newest item of furniture – a couch Bekhor had designed, covered with linen, underneath which he'd packed sheep's wool to make a softer seat. Gomer was next to him, and Adah soon noticed Naamah slipping into the room behind her.

'Ima, we've had an excellent day,' Juval said.

Adah had heard about Lamech's surprise project providing for the women and had taken a keen interest. She pulled up a chair as Shua entered with drinks for everyone.

'We've found husbands for five more women,' Gomer said. His eyes flickered to Naamah, who had settled on a woven rug near his feet.

'What sort of men are they?' Adah asked.

'Willing men. Is there a better kind?' Juval joked.

Adah tutted.

Gomer took a cup and thanked Shua. 'Actually, we are taking pains to ensure the women approve of their husbands. When the men come forward, we identify the neediest woman...'

'Those closest to giving birth or poorest,' Juval interjected.

'...and we let them meet each other,' Gomer said. 'Today, ten candidates spent the afternoon together in a group. Tomorrow, they will each come to us – women included – and state their preferences and then we will match up the best couples.'

'So far the system is working very well,' Juval said.

Gomer coughed. 'Of course, the circumstances are far from ideal. Yet, I think we stand a real chance at redeeming them.'

Adah's gaze fell on Naamah, who was looking up at Gomer adoringly. Gomer had taken Naamah's hand and was stroking her palm. 'I'm pleased you are doing your best for them. I find it hard to believe any woman would choose the lifestyle they've been dealt.'

'Well, some come from—' Juval began, but Naamah's eyes left Gomer and fixed her brother with a stare.

Juval laughed and glugged his drink. Naamah clearly didn't want her beloved having any clue that Juval might have associations with those women.

For the first time Adah wondered, *What if one of them is carrying my son's child? Would we ever know?*

'Gomer, how lovely to see you.' Tzillah walked in, wearing the shorter, lower-cut tunic, and bent over Gomer to kiss his cheek.

Naamah flushed at her mother's flirtatious behaviour, but Gomer merely laughed.

Tzillah perched herself on the edge of the couch and crossed one leg over the other. 'So, have you finished my daughter's home yet, Gomer?'

'Abba has given me a plot of land, and the materials. But Eber is being stubborn. He doesn't want to lend me any workers – says I should build it all myself. I am going as quick as I can, but I keep getting distracted carving intricate patterns on the doorways when I should be building more rooms.'

'I don't require much,' Naamah said. 'A simple house like Eliana's would be fine. I just want to be your wife.'

'Who's Eliana?' Gomer asked.

'Ima Adah's friend. I visit her sometimes with Yaval.'

Though not with me. I haven't been for so long, Adah thought.

Tzillah pinched Naamah's cheek. 'Nonsense, Naamah. You are the daughter of the best builder in the city, and we have the greatest house ever constructed. Lamech will never allow you to live as a pauper. Gomer must build you something impressive and his family must provide the means. It's a show of faith on Kenan's side. A promise that they will look after you.'

'And I will,' Gomer said. 'Eber is just being difficult because he's jealous. Perhaps I will bypass him and ask Dania for help instead.'

Naamah tentatively stroked Gomer's knee. 'You will fight for me, won't you?'

Lifting her fingertips, Gomer's lips brushed over them as he looked into her eyes. 'I would die for you.'

ADAH WAS SWAMPED in fabric. A season had passed since Naamah's engagement to Gomer, and she'd just taken delivery of Tzillah's order for the wedding. It was far too much. What were they to do with it all? Tzillah had already set her favourite seamstress to task on Naamah's dress, so one could only assume this fabric was for decorating the hall, or perhaps for setting Naamah up in her new home. Bed linen – could that be it? No, surely it was too fine.

'What is all this?' Adah heard Eliana's melodic voice from beneath the sheet she was folding. Pulling her head out, she beheld the welcome sight. Eliana was in her living room, and next to her was Shimiel.

'Abba. Eliana!' Adah threw the sheet down and jumped over it, trying to tread on as few spots as possible as she traversed towards her loved ones. Once there, she threw herself into their arms. 'It has been so long.'

'Yes, it really has.' Eliana chided. 'So long that we thought we better come and get you. Honestly, Adah, you've always been hopeless, but it's been a full cycle of the seasons since I saw you. Even you can do better than that.'

'Oh no, has it really been? Surely not so long for you, Abba?'

He shook his head. 'Close though. Little Yesha has grown the span of my hand since you last saw him.'

'Oh, Abba. I'm sorry.' Yesha was her youngest sibling – eleven years old now – though she barely knew him.

Eliana tutted. 'Now, we've already seen Shua and she's making herb tea, but I don't know how we're meant to sit down.'

'Let's go to the garden,' Adah said. 'Tzillah can sort this out when she gets back.'

As they had tea, Adah enquired after Rivkah and her half-siblings, interested to know how the farm was coming along with several extra people to manage it and the threat of the tanninim extinguished.

'I have to say, your husband has certainly redeemed himself in many eyes by getting rid of those beasts,' Abba said. He looked around, checking Lamech was nowhere to be seen. 'You know I have no great love for him, Adah, but he did a good thing there. It was dangerous trying to survive on the land.'

'My parents have moved back to their farm too,' Eliana said. 'It took a while – they were quite traumatised – but I'm so glad they've been able to go home. Not least because my house feels large now. Did you know that Elias is engaged?'

'No. That's wonderful. Who to?' Elias was Eliana's third son.

Apparently, the betrothed was the daughter of one of Eliana's *dear friends* – she had many. 'We will be sisters now. Isn't that wonderful? Though, I will have just five young ones left at home, and of course Mela, who still holds out for Yaval.'

'You know about that?'

'Of course. I know everything. Except his intentions...'

'I wish I could tell you. He loves her, Eliana. Truly. I think he must be waiting until he's established in Lamech's business. The covenant has gone a long way to help, but he's still trying to win his abba's favour.'

'Why? Why can't he just marry whom he wants?'

Adah sighed, her heart heavy. 'You know it doesn't work that way in this family.'

Abba slapped his knee and stood up. 'Well, I think it's high time we got you out of this house. Rivkah has prepared one of her famous stews, expecting you to join us for dinner. Are any of my grandchildren here? They are most welcome too.'

Fear tightened itself around Adah's already heavy heart, making her chest constrict and her breathing difficult.

'Adah?' Her abba looked about.

'No,' she managed to say. 'They are all working.'

'Oh, that's a shame. Just us then.' He spun on his heels and started skittering towards the archway, as much energy in his body as he'd always had. Yet Adah's feet remained firmly planted, weighed down with stones and unable to move.

Eliana reached forward and grabbed her arm. 'Come along.' She tugged, sending Adah off balance. 'What's the matter? Don't you want to come?'

Adah shook her head, then nodded. 'I do. Of course, I do. I just haven't left the house in—'

Eliana's brows drew together in concern. 'In how long, Adah?'

'I... I cannot recall.' But she could. She knew exactly how long it had been. She hadn't left the complex since the day after she was attacked. The last time she saw the hills was when she climbed the old watchtower to fetch Yaval for his banquet. It had been almost a year.

'All the more reason to get you out of this place.'

They took her arms, one on each side, and led her unyielding legs through the archway and the courtyard, up to the gatehouse.

'Good to see you, mistress,' Avram called as she nodded and stepped into the street.

Immediately, poverty hit her. Lining up against the walls of her home were men, women and children, most of them slumped in various states of weakness-fuelled anguish, all of them with little more than rags covering their skin marked with pox, sores and insect bites.

Several groaned as they passed. Those strong enough held out their hands, recognising the rich man's wife who used to bring them food on occasion.

'I... I'm sorry. I have nothing,' she stammered. Pulling her tunic over her nose and mouth, Adah realised why she'd thought there was an issue with the supplies in their storehouses for many moons past. The smell of the bodies outside had made it over the walls. No wonder Shua had raised her eyebrows every time Adah had asked her if she'd checked for dead rats.

'Hurry along,' Abba muttered, 'before there's any trouble.'

'But I should feed them.'

'You can organise that when you get home,' Eliana confirmed. As if to prove the point, a hand grasped Adah's ankle suddenly and the feeling transported her immediately back to the alleyway she'd been seized in. Instinct kicked in. She squealed, kicked and trod on the hand, then started running, hoping to find relief in the next street.

There was none. Bodies lined this too.

'How long has it been like this?' she panted when the others caught up. 'What has happened?'

'You don't know?' Eliana's face betrayed her disgust. 'Adah, you are the only person of my acquaintance who has the power to change any of this, and you don't even know?'

'The children mentioned sickness in the city, but I had no idea it was this bad. Lamech tells me nothing.'

'Has he forced you to stay inside your home?'

Adah shook her head. *No, he had not. Fear forced her.*

'Come on,' her abba said. 'Let's get out of the city. Then we can breathe and talk freely.'

The further they got from her home, the fewer people were on the streets and the more Adah was able to relax.

'Those most unfortunate crowd around the homes of the rich, hoping for charity,' Abba explained.

As they left the gates behind and started ascending the hill, Eliana looked behind her. 'There's a man following us.'

Adah didn't need to look. 'That'll be my shadow.'

'He follows you everywhere?'

'Yes.'

Eliana smirked. 'He can't have been very busy recently.'

'No. He's obviously lost his touch, or you wouldn't have noticed him. He's been with me since the twins were born.'

Eliana softened a little. 'Does Lamech trust you so little?'

'He says it's for my safety.' *And he's right. Shadow killed the two men who attacked me. But who killed the old man?*

'Probably just as well,' her abba confirmed. 'There are so many in dire need, it won't take much to send them over the edge.'

Adah thought about the men who had attacked her. She hadn't seen their faces until they were dead. Had that been why they'd done it – dire need? That didn't make sense, though. She had been trying to help. She'd been giving out food. And they had wanted something else. Her feet froze again, and Eliana had to wrap her arms around her and push to get her moving again.

'What has happened? Why are so many sick?' she asked at last.

'One plague after another ravages the city,' Eliana said. 'Some of it seems to have been brought in by Barsabas' army – women were the first to fall prey to that. Other diseases have been getting steadily worse over time. The last plague to hit was so contagious, it ran through the poorest neighbourhoods like a wildfire.'

Her abba skipped out in front. 'The best thing we can do is get out of the city and move back to our farms. Overcrowding seems to make everything a lot worse.'

Eliana strode ahead and turned. 'Yes, the air feels much thinner out here, don't you think Adah?'

She looked about, drinking in the countryside for the first time in so long. After taking a long, deep breath, she smiled. 'Indeed, it does.' *If only I could stay here.*

CHAPTER 51

The following morning, Adah woke at dawn filled with conviction. After hastily throwing on an old tunic, she pattered outside. She was pleased to see Avram in place at the gate; she'd never built a rapport with the nightwatchman.

'Shadow?' She called out as she passed through the courtyard, hoping he would come forward. She still had no idea what his real name was. 'Shadow.'

After a few moments, the familiar form stepped out from behind a column.

'Good. I have a job for you. Come.'

Shadow lifted an eyebrow then rubbed his eyes. It was funny to see him sleepy. She'd only ever known him to be alert and efficient, but she supposed that waiting for something to happen for many seasons would take its toll on anyone's watchfulness.

She strode over to Avram at the gate and beckoned Shadow forward. 'Those people out there. I want to help them. I need you two to let them in, no more than four at a time, and take them to the garden. There, I will minister to their wounds, feed them and provide them with new clothes. As soon as Leah is awake, I'll send her to market for supplies.'

Shadow's eyes widened and for only the second time, she heard his voice. 'Mistress, the master will not like it. He has been at pains to protect your family from this plague, and from other dangers.'

'I don't expect anyone else in the household to help. I will tend them myself.'

'What if you catch it, mistress?'

Strange that she should have so little fear of that, when terror usually gripped her like a fiend in an alleyway. Yet this instinct for self-sacrifice that she'd so often felt as regards her children, now extended to those innocents outside, shaking out her fear like the dust on a rug. She no longer needed it.

'I don't really care. If I die, at least I will know I've lived for some good purpose.'

'Of course we'll help you, mistress,' Avram said.

Shadow still looked unsure. That was understandable – after all, it was his job to protect her, but she fixed him with a pleading glance. 'Do you have family?'

'There's not much time for that, mistress.'

'Has anyone you know died from these plagues?'

Shadow's face fell, and he investigated the earth. 'Yes.'

Adah reached a hand forward and touched his with it. He flinched. 'Do this for them,' she said. 'If Lamech objects, I'll deal with it.'

That day, Adah ministered to three groups of people, the worst of those directly outside the gate. As soon as it became known that she was helping, people started hustling to be seen next, but Avram and Shadow's formidable guard, and a couple of forceful removals, soon reinstalled patience among those on the street.

Adah knew she was putting the men at risk also, and felt a certain measure of guilt for it, but the conviction that this was the right thing to do remained. For the first time, Shadow became a person. She learned his name, though she'd thought of him as Shadow for so long, she couldn't quite adopt it.

He gave a little smile, the most she'd seen cross his face. 'Don't worry, mistress. Shadow will do just fine.'

She noticed that his eyes were green like the hillsides and his hair, which she'd always thought of as black, was actually dark brown with streaks of blonde in it. She wondered what it would be like to dedicate your whole life to a job, so that you couldn't live outside the complex or have a family of your own. It was the same for Shua and Leah, she supposed, though it seemed different somehow for Shadow. At least they could go out when their work was done, and they had days off. Avram went home every night to his wife, and several of his children worked for them as general help. Whereas Shadow must be constantly alert.

As she tended the sick in the garden, Avram stayed guarding the gate, but Shadow stood watch over her, in case of any trouble. 'Desperate people can do desperate things,' he said.

When Yaval entered on his way to see the goats, Adah asked a favour of him. 'I have a job for you.'

'I'm terribly busy, Ima. I've been working with Eber to review practices at the quarry.'

'This job requires a day out on the hills.'

'Oh. Well in that case...' Yaval grinned.

'I'm going to need a lot more of these herbs.' She pushed a few varieties into his hands. 'If we get them all from the marketplace, Lamech will baulk at the resulting trade.'

Yaval ran the stalks through his fingers. 'Yes, I know where to find these. I'll gladly take baskets and fill them up. Ima – why the sudden action?' he asked as he motioned to the gatekeeper's son to join him.

Adah chewed her lip. 'I'm not sure. I just... I must do something.'

The truth was that the conviction she'd woken up with was like nothing she'd experienced before. It filled her entire soul, from her gut to the pressure behind her eyes, she knew it was something that could only be released by doing the right thing. As she knelt, dipping cloths into warm, salted water and cleaning dirt from wounds as she would clean out a goat's maggoty hoof, she felt an intense sense of peace.

Peace reigned over the whole enterprise as the pitiable, wretched persons – who had never seen luxuries like those that filled every space of her ornamental garden – stared with wide-eyed fascination at their surroundings. It was the perfect distraction from their pain.

Leah kept a steady stream of food coming, placing fresh bread, fruit and salted meat just within the entrance to the garden, but she didn't let Leah get close to the sick. Adah wasn't worried that Lamech would notice the food. They provided far more at the banquets so frequently given.

The peace in her heart didn't cease until she was finishing for the day. Shadow had seen the last group of people out and Adah went to enter the house for the first time since she'd risen at dawn. Suddenly, an intense burning behind her eyes stopped her in her tracks.

Ah! Am I sick already?

The answer came in the impulse to strip off her tunic.

'Leah,' she called, as she pulled it over her head.

'Yes, mistress?' Leah barely batted an eyelid as Adah stood naked in the secluded inner courtyard.

'Would you bring me a fresh bowl of salted water and a clean tunic?'

Leah returned directly and Adah washed herself from head to toe. As she did so, the pressure behind her eyes abated. *That was what it meant, then.*

Once dressed in her clean tunic, she left instructions about the filthy one before going indoors.

'Feeling better?' Tzillah queried, looking up from swathes of fabric covering her lap and beyond.

'What do you mean?' Adah asked, suddenly realising she hadn't eaten herself.

'Your little project today. Has it given you satisfaction?'

'Yes.' Adah smiled. 'Yes, it has.'

Tzillah smirked. 'Well, enjoy it until the novelty wears off. Just don't bring the plague into my house before the wedding.'

THE FOLLOWING WEEK, Adah was in the garden tending her first round of daily patients when she heard a ruckus coming from the courtyard.

'Just leave me alone!'

'But Naamah, please—'

'I don't want to speak to you. I don't want to see you. I can't believe you would do this.'

Adah poked her head through the archway to see Naamah fleeing into the house, in the previous night's clothing, and Juval following her. What was going on?

Shadow raised his eyebrows.

'I think we're done here,' Adah said, as she cleaned off the last person's feet. 'After they've finished eating, would you see them out?'

Shadow nodded.

Leah had already left salted water and a tunic in the courtyard, so Adah swiftly washed and changed, then made her way into the house. Juval stood in the living area, banging his fist against the wall. Naamah was gone.

'My love, what's happening?' she asked, looking around for Tzillah, who wasn't there. They were alone.

Juval turned to her. His face was streaked with tears and his eyes betrayed a sleepless night.

'We spent the night at Eber's – you know he has his own house? – Naamah, Gomer and I, and some other friends. There was a party. I drank too much. I…' He slammed his hand into the wall again. 'Oh, Ima. What have I done?'

Adah cradled his shoulders and held him as sobs racked his upper body.

'It's all his fault… No, I can't blame it on him. It is my disgusting mind. I have battled. I have fought. I cannot win. Oh why, Ima? Why?'

She had no idea what he was talking about, except that it was clear Juval had done something he deeply regretted. 'Whose fault?' she asked gently.

'Azurak.'

'Azurak?' What had he to do with their party? He never joined the young ones in their exploits. He was far too subversive for that.

Juval drew away from the wall and threw himself into a chair. Adah gently lowered herself next to him and waited. After a while, he spoke again.

'It was something he said, Ima. He mentioned The Wanderer and his wife…'

The Wanderer – Azurak mentioned him?

'He said they were siblings. It was just in passing, but it stuck in my mind…'

Adah's eyes widened. *What could this mean? Surely not—*

Juval rubbed his eyes then pulled his hands down, leaving them on his cheeks. He looked up at her, as if willing her to understand so he needn't explain. 'Married siblings.'

She had to say something. 'You… you love Naamah. You told her?'

'I kissed her.'

Adah's hand flew to her mouth. She bit down everything she wanted to scream out. *No, Juval. Why would you do that? She is your sister! She loves Gomer. She trusted you. Why, Juval, why?*

Instead of screaming, she just nodded, needing him to know he could continue. For he was her son too, and she loved him unconditionally, even if at this moment she wished to flee from the room.

'Everyone was asleep, lying all over the floor and cushions. Naamah and I were next to each other. She opened her eyes sleepily. I reached forward, I couldn't help myself. I didn't want to, Ima...' He rubbed his eyes again, then stared at the floor. 'Gomer saw it.'

Adah's chest tightened. She hadn't thought it could get any worse.

Juval's eyes welled. 'You hate me now.'

She wanted to deny it, wanted to pull him into her arms, but she could not. Disgust welled up inside her like a rotten egg, and she wanted to spew it all out. It was all she could do to stay silent and still. He had violated his own sister. He had ruined her chance at a loving marriage. He was... he was...

She sank her head into her hands. *He is just like his father.*

Juval waited a moment, then spoke again. 'What are we going to do, Ima?'

Slowly she lifted her head and fixed her gaze back on her son. 'How did Gomer react?'

'He ran from the house. Naamah pushed me away and followed him, but she couldn't catch up.'

'Where might he be now?'

'I don't know. At his house. Or maybe, the quarry? He went in that direction.'

'I will go to him.'

'Let me come with you—'

'No. Shadow will come. You stay here and stay away from your sister.'

Adah fled from the room, but she couldn't allow her emotions loose. Before she reached the outer gate, she spotted Tzillah coming in. 'Cancel all your plans and go to your daughter,' she said. 'Tell no one what she says. Just stay with her.'

Tzillah furrowed her brow, but Adah left no room for argument, pressing onwards, confident that Shadow would not be far behind. She pushed her way through the crowds of sick lining the streets, forcing herself not to get distracted as she headed for the eastern gate. *They won't hurt you, and this is more important.* Once outside the city, she breathed more easily and slowed her pace somewhat.

Shadow caught up with her. 'What is happening, mistress? I can see your panic.'

'I need to find Gomer. Stay behind, out of sight.'

When she entered the quarry, a quick word with the foreman on duty ascertained Gomer's whereabouts. Eber was nowhere to be seen. She pressed on to the rear of the site, not stopping to marvel at the huge piles of stone they were hauling around, or the sandstone cliff-edge being chipped at by fifty or so men holding sharper, harder rocks.

Gomer was among them, putting all his effort into the task at hand, like the stone was his enemy. No creativity for him today – this was pure fury. She called his name.

He turned his head, and she saw the redness of his eyes, blood vessels broken by grief. Realising who she was, he returned immediately back to his task with gritted teeth.

'Gomer. Please let me talk with you.'

He ignored her.

'I won't leave until you do. I have all day.'

Gradually his arm dropped. He sniffed back his passion, collecting himself enough to realise that he didn't want to have the conversation in front of his peers. 'Follow me,' he said, jumping down, dropping his tool and making for a quieter area where no rock was currently being hewn.

Adah began. 'Naamah loves you.'

Gomer choked. 'She kissed him.'

'He kissed her.'

'It makes no difference.'

'It makes *all* the difference.'

Gomer sniffed again and drew in the dirt with his foot.

'Did you see her kiss him back?' Adah asked.

He did not respond.

'Did you?'

Gomer looked up. 'No.'

Compassion for this young man swelled in Adah's heart. She knew what it felt like to be betrayed. 'My son is a confused person. He's had Naamah's attention all his life; he doesn't know how to live without her. But he can. And he will.'

'It is disgusting.'

'Yes. He is... very susceptible to influence and too much like his father.' She considered Azurak's words to Juval. He said they'd been 'made in passing,' but Adah knew better.

'I thought Juval was my friend.'

Adah instinctively reached forward but stopped herself. 'I know. I'm sorry. All the same, Naamah does love you.'

Gomer stamped the foot he'd been drawing with. 'How can I marry into such a family? I want nothing to do with... with any of you!'

'I understand. Yet, I was hoping you would marry into our family precisely so you can take Naamah away from all this. I have been protecting her for many years. Now, Yahweh has given you the task. Please consider it again.'

The young man shook his head. 'You ask a lot.'

'Please.'

He was still staring at the ground. Adah ventured a step forward and when he looked up, she caught his eye. 'Do you love her?'

'You know I do.'

'Then do this for her sake.'

'What about Juval? What if he tries it again?'

'He is already disgusted with himself. I don't think it's likely. And she doesn't want him.' She stared deeply into Gomer's eyes, hoping that somewhere he would see her trustworthiness.

'Alright. Tell Naamah I will wait for her at my father's house tonight. We can talk.'

Adah wanted to throw her arms around him, but she contented herself with a small smile. 'Thank you, Gomer. You are a good man.'

CHAPTER 52

As Azurak watched Adah exiting the quarry, fury mounted in his chest. His passing comment to Juval had worked perfectly. He had witnessed the young man grow increasingly agitated, had known it was only a matter of time before his self-control failed. To think Gomer had seen it too – it was perfect.

But no, Adah had to step in, didn't she? Had to step in and ruin everything. Oh, how he hated her. If it wasn't for Lamech's continued, irrational passion for the woman, he'd be tempted to dispatch her now. Instead, he'd have to dispatch someone else.

From his viewing point atop the cliff, he considered the sight below. It was the middle of the day and there were far too many people about to do anything at the quarry. He thought through the other things he needed to do that day. There weren't many. He'd long since stopped overseeing individual building sites, allowing foremen under him to do the arduous work while he oversaw Lamech's other… activities. Since Barsabas' armies had left, his chief role – enforcer of order in the camps – had ceased to exist.

Shame. He'd enjoyed rallying the soldiers behind iniquity. What sins they hadn't been committing when they arrived, they'd certainly been committing by the end of it. And his biggest triumph had been getting Juval involved, training him in the ways of his father. Adah had no idea how well he'd succeeded in corrupting her son. And the best part? Everyone blamed it on Barsabas. Lamech could stand as a beacon of light in comparison to that man.

There was a very real risk his current project would backfire. He'd have to be very careful. Lamech wouldn't approve, that was the trouble. Most things he suggested, Lamech agreed with, so long as they could be passed off as his own idea. Yet he had taken a strange liking to Kenan and his artistic, sensible son, and he wouldn't like the idea of his second-in-command interfering, even though it was for his own good.

But interfere he must. For Azurak could not allow Gomer to marry Naamah, and it wasn't just because his own lust kept him awake at night and distracted his mind. He needed an influenceable Eber at the helm of his father's business. Azurak had been grooming him for some time and neither his own passions, nor Naamah's, nor Gomer's could interfere with the future he had planned.

Gomer had to go.

His fingers ran over the hilt of the knife Tuval-Kayin had given him. It was a piece of art. Almost the colour of copper, but strong like flint, and far easier to handle, thanks to its narrow blade, sharpened to perfection. This blade could kill swiftly – skilfully in his hands. Yet it was also traceable. No weapon of Tuval-Kayin's could be used, not without pointing suspicion at Lamech.

Azurak looked about for a good place to spend the remainder of the afternoon until the quarry emptied, and he could figure out a way to enact his intentions. Then he spied it – a boulder already hewn but left abandoned on a ridge. The track up to it was empty. He tutted under his breath. An accident waiting to happen. It was ideal.

Sliding over the cliffs like a snake, he reached a spot where he could settle near enough to the boulder. Then he pulled a piece of grass to chew on, laid back and closed his eyes.

When he opened them, most of the workers had left for the day, but Gomer remained. He was always one of the last to leave, being oddly conscientious, even though he cared little about the work. It was because he liked going around at the end of the day, inspecting the rocks, seeing if any of them might be useful to him. He had a strange mind, that one.

Azurak shuffled further down, picked up the digging stick discarded near the boulder and tried it. It was too short. Checking no one was looking up, he lifted himself higher and spied a much better branch nearby. After retrieving it, he slipped it between the rock and the cliff edge. Then he waited.

Three workers made their exit. Just Gomer was left. Azurak knew that Eber would be on the other side of the quarry overseeing another group of men, but too far away to see anything. It was time.

Disguising his voice, Azurak cried out.

Gomer, about fifty paces off, looked up.

'Help, somebody help me,' he continued.

Gomer looked around, trying to ascertain where the voice was coming from. Then he took a few steps.

'I'm stuck.'

Gomer picked up the pace. 'Don't worry, friend, I'm coming.'

Almost there.

Gomer found the track leading up to the boulder, then started scaling it. 'Are you high?'

'Beyond the ridge. I can't move.'

Just a little closer.

Azurak pushed the branch down hard, then pulled it towards him. The boulder didn't move far enough. He wedged it further, then pulled with all his might. The boulder rolled slowly as the branch snapped. Leaning back against the crag, Azurak put his feet against the rock and pushed.

It tipped over the ridge.

Gomer heard it. He raised his head, eyes widening in terror as the rock hurtled towards him. There was no time or space to escape the narrow track.

The boulder's release revealed Azurak's position. A flicker of recognition crossed Gomer's eyes before he threw himself down, covering his head. The rock crashed on top of him, concealing his body with a satisfying crack.

Azurak paused. *Now what?* Should he make sure Gomer was dead, or leave immediately?

He glanced around again, checking no one had seen him. The men on the other side of the quarry, some two hundred paces away, had heard the noise. They were running his way. Slipping out from his crevice, he pulled himself up and over the cliff edge, then ran.

CHAPTER 53

Something had happened with Barsabas, a discovery of sorts, and his messenger was at the city gate. The news, relayed by Azurak, interrupted Lamech's breakfast.

'He's demanding an audience with you, master,' Azurak whispered, his face unreadable.

Anger seethed in Lamech's chest, but he would not let it show. Lamech rarely joined the family to break fast, but he had been doing so since the tragedy two weeks before, as a sign of solidarity with his daughter. Tzillah had made it clear, in no uncertain terms, that she expected his presence, and strangely, he'd been rather enjoying it.

He looked over at Naamah, sitting head down, hair and face unmade, food untouched before her. Despair, that's how he might best describe it. Had he ever felt what she was feeling? The closest he could recall was the day Adah fled his father's house, and he had to fight to win her back. Then, fear had projected him into determination. By contrast, Naamah sat vacant, overwhelmed by her loss, for there was no recovering it. Gomer was dead.

'Make him wait. I am eating,' Lamech replied.

Azurak lifted one brow, glanced at Naamah, then bowed his head. 'I will wait for you by the gatehouse.'

Lamech considered Tzillah. His second wife gave him a small, grateful smile, then took a bite of bread. Lamech sighed. He'd better get on with it. Quickly finishing the food before him, he stood up, gave Naamah a brief hug, Tzillah and Adah a kiss, and the boys a pat on the shoulder.

'Do you want me to come with you, Abba?' Juval asked.

His second son was increasingly interested in his business since taking on the fallen women and had done very well at walking the line between outward compassion and advantageous action. Lamech could tell something had happened between him and Naamah – why else would she be refusing his comfort in her grief – but his wives seemed to be dealing with it, so he need not concern himself. Besides, it had given Juval greater focus.

He considered his son's question. *No.* If Barsabas had in any way discovered the details of Azurak's duplicity, it was better Juval knew nothing about it. 'Thank you, son, but you needn't trouble yourself.'

Leaving no time for argument, he exited and strode towards his second-in-command.

'Have they discovered what you did?'

'I don't know,' Azurak said. 'The man wouldn't speak to me but demanded to see you specifically.'

'And the elders?'

'No request for them to convene as yet.'

That was a relief. Spontaneous duplicity was hard enough if you were deceiving one person, let alone two interested parties with different objectives. 'We cannot risk anything being overheard.'

'There is an ill-tended field a short walk to the south of the gate.'

'That's ideal. Stay by my side, Azurak. And try to look innocent.'

The messenger wasn't happy about being escorted to an empty field with no witnesses. His eyes flitted around, and his feet danced over the ground like he was walking on hot ash.

'Stand still, man,' Lamech growled. 'Now tell me what you have to say.'

The jittery man spat out his words. 'There are no Iradites. My master has done a thorough sweep of his land and hasn't found a single trace of an army.'

'Not a year has passed. Perhaps they are still amassing their fighters?'

'Why would they send such a clear message if they were not ready to fight?'

Lamech snorted. 'How should I know? I am not the one who took their lands.'

'My master believes they did not send the message at all. Someone else did.' The man fixed him with a knowing glare, though the trembling in his hands betrayed how scared he was.

Lamech took a step forward. Why would Barsabas send such a weakling as his emissary? If he had evidence, he would be here with his army, demanding a reckoning. Instead, he had sent this scrawny, middle-aged man, with no power to frighten them into admitting their part. What game was he playing?

The man quaked before him, which was rather satisfying.

'Tell your master, we are very sorry to hear there has been no justice for his son but are also glad he is not under attack.'

'My master wants assurance that, in return for leaving the situation be, you will aid him against any future attacks, providing your hunters to reinforce his fighting men in his efforts to establish peace.'

Ah, so that was Barsabas' game – blackmail. He had his suspicions, but no evidence. He hoped that by dangling those suspicions before Lamech, he could scare him into reassigning his fighters to Barsabas' army, leaving Lamech's city entirely defenceless. An easy target for Barsabas' next assault.

Lamech looked at Azurak. What did he think? How confident was he that he had covered his tracks?

Azurak, almost imperceptibly, shook his head.

Lamech turned back to the messenger. 'Tell your master that I owe him nothing. He violated my sister's honour. He should be grateful I let him go without demanding recompense.'

The scrawny man slid back from his shadow, chewing his bottom lip. 'My master also said that if you did not provide your word, he would send a delegation to the elders, suggesting your involvement.'

Lamech clenched his fist. It would be easy to land it in this man's face, then leave Azurak to clear him up. Yet that would almost certainly lead to worse consequences, which Barsabas well knew. They had killed Barsabas' son. It had not been exactly what he'd had in mind when he'd asked Azurak to create a little chaos, but the deed was done. Was his reputation with the elders strong enough to withstand such an accusation? Possibly not. This could ruin everything he was trying to achieve.

'I cannot promise him armies. Not yet. Even so, I do not wish to make enemies with my brother. What else might your master accept as a show of good faith?'

The scrawny man's eyes lit up and a crooked smile spread across his face. Lamech tried to smile back, but the face really needed his fist in it. It was all he could do to keep his hand by his side.

'Your daughter,' the messenger said. 'He would take your daughter as a wife for his son, Anak.'

ADAH COULDN'T BELIEVE her ears. Poor Naamah was in mourning, devastated by the loss of the man she loved, and Lamech would stoop so low to ask her this?

He had returned furious from his meeting with the messenger. He and Azurak had clearly had an argument on the way, for Azurak's face also looked like a thundercloud – indeed she'd never seen such emotion on it.

Lamech knelt before Naamah as she sat on one of the wicker stools in the living area, unusually humbling himself. He took her hands in his and stroked them. 'I wouldn't ask you unless there was no other option.'

Azurak's eyebrow raised. He wanted to say something – Adah could see he was holding back, trying to submit to his master, though it was killing him.

'I thought you got on with Anak?' Lamech said.

Naamah rubbed her nose, her bloodshot eyes filling with tears. 'I used to. Until he started leering at me and allowing his hands to wander under my tunic.'

Adah shivered. Just like Methushael had done to her. Lamech had hated that. Would he hate it happening to his daughter?

Her husband's jaw stiffened.

Azurak took a step forward. 'We should also consider our obligation to Kenan.'

Lamech shot him a vehement glare.

'What obligation?' Naamah whispered.

Lamech's shoulders sagged. He stroked Naamah's hand. 'Azurak thinks it would be better if we honoured our commitment to Kenan's family and found another way with Barsabas.'

'What does that mean – honour our commitment?'

'He wants you to consider marrying Eber.'

Naamah's eyes opened wide, and her gaze swept from her abba to Azurak, past her ima, and then rested on Adah. Adah's heart sank. What a position for her poor girl to be in. She had suffered betrayal from her brother, the crushing death of her beloved, and now she was being asked to choose between marrying two men she didn't like while still in mourning.

'I have told the messenger he must give us a day to consider.'

'But I don't want to marry either of them, Abba!' Naamah sobbed.

'My daughter, if we do not give Barsabas something, it could mean war between our people. Endless fighting. Think how many could die? Now, Azurak and I will do our best to come up with an alternative, but this was Barsabas' only offer. If we do not accept it, and he invades the city, we will need all the friends we can get. Having Kenan on our side will ensure the elders collaborate with us to avert disaster. If we scorn both prospects, we are on our own. Do you understand?'

As tears flowed down Naamah's cheeks, Adah couldn't help but intervene. 'What makes you think Kenan will turn against us if she doesn't marry one of his sons? He doesn't seem to be an unreasonable man.'

Azurak flashed her an angry glare. His fingers ran over the hilt of the blade tucked in his pouch. She knew it was there, for Lamech had one the same. What was Azurak's part in all of this? Why was he so determined to see Naamah in Eber's clutches?

Lamech, unaware of Azurak's expression behind him, rose and turned to her. 'The wedding was scheduled for next week, Adah. We have already put things in place and acquired elements of the betrothal agreement. My preference is satisfying Barsabas and laying this whole situation to bed, but I hear what Azurak is saying. We've worked hard to win Kenan's trust; I don't want to break that now. And whatever you may think of me, Adah, neither do I want to send my daughter into Barsabas' clutches. So, Naamah, you have a day to decide your preference. But decide you must.'

As the two men left the room, Naamah broke down, and Adah enfolded her in her arms, wishing she could do something more.

'Ah, men!' exclaimed Tzillah and joined the embrace. 'What have you done to upset Azurak?'

Adah kissed Naamah's head. 'I refuse to play his games.' *Yet he's winning anyway.*

'Be careful, Adah,' Tzillah murmured. 'He is one enemy you don't want to make.'

CHAPTER 54

'So, what do we have to offer Barsabas besides my daughter?' Lamech asked as they strode away. 'What's good enough to satisfy him?'

'Last time you lent him your services.'

'I'm not going north again. There is too much at stake here. From now on, we secure our position, Azurak. We have laid the foundations, now we must build walls so impenetrable, no rumour can threaten them.'

'Yes, master. How about Tuval-Kayin?'

'I'm not giving Barsabas my son.'

'No, I mean his metal. Barsabas would be interested in that.'

Lamech thought for a moment. 'No. Tuval-Kayin is my secret weapon. He will be the advantage we have over Barsabas if it comes to war. In fact, we must instruct him to make more weapons immediately – just in case.'

'I will go to the forge directly.'

'Then spend the rest of the day doing some digging. Discover what Barsabas lacks, so we can find a way to bribe him.'

'Yes, master.'

Up ahead, Lamech spied one of the elders – a less prominent one, but someone he'd been keen to get on his side, for he suspected him of being less morally astute than others. He'd seen him in the tavern on several occasions. 'Ah, Naman, my friend. How is your new wife?' As Naman approached, Lamech dismissed his second-in-command. 'Come to my house tonight to finish our discussion.'

Azurak nodded and left.

'Lamech,' Naman said, slapping him on the back. 'I must congratulate you on your son, Juval. A very impressive young man.'

'You are pleased with your wife then?'

Naman was at least five hundred, and from what Juval had told him, had acquired a wife in her first century from Juval's program. They'd discussed it because Gomer had been unsure about granting the request, and Juval had needed his father's support to overrule him.

'Yes, yes,' Naman said. 'The baby was born a couple of weeks ago. She dotes on him, and I was pleased to adopt another son, for I had mainly girls, you know.'

'And your first wife – she is happy with the arrangement?' His first wife was as old as him.

'Oh, well.' Naman chuckled. 'I daresay she'll get used to it. I am looking forward to the young lady being recovered from the birth.' Naman wiggled his eyebrows.

Lamech laughed. 'Of course you are. Then you receive the reward for your charity, hey, my friend?'

'She's a good mother, though. I thought she might be a little wild; in fact, I hoped she might be.' Naman winked. 'However, many of these girls have just been dealt a bad hand, wouldn't you say? They're not bad at heart.'

Lamech thought of the games they often played in the tavern, taking small bones and rolling them to see who could get closest to a cup. Invariably, the shape of the bone determined who won more than the skill of the thrower. He supposed it was like that for many women. They did not choose the families they were born into – the bones they were given to throw. 'Still, most can choose whether to work an honest living or a dishonest one,' he concluded.

'Fortunately for us, many choose the latter.'

Lamech laughed again. He'd had no idea Naman was such a bold sinner. He must be skilful at duplicity to keep company with the elders.

'What is your trade, Naman? I forget.'

'Fabrics.'

'I wonder whether there is some deal we could make that would be mutually beneficial.'

Later that day, Lamech was holding forum in his courtyard when a bedraggled-looking man entered. Lamech made sure to open the gates once each full moon, so that any workers could come and air their grievances. It gave the impression of an employer who had their interests at heart and had been extremely successful in recent years as a peace-keeping device, particularly amongst the slaves.

The afternoon had been quiet. Azurak must be dealing with most issues effectively. Lamech leaned his chair back and ushered the scruffy man forward. He looked like a slave.

'Master Lamech.'

'Welcome. What can I do for you?'

'My name is Yosa, son of Ebed. I have been under your care for two years, master, working on your sites as a labourer.'

'Very good. Go on.'

'The terms of my deal were that I would work for two years as payment for a debt to the man who used to supply my grain. He handed me over to you, for you were building a home for his son. Now I have worked my time, I... I should be free.'

Lamech lifted his hand. 'That is wonderful news. Congratulations on earning your freedom.'

'So... so, I am free then?'

'Of course. I will ensure that all the information is correct when Azurak arrives— Ah, here he comes now.'

Azurak entered through the gateway and strode over.

Lamech held out a hand of welcome. 'Azurak. Yosa here claims he has worked his debt.'

Azurak narrowed his eyes, studying the man's face. Often people looked quite different after their time of hard labour. 'Who was your debtor?'

'The farmer, Tiras, son of Ripat.'

'Ah, I remember,' Lamech exclaimed. 'When did we build his son's house, Azurak?'

'Two years hence, I believe.'

'Then the dates match up. Very good. You are free then. What work will you go back to, my friend? I take it you were not a farmer.'

'No, master. I was a tanner.'

'A tanner? A good trade. Where is your workplace? I must visit you and make an order.'

The scraggly man looked at the ground. 'I lost my property when I could not pay my debts. Tiras seized it, for it was near his land. He uses it as a barn now.'

'Ah, I see. Was this for the same debt?'

'No. Twice I could not fulfil our trade. The first time, because a tannin destroyed my flock. The second, because I had no property in which to work, and we had an unusual amount of rain. The skins would not dry outside, and we were living with my married daughter inside the city.'

'You couldn't take the skins with you?'

'No, master. No one will allow a tanner to work inside the city.'

'I suppose the smell is rather... shall we say, pungent?'

Yosa gave a slight smile. 'The worst, master.'

'So, how do you intend to re-establish your business now you are free?'

'I will have to acquire another piece of land and build another home.'

'Have you saved anything you could trade for this land?'

The man shifted uncomfortably. 'How can one save when one gets given nothing except the minimum needed to survive?'

'What about your wife; does she also work for me?'

'No. My wife weaves when she can find the time, but we have eight children, master. Anything she earns gets swallowed by them.'

'I see. We have provided for this family though, haven't we Azurak?'

Azurak bowed his head. 'Of course, master. You are more than generous. For it is one man that labours for you, but ten people who are housed and fed.'

'It does sound like they have struggled though.'

Yosa stepped forwards. 'Indeed we have, master. Pardon my saying, but the rations are so meagre that the smallest of my children are starving...'

'Then you should not have had so many children,' Azurak sneered.

'Now, now, Azurak. That is no way to speak to a man who has worked hard for us.' Lamech shifted his gaze back to the worker. 'I will personally take it up with the overseer in charge of the rations.' Yosa needn't know that the overseer was Azurak. 'Now, as to your work, I have a proposal for you.'

'Yes, master?'

'I build things, as you know. I have land, as you know. How about you work for me for another two years, and at the end of it I shall give you some land, with a basic property already installed, which you can expand to suit your growing family. How does that sound?'

The man opened his mouth, closed it again, paused, then spoke quietly. 'I would rather find my own way, working for myself.'

'But how are you going to work without a workplace?'

'We'll... we'll find a way.'

'And your family – where will they live, once you vacate the housing we provide?'

'We can move back with my daughter, temporarily.'

'In the city?'

'In the city.'

'Where you cannot conduct your trade.'

'Yes.' Yosa lifted on and off his bare toes. Honestly, did these people never plan what they would do once free? It was a good job his own business was going so well. He dreaded to think what they would do without him.

'And how will you feed so many hungry bodies?'

'I will work.'

'That will be difficult without a workplace.'

Yosa reddened. 'We'll find a way.'

'Alright, my friend. I wish you all the best and, if you change your mind, my offer still stands.'

'Thank you, master. Farewell.' The scruffy man scurried away, looking unenthusiastic for a man who'd just earned his freedom.

'That was altruistic of you,' Azurak commented. 'What a fool for not taking it up.'

'Oh, he'll be back. Have a heart, Azurak. And a head. This is the way we secure long-term, cheap labour and maintain the impression of being generous. It is all about impressions, as I tell you, time and again.'

'Speaking of impressions, your wife is doing you a favour,' Azurak said.

'Which one?'

Azurak grinned. 'The one who normally causes trouble.'

'Indeed? What is Adah up to?'

'She's caring for the sick inside these gates.'

Lamech bristled. *She's doing what?* How dare she threaten their family with the plague? His legs found purpose and he moved to stand.

Azurak stopped him. 'The elders love it. She's the only one who dares in the whole city.'

Lamech allowed his bottom to retouch his chair. 'Is that so?'

'Everyone else is terrified of the plague. Some are leaving their own family to starve in the street. Even some healers are staying clear. Not your wife.'

'Interesting. How might we minimise the threat to us?'

'She's already restricting the sick to the garden, limiting the numbers and washing before she enters the house.'

'Who is helping her?'

'Avram and Tzel.'

'She's won over her tracker as well, has she? Clever Adah. Very well, we'll let the matter rest. Now what have you discovered about my adversary?'

'Precious little; Barsabas is too wealthy. But I did have an idea.' Azurak looked around, checking no one was in earshot.

'That bad, is it?' Lamech smirked.

His second-in-command sat on the ground crossed-legged and lowered his voice. 'The Kohan of Nachash.'

'Barsabas' serpent priest?'

Azurak nodded. 'Let him into the city.'

'Why would I do that?'

'It is the only thing Barsabas values more than power. He is very attached to the priest's ways and moans about how strict things are here. He sees it as a kind of mission to promote alternative worship.'

'Yes, I remember. Yet, why would Barsabas let his priest come here?'

'Oh, there is more than one. They could send us an apprentice.'

'It's a dangerous move, Azurak. How could we do it without being accused of flouting Yahweh? Remember who the founder of this city is. Chanoch is loyal, as are most of his immediate family. We don't have the advantage Barsabas has north of the lake.'

The idea also made Lamech feel a little sick. Though he had no great love for Yahweh Elohim, the Creator had once answered his prayers. If he disowned Yahweh in favour of other elohim, might his two sons be taken away? Moreover, several of the practices he'd witnessed in the north had disturbed him – though of course, he'd never admit that.

Azurak continued. 'I've thought about that too, and I think I know the answer: Juval's songs. Juval is extremely popular; he already goes from house to house in the city providing and teaching music. He already has the right temperament.'

'How so? My son is not as bad as them.'

'The priests celebrate promiscuity. You know this – it's why Barsabas was pleased to endorse your marriage to Tzillah.'

'That, and I paid him dearly for it. What has that to do with Juval?'

'You know his disposition…'

Lamech shook his head. 'I have tasked Juval with clearing up the city's wayward women. We cannot openly encourage more of them.'

'Openly? Who said anything about openly?' Azurak tilted his head. 'Songs. Parties. Dancing. Wine. Slipping in lyrics here and there that promote alternative worship. There are already stories about Leviathan circulating – the Lord of Tanninim, the Great Serpent. People are exhilarated by what they don't understand. It will be an easy task to imbue the serpent with the status of elohim. Besides, the Kohan claims to see the future in the sun, moon and stars, and the will of the heavenly host via the serpent's tongue.'

'I don't know. Many resist the idea of more than one elohim.'

'I disagree. Yahweh is hard to comprehend. It is easier for people to worship what they can see, than what they can't. They must only tilt their head to witness the wonders above. Whereas Yahweh – what evidence do we have He even exists? And consider the disposition of the people. According to the Kohan, the heavenly host require appetites from humans that men, in particular, are all too happy to gratify. Juval is perfectly placed to help us. You've always said he's extraordinary. It's time for him to be revolutionary.'

Though his enforcer was good at stroking his ego, Lamech shook his head. Azurak wasn't considering the downside of promiscuity. 'Juval's task in providing for fallen women is almost done, and I don't want it to continue. What would we do with the women involved in this alternative worship?'

'That's simple. They enter the service of the priests. They get legitimised.'

'And the babies?'

'Babies are easily disposed of.'

The thought made Lamech shudder. He wasn't so hard as that. He shook his head. 'It still won't work. The elders are loyal to Yahweh. They won't allow it.'

'Yes, but the next generation are not loyal. They are enjoying their multiple wives and their freedom. They thank you for that – you inspire them. Give them more, and they will love you. All you need do is quietly point people in the right direction if they happen to ask. Then, when the current elders pass on, you will be at the forefront of the new society.'

'We have no idea how long it will be before they pass on. As far as I'm aware, the first man, Adam, still lives. Besides, it's too risky. I have tried hard to build a different impression. If this worship is traced back to Juval, or to me—'

Azurak lifted his hands. 'Until the time is right, you deny involvement. You have no mark, after all. But Juval already has the mark of the nachash…'

'That mark was just a prank by the soldiers.'

'A prank that many other men in the city have also. And many women. The appetite for this is greater than you realise.'

But did he have the appetite for it? Just because he enjoyed multiple women and had drunk blood at his second marriage ceremony, didn't mean he approved of those practices spreading to the whole city. He had no love of chaos. Or chaos creatures.

'You are concerned,' Azurak said.

Lamech nodded. 'I don't want things getting out of control.'

The corner of Azurak's mouth twitched. 'Then we control them.'

Lamech thought through the implications. Was it worth angering Yahweh? Then he thought of Barsabas, his continued success despite his open apostacy, and the way Methushael still favoured him. Barsabas had lost a son, something Lamech could not afford to do. Yet, if they didn't offer this alternative, he would have to give Barsabas his daughter instead…

'If we do this, Azurak, I need you to take a step back from the forefront of my operations.'

Azurak looked offended. 'Have I angered you, master?'

'Not at all, my friend. It's just that you have become – how should I say it? – bolder recently. I wasn't expecting Barsabas' son to fall prey to such an unfortunate incident, and I suspect that might not be the only unfortunate incident that you've been involved in. A certain accident, perhaps?'

Azurak's nose twitched.

Lamech was surprised – he was usually so good at hiding his reactions. This wasn't the time to lose his second-in-command. 'I am not reprimanding you, nor asking you to stop, Azurak. Yet, if things need *further control,* as you've suggested, then we need to be extremely careful. Our relationship need not change, but we should allow safer people to give the appearance of management, while you reside in obscurity. Do you concur?'

Azurak visibly softened – well, as soft as he ever got, which wasn't very. 'Yes, master.' A slight smile contracted his lips.

'Excellent. Then there's nothing further to discuss until we see what Naamah decides.'

There was time for one more visit before the day was done. Lamech had not been to his concubine for some time, but she had sent word that she desired to see him a week ago, and frankly, he could do with the distraction.

When Lamech pushed aside the wooden door to the house he'd provided her, he immediately noticed the change. Tamar looked exhausted.

'Master.' Tamar bowed to him and approached, the scent of lavender and rosemary wafting with her dress, ready to render the services he usually required quite swiftly.

'You asked for me,' he said.

'Yes. Forgive me, master. I would not normally do so but...' She kissed him and ran her hands down his torso. 'I have good news.'

He stepped back and inspected her. Nothing was obvious, so he lifted her dress. There was a small rounding of her midriff.

Tamar smiled.

'Good. Do you know how far along you are?'

'You haven't visited for a full season, master, so it must be longer than that. Perhaps halfway. It is my first babe and my mother always carried small.' She approached again and caressed him.

He pushed her away. 'I shall not touch you while you carry the child. Tzillah carried small, Adah did not. It will be a challenge to confine Tzillah for any amount of time, but we will have to try.

Besides, you look more like her.' He suddenly chuckled, imagining them tying Tzillah to the bed, or stuffing her undergarments to keep up the pretence.

'What do you mean, master?' Tamar asked.

'You've always known this is a business transaction. If the child is a girl, you may keep her here, and I will support you. I am a man of my word. If it is a boy, Tzillah will claim him as hers. You may stay with us to nurse the infant until he is weaned. This was our agreement.'

'I believe it is a boy, master.'

'How do you know?'

Tamar stroked her bare midriff. 'I just do.'

'Adah always said she could sense it as well.'

'Will you continue to visit?'

'I will call in from time to time to check on your welfare. Goodnight, Tamar.'

As he strode towards the tavern, he hoped Tamar was right. Confining Tzillah, then claiming the child had died, would be far more difficult than claiming a quick labour with no time to fetch the healer. And if he did have another boy, perhaps he need not worry so much about angering Yahweh.

PART THREE

CHAPTER 55

← ——

City of Chanoch, 750th year of Wandering

A pounding outside rouses Chanoch from slumber. He immediately sits up. His heart knocks faster than the knock of fist on wood. Have they come for him? Is his time over? He swings his legs around and lifts himself from his mat, then stretches his arms out in front and counts the steps until he must turn.

'Coming, coming,' Chanoch mutters as the pounding continues. It is hard to move quickly in the pitch black of night. He turns, relieved not to hit the wall, then a sliver of light greets him, along with a gentle breeze. The moonlight is trying to break through the small square hole in the door.

'I'm here. What is it? Have they come for me?'

'No, master.' It is his guard, a man employed from necessity not desire, who doubles as the groom for Chanoch's kavash. 'There are two people requesting an audience.'

'At night?'

'They don't look dangerous. They are waiting inside the gate.'

'What are their names?' Sometimes his guard isn't the quickest to divulge basic information.

'Oh. Juval and Adah, master.'

'Adah?' This is unusual and must be significant. 'Let them in, let them in.'

As the guard hastens to do his bidding, Chanoch hobbles about for the items needed to light a fire. Before he's secured any of them, a knock sounds again. Sliding back the bolt, Chanoch eases the door open, still finding the sensation of metal under his fingers and wood sliding smoothly over a rail, peculiar. He'd had one of Tuval-Kayin's workers install the door several years hence for the sake of his ailing wife. Though it felt like an extravagance at the time, he was grateful for it as his body grew weaker. He'd passed into his seventh century recently, one year after he'd introduced The Wanderer to Lamech, and his life had abruptly become perilous.

Adah and Juval shuffle into the house. Chanoch slides the door closed behind them and bolts it back. He can hear their heavy breathing better than he can see their faces. 'Sorry, I haven't had time to light a fire.'

Adah speaks softly. 'Don't apologise; it's the middle of the night.'

'Indeed.'

Silence. Are they going to explain why they are here? This woman he has failed so many times and her wayward son.

When no information is forthcoming, Chanoch starts fumbling for his flint again, banging into several items on his way to the pit where his cooking fire burns during the day.

Adah speaks again. 'Chanoch, please don't trouble yourself. We won't stay long.'

'You won't?'

'We don't want to put you in any danger. I just need your help to escape.'

'To escape?' So, she has finally decided to leave. After all these years. But where is her tracker? And can her son be trusted?

Adah must sense his reservation for she continues. 'We planned this night as soon as we found out about Shadow's wife, but Azurak was supposed to be occupied.'

Chanoch barely understands what she is saying, but he catches the bit about Azurak - *supposed to be occupied*. Does that mean Lamech's enforcer is on the way here? A chill shoots down Chanoch's spine. Azurak has been watching him for some time, Chanoch's own version of Adah's 'Shadow', always on the lookout for a slip up. Might Azurak soon be pounding on the door, instead of the guard, dragging Adah back to her home to be imprisoned for good?

What a turn of events. Chanoch could never have imagined this consequence of his rash decision to drag his parents into Lamech's business.

'Can you help us find The Wanderer?' Adah asks.

Chanoch jumps from his thoughts. 'You want to find my abba?'

Now his eyes have adjusted to the dark, he can just about see her nod.

'He's my only hope.'

CHAPTER 56

City of Chanoch, 743rd year of Wandering

Adah surveyed the room before her. Dusk was dissolving the shadows on the wall and nearby, Lamech's concubine, Tamar, nursed her third infant. It had been six years since Lamech had announced he was expecting another child, and he'd shown no inclination to cease his attempts at gaining more sons. The babe across the room was the second child they'd adopted, since the middle one Tamar birthed had been a girl.

As the babe dropped off into a contented, milk-full sleep, Adah considered the woman whose scent of lavender and rosemary had alerted her to Lamech's activities years before. She was tall and slim, with rich, long hair that fell in dark waves to her waist. They were alone in the room, the adults being out and the eldest child in bed. Adah studied Tamar's delicate, long fingers as she rubbed together her own coarse ones. The skin on her knuckles was raw from frequent handwashing, though less so since the plague had calmed.

With Tamar's first son, Lamech had been careful to keep Tzillah from public appearances for a while before the birth. He'd put about the story that she was pregnant and feeling unwell with it. After the birth, Tamar moved in with them temporarily to nurse but stayed out of sight. She had barely spoken to Adah that first time.

When Tamar became pregnant again within a year, Tzillah had refused to be confined, insisting on continuing her life. When Tamar's labour produced a girl, everyone had been relieved that no pretence was necessary.

'Imagine pretending I'd lost a baby, Adah? How incredibly insensitive to those who have,' Tzillah had said.

Indeed, Adah thought. *You have no idea what it feels like, but I'm glad you at least considered it.*

Before two more years had passed, Tamar appeared again, two seasons into her third pregnancy.

'I'm still not pretending,' Tzillah said. Lamech laughed, told Tzillah to be a good girl, and carried her to bed. That was the last protest Adah heard. Tzillah didn't pretend, and she didn't need to. Just as they'd gradually accepted his second marriage, the city accepted Tamar's second son was Tzillah's, despite all evidence to the contrary.

Besides, having multiple wives was popular in the city now. The plague had reduced numbers for a time, hitting the men hardest. Hunting also continued, taking men at an increasing rate as they went further afield to conquer more dangerous terrain and creatures. So the ratio of women to men increased, adding to the conviction that it was better to have multiple wives than leave the women to fend for themselves.

Despite the acceptance of his way of life, Lamech didn't spend much time in the home of his concubine. She hadn't lived with them this time because her daughter needed care, and Tzillah's chamber continued to keep Lamech happy most of the time. It was just unfortunate that Tzillah had produced no more children herself, despite her efforts to keep their husband close.

'That doesn't bother me,' Tzillah had said when questioned. 'You know how much I hate pregnancy, Adah. And I'm not exactly a natural mother like you are. I don't mind adopting someone else's children if you and Shua do the work.' She'd flashed Adah a cheeky grin, making Adah wonder whether she hadn't contrived some way of preventing herself from conceiving.

'Aren't you jealous, though? You would have been before,' she asked.

'I hate him sleeping with her, it's true. But I know Lamech loves me, in his own way. He doesn't love Tamar. She's just business, Adah.'

Funny sort of business, producing sons. Almost like children were a commodity to be traded and not your own flesh and blood.

Despite all this, Adah didn't dislike Tamar. Though clearly a woman of questionable lifestyle, she knew her place and didn't assert herself. Unlike Tzillah, Adah felt neither envy nor sorrow at Lamech's continued betrayal. The door of her heart had long since closed, leaving just a small opening for his other children.

As Tamar stood to leave, Nahar, Tamar's eldest, snuck into the room, his face wet with tears, his hair standing on end like the legs of a dead beetle, and his tunic soaked with sweat. Longing flashed across Tamar's face, communicating everything Adah suspected, but Tamar would never confess.

'Did you have a bad dream, Nahar?' Adah asked, turning to him. Nahar nodded and held out his arms to her. Though he was approaching five years old, he was still soft at heart. *Long may he remain so.*

'How about going to Tamar?' she asked, raising an eyebrow at the other woman in the room. Tamar's eyes widened and she shook her head. Nahar's brows drew together. He barely knew his real mother, and certainly didn't know she *was* his real mother.

'I'll take the baby.' Adah stood, rejecting Tamar's refusal. She retrieved the little one and left the room to lay him in his crib. When she returned, Nahar was on Tamar's lap, settling into her embrace. She had wiped his tears and was kissing the crown of his head. Now her eyes closed, and she rested her chin on his hair, just for a moment.

'Is it hard?' Adah asked.

Tears pricked at Tamar's reluctantly opening eyes. She spoke in a whisper. 'I shouldn't be ungrateful. I have it so much better than many.'

'That's not what I asked.'

Tamar chewed her lip. 'Of course it's hard.' Then she lifted Nahar from her lap, placed him gently down, wiped her eyes, and strode purposefully from the room.

Adah took Nahar's hand. 'Come, my dear. Let's take you back to bed.'

'Where is Ima?'

Your ima just left. She is the one that loves you, but she must leave you, Adah wanted to say but didn't. For Nahar was asking after Tzillah who wasn't often there.

'She's at dinner with Abba. I am here to watch over you.'

Nahar sniffed, nodded, and allowed himself to be led back to bed.

Yaval's pet wolf followed them. Adah thought it amusing how he protected the little ones now, just as Yaval had said he would. As she sat by Nahar's bed singing him to sleep, she thought back on the cub's recent entry into their lives:

'Ima, look what I found!' Yaval had burst into the room, in the way only Yaval could – arms complete with a large bundle of tanned fur and glee plastered on his face.

Lamech looked around and immediately soured. 'What are you doing? Get that thing out of here.'

Nahar jumped up and crowded Yaval, who revealed the contents of his arms. Nahar loved his eldest half-brother, who brought home the most exciting presents.

Lamech stood. 'I said, get it out!'

'But Abba, it's an orphan.'

'*Now* it is, but I have no doubt you plucked it from some poor mother's grasp just so you could experiment on it.'

Plucked it from some poor mother's grasp – just like you did with Nahar. Adah massaged a bruise on her arm, keeping her thoughts to herself. Years of living with Lamech's unpredictable rage had taught her the wisdom of silence.

'I didn't,' Yaval protested. 'I know it's an orphan because I found it lying in its mother's paws – she was already dead.'

'If that's true, where is the rest of the litter?'

'I can only assume they were eaten by whatever killed the mother. She was horrifically mauled. This little one must have seen the whole thing, poor beast.'

'Was there lots of blood and guts?' asked Nahar.

'Loads,' Yaval confirmed, 'but you shouldn't be interested in that.' He ruffled his little brother's hair.

'Can I see it? Oh, take me, Yaval. Say you will.'

'Absolutely not.' Lamech picked Nahar up by the collar and plonked him, arms flailing, back on the floor. He stood between his two sons. 'Yaval, you cannot keep that wolf-thing in my house. It is a wild animal, known to hunt and kill humans.'

'It's just a cub.'

'And where is its pack? You'll have beasts following your scent and howling at our doors.'

'The dominant male has already moved on.'

'Dominant male?'

'The pack has one male that leads it. I've been watching them; I know their patterns of behaviour, Abba. The dominant male decides where the pack goes. They didn't come back for this little one but moved on. That means he's been rejected.'

Lamech stepped forward, backing Yaval against the wall. 'Then give it to me. I'll dispatch it if you haven't the courage.'

Yaval cradled the furry bundle. 'I shall not. I'm keeping him.'

Lamech slammed his hand against the wall near Yaval's head. 'Defy me again and you will not eat for a week!'

Adah squeezed her eyes tight shut again. *Don't hurt my son. Yahweh, protect him.*

Yaval's cheeks darkened, yet determination set his face to flint. He lowered his voice to the level Lamech used at his most intimidating. 'Abba, I know these creatures. I understand them. I can bring him up – train him.'

Adah couldn't see Lamech's face, but she noticed his shoulders relax slightly. She could picture his expression as he snarled the next words. 'I have given you a job to do – several jobs – and still, you insist on running about in the wild when you should be working. You disgust me.'

Yaval still didn't flinch. 'If he eats from my hand, in time he will protect us as he would his own pack. Think of the benefits.'

Lamech lowered his arm. 'You truly believe you could achieve that?'

'I do.'

'It has never been done before.'

'Neither had keeping geese.'

'Geese don't tend to be interested in killing people.'

At that point Tzillah had chortled, breaking into the tension. 'I beg to differ. They're always chasing me. Nasty creatures.'

Adah suppressed a smirk. *Thank you, Tzillah.*

Lamech relinquished his position, and his posture assumed a lenient pose. 'I will give you one chance. But if I ever catch that creature baring his oversized fangs at one of my sons, I shall slit its throat.'

Fortunately, Lamech hadn't done so, and 'Fang' was now part of the family. He was usually to be found at Yaval's heel, but in the evenings, he stayed at home – for he was still just a cub and needed his sleep like the rest of the little ones. Adah rather liked having him there and stroked his fluffy head with one hand while she stroked Nahar's hair with the other.

IN THE NORTH of the city, Eliana was having a heated yet whispered discussion with her husband, mindful of their slumbering children on the opposite side of their cramped hut. Mela was next to her, cross-legged on the sheepskin in the centre of their living area.

'We cannot expect her to wait for him forever,' Manon was saying. 'Besides, I'm not at all sure I want to associate with that family now.'

Eliana interjected. 'But Adah is my oldest friend—'

'Whom you rarely see.'

'—whom I love with all my heart.'

'And Mela is well beyond forty years of age…'

'Which is still young. Many women don't marry until they are older. And most men don't. You were fifty before you married me.'

Manon fixed her with a stare. 'That's beside the point.'

'Hardly.' Eliana reached forward and took her husband's hand, running her fingers up his arm. 'For you still look young to me, my love, and just as handsome as the day I met you. Your second century suits you well.'

This caused Mela to stamp her foot. 'Oh, Ima, stop it! Do I not get a say at all in this discussion? It's my life.'

While Manon stared at his fingernails, Eliana turned to face her daughter, grinning. 'Of course you do, my love.'

'Then stop getting distracted and let me speak. Every time we try to talk about it, you and Abba get into an argument, and your arguments always finish with a passionate make-up.'

Manon coughed. 'You're right. Sorry. We just want you to have what we have. We have sought good matches for all of you, but the most important thing is that you find someone you love, who will commit to you for life. That could be a short time, but as far as we know, it could be a thousand years. The Wanderer has not died yet, and he must be eight hundred by now. The Creator didn't specify the number of years we would live.'

'Yaval is the man who will commit to me for life. I know it, Abba.' Mela's eyes shone in the small amount of light given by the fire.

'He has offered you nothing, nor us,' Manon protested. 'And five of your younger siblings are married now.'

'He has given me his heart. I love him, Abba. I will wait another hundred years if I must.'

Eliana reached forward, placing a hand on Mela's knee. She could understand both points of view, feeling them both keenly in her soul. 'You know there will always be space for you here. Even so, we need some assurance from Yaval that he is serious.'

'I am.'

Eliana turned towards the voice in the doorway. Yaval let down the woven fabric entrance and entered, greeting them all with a kiss. Eliana motioned to the bread and oil on the table. 'I'm afraid we have little food to share, but of course you are welcome to join us, as always.'

Yaval reached into the leather bag slung over his shoulder. 'I have brought you cheese from my goats, goose eggs and some pomegranates from Sav's tree. Sorry I'm late – I visited him first.'

Eliana did like Yaval, who always came bearing gifts, just like his ima. He placed his offering on the wooden board in the centre of the sheepskin and sat with them. 'I am not afraid to admit my love for your daughter, nor afraid to defy my abba to marry her. I initially hoped he would come around once I had pleased him in the business, but he has not. Consequently, I am seeking a way we might be together that doesn't put Mela in danger. Her safety is my main concern.'

Manon shook his head. 'That is another reason I am reluctant to let her marry you. Please don't misunderstand me – I like you, Yaval – but I do not trust your father.'

'I understand. I don't trust him myself.'

Manon stroked his chin. 'Tell me what you are doing to seek this *safe way*.'

Yaval's mouth twitched into a slight smile that betrayed hidden pleasures. 'You know I've always loved wandering the hills. I am not cut out for city life. Never have been. My heart yearns for grass beneath my feet and freedom to run through a meadow, to live off the land, to swim in the sea.'

Eliana grinned. 'You sound like Mela.'

'Exactly. I want to take her away from here. Yet, I know that means taking her away from you.'

Eliana couldn't deny that would be hard. Mela had been part of her life for so long, not just her daughter but her companion, helpmate and friend.

'And when you take her away, what then? Where will you live?' Manon asked.

'Recently I went travelling for a few days, on the pretext of scouting some metal with Tuval-Kayin. I left my brother as soon as we were out of sight of the city. Fortunately, he's used to my escapades, and I don't think he'll have told Abba. I followed the river all the way to the Great Lake, but finding the water there unsuitable, I went north again, towards the sea, following a stream that seemed to hold fresh water. After a day's hiking uphill, I came upon a meadow so luscious that herds of long-horns, deer and wild goats all grazed together. Of course, long-horns are unsafe, so I didn't linger, but sought shelter for the night in the nearby hills.'

'Did you find shelter?' Mela asked. She had leaned forward, chin on hands, and was gazing into Yaval's enthusiastic face.

'Yes. It was already dark, but thickets were plentiful, so I crawled into one. At dawn, I went exploring again, soon discovering a cave with a perfect glade outside it, which has certainly been inhabited before.'

'How do you know?' Eliana asked.

'The position of the stones outside. Though the glade is rather overgrown and the cave empty, there was a definite grinding stone near a dip where a fire has been frequently lit, and around the grinding stone, purposefully placed boulders.'

'So, you think we could live there?' Mela's eyes sparkled.

'The water is fresh. I tried it to make sure. There are garden areas around the site, fruit bushes and pistachio trees, and little pools where one might bathe. It's perfect.'

'It sounds like it may be someone's home,' Manon said.

'Perhaps it belongs to The Wanderer?' Mela said. 'What if we went there and he found us? What would happen then?'

'There's no need to be afraid of The Wanderer,' Eliana interjected. 'Your abba met him once. He was gruff but generous with his trade.'

'But that was when he came to you,' Mela insisted. 'It's different if we steal his home. He might kill us and eat us. My friend said he's been known to—'

'Don't be ridiculous, Mela. Those stories are a load of old nonsense. You friend deserves a good talking to.'

'Still, there must be a reason why the cave was abandoned,' Manon cautioned.

'I suppose.' Yaval's enthusiasm waned slightly. 'Yet, if it is The Wanderer's, they might use it seasonally.'

The chief concern on Eliana's mind had little to do with her ancestors. 'How many days walk from the city is it?'

'It took me three to get home, coming more directly.'

She supposed that wasn't so bad. It wasn't like going all the way west, beyond the mountains, as Ruhamah likely had by now. As a child, he'd been fascinated by the stories of Eden and, though he knew the Garden was out of bounds, there was plenty more to the land than that. To be closer to where Yahweh walked – that had always been Ruhamah's desire. Still, she missed her brother terribly. It had been so long...

Manon licked his fingers, savouring every last taste of the goat's cheese he'd been enjoying. 'The word *north* troubles me. We hear many stories about the iniquity of northern people.'

'Oh, it's not as far as Barsabas' lands. It must be a week's walk at least from the coast.'

'And how do you think your abba would react to you disappearing?'

Yaval chewed on his lip. 'It's hard to know. Though I established one covenant for Abba, I haven't done much else. He doesn't rely on me for the vineyard either. I help, but I'm certainly not as good as his current manager. The most use I am to Abba is in training kavash for his scouts.'

Manon placed his hand on the table. 'If you are no farmer and no tradesman, how do you intend to support my daughter and any children Yahweh may bless you with?'

Eliana bit her tongue. Her husband was usually far more sparing with his words than she, but where his eldest daughter was concerned, he didn't hold back.

'He is wonderful with animals,' Mela said, smiling. 'We will leave with a bag each of eggs, carrying a hen and a goose to sit on them at nightfall.'

Eliana chuckled. 'I can just see you two riding a kavash through the streets, poultry in arms.'

'In all seriousness though,' Manon said, 'You need more than that.'

Yaval nodded. 'I know. I intend to return to the cave and explore the area further as soon as I get another opportunity. Will you grant me time for that?'

Not waiting for her husband, Eliana placed her hand over Yaval's. 'Of course, dear. Won't we, Manon?'

'Alright,' Manon said. 'Also, try to ascertain what Lamech will do. The last thing I want is the city's most powerful man hunting my daughter all over the countryside.'

'That concern is the entire reason for my delay. Thank you for your patience.' Yaval grabbed what was left of the flat bread and tore off a piece with his teeth, smiling all the while at Mela.

CHAPTER 57

An arrowshot from Eliana's home, Naamah kissed her two almost-sleeping children goodnight and snuck from their room, trying to keep her footsteps as light as possible. Eber wasn't home, which wasn't unusual. Her husband rarely came back before the moon was high in the sky, preferring to keep company with Juval late into the night, even during the working week. Naamah didn't mind anymore; his absence quelled her conscience regarding her own, and if it kept Juval out of the way, so much the better.

Slipping into the darkness of her chamber, Naamah stripped off her practical, daytime tunic. She felt around for the oregano stalks bunched on the table near the narrow aperture in the wall, through which she could see a slight crescent of moon. After dipping the stalks in saltwater, she rubbed them under her arms and over her chest, then felt for the clean dress that she'd left hanging by the bed earlier.

Her housekeeper was dozing in a chair near the front entrance. Naamah whispered in her ear, 'I'm going out. The children shouldn't stir now.'

The woman moaned a response, and with permission granted, Naamah slid back the outer door to her home, nodded at the nightwatchman and glided into the passageway.

This was the part she hated the most – wondering if there was anyone there when the moon was too slight to light up bodies slumped on the streets. She had taken about five steps when a hand slid into hers. For a moment her heart leapt in fear, until she recognised the feel of his fingers and the scent of the man who'd taken her hand.

'It's me,' he said. 'I have been waiting. The night is too dark for you to walk alone.'

Turning towards the voice, her lips met his and she submerged into them, allowing her relief to transform into passion. When they broke apart for air, she felt his lips twitch into a smile. After another gentle peck, he tugged on her hand. 'Let's go.'

It was a short walk to her lover's simple one-roomed dwelling. Once inside, the warmth and meaty smell hit her. The embers of a fire smouldered in the hearth, with a roasted rabbit on a spit above.

'Are you hungry?' he asked, striding to the fireside, slipping on a leather glove and lifting the spit from its stand.

A rumble in her stomach confirmed she was. She hadn't even realised.

'Yes,' she replied. 'But first, I want to do this.'

The kiss in the passageway had kindled the fire within. The passion that had died with the death of Gomer, and had never ignited for her husband, was being stoked by the man before her. The man who had terrified her when she was younger but had displayed such compassion and tenderness after Gomer's death. The man who had offered her a way out when her father would have thrown her to the wolf, Anak.

She knew he was dangerous, but the thrill of fear, the excitement of something forbidden, and the awareness of fervent desire on his part, all contributed to her uncontrollable yearning. With him, she was not just a mother or an ally, she was a woman. A goddess.

AZURAK FELT THE WARMTH of the sun on his bare shoulders before his closed eyelids registered the brightness of dawn. He stirred, stretched his arms, and contemplated the woman sharing his bed. Then reality hit.

'Naamah.'

Naamah groaned as he stroked her copper hair.

'Naamah, wake up.'

When she refused to move, he kissed her neck, tenderly easing her into the land of the living. 'We fell asleep. It is dawn. You must leave,' he whispered.

Naamah's eyes flew open and rested on him a moment before they flicked to the aperture through which the sun was shining so brightly. 'Curses!' she exclaimed and jumped out of bed.

She rushed around, flinging on her tunic and sandals, then grasped the wooden door, ready to slide it open. Azurak placed a hand on her shoulder. 'Hush. Breathe. Remember not to look guilty.'

She turned panicked eyes to him, and he immediately craved her delicately proportioned features. Controlling his urges, he touched his lips to hers, rubbed an errant smudge of kohl at the edge of her right eye, then smoothed out a little knot of hair. 'Perfect.'

'I'll see you again?'

'On the third day.'

'Assuming Eber hasn't found out.' Naamah's mouth twitched.

'You know how to warn me if he does.'

She nodded. They had decided on their code the second time she had come to his home. Azurak had every confidence he could rescue her from any trouble.

'Before you go,' he said. 'The regulations we discussed are being brought before the elders in a few days. Can I count on Eber's input?'

Naamah raised an eyebrow. 'Eber is not an elder.'

'He has his abba's ear, and you have his.'

Naamah gave a slight snort. 'Usually it's him I have to sleep with to get his ear, not you.'

Azurak placed his hands on her shoulders. 'This is important. It is in Gomer's memory – you know that. If these regulations don't pass, who knows how many innocents will die? You must suggest what we discussed.'

Naamah's eyes flickered to the floor and her shoulders sagged. She nodded. 'I appreciate all you've done to ensure Gomer's death was not in vain.' Her eyes joined his again and she stroked his cheek. 'You are the only one who seems to care that I lost the man I loved.'

'Everything that pains your heart, pains mine. Though, dare I hope, you love another man now?'

The gloom in Naamah's eyes was replaced with a spark. 'You are coming close, Azurak. Coming close.'

He slid the heavy door for her and checked the street was empty before seeing her out. 'Be careful.'

'I will.' And she left.

EBER WAS IN HIS FAVOURITE chair, distractedly chewing on some oat flakes, when Naamah walked in. 'Where have you been?' he asked, narrowing his eyes.

Naamah held up the fruit and grain she'd collected on the way home. 'At the market.' Pulling out all the tactics she'd seen her mother use when she was growing up, she smiled her best smile at her husband, who narrowed his eyes further.

'You weren't at the market when I got home last night and found our bed empty.'

Naamah could feel the heat rising on her cheeks. She turned from him and started putting things away. 'Oh, my friend Sarai sent a messenger for me – you remember the one whose husband is a chief of Abba's hunters? She gets scared at night sometimes. She didn't want to be alone. Said she kept hearing noises. I went over there but it turns out it was just an owl…'

Naamah had thought up the story on the way home. Her friend was often a convenient excuse to get away. As she settled into her lie, the warmth diminished, and she felt it safe to approach her husband again. 'How was your evening?' she asked, placing a gentle kiss on his lips.

He pulled her closer until she fell into his lap. 'You know that jealousy sets me on fire,' he said. 'I was imagining you in another man's bed.'

Naamah laughed. Her laugh was probably too shrill, but Eber didn't seem to notice as he kissed her hungrily.

'Don't go out again without telling me. You don't want me to worry, do you?'

She fluttered her eyelashes. 'But how am I meant to tell you when you are never home?'

Eber growled. 'Would you like me to be home more?'

Her slight hesitation was enough to anger him. He threw her from his lap. 'You don't want me. I knew it.'

'Eber…'

'I have loved you, Naamah. I have loved you with passionate violence since long before you were betrothed to my brother. I couldn't believe it when his accident propelled you into my arms. It was the most unexpected joy after the grief of losing him. Yet you have never loved me. The best you have given me is either mild indifference or flagrant pretence.'

Fear mounted in Naamah's chest. *He knows... He knows. No, he doesn't. He is just angry because you don't love him as you loved Gomer – and that, he knows.* How to calm the anger? What was it that had justified the risk she took in seeing Azurak? Of course, Eber's own actions.

Taking a deep breath, she dared to approach his rage. 'I asked you a question too. I asked how your evening was.'

Eber breathed through his flared nostrils and fixed his eyes on hers.

Keep his gaze, don't look away now.

She continued. 'I know you were with Juval. And I know what his nights are like. I know about the women. I used to be there, remember?'

Eber clenched his fist but kept her gaze.

She bent low and spoke softly. 'Tell me you have not slept with another.'

He didn't waver.

'Tell me!'

Eber's stance broke. He rubbed his nose and murmured, 'I cannot.'

'And yet you have the audacity to accuse me.'

Eber closed the gap between them and grasped her chin in his hand. 'It is not what you think. They are not common harlots.'

'What difference does that make?'

'It's part of our worship. I do it to protect my family.'

Naamah stared her husband in the eye. For the first time, she wished she hadn't broken off all communication with Juval. Then she might know what he was talking about. How could fornication be worship? 'I don't understand you. All I know is that you have been there, while I have remained here night after night, faithfully raising your children, and never questioning you.'

Eber's eyes turned hard. 'Prove it, wife. Prove your faithfulness right now in our chamber.'

Naamah gulped. 'Don't you have work to get to?'

'It can wait. This – you – you are my priority.'

She closed her eyes. *Alright, Eber.*

Careful to be neither indifferent nor flagrantly pretentious, she pictured Gomer, the brother she'd really loved, as she leaned in to kiss her husband.

Later, after Eber was satisfied, and Naamah felt reasonably sure she had regained his trust, she rolled over and dared to broach the other topic close to her heart. The one Azurak had reminded her of.

CHAPTER 58

Chanoch scratched his head as he listened to the fourth discussion of justice regulations brought to the company of elders. Ever since the accident that had ended Gomer's life, there had been calls for greater regulation of dangerous activity, tighter controls and harsher punishments for offenders. Chanoch had resisted them all. During his earlier years, he'd overseen the setting up of prison houses to confine the most dangerous members of society and he'd made a point of visiting them, telling the prisoners about Yahweh and seeking their repentance. Some visits met with success, others did not.

He far preferred this slow, steady approach to the ones now being espoused by the younger elders, though he could understand why they felt the need for change. With the swelling of the city population, the prison houses were overcrowded, and few changed their ways sufficiently for release.

The reality was, the council hadn't capacity to deal with every case, and most offences didn't involve severe danger to others. Only the worst cases tended to be brought before the elders, the rest being dealt with informally between families and businesses. The chief concern was how to deal with accidents that had caused death – those like Gomer's – and how to ensure punishments were consistent and fair.

Many felt that to control acts of revenge, all offence, whatever the motive, should be repaid like for like – those who caused the death of others should meet with death themselves, those who stole should have possessions removed. The first difficulty with this approach was proving the offence beyond doubt. The second was obvious – surely accidents could not be treated the same way as intentional offences? The third was how to take something from those who had nothing.

The fourth was that these *like for like* punishments left no room for mercy.

Having lived with a father who had experienced Yahweh's extraordinary mercy, Chanoch was keenly aware that what was reasonable was not always what was right. His father had spent his life as The Wanderer – a fugitive, whose love for farming was denied him. Yet, his act of murder had not been repaid. If Yahweh acted justly in meting out mercy to The Wanderer, then there must be space for mercy within any justice system.

They'd been discussing the discipline of negligent workers (and whether it needed to be harsher) for some time when Lamech stood up, raising a hand to speak. As the owner of the largest construction business in the city, he'd been invited to sit as an honorary member of the council for this discussion, as many tragic accidents happened on sites like Kenan's and Lamech's.

'Within my business, my foremen are responsible for checking their sites regularly and ensuring nothing has been left unsafe,' Lamech was saying. 'Their superior experience makes them liable for the mistakes of their workers. Responsibility should lie there, not just with those less fortunate.'

Lamech was right – why should labourers be the ones constantly punished? Yet Chanoch was surprised to see him state such an opinion when he had the largest workforce of slaves, justified by this *like for like* principle. Slaves were those who had nothing to pay with but their own lives, or those of their children. What game was he playing?

'So, extend the rules to everyone,' one speaker replied. 'Foremen can exercise discipline against labourers who cause undue danger to others, but, if bad practice is found on their watch, the same discipline may be given them.'

'Then where will it stop?' another said. 'Who will mete out these punishments? It sounds like a recipe for constant accusation and little action. Better to deal with things quickly than drag everything before the elders. I for one am sick of these constant meetings.'

There was a ripple of agreement, and Chanoch didn't blame them.

After a little more discussion and interjection by several others, Kenan at last spoke. 'I lost my son to negligence, as you all know.'

'May Yahweh bless his soul with peace,' the elders chorused.

'Do I want justice?' Kenan said. 'Of course. Do I want to ensure others do not face the same fate? Of course. All the same, I don't believe that meting out harsh punishment on an entire generation will get justice for my son. At the time of Gomer's death, the accident was investigated, and it was never established who had left that boulder cut and untended. Increasing the effectiveness of such enquiries and establishing set penalties seems to me better than allowing sporadic discipline across the board.'

A murmur of agreement rippled through the council.

'The question is,' Kenan continued. 'How is it best done? Discipline cannot be left to each individual business owner, nor can we, as a council, hear every case. I have been discussing this with Eber, who, has management over most of my quarry.'

With Eber? Since when did we consider the opinions of one so young? Chanoch thought as Kenan continued.

'He asked why we don't set up a separate assembly to deal with these cases? One that can be properly managed by those who have time to conduct thorough investigations where harm has occurred to any individual in the city.'

'Does that include harm from hunting?' a female elder said, who had lost a husband to the hunt.

'What do you think, Lamech?' Kenan asked.

Lamech waved a hand. 'Hunting is a very different matter. All who join the hunt are aware of the dangers. Indeed, often it's the danger that entices them, for they are the sort who enjoy the thrill of it. I am concerned for those who do not sign up for danger – for miners and builders who are just trying to earn an honest living.'

'Lamech is quite right,' Kenan replied. 'Which is why those who create danger for others should be dealt with most severely.'

'A moment ago, you were saying we shouldn't mete out harsher punishments,' Chanoch's daughter, Selah, interjected.

'To the entire generation. Not to the culprits. Breaking blood covenants results in death. Why not negligence?'

Chanoch was stunned to silence. His grandson's words had the impression of logic, but he feared they crept remarkably close to legitimising revenge killings.

'May I speak again?' Lamech stood once more, and Chanoch nodded. 'Kenan, my friend. I understand your sentiment. Truly, I do. To lose a son and never see the perpetrator brought to justice is a terrible thing indeed. Yet, there is a real danger that the assembly you speak of will be – shall we say – less than independent? It must not be the case that what is set up to provide justice in practice provides the opposite.'

Nodding and signals of approval met the speech, and Chanoch once again found himself agreeing with Lamech.

'Then we should nominate independent persons to oversee it. I suggest that nobody connected with any business where accidents regularly take place is involved.' Kenan said. 'I own a quarry, and I fear my grief may produce injustice. I am not a suitable candidate.'

'They should also be Yahweh worshippers,' Chanoch said. 'That is not a given anymore.'

A different elder spoke up. 'Goodness is not restricted to Yahweh worshippers, Chanoch. The Creator gave us all dominion over the earth. I would hate to see people unfairly punished because they do not strictly adhere to one faith.'

'Yahweh's principles of justice are the bedrock of this council,' Chanoch replied. Worry was rippling through his stomach.

'And no one is suggesting this council be disbanded, Sav,' Kenan said. 'This separate assembly is for smaller cases, to take the burden off individuals such as yourself. Let us choose those experienced in management of small businesses, who have no workers currently involved in quarrying, mining, building or other dangerous activities.'

Chanoch scanned the room. One obvious candidate was Naman. He had a small family trade in fabrics, and little ambition to expand it. Moreover, he had taken negligible interest in the discussion so far. Yet, he had two wives. Could he be trusted to represent Yahweh's principles?

'I think, as elders, we should discuss and agree on a standard range of punishments beforehand,' Chanoch said. Though he was still unsure about the whole initiative, they could set the correct precedents and safeguards.

Several people groaned and one man spoke up. 'Oh Chanoch, you always make everything last forever. Let us entrust those details to a smaller group. We can bring it up again later if there is need.'

Chanoch glanced at his daughter. He needed her support. Yet, she'd clearly had enough as well, for she just shrugged.

'I nominate Selah,' Chanoch said. Her disinterest was an asset. Selah rolled her eyes, a gesture that looked rather ridiculous on her six-hundred-year-old face, but took him right back to when she was a little girl.

'I nominate Naman,' Kenan said.

Two more people were nominated before Chanoch spoke again. Four seemed a safe number. 'Do any of the candidates have objections?'

Selah opened her mouth, but he fixed her with a look that said, *Don't let me down.* She closed it again and shook her head.

Naman spoke up. 'How am I meant to run my own business and undertake this task at the same time? I don't have a large workforce like some here.'

'I am willing to contribute to the running of the assembly, trading my goods as wages for those you hire to help,' Kenan said. 'All I would ask is that you commit personally the time required to oversee it. Are others willing to contribute?'

'I am,' Lamech said, and ten others also agreed.

'In that case, the matter is settled.' Chanoch stood and raised both hands, the signal for a matter's approval. The four nominated persons copied him. 'We will review your progress in two seasons' time.'

'Now, Lamech. I believe you had another matter you wished to discuss while you were here?' Kenan said as they all sat back down.

'Indeed, and it is no less lofty than the last, I am afraid.'

Kenan gestured. 'Please take the floor.'

Lamech made his way forward to his usual position in the round before the council. With the conclusion of the previous discussion, he was no longer one of them, but a petitionary once more. In that very spot, Lamech had made and been granted so many requests, some of which had changed the city irrevocably. What would he ask for now?

'I must begin with a confession,' Lamech said.

This made Chanoch curious. Lamech, confessing? He was being surprising today.

'Around five years ago, I withheld something from you fine men and women, which I shouldn't have withheld.' Lamech, ever the gifted orator, coughed into his hand and lowered his shoulders, giving the impression of deep humility.

'Cast your minds back, if you would, to when Barsabas was here, and the night he heard the news that his son had been killed in a raid. Shortly after he and his armies left, a season or so I suppose, Barsabas sent a messenger to blackmail me. He accused me of attacking and killing his illegitimate son.'

Whispers and mutters filled the surrounding area.

Lamech raised his hands. 'I knew the accusations were unfounded and there could be no shred of evidence – after all, I was here the entire time Barsabas was, caring for his men from my own provisions – even so, I feared what Barsabas was capable of. I am ashamed to say that I didn't feel able to come to you, the council of my elders. I should have sought your advice; I should have told you the truth, but I was afraid you did not trust me enough to assume my innocence.'

That part was true. Chanoch would never assume Lamech's innocence in anything. Yet could he have had anything to do with it?

'Baseless though they were, Barsabas' accusations frightened me. Especially when he claimed the only way to satisfy my supposed debt was by giving him my own daughter. A daughter for a son. Can you imagine? Exchanging my innocent Naamah's freedom for his silence! The thought disgusted me, as I'm sure it would every parent here. We all know how Barsabas' people treat their women and how hard Juval works to ensure the women of our city are cared for. Indeed, even now Barsabas' disgusting rituals invade our taverns and private parties. Now, we must be more vigilant than ever in protecting our people.'

Choruses of *Yes, Agreed,* and *Amen* followed this speech. Chanoch, though, was now on guard. For he knew that Juval was complicit in some of the rituals. Adah had confessed it to him some time ago and asked for his advice.

Lamech waited for silence before continuing. 'Of course, I could not give Barsabas my Naamah. Besides, we had already promised her to Kenan's family, with whom she would be safe. Still, that left me with a problem. My friends, I have been paying tribute to Barsabas all these years, fearing his unjust retribution on our city. I have been trying to protect us all from his barrage of evil. Still, he persists in threatening my family. A few weeks ago, he sent men to my father's farmlands, demanding that we hand over my sister, Dinah. Dinah, understandably, has no desire to return to her filthy husband, who treated her with such contempt, piling shame upon her before abandoning her here, far away from her beloved children whom she has not seen since. Yet Barsabas demands her back, despite the fact he has married multiple other women since leaving her. If we do not surrender Dinah, his army will once again appear at our gates, and this time, not to defend us, but to attack.'

Chanoch's chest tightened as several elders stood and shouted. His eyes throbbed as heated discussions progressed all around him and he tried to concentrate on all Lamech had said. His city, under attack? Of course, innocent women like Dinah must be protected. Yet at what cost? It was Methushael who had married his daughter to that monster. Where was he now? Besides, Methushael and his son shared a disposition to increase their power at any cost... just look at what Lamech had done to Adah. Lamech wouldn't put the whole city at risk, though, would he? Surely this couldn't be another power play.

Lamech motioned for quiet this time. 'My friends, my friends. Please.'

Gradually everyone sat back down and held their tongues, except Kenan, who said, 'What would you have us do?'

'I suggest we form our own army, stationing hunters around the city walls and scouts back on the borders of our farmlands, as we did when the tanninim attacked. Every able person should be trained to fight. I have a selection of kavash capable of carrying the scouts. They can outrun Barsabas' men. Moreover, we have another advantage Barsabas knows nothing of.'

'Which is?' Kenan asked.

'My son, Tuval-Kayin. Tuval-Kayin has been supplying farmers with metal tools for some time. The blades are light and adaptable. He assures me that the same metal can be used to make defensive weapons, and those already crafted into tools could be repurposed. Let us equip our farmers to defend themselves, sharpening their sickles into swords and learning evasive manoeuvres.'

The thought of tools being turned into weapons unsettled Chanoch, as did any talk of violence. He spoke again. 'We have noticed the expansion of your forge. Yet only the wealthiest farmers have these new tools, and their efficiency increases the gap between the smallholders and the landowners. Something several have complained about.'

Lamech shrugged. 'We set a fair exchange. I do not control who has enough to trade and who does not. Yet there is a way to ensure more access. The forge is currently worked to capacity – I have no more men to give it. It could be expanded still if you donate me people to assign to Tuval-Kayin. Additionally, we can produce more weapons if we train others to join the metal-hunters and find more ore.'

Another elder spoke up. 'You said every able-bodied person should join your army. Now you want metal-workers and metal-hunters. We seem to be running out of people here, Lamech.' Despite the seriousness of the occasion, a chuckle escaped the lips of some.

Lamech took a step back. 'You are right. My ideas run away with me. I am just passionate about defending our people. I have given Barsabas everything I can – he will never stop wanting more. Several of you have already formed your own groups of fighters to defend your assets. In the first instance, send them to me. Let us unite into an army with better weapons, ready to defend our families at the earliest sign of attack.'

Those who had already hired fighters seemed to approve of this idea, and a lively discussion broke out. Others began speaking of people in their extended families who did not work an honest day and could do with being relocated to the forge.

'Eber has acquired a new quarry near the eastern sea,' Kenan said. 'We can donate any ore we find to Tuval-Kayin, and some workers I expect.'

As Lamech's rallying call took effect, Chanoch could not prevent himself from standing. 'Stop. Wait!'

The others immediately halted their discussions.

Chanoch took a deep breath. 'Are we sure that peace has failed? Might there not be another way than the escalation of violence? I appreciate your sentiment, Lamech, and your willingness to defend the innocent. Yet, could we not invite Barsabas here? Surely if he knows the whole council is on your side, he will listen to reason?'

'And risk divulging our secret weapons?' Naman said. 'That does not seem very wise.'

'It is if there are no secret weapons to divulge,' Chanoch replied.

'Not so,' Kenan said. He rarely stood against Chanoch, and it was rather a shock. 'I apologise, Sav, but I'm with Lamech on this one. We must prepare for the worst, or it might catch us off guard. If Barsabas' armies march out now, they could slay everyone in the city before the season is out. However, I take your point. We should try mediation as well. Let us send a delegation to Barsabas.'

A ripple of agreement ran through the council.

'Very well,' Chanoch conceded. 'Volunteers for the delegation?'

Four people stood.

'Lamech should accompany them with a guard,' Kenan said. 'But, in the first instance, stay out of sight. Your presence could make things worse.'

Chanoch's heart felt heavy as he left the council to disperse to their separate homes, and no doubt discuss the news with their families. Had it really come to this – a potential war?

CHAPTER 59

'Azurak. Open up.' Lamech pounded on the wooden door until it slid open, and his enforcer's face appeared.

'Master?'

Lamech could understand Azurak's surprise. He hadn't been to his house before, at least, not in it. Azurak was usually at work before dawn.

He stepped inside and surveyed the place. It was a mess. And tiny. Both surprised him. 'You know, you could have a lot better home than this,' he said, running his finger over the rough clay walls. You only have to ask.'

'This suits me fine. I like the view.'

Lamech strode to the aperture and gazed out. It was true, the view lent it a certain charm. Stretching before him, all the way to the bottom of the valley, was his vineyard. The vines, perfectly aligned by his excellent vine-keeper, were good enough to rival Lemuel's. Was Yaval at work there? He couldn't see him. Lazy boy – it was almost midday.

His gaze alighted on the old watchtower to his far right, between Azurak's home and his own. 'We will need more of those,' he said, pointing.

'Master?'

'Do you have no other words today, my friend?'

Azurak looked half asleep, unusual for him. Lamech's eyes roamed over the rest of the quarters, catching on the linen flung lazily over a bed. Was that a strand of copper hair? Surely not—

He turned to his second-in-command. 'Are you bedding my daughter?'

Azurak's eyes widened, revealing something between shock and guilt, before he swiftly switched to his standard controlled antagonism. 'Why would you ask that?'

Lamech pinched the strand of hair between his fingers and held it aloft.

'Oh.' Azurak relaxed. 'That belongs to the tavern girl, Alina. Have you had her? She's good but prefers to come here. Rather inconvenient.'

He had never heard Azurak spout such rubbish. Was he losing his touch, or was it just the Naamah effect? Perhaps she made Azurak lose his wits the way Adah used to affect him. Stress on *used to*. Lately, Adah had just been tiresome. Even so, she still managed to send him into a rage on a regular basis. Why was it she made him so angry? He'd never quite figured it out. Whatever it was, she deserved everything she got.

Lamech opened his fingers and the strand glided to the floor. 'Just make sure Eber doesn't find out or you're a dead man. I require you alive for the next stage of the game.'

Azurak's face remained passively neutral, except for the slightest twitch of his upper lip.

'Is there anywhere for me to sit down?' Lamech looked around again. He thought he could spy a wicker chair beneath a pile of clothing and weapons. Azurak picked up the pile and shoved it on the bed, then stood back.

'As I was saying,' Lamech continued. 'We will need some more watchtowers. Seven or eight stationed around the walls should do it.'

Azurak stood in front of him, completely still. 'I assume the meeting was successful, then?'

'Yes. I thought you would be waiting behind the trees, desperate to know what happened. You've put so much work into it.'

'I was staying out of the way as you suggested, Master.'

'Hmmm.' He considered Azurak's darker-than-usual shadows. 'Anyway, it all worked out magnificently. They took every piece of bait I offered.'

'So, the second council will be set up?'

'Yes. An independent assembly or some such nonsense name.' Lamech felt his mouth stretch into a grin. He allowed the grin full sway over his face, suddenly revelling in the elation of the moment.

From deep in his chest laughter sprang up, filling the small house. 'Of course, thanks to you, it will be no such thing.'

'Naman was chosen.'

'By Kenan himself. Oh, our elders played their part excellently, my friend. Naman's disinterested face – brilliant, it was! He even got everyone paying him for his services.'

The bubbled laughter spilled out again and this time, Azurak allowed himself half a smile.

Lamech thought for a moment. 'The only trouble might be Selah.'

'Selah?'

'Yes, Chanoch's little fly in the ointment. Still, I suspect she can be easily influenced, or replaced.'

'Tell me about the war.'

'They want to send a delegation first. I suspected as much, despite my brilliant performance. I had them lapping up every insincere word as though I were the Deceiver himself. They were beautifully riled – you would have loved it. Everyone is on board – even the old man to an extent – and ready to send us their spares.'

'So, we expand the forge?'

'Oh yes. I shall tell Tuval-Kayin the good news.' Lamech stood up, suddenly anxious to see his favourite son. 'Get the slaves building those watchtowers immediately. As soon as I know more about the delegation, I'll tell you, and we can formulate a plan. We may have a nice little trip to go on.'

'You want me to join you? I thought I would manage things here.'

'No. They asked me for a guard. Who better than you? Besides, it'll get you away from my daughter for a while.' He couldn't help a slightly wicked wink at Azurak's expense.

His second, of course, just nodded his head.

'Oh, Azurak. Have a little fun, would you?' Lamech nudged the man in the shoulder and departed.

A RIDER WAS DISPATCHED immediately after the council meeting, returning a week later with news that Barsabas had agreed to meet their delegation on the first day of the new moon at the Great Lake. When Lamech returned home early a few days before the new moon,

Tzillah was delighted, until he'd revealed his intention to leave with the delegation the following morning.

'Must you go?' Tzillah asked, smothering him in kisses from her position on his lap. 'Aren't you needed here?'

The last few weeks had been a flurry of multiple meetings to ensure all would continue smoothly in Lamech's absence. The construction of extra watchtowers and assembly of a haphazard group of hunters and fighters into an organised army had begun. As Lamech sat on his couch, he felt exhausted but pleased with his second wife's attention. Nahar played sticks and bones at his feet. Lamech was meant to be playing too, but aside from the occasional roll, he largely ignored the game.

'But I need you,' Tzillah moaned, and Lamech threw Adah a glance that said, *If only you cared as much as she.*

Adah blushed and dropped his stare, focusing her attention back on the sewing in her lap. He noticed she carried a bruise on her neck and wished she'd cover it with a shawl as she did when she left the house. The other day, he'd overheard Yaval encouraging his mother to escape, but to his relief, Adah had refused. She still felt a duty to her household.

'You don't need me as much as the city does, woman,' Lamech responded to Tzillah.

'Oh, you men and your power. Can't we all just get along?' Tzillah pouted.

'Not unless you want me to feed Dinah to Barsabas.'

'Tush. Barsabas doesn't really want her. He has plenty of women.'

Lamech caught his first wife's eye again and they shared a knowing glance. Barsabas' passion for Dinah might easily resemble Lamech's for Adah. Passion bound up in equal parts hatred and desire. He couldn't live with her; neither could he live without her. Adah swallowed and gave Lamech a single nod before he turned to his second wife and dissolved Tzillah's glares of hostility with his lips.

THE ALMOST-SILENT BREATHING of Lamech's companion tickled his right ear. He wished the man hadn't eaten dried meat that morning; the smell was quite off-putting. They were squashed together within a thicket on a hill overlooking the Great Lake, spears at the ready and stone daggers tucked into their belts. Lamech hated leaving behind his beautiful bronze blade, however, he couldn't risk its discovery at this early stage of the game. In his hand instead was a small copper disc, which he was running through his fingers as he waited, being careful to keep it in the darkness of the undergrowth.

Twenty paces to his left, Lamech could see Azurak high in a tree with a bow in hand, so well camouflaged that Lamech wouldn't have known he was there if he hadn't singled out the position himself the day before. Azurak's cloak almost perfectly matched the leaves of the tree thanks to the dyeing method Naman's family had devised recently. The elders knew of Azurak's presence also, but it was essential that Barsabas didn't. Though the bow was merely the back-up plan, Lamech didn't need Barsabas having any more ammunition against his enforcer.

The previous week, Tuval-Kayin had revealed his new arrows with pride – small, thin tips, so tiny they added little weight to the flying projectile that could reach ten times further than a spear – the deadliest weapon he'd created so far. Reluctantly, Lamech had forbidden those too for this excursion, insisting on flint-tipped arrows that could be left behind without revealing their secrets. Even so, he'd commissioned Tuval-Kayin to make many more.

Thirty paces to Lamech's right, back flattened behind a huge trunk, was another hunter – a woman. Lamech had argued with Azurak about her inclusion, but his enforcer insisted she was the best sling-thrower on their side of the lake. She'd been wielding the weapon against wild animals since she could walk, protecting her family's flocks. Now she stood, leather-clad and hair pulled into a thick blonde braid that reached her lower back. Her sling was the first part of Lamech's plan, should the negotiations go the way he anticipated they might.

The fifth member of their party, though, was the prime weapon on this outing. Hidden amongst Barsabas' people, now lining up forty paces in front of them by the north-eastern side of the lake, was a young man Azurak had been training since childhood. Born to a life-long slave and given to Lamech to increase the family food rations, a foreman had noticed his skill at the age of eight, when he was fighting with another slave child over a piece of bread. The foreman had dragged him to Azurak's feet and there, he'd been made to demonstrate his swift, subtle attacking method. The child could render someone unconscious with a swift pinch to the shoulders, could slit a hamstring and disappear before anyone realised, and could steal without being seen. In short, he was the perfect spy.

Now, after ten years of training, the spy was loyal to his master, devoid of conscience or remorse, and most importantly, he'd been stationed in Barsabas' territory for the past two years. Through his intelligence, they had learned Barsabas' plans and weaknesses, allowing them to dodge all attempts to capture Lamech's covert metal-hunting teams in the north. For Barsabas had bitten at the chance to install his kohan in the city of Chanoch, which had kept him content for a time, until he'd realised Lamech's metal-hunters were stealing his ores, and war had become a real possibility again.

As the delegation of four elders greeted Barsabas and his men, the early-morning sun glinted off the lake, making it hard to see. Yet, Lamech noticed his spy subtly nod in his direction. He knew they were there. He had received the message. Beyond the delegation and guards, a herd of shaggy-haired long-horns grazed casually in the grass adjacent to the water. Straining his ears to hear what the men were saying, Lamech waited.

'You summoned. Here I am.' Barsabas raised falsely humbled hands before the elders of Chanoch.

Selah stepped forward one pace. 'We have come to negotiate peace. State your claims against us that would lead you to threaten our city.'

'That's easy. You murder, you hoard and you steal.'

Selah tilted her head. 'I am aware of no such activity. Would you care to elaborate?'

'My fight is not with you, daughter of Chanoch, but with my own kin. Yet, as you insist on bringing an official delegation, it is evident that you support my enemies. Is this the case?'

'We seek to protect our own, that is all. Name the charges.'

'Someone from your city had my son killed. I have good reason to believe it was my wife's brother, Lamech.'

'Impossible. Lamech showed you exceptional hospitality when you stayed with us, and he never left the city in that time.'

'Just because the deed wasn't committed by his hand doesn't mean he didn't orchestrate it.'

'I thought the Iradites did it.'

'If so, why did they not follow through on their threat? No Iradite has been seen near my borders since. By contrast, Lamech's men are everywhere.'

'What evidence do you have?' Selah replied. 'Show me one of these men.'

Barsabas' lip turned up. Lamech glanced nervously at his spy. Would this be the point Barsabas called the spy out, showing he hadn't been fooled all along?

'They have been seen multiple times in my land, stealing my ores.'

'Again, I ask you for evidence.'

'The witness of my men is evidence enough.'

Selah and Barsabas stared each other out, neither budging.

Naman stepped forward. 'I am astounded at your accusation of Lamech – a man who provides for the poor, sets up refuge for women sucked into your disgusting rituals, and whose wife tends the sick with her own hands. This man you accuse of murder?'

'Someone matching the description of his second-in-command, Azurak, was seen near the place my son was killed at the time of the murder.'

Naman laughed. 'Someone matching the description of Azurak? You match that description yourself. Perhaps it was you.'

A flint-tipped spear twitched. The spy's movement was barely perceptible, yet produced a swift copy as Barsabas' well-disciplined soldiers all lowered their spears towards the laugh, surrounding Naman, stopping the points a finger's length from his chest.

Surprise briefly crossed Barsabas' features at the unsolicited action, until he collected himself. 'Do you question my integrity?' he barked.

'There is no question of your integrity. You have none,' Naman sneered.

'There now,' Selah said, putting her hand up and gently pushing the nearest spear aside. 'We came here to establish peace, not to quarrel further. What do you want from us, Barsabas?'

Barsabas nodded and his soldiers retreated. 'I want justice for my son. I want my wife back. And I want the people of Chanoch off my lands.'

A third elder stepped forward. 'I was there the night you heard about your son. Lamech was as shocked as the rest of us – I saw it with my own eyes. And I heard your words to your wife. You treated her shamefully and said you cared not if she followed you.'

Barsabas' lip curled again. 'Well, I have changed my mind.'

'We do not believe in handing women back to husbands who mistreat them,' Selah said.

It was Barsabas' turn to laugh. 'Tell that to Adah!'

At the mention of his wife, Lamech's blood boiled. How dare Barsabas equate the way they treated their respective wives? He and Barsabas were nothing alike. His fingers itched to give the signal to his spy. He chewed his lip. *Control yourself, Lamech. Remember the long game.* He could not see Selah's expression from this distance, but she'd grown quiet, and it worried him.

The third elder spoke again. 'We will investigate the claims of our people on your lands and establish if any have strayed into your territory against our advice. As to the other things, we will not give you Dinah, and until you produce evidence, neither will we try Lamech.'

Barsabas motioned to his spearsmen who resumed their provocative stance. His voice lost its edge of calm. 'You are in no position to negotiate. I could send my armies to your gate within weeks and decimate your entire city before the season is out.'

'And how much trade would you lose if you did that?' the last elder said. 'Caravans regularly travel between our two cities. Your people would not thank you for cutting off the supply of their favourite foods.'

'Which is the only thing that's prevented me acting thus far. That and my foolish deal with Lamech.'

'What deal?'

Barsabas will tell them about the Kohan of El-Nachash. It cannot be. Lamech held the polished copper disc towards the sun and turned it three times.

It all happened swiftly. A huge longhorn raised its head, lowing loudly into the atmosphere. It flinched, then started to charge. On it went through the herd, hurtling forwards. One longhorn followed, then another. Soon, the entire herd were charging head-down towards the delegation.

Panic gripped the two parties of people, who split into chaotic runs of three or four, chasing after safety. A body slumped to the ground. Lamech watched as his spy withdrew a dagger, jumped away from a longhorn angled his way and followed the other fleeing soldiers. The cattle trampled the site where the body lay. Lamech knew to watch it, but no one else had been doing so. Their only concern was escape.

The delegation were running their way. After checking Barsabas was out of sight, and no longhorns had veered from the herd now careening over the northern hill, Lamech stepped out and guided the elders to safety. Three of them.

'Where is Selah?' They all looked around in panic, and Lamech joined them.

'There!' Azurak jumped from his tree and sprinted towards the spot where the meeting had been held. Hands flew to mouths. Cries of shock rose from the remaining elders.

Trampled in the dirt was a mangled mess of skin and clothing that had once belonged to Selah. Azurak reached her as Lamech broke into a run and dashed with the rest towards the sight.

Azurak turned the body over and lowered his ear to what loosely resembled a face. Then he looked up and solemnly shook his head. Behind him, Lamech heard someone retch. His own stomach churned at the sight, and he glanced away. The creeping claws of horror ripped at his gut, convicting him of guilt he had no intention of owning. The death was necessary, the associated command unavoidable. It had to look like the longhorns had charged unprovoked. He closed his eyes and breathed deeply through his nostrils as Azurak spoke again.

'Lamech. This was no accident.'

Back to the game. Lamech's eyes flew open, and he assumed a posture of disbelief. 'What?'

'Look here, master.'

Steeling himself to face the mangled mess, Lamech strode forwards to witness what Azurak had found. The two elders who had maintained their composure followed.

'There is a knife wound here. This blood left the body before the longhorns trampled it.'

'No!' Naman exclaimed behind him.

'See for yourself.' Azurak stood back, and the two elders crept forward, partially shielding their noses and mouths.

'He's right,' the other said. 'That is a knife wound.'

'Do you think—?' Lamech stopped short of vocalising a suspicion, needing it to be their idea.

'She was murdered,' Naman said. 'Barsabas has killed one of our people.'

'He must have used the longhorns as a distraction. She was very vocal in her disdain,' the other said.

Naman shook his head. 'No more so than the rest of us. We were united in our approach.'

'Perhaps she wasn't targeted specifically, but as a warning?' Azurak suggested.

'Why would they try to hide it if it was a warning?' Naman asked.

'Because Barsabas would never incriminate himself. He has been playing the victim all along,' Lamech said.

'How will I tell Chanoch? And Selah's husband; her children? She was the wisest of us all, and so well loved.' The man who had thrown up was sitting by his vomit, crying into the soil.

Lamech approached him. 'There, my friend.' He wrapped an arm about his shoulder and lifted him up, pulling him into a manly embrace. 'This is not your burden alone. We will tell them together, and hold a public memorial for her, as is fitting.'

The man shook in his arms, but amongst the shaking, nodded his head in gratitude.

Azurak removed his cloak and covered Selah's body, then two of them lifted her, ready to carry her home. As they departed, the woman with the sling slipped out from her position behind the wide-trunked tree. Lamech held back, allowing the others to walk on ahead, and met her.

She was trembling and whispered as he drew near. 'I didn't expect that.'

Lamech grasped her arm, and her sling fell limp in her hand. 'You did an excellent job and will be richly rewarded. It is not your fault it ended in tragedy. Barsabas' men murdered Selah. You understand?'

Her eyes widened, and she chewed her lip, nodding.

Lamech didn't look at her again as he squeezed her arm tighter and followed the others. 'If you ever confess to slinging the stone that started that stampede, or I hear wind of a single syllable in that regard, know this for sure: your body will end up like hers.'

The woman quivered in his grasp. It gave him satisfaction. This girl could defend her flock from bears, yet she shuddered at his threatening words and quaked at his touch.

Her voice cracked. 'I understand. You have my silence.'

CHAPTER 60

The city was in chaos. Selah's funeral had taken place the previous week, a protracted affair that saw a grossly carved image of her paraded through the streets for the people to grieve over, while her poor, trampled body was buried swiftly in Chanoch's family grave outside the walls bordering his home. The news that Barsabas had killed their beloved elder had travelled fast and people were terrified. War seemed inevitable.

Across all generations, people volunteered to train with the hunters and to work at the forge. Parties of metal-hunters were dispatched far and wide, though they were instructed to avoid Barsabas' lands.

Chanoch had graciously received Adah when she'd visited to offer condolences for his loss. His cheeks had looked thinner and his movements delayed, like it was a strain to stay in the world and not join his beloved daughter.

Adah was most worried for his wife, though. Being familiar with their humble home, she allowed herself leave to squeeze though the mourners in the central living area and enter Shiphrah's chamber. There she sat on the floor by the woman who had once held her hand as she grieved Lamech's betrayal and the loss of her infant.

Shiphrah's eyes opened a fraction and her dry lips, crinkled as pitted dates, parted slightly as she drew in a deep, heaving breath. 'Adah,' she exhaled. 'How are you?'

Adah stifled a cry as emotion welled within her. Here was the mourner – a woman who'd been dying for over a century – enquiring after her welfare.

'There, there.' Shiphrah tried to lift her hand, but it shook too much, and she was forced to lower it again. Adah wiped her own cheek, then Shiphrah's, as a little chunk of dried discharge dropped from the older woman's eyelid when a tear of her own escaped.

They'd shared the afternoon together in silent understanding, contrasting the wailing well-wishers on the other side of the curtain that sectioned Shiphrah's chamber from the living area. Those people offered constant condolences but knew little of their loss. Adah had left there late in the evening, oblivious to the darkness that accompanied her home, aware only that Shiphrah was not long for this world, and expectant of the additional loss her friend Chanoch would soon bear.

Lamech was proving a conundrum. Inside their home he seemed unusually cheery, but his expression changed the moment someone visited, or he went out.

'I can tell he's up to something,' Tzillah commented one day at the midday meal.

Juval was also on edge. 'Abba has tasked me as commander over a hundred men. He says I am one of the most experienced hunters we have, and I can ride, but I fear I lack the wisdom needed to make decisions affecting other people's lives. What if I call it wrong, and they are all slaughtered? I wish you would stand by my side, Yaval.'

'I want nothing to do with it,' Yaval said, picking up his wolf-pet from near Nahar and the little one, who were poking and irritating it. 'I told you not to do that. He will bite you, then Abba will wring his neck.'

'You never take responsibility for anything,' Juval huffed.

'I take responsibility for him,' Yaval replied, accepting a lick on the nose for his trouble. Yaval put the wolf back down and it bumbled straight back to the boys to play.

Juval rolled his eyes. 'I'd feel far more confident on my kavash if you were beside me.'

'You'll be fine,' Yaval said. 'You've been riding for years.' Juval often acted as Lamech's runner, riding out to manage his father's lands and building sites which stretched well beyond the city borders, covering land from the Great Lake to the eastern coast.

Juval sighed. 'I don't have a way with it as you do. I still need to get the whip out.'

'And that's why I hate handing them over,' Yaval said. He consented to train kavash to keep Lamech off his back but did so without using whips. Yet, the people he passed them to soon took them up. The only other person who refused a whip was Chanoch, who had adopted the original animals Lamech bought when they got too old to run at the speed required for a scout. Chanoch took them in out of pity saying they would be useful, though Adah couldn't think how.

As Juval continued to berate Yaval, Adah realised she'd need to break up the argument. 'Juval, have you heard from Naamah recently?'

Her son's face fell. 'Of course not, Ima. You know she won't speak to me.'

'I thought you'd been seeing Eber?'

'Yes, almost every day. But unless Naamah is hosting us at her home, she never gets involved. I don't think she sees her husband much.' Juval sighed, before sending a pointed look at his twin. 'I'm going to head to the training field. Unlike some people, I take my responsibilities seriously.'

Yaval ignored his brother and tucked into some more of Shua's excellent broth while Adah kissed Juval goodbye.

'I'm glad I didn't have twins,' Tzillah said. 'Mini-Kayin never argues with anyone.'

Adah chortled. 'That's because Mini-Kayin is never here.'

A growl came from the midst of the younger boys. Yaval jumped up. The little one had a hold of the wolf's tail and was tugging on it. Yaval dropped to all fours, pushed his brother aside and growled himself. The wolf continued to bare its teeth. Yaval drew closer, showing his superior size and complete lack of fear. The wolf took a step back. Then its lip dropped over its fangs. Yaval continued forward, snarling, backing the creature into the corner of the room, until its tail hit the wall and it dropped in submission. Yaval growled one last time. The wolf rolled over, baring its belly. Then Yaval reached a hand forward and stroked it. He scooped his pet into his arms and turned towards his half-brothers, sternness lining his face.

'I told you, *No*. Until Fang considers me his leader and you a pack to protect, you must not anger him. Abide by my rules or stay away.'

'Sorry, Yaval.' Nahar sniffed.

Yaval grinned and pulled his brothers into a hug. 'You're forgiven.'

'YAVAL, I NEED YOU,' Lamech said to his son that evening.

They were in the main living area – just the three of them – for the little ones were already in bed and everyone else was out. Tamar's youngest was cutting a tooth and Adah had been awake for a good portion of the previous night, wishing that Tamar was there to comfort the child herself, for he'd settle for no one else's heartbeat. If Lamech had sprung entertainment on her she would have struggled to control her tongue, so she was relieved it was just them.

Almost. For when Yaval and Lamech were in proximity, tension always reigned supreme, and Adah couldn't help but fixate on the scar drawn above Yaval's eyebrow, reminding her of the time Lamech dealt to her son what he often dealt to her.

She'd eaten a small amount of chickpea salad and bread, until fatigue had made her stomach sick. Now she longed to take herself to bed, though she feared the combination of heavy eyes and sickness would secure a night of unpleasant dreams.

Fang sat by Lamech's feet looking longingly at the bone Lamech chewed. The creature was devoted to food almost as much as to its young master. Lamech had softened towards it and occasionally picked a piece of meat from the bone and fed it to the wolf from his fingers.

'What can I do for you, Abba?' Yaval's look declared mistrust and misgiving, coupled with slight irritation that his abba was spoiling his wolf's training.

'You know what I'm referring to,' Lamech said abruptly.

Yaval reached to grab Fang then withdrew his hand. 'And you know my answer.'

Lamech's growl was akin to the noise Fang made when his tail was pulled. 'I can no longer accept your answer. War is upon us. You must train the kavash to take hunters.'

'How? They are frightened of weapons.'

'They might not be if you had used the whip on them.'

'What a ridiculous thing to say…' Yaval muttered. Adah's stomach churned like milk in a barrel. For once she wished Yaval would give in before Lamech lost it again.

Lamech threw his bone to Fang, who bounded across the room to fetch it. 'Start with Juval. His beast is used to him and surely won't flinch if he picks up a bow. Tuval is devising a breastplate the kavash can wear, so the enemy can't spear them. Coupled with your brother's genius, the kavash will give us the advantage we need over Barsabas. You must see that.'

'I see it, Abba, I just don't think it can be done.'

'That's nonsense. You know it can be done; you just don't want this war.'

Yaval stood. 'Of course I don't! Nobody wants this war.'

Lamech gritted his teeth. 'I meant you don't want to win the war. If you did, you would do as I say. If you don't do what I say, hundreds could die, including Juval.'

For once, Lamech was right. Juval's life was more important than the kavash – Yaval must see that.

Her son paused. He was thinking about it. Slowly he sat back down. 'I hate the idea that innocent animals will get slaughtered because men can't get along.'

Lamech finally appeared to soften. He reached a hand forward and touched his son's – just slightly. 'Yet innocent men will die if the animals don't aid us. Please, son. Do it for Juval.'

Now Adah desperately wanted Yaval to say yes. If he didn't and Juval died— It was unthinkable. She remembered something. 'Aren't two of Mela's brothers in the army as well?'

Yaval looked at her. 'They are...' A light flickered in Yaval's eyes. 'Alright, Abba. I'll do you a deal.'

Lamech raised an eyebrow. 'A deal?'

'I will train the kavash to take hunters if you let me marry Mela.'

'What?' Lamech scoffed. 'My eldest son marrying a weaver's daughter? You must be joking.'

'They are a respectable family—'

'With no influence whatsoever.'

'So what?' Yaval stood again. Fang whimpered as he placed his hands on the table before his abba, looking him squarely in the eyes. 'We both know I am not the son you wanted. I am a failure in your eyes. What difference does it make if I marry Mela? So...' Yaval paced towards the fireplace, then spun. 'I give up my rights as firstborn to Juval. There. I give them up!'

Lamech was mute. The silence penetrated Adah's tired, heavy head as painfully as a pealing bell.

Her husband chewed his bottom lip. 'You would give up your birthright for a woman?'

Fortifying himself, Yaval crossed his arms and stuck out his chin. 'I would. I do. Please, Abba. I will do as you wish – I will help you win this war – if you agree that afterwards I may marry Mela. Juval and Mini-Kayin can follow in your footsteps, but I never can. I will even leave if you want me to – you need never see me again.'

For the second time that night, Adah saw unusual tenderness sweep over Lamech's face. 'I don't want that,' he said quietly. Then slowly, he shuffled and stood, until his height was level with his son's, whose figure looked slight in comparison. Lamech chewed his lip again, turned and strolled towards the exit. At the doorway, he paused. 'You may marry your woman. Now train my kavash. All of them.'

Yaval's mouth dropped open.

'Are you leaving?' Adah asked. She wasn't sure whether to be pleased or not. It wasn't long since sundown, and the night was young.

'I'm going elsewhere.'

By *elsewhere*, Lamech meant to Tamar.

'Lamech.' Her voice surprised her. 'Do you need to? Don't you have enough sons now?'

Her husband turned, his eyes asking a thousand questions. 'Are you offering me an alternative?' was the only one that left his lips.

Momentarily, she considered it. Was it what she wanted? Then the weariness of the previous night impressed itself on her senses and she lightly shook her head.

Lamech snorted and left.

The air in the room felt lighter the moment he did. Yaval tilted his head. 'Are you unwell, Ima?'

'No, just exhausted. I am pleased about Mela. That was well played.'

Yaval hummed. 'Perhaps I am my father's son. We'll see if he keeps his end of the deal; I'll only believe it on my wedding night.'

Adah sighed and rubbed her temples. 'First, we must win this war. Oh, it's so awful. The thought of anyone dying—'

'I know,' Yaval said. He slid his arm under hers and helped her up. Fatigue took over as she stumbled to her chamber, and she was grateful for Yaval's arm, particularly as she slipped into bed.

'Goodnight, Ima.' Yaval kissed her forehead, then left.

CHAPTER 61

The winter came and went with no message received from Barsabas and no soldiers seen from the hastily constructed watchtowers. Though most of the council were keen to see justice for Selah swiftly carried out, they knew the longer they had to fortify, the better the chance of beating Barsabas at his game. So they waited.

Lamech grew impatient. He had expected at least some indication of Barsabas' readiness to fight. Yet, as he stood in the mouth of the cave at the forge, surveying a collection of bronze arrowheads, sickle-swords, rapiers, spear-tips and axes, he thought it better no attack was imminent.

The bronze-work was exquisite. His son was a true artisan. The larger pieces were not just deadly weapons, but had patterns etched into them, declaring the maker's skill for the bearer and the wounded to see. The smaller pieces, such as arrowheads, the newer workers had made, practicing with less of the precious ore. The weapons were excellent. There just weren't enough of them.

'What is this?' Lamech asked, picking up an almost flat, rectangular piece of metal, bowed slightly at both ends.

Tuval-Kayin smiled. He retrieved a leather head covering, slipped the disc into it and put it on. 'Tap it,' he said.

Lamech formed a fist and lightly tapped his son's forehead, drawing his brows together as his knuckles touched the hardened headpiece.

Tuval-Kayin removed it. 'I thought it would protect the skull from blows. We've yet to try it in practice-combat.'

'Clever,' Lamech commented. The heat from the forge was less intense up in the cave, where Tuval-Kayin assembled his creations and taught others to refine and sharpen them. Yet smoky smouldering still reached the nostrils, and warmth touched his feet from the furnace below ground. 'Will you need a tanner to create you more...?'

'Helmets,' Tuval-Kayin finished.

'Helmets. Yes.'

'That would be helpful.'

'I have someone. I'll send him.' The slave Yosa who had tried to earn his own way had predictably come back a few seasons later, starving and begging Lamech for work to sustain his family. Lamech had given him some, then set him up a new workshop in a suitable place outside the city, providing him with everything he needed in return for a limitless supply of leather goods.

It had turned out to be a brilliant arrangement, for Yosa was an excellent tanner, a man capable of not just processing skin, but also forming it into useful objects. Several times a week, Lamech's hunters dropped skins off at the tanner's workshop and a season later, they came back as goods. Lamech was so pleased, he even made sure the man's ludicrously large family was well fed. Sometimes his open-handedness astounded him; he was known as a generous man, and not without good cause.

Lamech turned his attention back to the collection of weapons. 'Is this all?'

Tuval-Kayin blinked and grimaced slightly. 'This is an immense amount, Abba. I thought you'd be pleased. Everyone is working hard; the ore doesn't come in as fast as we can break it.'

He considered his son, the boy who bore his image almost exactly, from the broad shoulders to the shape of his toes. The trace of Tzillah was just in the hair. He was proud of this son-in-his-likeness, more than Juval, who, though talented, was easily distracted like his mother. He never feared that fault with Tuval-Kayin – a permanent fixture at the forge.

'Why doesn't the ore come in?' he asked. 'Isn't Eber providing it? He promised...'

'Yes, but since we stopped collecting it from Barsabas' lands, the metal-hunters have struggled to keep up with demand.'

Lamech glanced around. Behind him, outside the cave, were ten or so men working hard at the anvil or grinding stone – sharpening, shaping and fixing. Before him, the cave was empty. He grasped Tuval-Kayin's arm gently and drew his son further into the darkness.

Once out of earshot, he spoke again. 'Why have you stopped hunting Barsabas' lands?'

Tuval-Kayin drew a sharp breath, though Lamech could no longer see his son's expression. 'We were given strict orders, Abba.'

'Not my orders.'

'Aren't we trying to avoid a war? If men are caught—'

Lamech suppressed a chuckle. 'What makes you think I am trying to avoid a war?'

His son's voice quivered. 'You're not?'

Lamech lowered his volume further, murmuring near Tuval-Kayin's ear. 'My concern is not whether we avoid this war. It's whether we win it.'

'I don't understand, Abba.'

'You are my son, Tuval. The image of me, and of your namesake – Kayin, The Wanderer. You know he killed his own brother? That is our legacy, son. That is our blood. We take what we want, and we repay the evil done to us.'

Tuval-Kayin nodded. 'Barsabas *has* mistreated Aunt Dinah.'

'Precisely. His people are a blight on these lands, spreading their filth all over the north and now, they want to bring it here. Have no doubt, your uncle would kill us all given the chance, and take our property for himself.'

'Then why hasn't he done so already?'

'He is playing a long game. But he doesn't realise I am better at it than he. And you, son? You are like me. We have the foresight to know the potential of humankind. We are not content to let life pass us by – to let the world affect us. No, we affect the world. We remake it in our image. Now, consider this long game. What do you need to achieve your aspirations?'

'I need more ore, Abba. Lots more. I know there is more in the north, in the mountains and in the marshland of the south. Different types too. The potential is endless; I can feel it.'

'And how are we to get this ore?'

'We could make trade deals, exchanging some of our goods – our city produces the best wine and wheat in the region. Labour too – building on our skills, training others, as I do here. This could go across cities. We could expand…'

Lamech stopped him. Tuval-Kayin sounded just like he had in his younger years. He had changed now. He'd learnt the benefits of speeding things up with a little efficiency and ruthlessness. 'Yes, yes. All promising ideas, which would no doubt work with the peaceful southern cities. Yet consider this scenario: Barsabas attacks us, mistaking how powerful we have become. War ensues for a brief time. Then we win. We banish him for his deeds, sending him to the Realm of Leviathan, or over the mountains. His lands become ours; his people work for us, retrieving more ore than you could ever need, and bringing it right here.'

Tuval-Kayin didn't reply directly. After a pause and a slow breath, he spoke. 'So, you're saying you do want a war?'

'I'm saying it has certain benefits.'

'But lives will be lost.'

'Shh!' Lamech reached for his son's arm and once he had a hold in the dark, he squeezed it. 'An unfortunate consequence of progress. A short-term tragedy for a long-term gain. Remember, we think beyond. We think ahead. We do what is best for our family. For our people.'

Silence reigned in the cave. Had he misjudged his son? Should he have kept quiet? Was it too early to reveal his hand?

Lamech decided to play his final piece. He dropped his hold on Tuval-Kayin's arm. 'Barsabas murdered Selah. His evil must be stopped. I'm not suggesting we start anything, just that we are well prepared for what is inevitable. If we need to raid Barsabas' lands to prepare for his attack, then so be it.'

A worker called for his son from outside the cave. Lamech felt Tuval-Kayin walk past and soon, he could see his silhouette against the light outside. Tuval-Kayin stopped, looked back and nodded. 'I understand, Abba. I will order the metal-hunters to resume their previous activities.'

And just like that, the piece fell into place, and the game was back on course.

SOMEHOW, Yaval did the impossible. A month later, he delivered to Lamech's commanders some improved mounts. Then lessons began, each commander taking it in turns to learn to ride with his weapon, as Yaval instructed from the side of the field, imploring them not to use the whip too readily, and running on occasionally to steady the creatures if they reared in protest. They responded to his touch – his gentle drawing near to their flank and conversing cheek to cheek – far better than to strangers.

Several times a week, Yaval would come home with an injury, so that Adah's concern multiplied further. Once, she tried convincing Lamech to call off the project, but he grew angry, accusing her of not caring for Juval, who would be more likely to survive battle astride a kavash than on foot.

Needing to keep her mind occupied, Adah joined a special project set up by the healers, tending battle injuries. Under the guidance of the oldest and wisest, Adah and the other volunteers learnt how to treat wounds, mix herbs for infection and pain relief, and even how to remove limbs that had been damaged irrevocably.

When she wasn't with the healers and needed an escape from the boys, Adah took herself to the vineyard, where the rolling hills and rows of neat, orderly vines, brought stability to her mind. She could escape worrying about everyone and everything as she concentrated on a little prune here or supporting a branch there. Yet, one day, worry invaded her place of escape.

Who is that? A solitary figure approached in the distance, limping then stumbling. His figure was unfamiliar and unwelcome against the backdrop of cultivated land. As he drew nearer, Adah saw blood – blood splattered on his clothing and dripping from his flesh.

She dashed to him. 'Who are you? What happened?'

The man, in his three-hundreds or so, spluttered a reply. 'A metal-hunter. I was...' he coughed and winced at the movement. 'Collecting north. We were ambushed.'

Collecting in the north – in Barsabas' lands?

Having reached safety, the man's legs gave way, and he fell into her arms. Pain shot through her back as she caught him, and they tumbled together to the soil. His eyes closed.

Adah glanced around. The discomfort shot up her neck. His weight had done her an injury. Spying a vine-worker about fifty strides away, she shouted, 'You! Get the master. Get the master, now.'

The vine-worker looked up, startled. His eyes opened wide, and he nodded, then sprinted towards the city.

It felt like half a day before Lamech came, though the sun didn't move in the sky, so it could have been barely any time at all. As he lay over her legs, Adah tried to loosen some of the injured man's clothing to free his airways. She bound his bleeding leg with a ripped section of his tunic. If only she could leave him to get some decent supplies, but he was too heavy, and she feared hurting him further by putting him down. Never mind herself. It was also a considerable walk to the stream where large skins for watering the crops hung from a wooden pole, taunting her. She was sure water would revive him somewhat.

Eventually, she spied Lamech jogging towards her, followed by Azurak and another young man.

'What happened?' he said, crouching and placing a gentle hand on her arm.

'He said he was metal-hunting in the north, and they were ambushed. Then he fell unconscious. Careful—'

Lamech lifted the body from her, and the release shot another pain through her back.

'Are you hurt?' Lamech asked.

'Yes. My back went as I caught him.'

'Azurak. Take this man to the healer on the tanner's street. I trust her. Be careful carrying him – there is a broken bone somewhere. I will see to Adah then join you.'

Azurak nodded and, together with the young person hovering behind, removed the unconscious man and carried him up the hill.

Adah breathed through the pain as Lamech helped her to her feet.

'Can you walk?'

She nodded.

Lamech tenderly stroked her cheek. 'I can carry you if you'd rather?'

She shook her head gently, immediately wishing she hadn't as her neck protested. She swallowed the pain down. 'I'll be fine. Can I come with you?'

Lamech's brow furrowed.

'I want to make sure the metal-hunter is well,' she persevered. 'I have some skill in healing; I can assist.'

His lip twitched. 'Alright. I doubt you can do much in your condition, though I would like her to check your back. But Adah?'

'Yes?' She looked into her husband's eyes. So often cold and angry, now they hovered between compassion and mistrust.

He shook his head and rubbed his brow. 'No. I cannot trust you...'

'Please, Lamech. I promise—'

'You must. You must promise that whatever you hear that man say, you cannot pass on. To anybody. There are things happening beyond your understanding and I can't have you running off to Chanoch about this.'

What could he mean? She knew he held secrets – many. What was he hiding that concerned this man? It was a foolish promise to make; she would probably regret it. However, curiosity forced her assent, like a moth compelled to touch fire. 'I promise.'

'Come then,' Lamech muttered, helping her up the hill. 'No doubt I will live to regret this.'

By the time they reached the healer's home, the injured man was laid out on the bed, stripped and washed. His major wounds had been bandaged and the healer was attempting to set his bone, but he'd woken, making the job far more difficult.

Seeing Lamech, the man's lip trembled, and his eyes closed.

Lamech approached the bed. 'Don't worry, friend. You are safe now. No harm will come to you if you answer all my questions.'

'And after that, keep your mouth firmly shut,' Azurak sneered.

The healer tutted. 'Now then. The last thing this man needs is an interrogation. Adah, I'm glad to see you; you may assist. The rest of you may leave.'

Lamech rolled his eyes, and the three men left the room.

'Thank the gods,' the healer said. *The gods... they were plural now?* 'It's always hard to work with men breathing down your neck.' The healer turned to the injured man. 'Now, my friend. If you want them to stay out, you must let us do this without too much fuss. It's going to hurt, but it's up to you whether or not we get Azurak in here to hold you down.'

The man nodded and closed his eyes.

'Good decision. Here's a stick for you.'

Adah placed the stick in his mouth to bite on as they worked. Just before they had finished, Lamech strode back in. He glanced at the man then wrapped his arms around Adah. 'How is my wife?'

The healer looked up. 'You were injured too?'

'It was nothing. Just my back.' Adah had borne it silently, conscious of the greater pain of the man on the bed.

'May I question him now?' Lamech asked.

'Yes, but go easy. He's had a great shock. I will give Adah a massage while you do.'

'I'm in awe of you,' Adah said, as the healer rubbed oil over her shoulders in the other room. 'When I stand up to Lamech, he—' she stopped herself.

The healer rubbed her neck. 'He what?'

'Nothing.' If her husband had this woman in his camp, his increasingly violent reactions were not for her ears.

'Your husband is well liked and respected. A powerful, charming man. Yet I know all is not as it seems,' the healer whispered.

Of course, if trusted by Lamech, this healer must be privy to some of his secrets as well. Did Adah want to know more about his plans, or was ignorance the better course? As the massage progressed, her pain intensified then gradually eased, and Adah came to no decision.

Murmurings from behind the curtain grew louder, then Lamech pushed it aside and entered. 'I am satisfied. You may let the man rest. Come, Adah. I'll escort you home, then I must call a meeting of the elders.'

Adah stood gingerly. 'Why? What's happened? Why was that man in Barsabas' lands?'

'He strayed accidentally. They were waiting for him. Killed three of our people and left him to die.'

'No!' Adah's hand flew to her mouth. Was it true? Had they really strayed accidentally? Either way, the killing was unforgiveable.

'I've had other news today that suggests Barsabas' army is coming. I'm afraid to say you healers better get ready for war.'

'We are ready, master,' the woman said.

Are we? Can you ever be ready to lose those you love?

CHAPTER 62

Lamech's army went out to meet springtime with war. At the helm, Lamech rode a kavash, with Azurak and Juval beside him and the other mounted commanders behind. News of Barsabas' fighters amassing on the borders had produced a quick mobilisation of all trained men and women, and hundreds followed on foot, most with weapons crafted from the forge.

Adah stood on the watchtower platform, holding hands with Tzillah and Naamah. Naamah's other hand gripped the railing, her knuckles whiter than a lily. They watched in silence as the glimmering army passed slowly before them, each weapon reflecting the light like the ripples of a river in high summer. Across the city, many others were doing the same, making use of the six or so watchtowers Lamech had built, and straddling the walls where no tower existed.

They kept watching until the steady stream passed over the northern horizon at noon.

'Now what do we do?' Naamah asked, releasing the rail and a breath.

'We wait,' Tzillah replied. 'It will take them some days to reach the borderlands at that pace. Let's get some wine.'

Adah didn't think wine would solve the problem, but she needed something after watching Juval go to war. The thought of her beloved being exposed to so much danger had almost induced her to contrive a circumstance that would force him to stay. Only Lamech's inevitable wrath had prevented it.

One company of healers had left with the army, laden with bandages and medicines, but Adah was in the second company, the ones who waited for the wounded to return. Hopefully in victory – not with Barsabas' army in hot pursuit.

When they passed Shadow, watching by the wall, and entered the house, Shua was surrounded by four hungry children, impatiently waiting for their lunch.

Leah was trying to carry dishes through the crowd. 'Come now, little master, you can carry something,' she said to Naamah's eldest.

He refused, saying it was women's work, and snickered to Nahar. Adah stepped in to help and, by the time they were all reclined at the table, things had calmed down somewhat.

'When is Abba getting home?' Nahar asked.

'We don't know,' Tzillah replied. 'Now eat your beans.'

'I hate beans,' Naamah's daughter said.

'They're good for you,' Adah replied, glancing at Naamah. She hadn't joined them at the table but was in the chair by the fire, holding tightly to its intricately carved arms, her face starkly pale against her copper hair. Eber hadn't gone to war – Kenan couldn't spare him – and, though Naamah seemed to tolerate her compulsory husband well enough, she didn't love him. Perhaps she was frightened for Lamech and Juval? Despite forcing her to marry whilst in mourning, Naamah still loved her abba, but enough to elicit this reaction? It was more likely that Juval remained highest in her affection, even though Naamah still refused to speak to him. Unless... Could there be someone else Naamah was petrified of losing?

YAVAL PUSHED HIS KAVASH as fast as he dared, encouraging her on with constant endearments. The saddlebags jostling at the creature's sides were stuffed full of additional medical supplies which he intended to get to the healers before dark. As he approached the rear of the camp, the last few skirmishes could be heard beyond the moans of injured men lying in and around deerskin shelters.

'They're further back,' he muttered to himself. 'Barsabas has gained ground.'

Yaval's heart tugged at the suffering as he scanned the bodies for his brother. None of them looked familiar. He cursed his father and the war as he dismounted and lifted the bags onto his shoulders, glad he had refused to get involved in the fight whilst ashamed it was happening at all.

He spied a senior healer, hands deep in a body wound, arms and tunic plastered in scarlet. Beside her was a fire, giving a little light to assist the treatment.

She looked up. 'Come quickly. Help me.'

Yaval threw the bags by the shelter then placed his hands around the upper arms of the injured man to pin him down while the healer stitched. The smell was almost enough to make him retch and he knew it would get worse when infection set in.

The healer nodded towards the wound. 'Did you bring poppy seed?' The pain-relief had been discovered by The Wanderer's wife, along with many other remedies.

Yaval nodded. 'Ima sourced it for me. It's in the bags.'

'This one might need it.' The healer tutted as she finished off the stitch and covered it in a paste of pomegranate molasses, thyme and sage. This man was now mercifully unconscious, but plenty of others still screamed in agony.

'Are you staying?' the healer asked. 'We could use you here.'

His eyes scanned the remaining patients. 'How many will live?'

'It's hard to say. That one, certainly not.' She pointed to a woman in the far corner of the tent, just visible. Where her clothing was removed, a flesh wound ran across her entire torso and midriff. All around it, purply bruising indicted the internal bleed, and the wound was oozing large quantities of pus.

Yaval's heart dropped as he recognised the face atop the mangled body. 'I know her. She's my age. Have you seen Juval?'

The healer shook her head. 'He's not been near here. As far as I know, he's fine.'

Relief eased slightly, but Yaval's chest still felt tight with worry. There were so many injured, never mind the mounds of wrapped, lifeless bodies he'd seen outside the camp. How many had lost their loved ones that day? All thanks to Barsabas, Abba and their foolish ambition. It was incomprehensible that they would embrace death – that destructive, disinterested force that took at will, waiting for no permission. Death belonged to the great enemy and had no place in the hands of men who turned it to their own means, trying to control it the same way they subdued the animals. How could any hope to conquer it?

'I'll take her back with me.' Yaval indicated the dying woman. 'I know her family. If she's going to pass, let it be in their arms.'

The healer nodded. 'As you wish. You can't travel in the dark though. Help us for the night, then return in the morning. She should survive that long.'

A groan nearby pulled the healer back into urgency and she got up to attend another victim. 'Yaval? It would be useful to know how many to expect at dawn. Perhaps you could find your father and ascertain his intentions?'

Seeing Abba didn't hold much appeal, but it would give him the opportunity to check on his brother. He nodded, grabbed a burning torch and headed towards the front of the camp. He pushed his way through soldiers who had finished for the night and were setting up campfires and distributing meat. How strange it was – two opposing groups, ready to fight to the death, sitting within running distance and doing nothing.

As he approached his father's tent, he heard voices inside. Abba's. One he didn't know. Then – Ah! Relief broke in and a smile spread across his face, dispelling the bleakness of his previous musings. Juval was alive!

Yaval wanted to run into the tent, but sense stayed his feet. They were discussing the battle. Tactics. He put his ear to the deerskin and listened.

'This whole thing could be over quickly if we take out Barsabas.' It was Lamech speaking. 'His life is worth far less than the lives of every other man here.'

'You mean, murder him?' the unknown man said.

'We don't need to stretch to the word *murder*. A strategic death for the benefit of others.'

'I'm not sure I see the difference, master.'

'Nonsense. What matters is victory with as few casualties as possible. Our superior weapons have prevented mass slaughter. Barsabas expected an easy win and hasn't got it. But the men are tired and depleted. We must act to save them.'

'What do you propose, Abba?' It was Juval's voice again.

A brief pause followed before Lamech spoke. 'I've already set the plan in motion. Azurak has left to meet my man on the other side. Before the sun has fully lit the sky, it should be over.'

The unknown commander spluttered, hesitated, then spoke again. 'So, you don't want me to ready the men?'

'Oh, I do.' Yaval could almost hear his abba's smile. 'But we are readying for capture, not battle.'

'Capture?'

'I intend to take Barsabas' entire army captive.'

Several gasps followed. 'How?'

He could picture Lamech's smirk perfectly. 'Just wait and see.'

THE SUN WAS PEEKING above the horizon, announcing the dawn of a new era. The culmination of years of planning and subterfuge. Azurak could see the back of his target's head, for Barsabas stood with his commanders at the battleline, holding conference. Barsabas' twisted black hair was fastened into a rough knot, revealing his neck, bound by an inked serpent with a two-pronged tongue, which kissed beneath his earlobe. Five stars encircled the snake.

From his position high in a tree, Azurak's arrowhead was perfectly poised to split the tongue from the serpent's head. With one eye closed and the other on target, he breathed slowly in and out, silently aware of his sling-bearer creeping to her post. Forming the third point of their triangle was his spy, three men to Barsabas' left, hand on hilt.

A war cry resounded – the blast of a ram's horn, followed by hollers from Lamech's men. Barsabas nodded to his commanders, who stepped back from their semi-circle into a straight line. Barsabas blew his own horn then raised his arm. His soldiers raised weapons.

Now.

Azurak's fingers released the nock and the jolt on his shoulder almost sent him off balance. It was the farthest he'd shot from such a height. As he grasped the branch below, his arrow sank true. Barsabas' head lopped forward. His knees crumpled as he collapsed to the ground. Then around him, the commanders fell one by one, by stone or sword, until just his spy was left, brandishing a bloody blade, staring up at Azurak's tree.

It was done.

ADAH WAS IN THE garden when she heard Avram call out, 'Young masters. Welcome home!'

Masters? Both of them? She'd been expecting Yaval's return but, could it be Juval too? Jumping up from where she'd been trimming a flower, she ran into the entrance courtyard, in time to see her two sons dismounting from their kavash. Juval held out his arms.

'My boys!' Adah's feet couldn't carry her fast enough and soon, she was melting into Juval's chest as he held her tightly. 'Is it over?' she asked, reluctantly pulling away to look him up and down, checking for any injuries.

'Yes, Ima. We won. All of Barsabas' commanders fell and we captured the army swiftly. Abba is travelling north to set up a new command in his lands. He tasked Azurak and me with getting the rest of the army and the new slaves safely home. We've just arrived.'

Adah pushed the word *slaves* from her mind as she grasped Juval again, focusing on her son's vibrant heartbeat. Then she kissed him and embraced Yaval, before hearing a squeal behind her.

Naamah was standing, hand clasped to her mouth, between the colonnades. Then she too ran and threw herself in Juval's arms, weeping loudly.

Juval kissed the top of Naamah's head, smiling broadly.

Adah felt Yaval squeeze her middle. 'Finally,' he whispered. 'It's about time they made up.'

It was a number of weeks before Lamech returned home. By then, all in the city had heard of his victory, and none openly disagreed with his methods. Not even the elders. He was proclaimed a valiant hero, master tactician and the saviour of countless lives.

They raised banners at the gates as Lamech's company rode through, and cheers accompanied a parade through the streets where women – grateful for the return of their husbands and sons – cared little for the hooves of kavash as they wrestled to press gifts into the heroes' arms.

When Lamech entered Adah's bedchamber that evening after an extended welcome at the tavern, he swept her into an embrace.

Excitement dominated his presence. The glint in his eye hinted at the triumph without and within. His confidence wasn't surface-deep anymore; it ran through his veins and sweated from his pores. *I am man,* it said. *I have conquered.*

CHAPTER 63

City of Chanoch, 750th year of Wandering

Chanoch leaves Adah and Juval by the burnt-out embers as he lights a piece of oiled linen, wrapped around a branch, and takes it to the back of the house. *She is asking for my father. Should I trust her?*

Four seasons ago they'd stood together in Lamech's courtyard, discussing whether Yaval and Adah could see his parents again. They agreed to it then. But things are different now. This is the first time he's seen Adah since that day.

He also knows they are watched - penned in like wild animals waiting to be broken. The danger increases with each passing day, each whisper in the marketplace, each retelling of The Wanderer's story. The city is stirring, discomfort is increasing. And Lamech blames him.

Was it the right thing to do, taking his parents to that party? For the past few centuries, they have stayed safe by moving from place to place, never revealing their whereabouts to any but the closest family members. By exposing his connection to them, Chanoch put them in danger. Asking them to challenge the most violent, powerful man in the region placed a target on their backs.

Now the enemy's wife wants their help.

Chanoch's foot hovers above the top step leading to the cellar. *Yahweh, what should I do?*

He receives the same answer he always gets: **'Do what is right.'**

Not immensely helpful when you don't know what the right thing is.

'Yes, you do.'

Chanoch leans against the red stone wall and closes his eyes. *My abba's mark.* The picture of the scar, that traces Kayin's face from his right eye to his upper lip, flashes clearly into Chanoch's mind.

Of course. Yahweh protects my abba. His mark proves that, and Yahweh certainly doesn't need my help. But Adah? Adah does need me… 'Alright, I'll do it.'

He steps boldly down one step. Then another. Soon he is securely in the underground cellar, surrounded by stacks of wheat, cheese and wine. He holds his torch aloft and spies the tiny hole in the wall - right at the top. After strolling to it, he runs his hand along the slit until he feels the silkiness of a feather. Drawing it close to the flame reveals its colour. Not white, black, nor brown, but grey.

They are in the hill-country then.

He replaces the feather, ready for the messenger to swap the next time he visits. He doesn't know who the messenger is - it's safer that way.

Time to return to Adah and ready the kavash.

CHAPTER 64

City of Chanoch, 745th year of Wandering

Once the dead had been buried and the wounded had recovered sufficiently, the elders declared a seven-day festival to celebrate their victory which would commence on the second Shabbat following the announcement.

'I agree we should celebrate,' Eliana said, as Adah had lunch in her house the day they heard the news. 'But what about those who've lost loved ones? Many died before the victory came. Shouldn't we hold a memorial first?'

Eliana, with all her connections, knew many affected families and she had been busy preparing food baskets and condolences for each acquaintance, which Adah contributed to from Lamech's supplies.

'Perhaps it will be part of the festivities,' Adah replied. 'I'll speak to Lamech about it.'

Lamech hadn't grown angry with her once since his return, though she'd been especially careful not to provoke him. Strangely, she'd enjoyed the unexpected return of his pleasure. He was like the Lamech of their early days – funny and attentive, proud and keen to please. Only the glint in his eye frightened her – the knowledge that at any moment, he might snap. So, Adah feared asking him about holding a remembrance from the moment she'd promised it to Eliana.

At dawn the next morning, as she lay in Lamech's arms, she took a deep breath and did it. 'Will there be a remembrance for those who gave their lives as part of the festivities?' she asked, kissing his lips before he could answer, to soften the question.

Lamech groaned and kissed her back. Then, slowly, his eyes opened, and he stroked her cheek. 'I hadn't thought about it. But that is an excellent idea.'

'It is?' Relief swept through her.

Lamech chuckled. 'Don't look so terrified, little mouse. What better way to win people's hearts than to honour their dead?'

Adah wasn't sure that was the right motivation, but she wasn't going to question him again. 'Do the elders know the names of all the fallen? I can organise something if you'd like?'

'I'll find out when I meet with them tomorrow. They'll be pleased you suggested it.'

'You'll confess it was my idea?' She'd assumed Lamech would claim credit for himself.

'Of course. They approve of you. It will lend the whole thing legitimacy.' Lamech sank back into the bed and sighed. 'This is what I always wanted, you know.'

Adah couldn't resist tracing his beard with her finger. He looked so at peace, like she'd never seen him before. 'What is?'

He fixed her eyes with his. 'A family I could be proud of, at the forefront of society, shaping the future. We have overtaken them all, Adah.'

Adah forced her face to relax against the instinctive inward pull of her eyebrows. She lay down and snuggled into his hold. The conversation had shown her the best way to influence her husband. All those years fighting against him, trying to correct him, had achieved nothing. He'd never done what she wanted but had battled her at every turn, in every way. By contrast, Tzillah knew how to handle him, pandering to his pride and helping him think her ideas were his.

If she ever wanted Lamech to change, she'd have to transform him slowly, with cunning and affection. Yet, as the knowledge sank into her heart, she realised the best she could hope for was to filter the powerful river of influence secreting from their household. The river would still carry dirty water.

'Will Chanoch be there tomorrow?' Lamech stiffened at her unexpected question. 'I haven't seen him in so long,' she qualified.

'I don't expect so. He hasn't attended anything since Selah's death.'

Adah nodded. Her poor friend. The only man holding back the tide of immorality sweeping through the city was bereaved and exhausted. Had he given up at last?

She ran her hands over Lamech's chest, and he relaxed again. 'I expect that makes things easier for you. Is Kenan still on your side?'

'He is. Eber is an invaluable ally; Azurak was right.' Lamech turned until his face was level with hers. 'You don't usually talk business with me. You're not going to chide me, are you?'

Hadn't she just resolved not to fight him? Adah shook her head gently and smiled. 'Of course not.' She kissed the end of his nose. 'Tzillah once mentioned that you talk to her about these things. I'd like you to be able to talk with me.'

Lamech lifted an eyebrow. 'Really?' As she nodded, he grinned. 'Alright, little mouse. So long as you promise to be on my side.'

That was a step too far, but rather than admit it, she smiled and kissed him again.

ADAH'S RESOLUTION to be her husband's ally was severely tested at the festival.

As owners of the largest complex in the city, the principal festivities were held in their home, which they opened to all families involved in the battle, to visit in turn over the seven-day period. Adah designed a memorial in the colonnade, commissioning Bekhor to carve an archway from wood, displaying something relating to each deceased person on its tresses, from favourite flowers to specialist trades. She was amazed Lamech's brother completed it in time and not surprised when he told her he'd hired ten other artists to help, each working on one section of wood.

Around the archway at the colonnade's entrance, Adah planted raised beds of medicinal herbs representing the treatments used in battle by the healers, surrounded by flowers in the colours of the war banners. In the centre of the colonnade, a fire burned throughout the seven days. Adah hired two young men just to keep it alight.

On a platform nearby, the one Yaval had sacrificed his goat on, hired singers and musicians took turns to lament with a song Juval wrote for the occasion. The effect of the arch, planting, fire and music was the perfect balance of respect and remembrance, sorrow and thankfulness.

After the visitors had paid their respects, servants ushered them into the main hall where Lamech's famous hospitality awaited. Adah had left Tzillah and her husband to design the celebration feast – a decision she regretted the moment she entered the hall that first evening, after the last group had passed by the memorial.

The festivities were well under way, and numerous empty jugs signalled the quantities of wine consumed. Adah had never heard songs to other elohim before, nor seen the rituals, though she'd been aware of their existence. The lyrics arrested her almost as strongly as the sight of Naamah and Juval together on stage.

From the moment Naamah had dashed and flung herself into Juval's arms all was forgiven, and now, Adah could sense the fire between brother and sister as they performed together again after so many years. Their harmonies blended perfectly, just like old times, except they sang of the glory of the stars, and the freedom El-Nachash offered, praising him for the recent victory. How could they attribute victory to the one whom Barsabas worshipped? It made no sense. As the song finished, Eber escorted his wife onto the dancefloor, leaving Juval with another singer.

Naamah was stunning; there was no denying it. Even after birthing two children, she commanded attention in the room as she danced. All around, men sacrificed their wives for Naamah's waist-length copper hair and voluptuous figure. Her innocence had departed. She threw her head back and laughed as Eber took another woman and Azurak claimed Naamah's dance for himself, snaking his arm around her waist.

It was true then. Azurak had won her. Adah had suspected it but had dared hope she was wrong. Though they stopped short of public affection, the looks passing between them brooked no argument. Why didn't Eber do something? Adah scanned the room for Lamech and found him on his favourite couch on the stage, near the right-hand pillar. Tzillah was nearby, but she wasn't the woman feeding him grapes one by one. That was Tamar, in a sheer garment that barely covered her nakedness. Lamech had one hand possessively on Tamar's bare thigh.

Lamech flaunted his concubine in public? What place had Adah been transported to? Only days before, he'd declared his pride in his family – in her. She felt someone tug at her arm. It was Yaval. Fang sat at his feet, watching his master's every move.

'Are you shocked?' Yaval said.

She swallowed and nodded.

'This is what's been happening in other houses for several years.'

'But why would your abba bring it here? Surely it will ruin him?'

Yaval shook his head. 'He knows several of the elders are already involved. Look about you, Ima. There is Naman, with his second wife and his concubine. Three paces from him is Asher – a man of six hundred years. See his companion?'

'Is that—?' Adah gasped at the woman with star motifs tattooed over her breasts. She was huge, like the figurines on the market stalls.

'Yes. She is a senior woman in the worship of the stars. Few elders refuse her, for she claims to bring fertility.'

Adah turned away and covered her eyes. 'How have I missed this. Am I so blind?'

'Abba has kept you busy raising his other children. Besides, until this point, he's been careful to distance himself from any involvement. Even now, he displays Tamar, but she is not one of them. She belongs exclusively to him and doesn't bear any ink. Abba is an expert at walking between two worlds.'

'I have underestimated him. I thought his fight against Barsabas was against this evil. I thought...'

Yaval wiped the tear that tickled her cheek. 'His fight was a power grab and nothing more, Ima. Whatever he dressed it up as.'

Adah scanned the room again. 'Kenan isn't here. Nor several other elders.'

'No. He has invited the remaining Yahweh worshippers to the final night of the festival. That will look quite different to this.'

'Adah!' Lamech had seen her and was beckoning. Adah wanted nothing more than to flee the room and try to forget what she'd seen. Yet Lamech's look offered no escape, and she told herself she must obey him and hide her shock for the sake of her earlier resolution. As she made her way towards her husband, she passed several inebriated and entwined groups of revellers.

Tamar moved to the side as Lamech grabbed Adah's hand, pulling her onto the couch. Then he cupped the back of her neck. His breath was thick with wine, but she knew he was fully in control of his senses.

'Your memorial is magnificent,' Lamech said.

'It feels rather pointless now,' Adah murmured.

Lamech pulled on the braid lodged between his fingers. 'You don't approve of my party?'

Her bottom lip was trembling. Her eyes started to water as he pulled tighter, his stare unwavering. She plied her lips upwards. 'It's not what I expected. But I'm sure you know best.'

'I do, Adah.' He tugged her head forward and bit her lip as he kissed it. 'I do know what's best. You see the people in this room?' His other arm motioned wide. 'They have faced death for the sake of this city. Terror has gripped their hearts. They need to release that terror and give their emotions free reign. Celebrate without holding back.'

'But isn't restraint a good thing? Doesn't it protect us?'

Lamech laughed. 'Oh, little mouse. When will you learn? Restraint is what keeps people locked in poverty, in a pitiful, mindless existence. This though – this will transform us. Transform us into people with freedom. When men throw off their shackles, they can flourish into their endless potential as I have.'

'And what about the women?' The words were out before she could stop them. She bit her tongue. If her legs had been free to kick herself, she'd have done it.

Lamech's nose twitched, but he controlled himself better than she. 'Look at Naamah. She has found freedom. Does she look unhappy to you?'

Adah turned to face the centre of the room once more. Naamah was delirious in Azurak's arms and though Eber's eyes were trained on his wife, he did nothing to interfere, as several inked women attended him. Neither did Juval who stared also.

When she didn't answer, Lamech spoke softly again. 'Does it bother you that much, me having other women?'

Adah wasn't sure why the conversation was now about them, but she delved into her husband's eyes, seeking the cause. Could it be that he still loved her, that he might still change? Did any goodness remain?

'I worry about you,' she answered.

'Even though you don't love me?'

Adah's heart quickened. 'A part of me will always love you, Lamech.'

'But only a part. The rest of it despises me, as I so often despise you.'

She wanted to refute him, but Tamar's uncovered midriff within her eyeline prevented that.

One side of Lamech's lip twitched into a half-smile. 'So, we are the same, you and I.'

Adah met his gaze once more. 'No, Lamech. For you take other women at will. Yet you denied me the desire of my heart.'

His eyelids narrowed. She waited for him to flip – to hit her or throw her off. Instead, he edged forward until their noses touched. 'And still, you remain.'

CHAPTER 65

Adah pushed her way through the crowds in the marketplace. She needed to find something special for Mela, and she knew just where to look, if only she could get there. The marketplace had increased in size considerably since peace was established after Lamech's war. New trade deals were struck with the lands in the north, south and, occasionally, the west. Even on Shabbat, the traders came, and no one refused them entry.

Adah passed stalls selling everything from fine linen to little statues of animals. Among those tables, she spied carved images of serpents, tanninim and the fertility woman. They couldn't be just for children to play with. One copper armlet looked just like the one Tzillah received on her wedding day. Though Tzillah didn't wear it, she'd shown it to Adah once.

Before she reached the trader she sought, she spied Tuval-Kayin unloading some knives and sickles onto a table. She waved. 'What brings you here, Mini-Kayin? I don't normally see you outside the forge.'

'Ima Adah, please don't call me that in front of my workers,' he hissed.

'Sorry. An old habit. Though not as tall as The Wanderer, you certainly don't deserve to be called *mini* anymore.' The top of her head only reached the curls at his shoulder. 'So, why are you here?'

'It's almost harvest time. The farmers need new tools, but my men forgot to bring down the bundle I'd prepared. I'm expecting some wealthy customers to pass through today.'

'Why today?'

'There's a feast for El-Nachash in Barsabas city – sorry, Leviathan city – old habit.' Tuval-Kayin grinned. 'They are staying here on the way.'

'Farmers?'

'No, merchants. They want my tools to sell to the southern farms.'

'Ah, I see. Well, try to be back for dinner tonight, won't you, love? It is a celebration for Yaval and Mela.'

'I will try, Ima Adah.'

Adah said goodbye and pushed her way through one more crowd of people before she reached the stall of her favourite jeweller – a woman trader, which was rare these days.

'Mistress Adah, how good to see you again,' the stallholder said. 'Tzillah was here the other week, but she told me you never come to market nowadays.'

'I usually don't. Today is special. My son is getting married, and I want a gift for his betrothed.' Adah eyed up the delicate beads of copper on leather necklaces, the exquisite gemstones and luxuriant fabrics. 'How do you make all of these?'

'We are developing new techniques in the west,' the stallholder said. 'The climate is different there and our animals have softer wool. There are also other plants we can use for fibre, not just flax. The stones I collect on my travels from several different suppliers. Though this...' She held out one stone which was jet black with white bands, 'comes from my home.'

'It's wonderful. Do you craft it that way?'

'No, that's beyond even my skill. The Creator made it thus. From what I can gather, onyx is found only in Havilah.'

Though stunning, Adah wasn't sure about the stone and ran her fingers over a blue scarf she liked best. 'How do you get it this colour? I've never seen one so vibrant.'

'Ah. That is a trade secret, my dear. If you want something really special, may I interest you in this?'

The woman held out a nugget of metal, more yellow than copper, and shining as brightly as the sun.

Adah gasped. 'It's stunning. What is it?'

'Gold. It's found mainly in water, in the streams of my land. Few know it exists yet, but I promise you, the future lies with this metal, for it doesn't tarnish like the others.'

Adah rolled it in her finger and the nugget gleamed. "It's soft though, isn't it? Will it have to be mixed to be useful?'

The stallholder smiled. 'This will not be used for tools. It will be for beauty – a sign of status. Mark my words. Give this to your new daughter and one day, she may trade it for far more than I ask for now.'

That sounded ideal. Lamech had finally, reluctantly, given his consent for Yaval to marry Mela, but only if he completely dissociated himself from his business, leaving Yaval with no means to support his new family. Furthermore, Lamech had claimed full ownership of the kavash, saying Yaval would have to rear his own herds if he insisted on marrying his *little inconsequential wife*. It was all intended to force Yaval to give in and abandon Mela, but Lamech underestimated his son. *He has the same passion for Mela that you had for me,* Adah wanted to say, but she didn't dare.

All Yaval had to his name were the geese, Fang and whatever goats Adah gave him. They could do with an investment that would grow in value – something Lamech need not know about. But should Adah trust this trader, whom she barely knew? What value could there be in something merely for decoration?

'That scarf, I want that one!' Pushing to the front of the crowd was a young woman Adah recognised, a daughter of one of the elders.

'How much?' her father asked, rolling his eyes.

'That one is special. It is worth at least five skins of wine, or a cage of birds,' the stallholder replied.

'For a scarf?' The man huffed, then nodded her way. 'Ah, Adah, how are you? My daughter seems to have expensive taste.'

'This trader is the best on the market. Her quality is unparalleled,' Adah said, clutching the gold nugget in her fist.

'And, if I don't do what my girl asks, I shall never hear the end of it.' He rolled his eyes again. 'Give it to her,' he said to the trader. 'If you come by my house later, I will have your payment ready. It's the largest house on the fourth street east.'

The young lady squealed and kissed her abba's cheek, then grasping the scarf, she flung it over her hair and wrapped it around her neck. 'Does it match my eyes?' she asked everyone looking, then pranced off to the next stall.

Adah chuckled. 'I suppose that answers my question. People will pay for beauty alone.'

'Beauty is the commodity of the future,' the stallholder confirmed. 'I should know. It's my trade, after all.'

'Very well. She held the gold out and dropped it back into the woman's hand. 'Does it only come like this, or is there some crafted item I could gift her?'

Adah chose a stunning bracelet with gold leaf motifs around a leather band, and rather guiltily asked the trader to add it to Lamech's account, knowing he would assume the purchase was Tzillah's and not question it. Then she squeezed her way out of the bustling marketplace, but not before filling her basket with unusual looking fruit, apparently from the southern marshlands.

She was nearing the Elders' square on her return journey when she stopped short. Ahead were two loops of rope hanging from the branches of the trees that surrounded the square. Dangling from the rope – two dead men. Adah stepped back, almost colliding with a huddle of street children playing a game of sticks and bones.

'Watch it,' a girl said, and Adah mumbled an apology.

How could everyone be walking by, ignoring the sight? Only a few turned their heads, then swiftly looked away, muttering under their breath. Though she didn't want to look, Adah forced her eyes up to consider the bodies. One man was old, his grey beard testifying that he'd reached his six-hundreds at least. The other was younger and displayed arms inked with nachash.

'You looking at them bodies, missus?'

Adah nodded at the street boy who had asked the question, still hunched over his handful of bones.

'Do you know what happened?' she asked.

'The nasty looking one was one of Barsabas' people, plotting against the city or something. But that one was found guilty of causing accidents.'

Causing accidents? 'How do you cause an accident? Surely accidents are... accidental?'

'In the workplace, missus. It's the new laws. If people aren't careful, and if someone else dies, or nearly dies... they have to pay.'

The girl who'd spoken earlier looked up from the game; she was no more than seven or eight. 'They said it's to protect us.'

'You?' Adah asked.

The girl turned back to the game. 'The workers, I mean.'

Surely these children didn't work. Where were their families?

'Why does nobody care?' Adah asked, considering how everyone carried on as normal, including the children.

'We see death every day. We're used to it.'

Forcing her feet forwards, Adah took a few steps towards the hanging figures. The older man looked familiar. 'That's my husband's slave,' she muttered.

The boy heard her. 'Yes, a slave, missus. Someone no one wants anymore, I reckon.'

Shock multiplied in Adah's belly. The lifeless eyes held her reluctant gaze, for now she couldn't pull herself away even though she wanted to. 'Why... Why would you say that?'

The boy came to stand by her side. She realised he was older than his skinny, hunched frame had suggested, for he exceeded her in height but was exceptionally malnourished.

'His hands, missus,' he said. 'They're all curled in, look. He's no good for nothing. And look – he's lost a foot too.'

So he had. A slave with no foot would be a great inconvenience. Could he have lost it in battle though, defending the city? Or by another of these 'accidents'? In any case, could it be true that he'd caused harm, or was this punishment some awful way of getting rid of him? Why not just free him?

'Still, I reckon its better being hanged than being left like that.' The boy pointed to an ancient man in the next alleyway, sitting in his own excrement. His gnarled fingers were cupped before him, but his face was between his knees. He couldn't even look at those he begged from.

Adah's legs went weak as the image of the old man Lamech had 'dealt with' flashed into her mind. He wasn't the same – they looked nothing alike – but she feared he was just as easily disposable.

'You alright?' the little girl asked, suddenly tender.

Adah nodded. 'What happened to that man?'

'He's no good for work neither. So they freed him. But he's got nowhere to live and nowhere to go. He just sits there...'

A crowd of women passed by, gossiping and barely glancing at the hanged persons.

'Your husband has slaves, then?' the boy continued.

Suddenly feeling exceptionally guilty, even though it wasn't her choice, she nodded again. The boy wrinkled his nose, like she had a bad smell about her, then snorted and rejoined his friends.

Adah had been heading home, but now she turned abruptly and went back the other way. She needed to see Chanoch, and she needed to see him now. As she paced the distance to the elder's home near the western gate, she rehearsed what she would say. Why were the men killed? What could warrant such an act? Even if they were murderers, The Wanderer's mark proved humankind wasn't meant to enact revenge. How could Chanoch stand by and let this happen? Was he still not attending meetings, all this time after Selah's death? Because there could be no other possible explanation... Why leave the bodies on display? And did her husband have anything to do with it?

She reached Chanoch's door. She banged loudly, expecting Chanoch himself to answer, but he didn't. A watchman was there. How strange. As he asked her name, a healer Adah vaguely recognised brushed passed her, leaving the house whilst wiping her eyes.

'I've no need for another pair of hands,' the healer said. 'I was already too late.' And she left.

Too late for what? Adah didn't think her sense of foreboding could increase any further after seeing the hanged men, but it did. Now intuition tightened her chest with fear – Shiphrah.

Chanoch's wife had lived far longer than anyone had expected. She'd been bedridden for so long. To survive her daughter by almost two years had been miraculous, given how wraithlike she'd appeared after Selah's death.

'This isn't a good time,' the watchman was saying.

Adah ignored him and pushed past into Chanoch's courtyard. Two kavash stuck their heads out of an open barn door. They looked old, like their master. The watchman's straw-speckled clothes made sense now. He was a groom for the retired animals Chanoch had taken pity on.

She continued to the main house and entered. Silence reigned. Tiptoeing into Shiphrah's chamber, Adah found them. Chanoch was bent over his wife's pale body, holding a limp hand. He didn't look up as she approached, nor as she knelt beside him and added her hand to theirs.

Adah stayed there well into the evening. Chanoch said nothing, and neither did she – none of the things she'd intended. Instead, she made him chamomile tea and fixed some supper, then left it on a plate near him on the floor.

'Thank you,' Chanoch murmured, when she whispered that she had to go. Yaval and Mela would certainly be waiting for her.

After squeezing Chanoch's shoulder, she wiped a tear from her eye and left the house. As she exited through the outer door opened by the groom, the healer she'd seen earlier was hastening down the alley, followed by two men.

'Has he moved the body yet?' the healer asked.

Adah shook her head.

'I didn't think he would. Come—' The woman beckoned the men inside and they nodded respect to Adah as they passed. Soon Chanoch would be saying goodbye to his wife for the final time.

CHAPTER 66

When Adah arrived home, she wasn't in the mood for what awaited her.

Lamech stood in the centre of the room, two paces back from the table and was delivering Yaval another lecture. Knelt next to her betrothed on the opposite side, Mela blushed intensely. Tzillah and Tuval-Kayin were there too, but mercifully, there was no sign of the little ones. Shua must have put them to bed.

'Adah. Finally!' Lamech said. 'Your son wants his wife to live here.'

Adah sighed and reclined near the food, which she picked at. 'Of course he does. This is his home, and you haven't let him build another.'

'He can build one. I'm just not going to give him any land, materials or workmen. Nor am I going to let that woman live in my house.'

'Lamech,' Adah groaned. 'Mela is the daughter of my best friend.'

'A woman I forbade you from visiting years ago.'

'What?'

'You heard me.'

Adah sank her head into her palms. She was exhausted and didn't have the strength to argue.

'I'd rather live with Mela's family,' Yaval said, 'but they have no room. You own more land than anyone else in the city. If you'd just give me a small piece...'

'I shall not,' Lamech snapped. 'You gave up your birthright. That was our agreement.'

'We'll leave then,' Yaval said. 'We'll leave, and you won't have to see us again. You can find someone else to train your animals.'

Though she heard Lamech's laboured breathing, Adah didn't open her eyes. She felt him plonk himself down next to her. 'You shall not leave,' he murmured while munching on a bone.

'You cannot stop me.' Yaval was pushing it tonight.

Lamech growled, echoing Fang who was put out by his anger. If Mela wasn't here, Lamech would have snapped by now. *Thank Yahweh that Yaval has Fang to protect him now.*

Pulling her face out of her hands, she reached for Lamech's fingers. 'Where do you propose they live if they can't live in the city, and they cannot leave it?' she asked softly.

Lamech ripped some more meat from his bone. 'I will not allow him to leave. If I do…'

'What?' she said, stroking his hand, trying desperately to look supportive.

His eyes turned to hers. 'If he leaves, you will.'

Adah's heart pummelled. What did this mean, this admission? Was it even true? Could she… Would she?

She couldn't think about it now. Instead, she smiled regretfully at Mela. 'I'm glad you are here anyway. Welcome to the family, my dear.' She didn't want Lamech terrifying Mela away. Not before the wedding, which was meant to be next week.

At the table's end, Tzillah finally decided to break the tension. 'Forgive our grumpy husband, Mela. He's just in a bad mood because the elders questioned the hanging.'

That made Adah sit up. 'I saw them earlier. How horrendous. Did you know?' She turned to Lamech, but his face of fury was fixed firmly on the empty wall in front of him.

'Of course he knew,' Tzillah continued. 'Azurak is the one who dragged the men to trial.'

'He did not,' Lamech spat.

Tzillah raised an eyebrow in mirth. 'Sorry, someone other than Azurak, acting under Azurak's not-so-secret direction, dragged the men to trial. The assembly has been in place for some time, but this is the first time the harshest punishment has been meted out.'

'What assembly?' Adah asked.

'Oh Adah. Do you ever pay attention to what's going on? People in the marketplace have been talking about it for ages,' Tzillah chided.

'I rarely go to the marketplace,' she replied, trying not to blush as her conscience bit back about her visit that morning.

Tzillah rolled her eyes. 'Perhaps you *should* leave and live in the wilderness with Yaval. You can hardly be more clueless than you are now.'

Lamech choked on his mouthful.

'After today, it does seem appealing,' Adah said, watching for her husband's reaction.

His eyes narrowed and he clenched his fist but said nothing.

'I don't understand how anyone could condone murder,' she continued.

Lamech towered over her, setting her in shadows. 'It's not murder, Adah. It's justice. The man you saw was dangerous – a traitor, conspiring to destroy our city and customs.'

'I saw two men, and one was no such thing,' she said. 'His inclusion looks like murder. You surprise me; I thought you cared what people think of you. People must know he is your slave.'

Lamech's face was turning a colour that matched the highlights in his hair. She'd failed, once again, to hold her tongue. Would she never learn? Sweeping his hand across the table, Lamech sent a cup crashing to the floor. Then he sat back down.

Knowing that hand would've struck her face if not for Mela's presence, Adah silently thanked Yahweh before changing the subject. 'Shiphrah died today.'

Lamech's eyes flickered in her direction. 'Chanoch's wife?'

She nodded.

'That's why you're late.' Lamech stroked his chin thoughtfully, then he got up and left the room, taking his plateful of food with him.

Chuckling, Tzillah refilled her cup. 'Welcome to the family, Mela. You're going to enjoy it, I'm sure.'

Seated on Mela's other side, Tuval-Kayin snorted. Adah was pleased he'd made the effort to be at the dinner, even if he looked like he'd rather be anywhere else. It felt like days since she'd seen him, although it was only that morning.

'How was the rest of your day, Mini-Kayin? Did you sell what you hoped for?' she asked.

As he glanced at her, his eyes were the image of his abba's, though gentler. 'Yes, they came by. They haggled, but merchants always do that.'

Adah smiled. 'I'm glad you were successful.'

'When did you see my son?' Tzillah asked, raising an eyebrow.

'At the market.'

Incredulity raised Tzillah's brows further. 'I thought you never went to the market.'

Adah stroked Mela's gift which she'd clasped around her own wrist for safekeeping, hidden beneath her shawl. Should she give it to Mela now? She glanced between Tzillah and her son. Did Tuval-Kayin know of this new metal? Caution told her not to reveal it in his presence.

'I was just picking up some fruit. Would you like some? I've never seen these varieties before.'

Tzillah's eyes narrowed but she didn't call Adah's bluff. Instead, she shrugged. 'Why not.'

It was late by the time Adah got Mela and Yaval alone to present them with the gift.

Mela's hand flew to her mouth and a tear ran down her cheek. 'It's so beautiful!'

'Keep it hidden until after you are wed. I'm told it will be worth far more in years to come, so I hope someday, it might do you a good turn.'

'Thank you, Ima,' Yaval said.

'And pay no attention to Lamech. Of course, you can stay here as long as you need to. I'll call on Naamah and see if Eber has any bright ideas about getting you a plot of land. Your abba isn't the only one with property in the city, and Kenan is fond of you.'

'Good idea. I hadn't thought of Kenan.' Yaval kissed her cheek, which filled Adah with joy but also apprehension. Juval had left home shortly after the war, for Lamech had given him a plot of land purely to spite Yaval – of course claiming it was a reward for his command in the army. She'd found Juval's loss hard, but at least he visited regularly. How long would it be until Yaval was gone too?

Her son was speaking her name.

'Yes, my love?'

'What did Abba mean when he said you'd leave if I did? I've encouraged you to leave him many times, but you never have.'

Adah chewed her lip. Was it right to tell him of the ultimatum?

'Ima?' Yaval persisted, until she sighed.

'You know you once asked me about Ruhamah?' she said, glancing at Yaval, then Mela, whose eyes lit up.

'My uncle?' Mela said.

Adah nodded. 'Your uncle. Likely you don't know, my dear, for you were young then, but Ruhamah and I... There once was a time we loved each other very much.' She turned to Yaval. 'This was after your abba married Tzillah. I left him, you see...'

'You did?' Yaval said.

She nodded again. 'I did. But I was already pregnant with you without knowing it. By the time I realised, I was in love with Ruhamah. We wanted to bring you up together, away from your father. Tzillah was carrying Naamah too.'

Was she making sense? She'd said everything the wrong way round.

Yaval shook his head. 'So, you were pregnant with Juval and I before leaving? Is abba really our father?'

'Of course! I mean, that's obvious, isn't it? Look at Juval.'

Yaval shrugged. 'I suppose. What happened?'

'Lamech found out. He forced me to return and be his wife again.'

'How did he force you?'

She considered the two sets of eyes imploring her to continue. It felt like betrayal to tell Yaval the truth about Lamech, but didn't her son already know what his father was like? 'He said that if I didn't return, he would take you from me by force and raise you alone.'

Yaval's eyes widened. 'I knew you stayed for our benefit; I didn't suspect he'd forced you into it. I suppose that explains why he set Tzel on you.'

Adah nodded. 'He's never trusted me to stay. Shadow is not just my protector, but my jailer.'

Yaval sat back in his seat and scratched the back of his head. 'How different my life might have been if abba had never found out.'

'My uncle would have made a wonderful father. I miss him,' Mela whispered.

Adah grasped her hand. 'I miss him too.'

She studied Yaval as he took a deep breath. 'If we left the city, would you come with us?'

Adah shook her head. 'He may fear it, but your abba would never allow it.'

'Suppose we were to find a way...'

'No, my son. You and Mela should go if that's what you want. You've always longed for the hills. I will stay here and do my best for Lamech's other children, as I have done my best for you.'

'You can't mean that. You have no relation nor obligation to them... Abba has enough women, Ima. It's time you cared for yourself.'

'I shall not endanger you. Lamech will let you go if he knows I will stay. But if I leave with you, he will hunt us down. And he always succeeds.'

'I should get home,' Mela said, standing. 'It's getting late.'

Yaval stood too. 'I'll walk you. But Ima, this conversation is not over.'

Adah nodded to satisfy her son. Though she knew it *was* over. She would never endanger him. She would never escape Lamech.

CHAPTER 67

Two years later

'I'm so pleased you're back,' Adah squeezed Yaval tightly, delighted to hold her son again. It had been several weeks since Yaval left the city, searching for a new place to live. Mela and their ten-month-old daughter, Ellie – named after Eliana – had gone too.

After Kenan had generously given them a small home with a yard for the animals, Yaval and Mela had tried to remain in the city. But they were miserable, longing for the hills, and Adah knew they must go. Of course, they hadn't confessed this to Lamech, but he'd taken little interest in their lives since they moved out and he became tied up with city politics. Adah couldn't recall him holding his granddaughter once.

Little Ellie squirmed in Mela's arms, trying to get down to play with Fang. When Mela obliged, the girl crawled after the wolf, who was running around the living area, sniffing everything as he inspected his old home for signs of change. Adah took the opportunity to give Mela an enormous hug.

'Sorry, Adah,' Mela said. 'I'm sure she'll cuddle you later.'

'Don't worry. Come, sit down. I'm terribly busy preparing for another of Lamech's parties, but I can work around you.'

'I'll help,' Mela said.

'Nonsense. You must be exhausted from your journey. Sit.'

Shua entered with some tea and raisin cakes.

'Perfect,' Adah said. 'How are the preparations for tonight?'

'Everything is in hand, mistress. You spend time with your granddaughter. Don't worry about us,' Shua said.

'Are you sure?' Adah knew that Lamech wanted everything perfect for this evening. He'd also recently returned, from a trip to Barsabas' old city, now named after the Leviathan, and had some important news to announce to the invited elders.

Yesterday, Adah had visited Chanoch to extend an invitation to join them this evening. Lamech hadn't asked her to, but she was worried about her old friend. Instead of becoming more sociable after the loss of his bed-bound wife, Chanoch had withdrawn further in the past two years.

When Adah considered her own tendencies to hide away, which Tzillah constantly chided her for, she could understand. When she'd questioned Chanoch about it, he'd merely sighed, put his head in his hands and said, 'There's so little goodness left, Adah. Another light has snuffed out and the darkness grows thick around me.'

She put out a hand to comfort him, and his eyes narrowed. He gently held her wrist and turned her arm over. 'These are not marks from bumping into something,' Chanoch said.

The purply-black bruising extending from her wrist to elbow was not as obvious as it might have been if her umber skin was lighter, but that hadn't stopped Chanoch noticing it several times. Usually she blamed it on clumsiness, though she wasn't clumsy at all.

Chanoch held her gaze, concern sweeping through his features as he waited for an explanation.

Adah's eyes flicked back to her arm, and she shook her head.

'Is it your husband?' Chanoch murmured.

Why was she scared to tell him? It made no sense to keep it from him; after all, he'd offered her sanctuary several times before. Yet this secret of years clung tightly to her chest, a knowledge that belonged within her household and no further.

Chanoch persisted. 'How long has he beaten you?'

'I... I need to get home.' After withdrawing her arm, Adah tucked her sleeve back over it and stood.

'Adah...'

As she reached the door, she glanced back momentarily and forced a smile onto her face. 'Come to the party, won't you? Several of your friends are invited.'

Chanoch's eyes had followed her as she left. In them she saw hopelessness, but not so great that he gave up altogether. He still cared enough to offer her kindness, and she knew he attended the elders' meetings most of the time, though not all. She knew because Lamech often moaned about it.

Her husband was on the elders' council now. Despite being far too young to be considered an elder, he was too prominent to be excluded. They relied on him as an emissary to Leviathan city, where he'd installed his own men in a second council under the authority of the elders of Chanoch. In reality, Lamech controlled the northern city in all but name.

These things she'd gleaned from Tzillah, Naamah and her continued efforts to be a listening ear to her husband, though he didn't trust her enough to tell her much.

'Ellie, come see your sava,' Mela said, pulling Adah back into the present.

The little girl looked towards Adah, but barging through the doorway at that moment came three hungry boys.

Naamah's eldest, who spent most of his time at their home, shoved straight into Ellie, knocking her over, and confronted Shua. 'Where's our food?'

'It will be ready directly, young master. We're rather busy preparing for this evening,' Shua said, patient as ever.

He huffed and stomped off, but Nahar picked up Ellie before her parents could, then jiggled her and sang her a song. Soon, she stopped crying and was passed to Adah who snuggled her close, noticing every tiny change since her last cuddle. She must savour each moment with this darling girl. Too soon, Yaval and Mela would be gone for good, taking Ellie with them.

'So, did you find anywhere promising?' Adah asked, sniffing down the tears.

'Yes, Ima. I think we have. Though…' Yaval paused.

'What Yaval means to say,' Mela continued. 'Is that we have a different plan now to what we originally intended.'

CHAPTER 68

'Yosa!' Lamech shouted outside the tanner's house. Unusually, it was raining, and he was getting soaked, but the smell was atrocious, and he didn't want to go inside. He was in a bad enough mood without contending to be heard with the tanner's tribe of children. 'Yosa!'

Yosa appeared under the door frame, pushing aside the attached skin, looking aged and even more bedraggled than usual. Lamech thought he might have smartened himself up by now. He'd been working his own business for years.

'Master Lamech. Please, step inside.'

'I'd rather not. Do you have somewhere else we may talk?'

Yosa nodded and led him round the back of the house. Skins hung everywhere, and some were thrown hastily over others, presumably just got in due to the rain. In the corner, just before a fence hanging off its post, was a lean-to roof, under which a fire burned with a pot on top. Yosa's wife was stirring it, with a small child hanging on her leg.

'Leave us please,' Lamech said.

Yosa's wife – tall, skinny and nervous every time Lamech had seen her, glanced at her husband.

'Go,' Yosa said, 'I'll make sure it doesn't boil over.' When she'd gone, Yosa turned to face him. 'How may I help you, master?'

Lamech took a deep breath. 'Tuval-Kayin tells me you haven't fulfilled all his orders.'

'Are they urgent, master?'

'Everything I commission is urgent.'

'It's just that I received an order from a new customer, and I've been trying to fulfil it...'

'Why would you need another customer? Don't I give you enough work?'

'Plenty, master, but I would like to expand the business.'

'Which you are entitled to, but not at my expense.'

'With respect, I must. You saw my wife there? She is so thin because she eats nothing – she gives all the food to the children. We need more trade to survive, and I am taking on extra workers to allow for it. We are preparing many skins, as you can see,' he gestured to the ones they'd passed. 'They are not ready yet, but my eldest son is now very proficient and—'

'Good. All that means you can fulfil my orders on time.'

Lamech turned about, intending to get back as swiftly as possible.

'But Master—'

He groaned. The roof was dripping water down his back, and he had several other matters to address before the party tonight. If the tanner intended to fight with him, he would soon feel his wrath. 'What?'

'I was trying to say that I must prioritise my other business. But I will get to yours as soon as I can.'

Anger rose in Lamech's chest. What did he mean, he must prioritise other business? What customer could possibly be more important than him? And hadn't they made an agreement...

'When I set you up with this workshop, you promised to supply me what I needed. Don't forget what you owe me,' Lamech said, raising his shoulders and puffing his chest out. If he had to back this man into the fire to make his point, he would do.

Yosa responded in kind, raising himself onto his toes and lifting his chest. 'I owe you nothing. I slaved for you for three years to pay for this workshop. In that time, I lost two daughters to the famine and a son to the plague.' A strange mixture of terror and courage dominated this man's eyes as they sparkled in the firelight. Lamech almost respected him. Almost.

'You promised to supply me with everything I needed,' Lamech snarled, taking a step forward. Surprisingly, Yosa did not step back towards the fire, but stood his ground, so that their chests touched.

'I have not failed to fulfil that promise. But you must take your turn with other customers. My family cannot thrive with only your—'

Lamech's hand was round Yosa's neck before he knew what he was doing. 'I am your master!'

'You are not. I am free!' Yosa spluttered. 'And I want a better life for my family.'

Enough of this insolence. Lamech pushed. The waif of a man tumbled into the flames, upsetting the pot of broth which tipped, splashing boiling fluid all over him. Yosa howled in agony as the shock of the burn turned to pain. Behind them, a girl shrieked.

Lamech spun. The girl was pretty; surprisingly pretty given her parents. He strode across the yard, and grabbed her arm, as a young man of a similar age ran out of the house – Yosa's son.

'What have you done to Abba?' the girl cried. Lamech glanced at the burnt man, who had rolled on the ground, covering himself in mud which stuck to his burns, creating a monster-like appearance. He dragged the girl towards her father, pushed her against the wall of the lean-to and pointed.

'This is what happens to people who defy me. I have done everything for your father. Without me, your entire family would be dead. Yet he repays me with insolence.'

'Get off her!' Yosa's son had reached him and was tugging at his elbows, trying to release his grip on the girl.

Anger always made Lamech lustful. The only way to rid himself of it was to be satisfied, to smash something or to smash someone. How many times he'd had to walk away from Adah to stop himself killing her...

He planted his lips on the girl.

'Get off her!' the brother shouted. Lamech felt the boy's fingers on his shoulders, grabbing and pounding.

Pathetic child. Like he could hurt me. Releasing the girl, he threw his arms over his shoulders and grabbed the young man. With a swift movement he pulled him up and over and threw him towards the fire.

'No!' Yosa roared, staggering up. Now the father launched himself forward with fists bared. Hands burnt and bloodied – useless for their occupation – struck Lamech's face. He gave a single punch back, and Yosa crashed into the wall.

A sharp pain shot through Lamech's flesh at the base of his back. He fumbled for the knife kept in his belt. It was gone. He spun again to see the blade in the hand of the boy, and his own blood on the tip. The boy's eyes widened in terror; he crouched as if he would run, but Lamech would not give him the satisfaction.

More screams accompanied Lamech's forward lunge. It was too easy to get the knife back – a trained hunter versus a child. Lamech extended his leg, causing the boy to lose his balance and fall. Then he crouched and swiftly retrieved the dropped blade before slashing at a nearby abdomen. Blood gushed forth. Far more than was seeping from the light scratch on his back.

'Korah!' Yosa sprinted to his son as the boy grasped his wound. Korah's face turned white. His eyes rolled back, and he dropped to the side, hitting the ground with a thud.

Have I killed him? The thought sent passion pulsing through Lamech's veins. The same exhilaration he'd experienced on the battlefield and afterwards. The fact the boy was barely twenty meant nothing. He'd attacked first. He deserved it.

Yosa held his son's shoulders as sobbing racked his body. Several more people ran from the house – the wife, with multitudes of children as scrawny as their mother. The child who'd hung on the wife's leg wailed. The girl he'd molested ran to her mother and hurled herself into open arms, howling hysterically.

Yosa looked up and fixed him with a stare. 'What have you done? Murderer!'

Yosa's appearance was horrendous, yet fire filled his eyes as his anger matched Lamech's.

'I will kill you for this,' Yosa cried. 'I shall be avenged!' Then the tanner ran, fists bared, shoulder down – straight into Lamech's knife. Yosa heaved a deep breath. The wife shrieked.

Lamech plunged the blade deeper. Tuval-Kayin's handiwork was marvellous. He'd enjoyed using it in battle, but he loved it now. Had the tanner not been injured, he might have thought twice about killing him. Yet, those hands would never strip skins again. They were useless. The rotting stench from Yosa's trade would soon permeate the man's own body.

Lamech's mouth twitched into a half-smile at the irony, as Yosa fell to the floor. 'Anyone else?' he asked, brandishing the knife at the huddled family.

CHAPTER 69

It was the greatest number of people Adah had seen in the banquet hall. Her old fears returned as she carried an empty pitcher of wine from the hall to the kitchens with trembling hands.

'Another one?' Leah asked, grasping a wine skin and pouring the contents into Adah's pitcher. 'We'll be breaking into the reserves soon.'

'I don't think Lamech will care,' Adah replied, breathing deeply. 'He's acting even more peculiar than usual. Like when he returned from battle.'

'Are you well, mistress?' Leah looked her up and down. 'You're off colour.'

Adah felt her head churning, except no milk ran off the cream. All thoughts clumped like butter behind her eyes. She put out a steadying hand and leaned against the wall. 'Too many…'

'Ima?' a familiar voice called her. It sounded like it was as far away as the mountains. Then arms enfolded her. She struggled for a moment, until something in her recognised the scent of her son and she gave up, sinking into Yaval's care. Her feet gave way.

When she opened her eyes, she was seated on a bench in the garden, wrapped in a blanket.

Yaval pressed a cup of water into her hand. 'Have you eaten? They're carving the boar.'

Adah nodded, sipping the water. It was too warm to refresh her, but the air outside was much cooler, and she felt relief from that. 'I ate earlier, before so many came in. I think if I tried to now, it would come straight back up.'

'The party is well advanced,' Yaval said. 'Perhaps it won't be long before they all leave?'

As her head started to clear, she was drawn back into the present. 'Lamech has entertainment planned. Some dancers are coming.'

'They just arrived.'

'Does that mean they'll put out that awful fire?' The presence of a fire in the hall beneath the cooking boar had intensified the stifling heat and smell. To counter the stench of sweat, Tzillah always burned herbaceous oils about the room during large parties, but they'd done nothing to improve the atmosphere that night.

'I don't know. Are you able to go back in?' Yaval placed a hand over hers.

'Must I?'

'Chanoch is here.'

'Oh no, is he?' When she'd invited him, she'd expected the party to be a gathering of respectable people. After all, Lamech told her he had announcements for the elders. Yet there were several here who attended Lamech's less reputable gatherings, and it might turn out to be something she didn't want Chanoch witnessing.

'Alright, I'll come and meet him.' *Perhaps I can persuade him to leave.* 'Where's Mela?'

'Oh, I sent her home a while ago. Ellie needed putting to bed. I was going to join them, but I was worried about you.'

'I see.' Putting a hand on the bench, Adah planted her weight into her feet. Yaval steadied her as she stood and took two deep breaths. She offered him a gentle smile.

'You are so strong, Ima,' Yaval whispered.

That deserved a chuckle. 'Oh, I am not. I often feel like the weakest, most pathetic creature on earth. Still, somehow we get through it and live another day. Though I often wonder if I shouldn't just give up.'

'Don't do that,' Yaval said, kissing her forehead. 'Please don't do that.'

The heat and noise hit her immediately as they re-entered the hall. Lamech saw her and beckoned.

'Here goes,' she muttered and Yaval squeezed her hand.

'Wife, where have you been?' Lamech asked as she approached, concentrating hard on putting one foot in front of the other.

'Getting more wine,' Adah replied, smiling and holding up the pitcher they'd retrieved on the way.

As Azurak briefly commanded Lamech's attention, Adah swept her gaze across the room and spied Chanoch right at the back, near the entrance. He hadn't ventured far into the party, but at least he'd been given food and drink, thanks to Shua who was serving him. Wonderful Shua.

Adah worked her way along the table nearby, refilling cups, one of which belonged to Naamah, whom she greeted with a kiss. Naamah had sung briefly earlier, but now the dancers were getting ready, discussing the order with Juval, in command of music as always. He had acquired several protégées in the last few years and a group of four musicians would play together for the dance.

As Adah put one foot on the step below, intending to cross the room to Chanoch, Lamech stood and called out. 'Friends! We must get down to business, before we are too inebriated to think straight.'

A chorus of laughter followed. Adah didn't pay much attention as Lamech announced new trade deals he'd brokered and the discovery of iron ore in the north. He'd told the family the details already and Adah knew he'd only called this party to show off. He could have – should have – saved it for an elders' meeting, but there, he wouldn't get the adoration he sought.

As Lamech talked about setting up new groups of metal-hunters, Adah concentrated on serving her guests, knowing that 'recruiting metal-hunters' was code for enslaving Barsabas' people to mine the ore. Most of those she passed didn't need more wine – they'd had plenty already – but serving them kept her mind off other things. Eventually she reached Chanoch and knelt near him.

'Your husband is doing well,' Chanoch said. 'I just wish he would conduct business in the ordinary manner.'

'Lamech does nothing in the ordinary manner. It's his life's mission to subvert the ordinary,' she replied. 'Have you seen his grandfather?'

'Yes, we spoke. Methushael isn't here though?'

'Oh no. Lamech hasn't spoken to him for a long time. Everything is more peaceful when they avoid each other. Bekhor is here though, with his family. And Dinah, on the far side.' Adah pointed to where Lamech's sister sat with her new husband.

'Do you still see Noa?' Chanoch asked.

Adah brushed off the memories of Noa's frequent snubs. 'She rarely comes here, and I won't go near Methushael. I only see her if we meet through Dinah.'

Chanoch nodded. 'I know how that feels. It's strange to think that almost everyone in this room descends from me in some way. I barely know any of them now; they have all distanced themselves, in one way or another. When I used to walk into a room, people would bow, or stand, or at least greet me. Now, barely anyone notices.'

'Does that bother you?' Adah asked.

Chanoch chuckled. 'Actually, no. It lends a certain anonymity which can be useful. My abba is more famous than I. Though nobody really knows him.'

'I would like to meet him one day.'

'You would?'

'Oh yes. The infamous Wanderer has always captured my imagination.'

Chanoch's mouth twitched into a half-smile. 'You've never mentioned that.'

Adah wondered if she should have done. 'It didn't seem appropriate, considering you're his son.'

'Yes.' Chanoch's smile reached full bloom. It transformed the worry lines on his face, and he looked altogether younger. 'To everyone else he is a legend. To me, he's just Abba.'

'It's true he's spoken of often, though less so now than when I was younger, I think. The trouble is that fireside stories get adapted and embellished. I don't know the truth, and neither, I suspect, do many others.'

Chanoch nodded pensively, his worry lines returning a little. 'Hmmm… there is danger in legend, I suppose.'

'Lamech wants to be one. If he succeeds, perhaps one day, hundreds of years hence, my sons will feel as you do.'

'Perhaps.' The smile dropped from Chanoch's face, and he patted her hand. 'I think you're needed.'

Adah followed his gaze to see Shua being accosted by an angry man for giving him the wrong drink. 'Excuse me,' she said, and stood, trying to ignore the rush of blood to the head. Before leaving, she glanced back at her friend. 'Thank you for coming, but don't feel you must stay.'

Chanoch nodded and resumed his meal. Lamech had ceased his business and sat down to have another drink. Some groups had grown louder with their wine and feasting; others had turned sleepy. After satisfying Shua's angry man with a refill of wine and another plate of food, Adah continued traversing the room, greeting those she must acknowledge.

When she arrived back at the stage, Lamech and Azurak were deep in a heated conversation. It was rare for them to argue. Spying a chair in the corner, Adah passed them and was just about to rest her legs when Lamech abruptly stood and called her.

'Adah and Tzillah, hear my words; you wives of Lamech, listen to what I say!'

This wasn't the way her husband usually addressed her. It was alike in tone to his earlier announcement about his business success. Why use her name when his entire posture was angled towards his audience? Her husband scanned the room for Tzillah, but when his second wife didn't respond, he grunted and turned to face Adah instead.

She was within grabbing distance. Lamech pulled her to his side, then his lips were on her ear. She smelt his breath, heavy with liquor, as he spoke. 'You look ravishing tonight, Adah. Play your part perfectly and we will have fun later.'

Play her part? In what game, exactly? She didn't like Lamech's games and could sense the force of the blood running through his veins. It wasn't just wine powering her husband. The peculiarity she'd noted to Leah earlier was heightened to intense proportions – heat and adrenaline dominated. Beyond Lamech, Azurak watched, beady eyes penetrating their master in anticipation of his next move.

As Adah squirmed away, not enjoying the clench of her husband or Azurak's stare, Tzillah finally looked up. 'Lamech, you old fiend! Leave Adah alone.'

His hold loosened slightly. *Thank you, Tzillah.* Adah never understood why Lamech tolerated – indeed, enjoyed – Tzillah berating him, when he hated her answering back.

Tzillah picked her way across the room, dodging the inebriated bodies slumped in various positions and stepping over one or two lying on the floor. The men were raucous by now and several grabbed her ankles, almost pulling her down. Unfazed, in typical Tzillah fashion, she kicked them off or swatted them over the head, providing further entertainment. Then she skipped up the steps and came straight towards them, before kissing Lamech full on the lips. His grip on Adah softened further, then he nudged her away and his arms encircled Tzillah instead. His brief glance held the words, *This is what a real wife does.*

Adah felt her cheeks warm as Lamech and Tzillah put on an elaborate display of affection, to cheers from the drunken crowd. She hoped to escape and was just backing away when Lamech spoke again.

'That's better!' he proclaimed. 'Now I have the attention of both my beautiful wives, and the rest of you despicable lot, I have an announcement to make.'

Another one? Yet this was different – not just because it started with their names, but because of Lamech's energy, stoked by the appreciation of his audience. He stepped into the centre of the stage then lifted one arm and spoke with a clarity that echoed through the hall:

Adah and Tzillah,
  Hear my words;
You wives of Lamech,
  Listen to what I say!
Today – this very day – I killed a man merely for
  wounding me,
  And also his boy for striking me.
If Kayin is avenged sevenfold,
  Then may Lamech be avenged seventy-sevenfold!

A hollow opened in Adah's chest. The same one she'd felt when Lamech dispatched the witness to her attack. The crowded room zoomed out of perspective, but Adah felt the stunned silence like a scream.

He'd killed. Again. Her husband; her lover – a murderer. Who was the victim this time – were they not important enough to name? Forever Lamech had dwelt in the shadows, tormenting her in the dark. Now he'd stepped forward and admitted who he was. Why?

She blinked tightly, trying to abate the pain in her ears as other noises began to filter through. Murmurs, whispers, chuckles. *They cannot accept him, can they? Surely not...*

Adah forced herself to focus but rather than Lamech, it was Azurak she saw. A smirk accompanied his beady eyes. That was the answer – Azurak had decided it was time. That's what they'd been arguing about.

The Wanderer's name had slid off Lamech's tongue so easily. All knew Kayin was untouchable. Yahweh protected him with an avenging curse – if any should kill Kayin, Yahweh would avenge his death seven times. Yet it wasn't that part of the legend that entranced Adah. She'd fantasized over his mark, his nomadic lifestyle, his mystery. Never once had she considered that his curse could be weaponised.

Yet her husband had. Clearly, he thought The Wanderer's legacy could be his own – that he could claim immunity in Kayin's name. How? When he did not even worship Yahweh, the supplier of Kayin's protection? Evidence of that was displayed about the room, from the boar to Juval's lyrics, from nachash-shaped ink to the presence of Tzillah by her husband's side.

They'd forgotten Yahweh. Or worse.

Naman stood and cheered Lamech's announcement. Then others did the same, incomprehensibly praising the murder. Their faith in her husband was so blind; he could do nothing wrong. He had led them to prosperity, to debauchery, to victory. Now he led them to celebrate the vilest excess he'd committed, and they loved it.

Azurak was right.

Somehow, Lamech's voice penetrated the screaming and pounding of Adah's thoughts. He was calling for more wine. More?

Tzillah nudged her elbow. 'Come,' she whispered, shoving an empty pitcher into Adah's hands. Adah followed Tzillah as she exited from the far left of the hall, towards the storehouses.

'Try not to look so shocked,' Tzillah said, as Adah stumbled along the passageway.

'How can I not? Aren't you?'

'Lamech is relying on our support. If we fail him now – if we show the smallest amount of hesitation – he could be dragged before the elders and expelled from the city.'

Adah stopped walking. 'You really think so?'

Tzillah rolled her eyes. 'He's taking a huge risk. Putting everything he's built on the line. Honestly, I'm furious about it, but the reaction in there proves it might work, and the unconditional support of his friends and family are essential.'

'But I don't want to support him!'

Adah felt the sting on her cheek before she realised Tzillah had slapped her.

'Wake up, Adah! The world is changing, and our husband leads the way. You can either come with us or step aside, but what do you think will happen to your sons if Lamech is destroyed?'

Images of Juval being dragged away with Lamech, perhaps even hung on the ropes Lamech likely contrived, flashed before her mind's eye.

Tzillah drew closer and lowered her voice, just like Lamech was wont to. 'I love you, Adah. But if you think I'm going to sit by and let you ruin my life, you're mistaken. Do we understand each other?'

Adah nodded. She would play her part in Lamech's game for now. What choice did she have?

CHAPTER 70

The night got worse. When Adah returned to the hall, she searched for Chanoch but couldn't see him. *He's left, horrified by what he's heard. It's his abba Lamech insulted. What if Chanoch never speaks to me again?*

The hired dancers had begun their performance, but though they dominated the stage, they didn't dance alone. Tables were pushed aside to make room on the floor where Tamar, Naamah and several women bearing ink also danced.

Actually, I'm glad Chanoch isn't witnessing this. I wish I didn't have to. The revellers were growing steadily more inebriated and lewd. Some swayed before the fire. Encouraged by lyrics about freedom, they stripped their clothing to the minimum and entwined their bodies.

Lamech had joined a table with Naman and the other elders who'd approved his actions. He was describing the events that afternoon, and Adah caught snippets of his decimation of an entire family, dressed up as self-defence. Adah knew it was no such thing – for which of his workers had ever dared rebel? And even if they had, she knew exactly how Lamech reacted to shows of defiance. She had plenty of testimony scars herself.

A stone sank to the bottom of the lake in Adah's soul. Whatever Tzillah feared, Adah knew the elders would believe her husband, just as everyone had always done. And rather than that being a good thing for their family, it was the worst. *Lamech will never change but will keep diving into immorality with both eyes open, and they will keep supporting him. If I ever manage to leave him, it will be 'Poor Lamech. What has he done to deserve his wife's betrayal?'*

She continued to serve the guests for some time, until her legs ached, and she sank onto a couch in front of a pillar. Lamech had retaken his former place on the stage and Juval had joined him, stopping to eat while the other musicians played on. Father and son sat together laughing, attended by Tamar and another woman Adah didn't know.

Nearby, even studious Tuval-Kayin had relaxed and was enjoying an animated conversation with Eber about stone-crafting tools. Was Kenan here? Adah's eyes swept the hall. Yes, there he was, on the far side of the room. He didn't look altogether comfortable, but he hadn't left. What was he thinking now? With her eyes angled that way, Adah caught a glimpse of copper hair – Naamah, with Azurak, behind the twin pillar to hers. Azurak's eyes flickered her way. They never lost concentration, never dimmed their intensity, even when attending to his affair.

Someone new entered the hall, from the passageway that headed to the colonnades, rather than the side openings others utilised to take fresh air in the gardens. Adah couldn't quite make out the figure in the shadow, but he was tall. Very tall. Then he stepped forward and she saw it, highlighted in the lamplight – a scar. *That* scar. It dominated the right side of his face, running in two lines, one straight from his inner eyelid to his upper lip, the other, from his outer eyelid to the centre of the first, then out again, across his cheek to the jawline.

No one knew what the symbol meant, but everyone knew its significance: Yahweh's mark. This man was The Wanderer.

Her entire life she'd wanted to see him – to see for herself. No longer did *Mini-Kayin* seem inappropriate for Tzillah's son, for Kayin was as imposing as the legend claimed, broader than Lamech and a head taller than Chanoch, who now stepped into the light behind his abba, holding a woman's hand.

Could that be The Wanderer's wife? The woman who'd chosen the life of a fugitive, though she'd done nothing to deserve it? *My grandmother many times removed, and the first healer.* A legendary figure herself, though always in the background compared to the man she dwelt with, whom everyone feared.

Everyone except Adah. For the racing of her heartbeat wasn't due to fear but excitement. She longed for him, dreamt of him, felt she knew him – though she did not. Now she finally saw him. The softness she'd detected in his face hardened as Kayin surveyed the room. He rolled back his shoulders, increasing his height further.

Chanoch was saying something to the woman – introducing people, perhaps. All three newcomers glanced Adah's way.

'Look at his eyes,' Adah felt her mother say as The Wanderer kept her gaze.

Yes, Ima. They are dependable eyes. They are Lamech's eyes – but not. For Lamech's failed me. Shall Kayin fail me too?

The Wanderer took a step forward. Now the light highlighted his hair but his face fell into shadow once more. He was old; she had to acknowledge that. She knew he must be living his eighth century, so why did she always imagine him younger? Yet, though his skin revealed the truth, Kayin didn't walk like an old man. There was no hunch, no apology. As the legend strode forward, Adah held her breath, determined to live this moment basking in his presence. The strength in his stride defied the streaks of grey that differentiated his hair colour from her husband's.

Wisdom streaks. Something Lamech lacks. Otherwise, he has Lamech's features, for sure. No – Lamech has his. How peculiar that I should marry someone who looks like The Wanderer. I never knew.

For the figure in her dreams and imaginings had never been clear, more like a hazy apparition than a man. And apparitions alter quickly when faced with reality. Yet, she still felt she knew him. Would his personality match her husband's too? Fear that she'd spent a lifetime getting it wrong nudged her insides.

Kayin didn't look at her again, though she wished he would. On his next step, he met Tzillah, for she was in the centre of the hall, still serving the guests. 'Well. If it isn't The Wanderer, come to grace us with his presence at last,' Tzillah exclaimed. 'Lamech, witness who has entered our humble halls!'

Adah's wasn't the only neck to crane towards her husband. Lamech threw Tamar from his lap and stood. How would he take this interruption? The Legend was sure to command more attention than him, yet Lamech's hospitality was famous, and he couldn't throw the man out. Chanoch surely knew that, or he wouldn't have taken this risk.

Lamech stuttered – the first time Adah had seen him struggling for words. Yet, he'd brought this on himself, hadn't he? His speech earlier that night, his claim on Kayin's promise...

Lamech, you fool. What have you done?

Adah saw the same fear on Tzillah's face as their eyes locked. Yet Tzillah laughed it away as quickly as it had arrived. Her laughter echoed. For the room suddenly fell silent as The Wanderer stepped centre stage, rendering Lamech speechless.

'People of Chanoch,' Kayin began. 'My son, the most senior elder of this city, has called me here tonight to tell you a story. We may be here a while, so I suggest you take a comfortable seat.'

Kayin's lip twitched briefly, like his own joke amused him. Adah wondered how he was feeling, addressing so many people after years of living in solitude. The twitch encouraged her. Something about his presence didn't just command her attention, and that of everyone else, it also warmed her heart.

He was a murderer, like her husband. She knew that – that was his legacy. Yet, he was also Chanoch's abba. The man who'd taught her friend how to be patient, repentant and forgiving. Therein lay the hope; therein lay the mystery.

He was here to tell a story… What story would he tell?

CHAPTER 71

The Wanderer's tale had continued until sunrise, and then, his wife, Awan, had spoken as well. He'd exposed his descent into depravity, then Awan had explained her journey to find Kayin and offer Yahweh's redemption. As Adah commenced cleaning the mess afterwards, she was still in awe that she'd heard the tale in full – something she'd been longing for her entire life.

But when Lamech re-entered after seeing out the last guest, fury filled the disordered hall.

'I shall kill them!' Her husband grabbed a pitcher and hurtled it. It wasn't empty. Wine splashed everywhere as the clay shattered into tiny pieces and scattered over a floor already littered with debris from the long, sleepless night of hosting.

Despite her fatigue, Adah's heart picked up pace. *Kill whom? Kayin, Chanoch or me? Likely, he'd enjoy all three.*

Picking up a nearby stool, Lamech tossed it across the hall. A leg broke off it, then another cracked as it landed, bounced, then crashed against the pillar. The midday sun basking the room in light did nothing to lighten her husband's darkness as he stomped closer.

'You. You told him to do this.'

Pain shot through Adah's neck as Lamech's fingers closed tightly around it. The blood ran to her head, and she choked, struggling to breathe while Lamech lifted her from the floor then pushed her into the pillar.

'Lamech!' Tzillah screamed, grabbing his elbow and tugging. He let Adah go and swiped back at Tzillah, sending his second wife skidding across the floor. Shua ran to Tzillah's side as Adah gasped, heaving in breaths. The restraint he'd shown while in company had vanished with the last guest. He was going to kill them all.

Lamech lunged for her again, but Adah side-stepped and using her last jolt of energy, bolted for the door. Then he roared.

The noise stopped her, and she spun to look at her husband. His face was red with rage, his knuckles white from squeezing his hands so tightly... Even so, he'd stopped. He was still.

Yaval burst into the room, followed by Juval and Tuval-Kayin. 'What's going on?' Yaval said, running to Adah and holding her up as her legs wobbled.

Lamech cleared his throat and spat. 'Ask your mother. She invited that man here to humiliate me. Though you are no better – I know you talked with him.'

Adah's cheeks almost coloured, aware that her conversation with Chanoch the previous night may well have contributed to The Wanderer's arrival, but she refused to feel guilty. Lamech had brought this on himself.

'You're angry about The Wanderer?' Juval said.

'Of course I'm angry! How could I not be? This was meant to be the night of my triumph—' The vein on Lamech's forehead bulged, but he stayed where he was.

Tuval-Kayin stepped forward. 'It was, Abba. It was a brilliant evening.'

'You call my humiliation brilliant?' Lamech snapped.

No, I wouldn't call it that either. Yet, The Wanderer was brilliant. Hearing their story was the highlight of my life.

Tuval-Kayin continued; if anyone could get through to Lamech, it was the son that pleased him most. Picking up a cup still half full of wine, he placed it in his abba's hands. 'The guests were fed and entertained, and everyone likes a good story. And your answer to the old fool was perfect. Who can question you now?'

When Lamech snorted, Tuval-Kayin persisted, 'You proved that your way brings success. Look around you, Abba.' Tuval-Kayin gestured to the grandness of the hall. 'It is just as you said. He claims following his Elohim brings blessing, but he is a pauper. You are victory. Don't let him get to you.'

Lamech downed the wine in one gulp, then dropped the cup, making Adah wince as another item smashed. 'How can I not? He told me I must repent – in front of everyone. Repent! Ha! He ridiculed my speech. Few laughed with me at the end. Everything I have worked for—'

'Is secure.' This time, it was Juval who approached his father. He put hands either side of Lamech's face. How peculiar it was, seeing her strong husband reduced and his sons ministering to him. Lamech had trained them well. They knew just what to say.

'Abba,' Juval said. 'The worship of El-Nachash and his host is secure in this city. Leviathan's hold is tight in the people's imagination. Yahweh means nothing to them now. The Wanderer cannot change that with one story which half the city didn't hear, and half the hearers slept through. The wife told a pretty tale for sure, with her songs and talk of restoration. But there's no appetite for it, Abba. Who wants to sing about Yahweh in quiet piety when they can dance to the stars and get whatever they want?'

'Then why didn't they laugh with me?' Lamech replied through clenched teeth.

'They didn't want to disrespect their ancestors,' Tuval-Kayin said. 'But this was Chanoch's last stand, Abba. Eber agrees with me. Before he left, he said the future is ours and Chanoch only pulled this act as a parting gift. Chanoch knows he's lost the elders. They belong to you now.'

Lamech grunted while Adah wondered at Eber's words. He likely knew more than her, for Kenan was often in Chanoch's house, and Kenan and Eber remained close. Lamech would believe Eber's word – but would that be enough for him to leave Chanoch be? It was true that her friend was weary, but he'd never give up trying to get the people to change. Even if it cost him his life. *Perhaps I take after him, in some way.*

'Come, Abba.' Juval winked. 'Let's go to the tavern and spread abroad some positive gossip. Maybe have a bit of fun while we're there, hmm?'

Just then, Avram burst into the room. 'Guards are here. For you, master.'

They didn't waste a moment but streamed into the hall – eight of them with weapons at the ready. At the helm was one of the elders Adah didn't know well.

'We've come to take you before the assembly,' the man said. 'We need your statement regarding the acts of violence that you admitted to yesterday.'

Lamech's sons stood between the soldiers and their father, but he just sighed and stepped forward, pushing Tuval-Kayin away to reach the armed men. 'I was hoping to get some sleep before you came, but fine. Take me.'

The elder raised his eyebrows, evidently not expecting the quiet submission. Lamech said one last word to his son before the soldiers led him away. 'Find out what you can, Juval; listen to what people are saying.'

Adah exhaled in relief once Lamech was gone, but Tzillah, quivering slightly after being struck for the first time, approached her. 'What do we do now? What will happen to him?'

'Nothing,' Juval said, turning to face them both. 'That was a formality, nothing more. Abba owns the assembly.'

Juval hesitated before leaving with Tuval-Kayin. The glance he shot her asked if she was alright. Grateful that he'd calmed Lamech down, even if every word disgusted her, she nodded and smiled gently.

'I'll stay and help you clear up,' Yaval said, grabbing some plates. Adah appreciated the sentiment. She could do with bed herself, but something was burning inside that gave her a strange burst of energy as she swept and wiped down the mess Lamech had made. The Wanderer's story – and his wife's – had ignited her soul. She felt the energy in Yaval too. It was the sense that life would never be the same again.

For whatever Juval claimed, Yahweh worship wasn't dead. Yahweh meant something to her. The name always had, but now – after hearing that story – the Elohim did too. He meant more to her than The Wanderer himself. And that... that was new.

Earlier that morning, after facing Lamech's wrath for delaying The Wanderer's departure, she had fortified her courage and run after Kayin and Awan, catching them before they reached Chanoch's kavash. She'd asked to hear them again and they'd agreed. She didn't know how she'd achieve it. Not now that Lamech had set Azurak to the task of watching them, and would no doubt tell Shadow to double his efforts watching her. Yet the story of how Yahweh had made impossible things possible – how he'd seen Awan safely over the mountains, how he'd changed a murderer's heart... It gave her hope. Perhaps He might see her to safety one day or might even change Lamech's heart.

Did she still want Lamech to change? Yes. For when The Wanderer challenged her husband, *'Will you listen to the words of an old man and turn back to Yahweh?'* her throat had caught. She hadn't been able to breathe for the brief silence while Lamech considered it, so much was her longing for him to listen. Seeing those two men opposite each other, so alike in looks and temperament, she'd seen what Lamech could be if he would only let Yahweh touch his heart as Kayin had done. He could be the Lamech she'd dreamed of as a young woman – the Lamech she'd adored. Better even. She'd dared to hope that her failed efforts to change her husband might not mean despair. Kayin was the worst of sinners – murdering his own, innocent brother. Still Yahweh sought him out, protected him, forgave him when he repented. If Yahweh loved Kayin that much, then surely, He loved Lamech too.

Yet, her husband dashed her hope as quickly as it'd risen with his stubborn refusal. Lamech would never go back on it now, as his outburst proved. He had chosen his path and wild tanninim wouldn't drag him off it. Yahweh offered redemption for the murderer, but the murderer must want redemption.

Envy for Awan flickered through Adah's heart. Awan found love in the end, though she'd had a long journey through grief and loneliness. Adah had lost people too. Her ima, Ruhamah and her babies. What was it the first-father Adam had said? *'Perhaps there will be others who do not easily bear children. Yahweh knows this, and He may have a different purpose for their lives.'* That was her. She was one of those who did not easily bear children. *So, Yahweh, what is your purpose for me?*

Adam had told Kayin and Awan to raise a generation of image-bearers in this land. They'd done that – Chanoch was one for sure, though she didn't know about his siblings. Yet she hadn't. The children she'd raised didn't bear Yahweh's image. They bore Lamech's. Which was exactly what Lamech wanted.

'Where does this one go?' Yaval asked, breaking into her thoughts with a beautifully hammered copper plate in his hands.

Yaval, my hope. The one child I've raised who stands a chance.

Adah approached her son and grasped him, pulling him tightly against her and resting her forehead on his shoulder. Tears pricked at her eyes.

'Ima?' Yaval held the plate aloft with one arm and wrapped the other around her.

'You must leave. Do not delay any longer. I must let you go,' she said, choking on her words.

Yaval stroked her hair, and she felt him nod. 'I was thinking the same, but I don't want to leave you. You're not safe here. I fear—'

'If Yahweh kept Kayin and Awan safe, He can do the same for me,' she said.

Yaval pulled away slightly. Tears filled his eyes also. 'Kayin has a mark of protection. You do not. Yahweh has made you no such promise.'

Fear flooded Adah's heart as her son voiced the insecurities that had kept her tied to Lamech for so long. Yahweh hadn't saved her mother, hadn't saved her babies, hadn't stopped Lamech finding her and dragging her back here, hadn't stopped his repeated blows. Why should He protect her now? She had no such promise.

Will You promise, Yahweh? Will You listen? Will You answer?

Her eyes must have betrayed the anguish warring in her heart, for Yaval shook his head. 'That decides it. I'm not leaving you with him.'

'But you must! You have a wife and daughter, and you are the hope of my life. If I produce one son who is good, I can rest in peace. You must go and I must stay, so you may be safe. That's all that matters. My life means nothing without yours. Go. I demand it. Go before Lamech realises what you're doing. Go.'

Salty tears dripped over her lips and her shaking chest, as Yaval pulled her closer once more and let his own sorrow loose.

CHAPTER 72

Yaval left. He gathered his little family, their few possessions and their growing number of animals and departed before Lamech returned, taking Adah's heart with him.

At her insistence, they didn't tell Adah where they were going. 'It's safer that way,' she said. Eliana knew though, and if Adah needed to reach them, she could do so through her friend.

Adah felt like walking death. Everything in the home irritated her, from the squeals of the children who weren't really hers to the wrong consistency of her bread dough. She sat in the goat pen with the two animals Yaval had left for her, feeling its emptiness in the absence of geese and chaos.

'What will I do without you?' she cried, sinking her head into the flank of the goat who'd come to nuzzle for food.

When Lamech found out, he was furious. As Juval predicted, the assembly had let him off without any punishment. When he'd shown them the knife scratch on his back, they'd deemed his actions self-defence and all he'd received was a warning to be more careful next time. He didn't even have to make provision for the widow.

'How dare he go?' Lamech said, pacing the courtyard where Adah found him after hearing him shouting at Avram about Yaval. 'Without saying farewell, too. What will people think when they hear that one of my sons has abandoned the city, stealing into the wilderness without a word? If he'd come to me, we could have thrown him a party, sent him off with gladness and made up some story that would justify it. What will I say to Kenan?'

It was nonsense. Adah knew Lamech would never have sent Yaval off with gladness. Besides, Yaval hadn't had anything to do with Lamech's business since he'd chosen Mela over it. Lamech cared less about losing his son than about looking a fool.

All the same, Adah tried to placate him. 'Anyone who knows Yaval knows what he's like. He's been wandering the hills since he was a child. They likely won't think it remotely strange. Besides, I'm sure he'll be back before long.' *Though I don't really expect that or wish for it.*

Lamech pierced her with a stare. 'Did you know?'

'Know where they were going? I have no idea.'

Her husband's eyes narrowed at her deliberate deflection. He paced her way, forcing her back against a pillar and put his hand to her neck once more. It still hurt from the previous assault. 'That's not what I asked.'

She gulped against the pressure and forced a smile. 'I am here.' It was hard to speak, and her words come out as a broken whisper. 'That's what worried you wasn't it? That I'd leave with him? Well, I haven't.'

Lamech's face didn't soften but he released her neck. Then he shouted without turning, so that Shadow's name pounded Adah's ears. 'Tzel!'

Shadow, sitting in his familiar perch in an alcove near the gate, jumped up and approached. 'Yes, master.'

'Regarding my previous instructions, they now apply indoors as well. You are not to let my wife out of your sight. Whether she is going out or staying in. You watch her always. Understood?'

Shadow nodded.

Adah's body tensed. 'What about when I need to relieve myself, Lamech, or wash, or… or Shadow does, for that matter?'

Lamech leered. 'You can work that out between you. If I must cope with my wife being in another man's sight, so be it. So long as you *are* in his sight.'

So, this was how it was to be. No more privacy. No more life. Shadow nodded and made to walk away.

'And Tzel.' Lamech said, in such a tone that Shadow paused and turned back. 'I know my wife has ingratiated herself into your favour. Still, remember what I warned you about. You prefer your own life to hers, I hope.'

Lamech didn't look at Adah again but stormed out of the gateway he'd recently entered.

After counting to ten, Adah approached Shadow. 'What did he threaten you with?'

Shadow didn't answer but climbed back into his alcove and started drawing on the wall with a small piece of limestone. Adah examined the picture. He'd clearly been drawing it for some time as it covered a length equal to his body. 'So, this is what you do to pass the time...'

Shadow grunted.

'I want to know,' Adah persisted.

Shadow grunted again. 'It isn't suitable for a woman's ears.'

'That bad, is it? Shadow, how many years have you served my husband now?'

'As many as your sons are old, mistress.'

'You didn't before that?'

Shadow shook his head. 'He employed me the day he dragged you back here.'

'You saw that?'

For the briefest moment, Shadow's eyes flickered her way, and she caught his compassion. 'You weren't the only one to lose their freedom that week.'

'So, you're a slave then?'

Shadow nodded. 'Your husband owns my life so long as I am useful to him.'

Adah wondered why she hadn't asked him this before. More than three decades they'd kept company, but she'd rarely seen him as more than something to be feared. 'Do you have a family, Tzel?'

He started at her use of his real name. Adah's lip twitched. Shadow showing emotion – that was new. He shook his head.

'Did you have one before?'

'I am an orphan. From the age of eight or nine, I lived on the streets. Azurak spotted my skill and contrived—' Shadow paused. 'Never mind.'

Adah instinctively reached a hand forward and placed it over his. She knew she shouldn't, but if they were to be better acquainted, she wanted it to be on better terms. 'Tell me, please.'

'Azurak watched me for several years – would come and play games with me, give me tips, that sort of thing. I owe him a debt, for I survived the streets when many do not. When I became an adult, he even found me a job. Yet, some of the tips he taught me weren't suitable for a working environment. I got caught stealing. I was being dragged to the elders when Lamech stepped in. He paid off my master in exchange for me. So, you see, I owe your husband too.'

'But you have no life. You sit here, always watching, never allowed to leave the complex unless I do. Do you ever go anywhere at night?'

'No, mistress. I have nowhere to go.'

'Have you ever wanted a family? A wife?'

Shadow continued to draw, and Adah noticed the picture he shaded in was of a woman and child. He did want a wife, then.

Shadow sniffed and wiped his nose with the back of his hand. 'I try not to think about it.'

And didn't succeed, by that drawing. Adah had a sudden thought. 'What if I ask Lamech to employ someone else? Not to replace you, but to work with you? You could have time off then.'

'Why would he agree to that?'

'As he says, we've grown too close.' Adah smiled her most charming smile, though Shadow wasn't looking anyway. 'It would give him assurance that I won't escape.'

'It won't work.' His fingers scurried over the stonework, expertly adding hair to the child's head. 'He knows I won't fail.'

What could Lamech have threatened this man with if he had no quality of life and no family? 'What is he holding over you?'

'I will not tell you, mistress. It is my burden to bear. Besides, my life is about to get more interesting.'

'Why is that?'

'I now get to watch all your arguments with your husband and watch you in the tub.' Shadow grinned, though he still didn't look at her. Adah felt a shiver run through her. Had she misjudged this man, or was he putting it on so she would give up?

'Fine. Don't tell me. I will find out another way.' That seemed to get a reaction, though it was so slight, she might have imagined it. 'As a matter of fact, I intend on having a wash now, for I smell after cleaning out the goats.' She grinned back sarcastically. 'Are you coming?'

Shadow didn't watch her, but turned around as she undressed and treated her with every bit of dignity she'd expected him to. Later, she found out from Avram that Shadow sometimes received one visitor – a young woman, of a similar age to him, dressed in servant's clothes.

'I always thought she was his sister,' Avram said. 'There seemed that kind of affection between them. But recently, I saw him kiss her and asked him about it. He said they grew up on the street together and protected each other; that kind of thing. Doubtless the master knows, and her life is what he hangs over Tzel's head.'

Adah thanked Avram and gave him a basket of fruit to take back to his wife. The next few weeks, she distracted herself from Yaval's absence by trying to figure out an answer to Shadow's predicament. How could she get the man his life back without setting her husband against him? She considered asking Lamech to let him build a room on the complex so his woman could live there with him but knew Lamech wouldn't allow such a distraction.

Eventually, Adah decided to visit Chanoch. Though she assumed Lamech would disapprove, she wanted to make sure he was well and ask after his parents. Additionally, he might have an idea to help Shadow.

'Where are you going?' The gatekeeper wasn't Avram, but the other one – the gruff one. He stood before the main entrance, blocking her way beneath the arches.

'A friend's house.'

'Which friend?'

Adah narrowed her eyes. 'I am the mistress of this household, and I don't have to tell you anything I don't want to.'

'With respect, mistress, I have my orders, and I am not to let you out without knowing where you are going.'

'I am following her.' Tzel stepped out from the shadows. She didn't know why he bothered staying in them, but old habits were sometimes hard to break. 'I will tell you where she's been on our return.'

The gatekeeper squared up to Shadow. 'There are certain *friends* the master doesn't want her to see. I fear him more than you.'

Adah's eyes travelled to Shadow's fingers, warming the hilt of his knife.

'Chanoch's,' she said. 'I'm going to Chanoch's.'

A deeper voice intruded. 'We cannot allow you to do that.' Azurak strode through the archway in front, free to come and go as he pleased. 'Good day, mistress.'

He hissed the last word, and Adah could almost imagine a nachash on his shoulders, with three heads surveying, scrutinising and spying in every direction.

'Why not?' she asked.

Azurak stood before her with arms crossed, mirroring the stance of the gatekeeper.

Three guards for one woman. It's almost funny.

'The situation is delicate,' Azurak said. 'Your husband is managing the fallout from The Wanderer's visit with his exceptional skill. The last thing he needs is you messing it up.'

Adah crossed her arms too. 'There would be no *delicate situation* if Lamech hadn't murdered those men.' The thought still filled her with disgust that she found hard to disguise in her husband's presence. She had returned to her earlier tactic of dreaming she was elsewhere when he visited her bedchamber. She suspected he knew it.

Her enemy narrowed his eyes. 'Regardless, Lamech would like you restricted, preferably inside the complex, until things have calmed down.'

Adah dug her fingernails into her arms, trying to resist flinging them at her captors. *I am not Lamech. I can control myself.*

'May Chanoch visit me?' she asked.

'No.' One side of Azurak's lip twitched into a cruel smirk.

'For how long do you anticipate this being the case? Am I to be a prisoner inside my home?'

'Of course not. You have permission to visit Dinah, Naamah, Juval – any of the family.'

'Not Eliana?'

Azurak shook his head.

'Why?'

'Because of her connection to your other son, of course.'

'What has Yaval got to do with any of this?' Adah demanded. They could not stop her contacting Yaval. *I need my son.* The stone walls of the complex appeared to grow thicker, the gateposts moved closer. The largest home in the city could still be a cell...

'Then I will visit Abba.' Adah strode forward, releasing her arms to shove the gatekeeper aside. Though she desired to push Azurak with all her might, she didn't quite dare and feared it would make little impact.

'I didn't say Shimiel,' Azurak said, but she ignored him.

'You said *family*.' That was enough.

'I expect a full report on your return,' she heard Azurak mutter to Shadow as her protector passed through the gateway.

Adah stormed down the alleyway. 'Can you believe this?' She threw the words back at Shadow, beckoning him to catch up. Shadow didn't respond, so she carried on. 'I've a good mind to stay at Abba's and force Lamech to fetch me, just to irritate him.'

Shadow's eyebrows raised.

'I don't care about the consequences. There's nothing he can do to me that he hasn't already done. I'm going to tell Chanoch. We'll pass his house. Hurry, Tzel!'

She was making a scene; she knew it. Several people had stopped to stare as she sped past, talking loudly to herself. She didn't care.

Shadow jogged and caught up with her. 'I don't think you should speak with Chanoch, mistress.'

'You won't tell, will you, Tzel?'

'Mine are not the only eyes your husband has trained on you. Nor are Azurak's the only eyes he has on Chanoch.'

'So, he has hired someone else? You are not my only guard?'

Shadow ran his fingers through his hair. He lowered his voice, so she had to draw close to him to hear. They really must look peculiar now. She slowed her pace.

'There are men living throughout the city,' Shadow said. 'Most in run-down old houses.'

'Those Lamech is determined to knock down?'

'Precisely. They watch from rooftops, doors and cracks in the wall. If you ever succeed in escaping, Lamech will destroy the homes of whoever lets you past.'

Fury quickened Adah's pace again. 'Are there any left whom my husband doesn't have a hold on?'

'Not many, mistress.'

'Argh!' She stopped dead, throwing up her arms. They'd reached the marketplace. Several women turned and gawked, gossiping to their neighbours. A child said to its mother, 'What is wrong with that lady?' and the mother tutted.

Adah felt the awkwardness. Though she didn't care how she looked, she didn't want to cause others discomfort. 'Oh – I forgot Nahar's birthday,' she said loudly, then approached the disapproving child. 'I'm sorry, my dear, I'm just so upset about it. He's about your age. Could you help me select a gift?'

This removed the stares immediately, and the boy wagged his head, pushed to his favourite market-stall and selected a toy he'd clearly had his eye on for some time. Adah gave the stallholder Lamech's name and took two, passing one to the child.

The mother immediately smiled and began declaring to all around how generous Lamech's wife was. Satisfied, Adah slipped away and strode towards the city gates. She stared longingly at Chanoch's house as she passed, trying to see him through the apertures in the wall, but she could not. However, she did notice two men opposite his gate, bearing the weapons of Tuval-Kayin. That was enough to convince her that Shadow was right. She could never visit Chanoch.

Her abba ran part way down the hill as she approached, then threw his arms about her and welcomed her home. He asked her all about Lamech – how could she stand to live with that killer? Was she safe; was she happy? Such was her mood, Adah didn't refrain from telling the whole truth.

'You must move back with us,' her abba exclaimed.

But Adah knew that could never be an option. She'd fled to him once before, when Lamech was little known and taken by surprise. He'd lacked the audacity to challenge her father then, but he did not lack it now. Whatever she'd claimed to Shadow, she did fear the consequences. If she stayed even a night, Lamech would likely drag her back and have them all flogged.

CHAPTER 73

Sunlight streamed into Adah's bedchamber, announcing the dawn. Outside she could hear her remaining nanny goat bleating, waiting to be milked. As the light flittered over her eyelids, she tried to open them. They felt heavy, one more than the other. She groaned.

Lamech had been particularly angry the night before. She'd done nothing. How could she? She hadn't seen beyond the complex walls for two seasons. He didn't even allow her to climb the watchtower anymore – no glimpses of what lay beyond, destroying her chance to imagine her son on the far-off mountains and the life he might be living. It was a battle of wills, and she had no will left.

The nanny continued, getting louder as the other goat joined her. Leah must be occupied. They can't have been fed.

Adah stretched out her toes and slid her knees up. *Ah!* The pain was excruciating – like she'd been in labour. Placing her hands either side of her torso, she shuffled back and up until she sat against the wall. Then she glanced over at Shadow, sat on the floor in the corner of the room. His eyes were closed, but she knew he was awake. He'd have entered during the night when he saw Lamech leave.

Adah lifted her linen cover towards her face to inspect beneath it. Bruises shrouded her flesh like a plague. *It gets worse every time. Next time, he will kill me.*

She fumbled for the small copper mirror by her bedside. In its polished gleam she could just glimpse the reflection of her eyes. Both swollen, but one bulging significantly more than the other.

'Mistress? Did I hear you wake?' Shua entered, walking in backwards through the linen over the doorway and holding a tray of breakfast. As she turned, she gasped. 'Oh, what has he done to you this time?'

Her faithful housekeeper approached and placed her tray on the wooden table vacated by the copper mirror which Adah dropped into her lap. The aroma of freshly baked bread and scented tea was more welcome than the brightness of dawn.

Shua reached out and stroked around Adah's ear, tenderly avoiding her bruises. 'I'm afraid it's too hot for a cold compress. Even our underground supplies are warm.'

'Never mind. I'll sleep it off once I've seen to the goats.'

'I was just going to do that. You're in no fit state—'

'I want to, Shua. I must do something.'

Shua nodded. 'I understand. There are no visitors currently, so you won't be seen, and we don't expect anyone later except Selene.'

Selene. Of course. That's what had set Lamech off. Shadow's woman was pregnant. Adah had dared ask if she might move into the complex. Stupid error. The words had slipped out before she'd consulted her brain. She should have approached Juval like she'd intended.

'Good.' Adah drank the herbal tea Shua pressed into her hands and felt considerably better. 'What would I do without you?' she asked.

'I wish you wouldn't ask that question. I wish you would leave here and never return,' Shua replied.

Her words bit into Adah's heart. It must have reflected in her expression, for Shua continued, 'I would miss you, of course. But I wish you would go for your sake.'

Adah shook her head gently, glancing again at Shadow, who hadn't reacted.

'Have you heard from Eliana?' Shua asked.

A little warmth trickled into her cold, aching chest. 'Yes. She sent a messenger boy yesterday. Yaval, Mela and Ellie are safe. Lamech has made no attempt to track them. They are wandering, searching for herds they might adopt.'

'So, your son goes the way of his ancient relative?'

A smile tickled at the corner of Adah's mouth. 'Yes. It would seem so. I am glad. It's better he wanders than settles somewhere Lamech might find him. Who knows when Lamech might have a change of heart?'

'So far, the only thing he's bemoaned is the absence of Fang. He doesn't even mention Yaval,' Shua said with derision. 'What are they living in. Caves?'

'I suppose so.' Adah's lip dropped and instead, her tear ducts prickled. She sniffed, blinking repeatedly to hold back the tears. 'I... I miss him so much.'

The sensation of skin on skin warmed her hand as Shua stroked it. 'It's Shabbat in two days. You'll see Juval and Naamah then. That'll help.'

Adah nodded. 'If my face allows me to keep company.'

'We'll sort it. We'll get through this, mistress.'

Get through it? Get through to what? Adah could see nothing beyond.

The goats were a welcome sight, though Adah's hands trembled as she milked, and her technique faltered. The nanny turned her head, as far as she was able with her neck fastened in a wooden stock, looking at Adah as if to say, 'What's the matter with you?'

Adah leaned her head against the goat's flank and muttered a reply. 'All my life I've been searching for something... something to give it meaning. Now it may be over, and what do I have to show for it? Lamech is worse than ever; Juval follows him. I failed Naamah, and Yaval is gone.'

The nanny shifted her weight to take Adah's, ignoring her mistress in favour of the food in the trough.

Adah continued, 'I cannot see my abba for more than a few moments and besides, he has his own life now. He doesn't need me interrupting and disturbing his happiness. Eliana is forbidden again, and I can't even join the healers anymore.'

She glanced at Shadow, standing sentinel by the entrance to the pen, pretending not to hear her. She'd tried to join the healers on occasion before Lamech became stricter, but they disliked having her guard present. No one in need called specifically for her, presumably because they feared the repercussions should any accident happen.

A sigh escaped her mouth. Her goat bleated impatiently, wanting the milk released. 'Sorry,' she mumbled, and continued as best as she could.

Shadow cleaned the muck from the pen, silently taking over when Adah's body failed and she sank her head in her knees, crying. As he handed her a cloth to wipe herself down, he caught her eye, and she thought she detected guilt there.

'It's not your fault,' she said. 'If I hadn't mentioned Selene, he would have found something else to beat me for.'

Shadow nodded almost imperceptibly and passed her a cup of water. They knew each other well now, and many a day would pass in silent company without it being awkward. Still, Adah couldn't count Shadow as her friend. For though she'd do what she could for him, and held nothing against him, the image of his bloodied stone withdrawn from her two attackers never left her. She knew that if Lamech demanded it, he'd use that knife on her.

As Adah wedged the gate closed behind her, she heard voices coming from the ornamental garden and women's laughter. It was Tzillah, with Noa and Dinah. They must have paid a surprise visit. Deprived as she was of friendship, she had a sudden longing to see her female relatives. She'd neared the entrance to the garden before she remembered the state of her face, then she stopped, remaining just out of sight behind the wall.

They spoke her name. Had they heard her approach? Were they calling her?

'What a disappointment she is.' It was Noa's voice. 'You know, I vouched for her when Lamech first introduced her to Methushael? I thought she'd make my son a good wife.'

'I remember.' It was Dinah this time. 'We all thought you were mad for standing against Abba, though Bekhor agreed with you. He's always had a soft spot for her.'

'Yes. If it weren't for that, your abba would likely have refused and seen it as an opportunity to teach me a lesson.' Noa tutted. 'He still valued Bekhor's opinion then.'

There was a pause while Noa sighed. Adah's fingers trembled as her palm rested on the wall. She held her breath, scared of discovery but needing to hear more.

It was Tzillah who spoke next. 'I just wish Lamech would let her go. It would be better for everyone. I don't understand why he keeps her here when she makes him so angry.'

'Do you finally want her to go then?' Dinah asked. 'Last time we spoke, you still valued her company.'

'It's no company now. Her guard is always present, hanging around the house, in everyone's business. I'm sick of it. I spend as much time away as I can, just so I can breathe.'

'Come now, Tzillah,' Noa interposed. 'You're just jealous. From the moment Lamech brought her back here, and you realised he loved her more than you, you've resented her. Don't try to pretend otherwise.'

'Of course I'm jealous—'

'It's only natural…' Noa said.

'But I can live with jealousy; I have done for years,' Tzillah continued. 'It's the effect she has on Lamech I can't stand. Do you know, when he takes me away with him, he is so charming – the best of men. But she brings out the worst in him. She always has.'

Sorrow ate into Adah's soul. Tzillah was saying nothing she didn't already know, but the fact she'd talk about it like this, behind her back…

'If only Lamech would speak with his father again; perhaps Methushael could talk some sense into him. Alas, he still refuses to enter our house,' Noa bemoaned.

'Well, you are always welcome here, Noa.'

Adah heard the chink of cups. Tzillah was likely pausing to drink. Adah's mouth felt dry too. Behind her, she heard the younger boys approaching. They'd probably realised their grandmother and aunt were here and were coming to greet them. Adah was just retreating towards the goat pen when Nahar ran round the corner followed by the little one.

'Hurry up! Sava won't give us treats unless we hu— Adah? What are you doing hiding behind the wall?'

Adah's neck stiffened at Nahar's loud declaration of her presence. When she glanced back at the garden entrance, Noa was there, hands on hips, staring at her. 'My grandsons,' she exclaimed, not taking her eyes from Adah. 'Dinah has sweet treats for you in the garden.' When the boys had passed, Noa grabbed Adah's arm. As her fingers dug into a bruise, Adah winced, and Shadow took one step forward.

'She doesn't need your protection from me,' Noa spat at Shadow, then turned back. 'What happened to you?'

Noa's hurtful words having sunk well into her heart, Adah didn't hold back. 'Your son happened.'

As Noa raised an eyebrow, her grip softened. 'This is what Tzillah was talking about. You heard us, I assume?'

Adah nodded, and, as her anger had not yet abated, added through gritted teeth, 'I'm sorry to be such a disappointment to you.'

She considered Noa through swollen eyelids as Lamech's mother pursed her lips and blinked for just a moment, before she dragged Adah into the garden. The boys were crowded around Dinah, pulling things out of her bag. Once satisfied, they raced off without giving Adah a second glance, but when Dinah's intricately painted eyes lifted, she gasped.

'Look who I found listening behind the archway,' Noa said. A flicker of shame crossed Tzillah's face. Dinah said nothing but studied her manicured fingernails while Noa continued. 'He evidently beats you. Even so, you cannot leave. We women must endure such things. It's our duty. Tzillah may wish you to go, but your son has already shamed this family. You will not.'

'I have no intention of leaving.' Adah knew better than to argue with Noa, and besides, it was true. At least, she thought it was. However, the part about shame she would deny. That wasn't Yaval's fault but Lamech's own doing, and Noa hadn't helped.

'Lamech may not invite us to his parties anymore,' Noa persisted, 'but I hear things, you know. You don't publicly support my son as you should. You pine and tremble and act like the world is your enemy, casting your suspicious glances and disapproving looks at Lamech's friends. Why can't you be more like Tzillah?'

This sparked her anger. 'If I was more like Tzillah then Tzillah wouldn't have been necessary.' Adah immediately felt her face warming. How had she let such words out of her mouth? It wasn't Tzillah's fault she hadn't lived up to everyone's expectations. She couldn't even raise her eyes now, couldn't look at the woman she shared life with.

Noa tutted. 'For sure, I've never met someone so stubborn. It's a pity. You used to be such a sweet girl. Beauty is wasted on you.' Then Noa laughed. 'Not that you look beautiful today. Well, I must go. I have several more visits to make and have been here far too long already. Dinah, come.'

Dinah raised a perfectly plaited head and tilted her chin. 'I shall stay longer. I have no pressing visits.'

Her mother's eyes narrowed but Dinah stared back, not shifting a muscle to rise.

'Fine.' Noa picked up her skirts and swished passed Adah, through the archway. 'Farewell, daughters.'

When she'd gone, Dinah released a long breath through pursed lips. Then Tzillah started to chuckle. *What was there to laugh about?* Adah stole a glance at her rival. Her laugh was in response to Dinah's expression and didn't continue once she caught Adah's gaze.

'I'm sorry,' Adah said.

'Oh, Adah, when will you learn?' Tzillah stood and pranced her way. 'I would slap you again if you hadn't already been beaten. Stop apologising! What you said was perfectly true, and nowhere near as bad as what I said about you. Now get yourself to bed and sleep off your bruises – you look awful. Dinah and I have dresses to try on.'

Tzillah left the way Noa had, beckoning to Dinah to follow. Spying the abandoned tea tray, Adah moved to pick it up, but Dinah caught her arm. She spun, shocked, but Dinah's eyes were not angry. Rather, she drew near and whispered. Shadow was far enough away not to hear. 'I disagree with Ima. I know what it's like to live with an evil man. If you want me to, I will help you.'

Adah couldn't believe the words gracing her ear. She thought Dinah loyal to Lamech; they'd always been close. She'd assumed…

'Don't worry about answering now. Just know that I have contacts in the north. If you need Lamech to go away for a while, I can make it happen. Think about it and send a messenger if you want to talk.'

CHAPTER 74

Dinah's words rattled around Adah's head for days. She couldn't escape the notion that the woman who once despised her would take pity and offer assistance. It forced her to consider if she wanted it.

Lamech left her alone once he saw her bruises and visited Tzillah's bedchamber, who made no secret of her pleasure. The giggling from the adjacent room brought home the words Tzillah had spoken. Though they'd hurt Adah at the time, she saw the truth in them. Tzillah would be happier without her. So would Lamech. Perhaps there was wisdom in leaving.

But how?

Shua had dressed Adah's bruises with a poultice. On Shabbat morning, she brought in clay paste to cover what remained. Adah's eyes were still blackened, but Shua managed to smooth paste and kohl so effectively that it looked intentional, then cut short her front braids to form a long fringe.

'There,' Shua stood back from her handiwork and smiled, then passed Adah the copper plate.

'Thank you,' she replied, feeling sure Juval would still notice, but hoping Naamah's children wouldn't.

Juval did notice. When he entered the hall at noon and bent to kiss her cheek, he whispered in her ear, 'Your painted face hides a secret, Ima.'

Remembering Shadow, she took the opportunity. 'May I speak with you alone before you go?'

'Of course.'

Juval had brought a woman to banquet with him. He introduced Adah to Kenan's daughter, Dania. She wasn't the sort of woman Juval usually favoured. Her beauty was in her bright, fiercely intelligent eyes rather than her figure, and the rest of her features were quite plain. Adah remembered she was joint overseer of Kenan's quarry, and a force to be reckoned with. They'd met years ago, at the covenant ceremony, when Juval had given her his seat on the stage.

After greeting Adah with a kiss, Dania sat next to her brother, Eber, completing the family surrounding the large table in the centre of the hall. The younger children took up one side, Lamech sat at the head, Tzillah at the foot, and the rest of them formed the other side. The spaces where Yaval, Mela and Ellie should be still shouted silently at her, but she was pleased to see Naamah and Eber getting along better.

The hall echoed without the crowds who frequented Lamech's parties, but this is how they'd hosted Shabbat since the extended family grew too large for the main living area. Shua and Leah soon appeared with dishes of food. Adah had long since given up insisting her servants rest on Shabbat. It was another battle she'd lost to the back of Lamech's hand.

The conversation around the table was more interesting than usual with Dania's fresh perspective. Eber joined in energetically where he would usually look serious, and Dania even managed to involve Tuval-Kayin. Tzillah fussed over her grandchildren and when Azurak briefly appeared to whisper something into Lamech's ear, Naamah didn't look his way but focused on Eber. Had she and Azurak fallen out?

'I like Dania,' Adah said, when she was clearing the plates with Juval's help. He'd stayed with her when the others rose and removed to the gardens, and Adah had dismissed Shua and Leah as soon as Lamech was out of sight, ordering them to take a rest.

'I thought you would.' Juval grinned. 'Abba won't though. She's too independent.'

'On the contrary,' Adah said. 'He prefers strong women. Look at Noa and Tzillah. It's me he dislikes.'

Juval put down a plate and lifted her face. 'Is that what this is about?' he asked, searching her painted eyes.

Adah turned away and continued stacking. 'You know we have difficulties. It's nothing new. Tell me why you chose Dania. She's... different.'

A smile spread wide over Juval's face. 'That's why. She makes me laugh, doesn't try to impress me – though she manages it without trying. Nor does she throw herself at me. It's refreshing, like a cool drink from a stream.'

'However did you convince her to court you?' Adah joked.

Her son laughed. 'With difficulty! She was not interested at all – said I was the exact opposite of what she wanted in a husband. Still, we've met many times through Eber, and gradually, I've brought her round.'

As her handsome, charming and gifted son grinned again, Adah thought how easily she'd have fallen in love with him if she'd been in Dania's position. It never surprised her that Juval had women fighting over him, and she knew that wasn't just her mother's bias.

'It's not official yet,' Juval continued. 'And I've warned her about our family. So had Eber, so she wanted to see for herself.' He gazed into the distance. 'I must confess, it will be hard…'

Adah raised an eyebrow. *What will be hard?*

'I'm not like Yaval, Ima. You know my struggles. My tendencies.' As his focus returned to her, he rubbed his hand through his glossy hair, reminding Adah of all the times she'd cradled him as a child and kissed his downy crown. 'Still, Dania is the first woman who has held my attention for longer than a few days, and the only woman I can see coming close to Naamah.'

'Will she expect to be your only wife?'

'Undoubtedly. And I don't know if I can do it.'

Adah chewed her lip. At least Juval was being honest. She could only pray that Dania would be a good influence and would be enough. *Please, Yahweh, redeem my son.*

'Now, what did you want to talk about?' Juval said.

Adah glanced at Shadow, leaning hunched against a pillar near the back of the hall. 'I need you to do me a favour. Do you still arrange marriages for unfortunate women?'

'On occasion. Why?'

'There is a girl called Selene who needs a husband.' In the corner of her eye, she saw Shadow straighten. 'She is expecting soon.'

'Who is the father?' Juval asked.

Adah motioned to her guard. Shadow's eyes widened.

'Him?' Juval said. 'How?'

How? Adah would have thought that obvious, but then, when *would* he have had the opportunity? He never left her side.

Shadow shifted his feet as Juval approached him. 'Are you the father?' Juval asked. They locked eyes for a moment, in a battle of wills, before Juval shook his head. 'It's not him.'

'What? Then who?' Adah exclaimed. 'I thought she was your beloved!'

'Speak, man,' Juval commanded when Shadow remained silent.

Slowly, but clearly, he spoke. 'Selene is a servant in the household of Shael, son of Jehu. Shael raped her. When it became clear she bore his child, he accused her of being a harlot and had her flogged in front of his wife. They hoped the child would die, but it lives and grows stronger. I expected them to turn her out, but they haven't. They mistreat her instead. I don't know what will happen when the child is born. Likely, they'll abandon it.'

As he spoke, Adah's hand flew to her mouth, her chest tightened so she could barely breathe, and tears sprang to her eyes.

Juval swallowed, not faltering in his gaze as he studied Shadow. 'What relation is she to you?'

Shadow hesitated. Collecting herself, Adah moved forward and laid a hand on his arm. 'You can trust Juval.' *I hope.*

'We grew up together on the streets,' Shadow muttered. 'She is the closest thing I have to family.'

'And would you wed her? Do you love her that way?'

The face of her guard hardened once more until it looked like bronze. 'I would do anything for her. Only I cannot so long as your father owns me.'

Juval nodded, backing away. 'So, we have a vulnerable girl in need of a husband, and a man who loves her but is not free to protect her. What about the child?'

A flicker of hope lightened Shadow's otherwise darkened features. 'If you can arrange our marriage, I would take the child as my own.'

Juval stroked his chin, ruffling the shortly cropped beard that accentuated his chiselled jaw. 'The elders give me freedom to judge these cases as I see fit. No one has taken much notice since Gomer died—' He paused. 'You say she's a servant?'

Shadow nodded. 'Yes. She is a servant, not a slave. Yet no one will hire a pregnant woman. They treat her like dung and get away with it, because she has no choice but to stay.'

'What if I hire her myself?' Juval said. 'My housekeeper could do with an extra set of hands.'

Adah's heart leapt, before sinking again slightly. Selene was a very pretty girl – not the best company for Juval when courting Dania.

'You would do that?' Shadow said.

'I assume that's preferable to me arranging a marriage with an older man, like I do for the other girls...'

'Yes.' Shadow replied abruptly.

Juval nodded. 'Leave it with me. I'll speak to Shael and see what I can do. If she pleases me, I'll ask abba about buying you as well, so you can be together.'

Shadow was lost for words. Juval scooped up a large pile of dishes and headed towards the kitchen.

Adah copied, scurrying after him. 'You'd do that for Tzel?'

'I assumed you hated your jailer, but clearly you care enough to bring this to my attention. Have I misjudged?' Juval asked, dumping the dishes in the kitchen courtyard near the water trough.

'No.' *Shadow isn't my jailer, your father is. Shadow's only doing his job.* 'He once saved my life,' was all she said aloud.

'Then I owe him a debt.' Juval placed his hands on her shoulders. 'You know that if I reassign him, Abba will only replace him with another? Someone you might not like so much.'

This had occurred to her the moment he'd suggested it. 'I know. Still, I want you to.'

As she dipped dishes in the trough and wiped them down, she considered her son and pride welled up again, not for his looks or talents but his heart. *He isn't lost yet. He still cares.*

Juval seemed to catch her thoughts. 'You know, Ima. I do think about The Wanderer's story.'

'You do?'

'I know the way I live isn't what you want.' He stroked the ink on his toned upper arm, reminding her of his other passion. 'I don't believe it all, you know. The alternative worship. I enjoy it,' he chuckled. 'I can't claim otherwise. But I have no loyalty to the serpent or his priests. If Dania asks me to, I'll give it up.'

If Dania asks you to. Only then? Adah had a thousand more questions, but she held her tongue, not wanting to push him away.

'I'd never thought much about the Creator, or his enemies, or what I was doing. Yet, The Wanderer spoke with such conviction, like there is a real battle going on. Perhaps...' Juval trailed off, looking into the distance once more.

'Perhaps what?'

He flicked his gaze back to her. 'It's complicated. I'm involved with Abba's business and can't easily change that. Now, enough serious talk. Let's join the others in the garden. We brought a new game with us. I'm desperate to see if Dania has thrashed them all yet.'

Adah didn't want to finish their conversation, but she knew she couldn't force him. Moments like these were rare and always on her son's terms. She looked back at the unfinished dishes as Juval pulled her away. She hadn't helped Shua much.

'Come on, Ima,' Juval said, tugging harder, 'or we'll miss the fun.'

CHAPTER 75

'Yahweh is love, goodness, kindness, joy, peace and patience. He is complete in justice and mercy, always faithful and true. This is what we must replicate.'

Ruhamah spoke the words from the mountains, calling tenderly to Adah where she teetered on the watchtower, gripping the railings. 'Adah, did you hear me? Are you coming to find Him?'

I heard you. I'm here.

'The wall is holding you back. I can see it. They are building it around you. Break free, Adah.'

I can't. There is no way.

'With Yahweh there is always a way. Look for it.'

How? I don't understand. I have tried to be those things – loving, good, kind… Even so, I find no joy. No peace. Where is joy when trapped inside these walls?

'The joy is in your heart.'

No, not mine. You took my heart with you to the mountains. Why do you speak those words anyway? Who taught you them? I have heard them somewhere before...

'Somewhere? Don't you mean from someone? They are my words, Adah. I am Havel.'

Havel? No, you are Ruhamah.

She peered intently, focusing her view over the plains that separated them. As she did, the figure in the mist on the mountains became less clear. As he beckoned to her, Ruhamah's face began fading.

No, don't leave me. Come back!

'Adah?'

This voice was near, right at her side. She turned, knowing whom she would find.

Kayin.

He smiled, and the upturn of his lips made his scar shimmer. 'That's the first time you've called me that. Are we friends now?'

We've always been, haven't we?

'Yes, in a way. Now come, I have something to show you.'

I can't come. The rope holds me tight.

It was noosed around her neck, like the ones that hung from the tree in the square. Two men appeared on her right and left. Dead men, hanging with their eyes glazed and tongues lolling, disabled legs swaying in the breeze.

Fear gripped her and she screamed.

'Take courage, Adah. Step out of the noose. Your feet are on solid ground.' Kayin held out a work-roughened hand.

Tentatively, she took it.

'There now, that wasn't so hard, was it?' he said, leading her on a step. There was no watchtower now, just a dry, dusty plain.

Where are we going?

'To the mountains, of course.'

Adah tried to look behind her. *Lamech must be here somewhere.*

'Stop looking behind. To claim your future, you must look ahead.'

'Mistress? Mistress.'

Someone was tugging at her shoulder. This was a female voice, familiar from somewhere. But Adah couldn't see her. She shook her head as Kayin withered into the dust. *No, not you as well. I'm coming. Wait for me!*

'Mistress, are you alright?'

Slowly Adah came around, opening her eyes to see Shua's concerned ones staring back at her.

'No. No, Shua. Why did you wake me? I was with him.'

'Who?'

Adah blinked. She couldn't remember. Was it Ruhamah, Kayin, or someone else?

'I heard you scream, mistress.'

'You did?'

An impression of very real danger planted itself deeply on Adah's mind. She sat up, searching for Lamech. He wasn't there. Only Shadow sat in the corner, his head against the wall and eyes droopy.

Then lyrics flew into her heart and before she knew what she was doing, she sang.

> *Why, soul, are you downcast? Why so wrought within?*
> *Put your hope in Elohim; give all praise to Him.*
> *You asked to hear Him. You asked for His voice.*
> *Now that He has spoken, obey and rejoice.*
>
> *I need your help now; I need you to be*
> *All that you have promised – sufficient for me.*
> *I need you, Yahweh, so walk by my side,*
> *And lead me onwards until I arrive.*

'Where did that come from?' Shua said, smiling. 'I've never heard you sing before. You have a nice voice.'

Shadow sat up straight. 'Awan sang it.'

'What?' Adah and Shua spoke together, turning to face Shadow.

'The night The Wanderer came. Awan sang that song. I remember.'

'He's right,' Adah mumbled. 'She did.'

'What does that mean?' Shua said.

'Mean?' she asked.

'Dreams can have meanings,' Shadow said. 'As street children, we used to talk about it all the time. Often someone would wake up with a premonition of some danger and they'd warn us. We'd flee to another place, and later find out there'd been a death or kidnapping where we'd slept. We learnt to obey those warnings rapidly.'

'No. Really?' Adah said. 'I dream regularly. I've always assumed it's my overactive imagination.'

Shadow continued, 'The night before I was dragged to the elders, I had a dream. In it, a man offered me a raisin cake. I was so starving, there was no way I was going to refuse it. Yet when I ate, it turned sour in my mouth, and I had to spit it out. I've often wondered if it was warning me about Lamech.'

'Lamech, why?' Shua asked.

'He saved you from the elders. It looked like something sweet, but it turned sour when you realised you'd been purchased as a slave,' Adah said.

Shadow nodded. 'Exactly.'

They sat silently for a moment, pondering. The details of the dream started to return, but Adah feared to share them with Shadow in the room. Yet if he was right, the noose seemed a clear enough warning: remaining with Lamech would lead to her death.

Eventually, Shua spoke. 'That song... Do you think Yahweh can speak in dreams?'

'Who else would be able to warn us about dangers?' Shadow replied. 'The Creator is the only one with foreknowledge.'

Adah was taken aback. 'Shadow, you never cease to surprise me. What do you know of Yahweh?'

Shadow scratched his head. 'Azurak wasn't the only one who scoured the streets, watching out for the children. Others did it with better intent. There was an old man – I never knew his name. He used to tell us stories about Yahweh Elohim. We'd clamour to see him when he appeared, for as orphans, no one had ever told us stories.'

'What do you mean, when he appeared?' Adah asked. It sounded so mysterious.

'Just that. Sometimes he appeared, sometimes he disappeared. We had no idea where he lived, or we'd have camped outside his door.'

Despite the seriousness of the moment, the image of twenty street children outside an old man's door made Adah chuckle.

'If Elohim speaks in dreams,' continued Shua, 'what did He say? I only ask because of that line you sang, *Now that He has spoken, obey and rejoice.*'

Adah's breath caught. Rejoice? Ruhamah had been talking to her about joy, hadn't he? Joy in her heart.

'Well?' said Shua. 'Is there something you need to obey?'

Adah glanced again at Shadow. As much as she wanted to, she couldn't share anything in front of him. Not yet. If she confessed that Ruhamah – or was it Havel? – and Kayin had both called her to the mountains, he would tell Lamech. He had to; it was his job to prevent her escape.

'I can't exactly remember, but I know there were two scenes, two people. They were different, but alike in some way...'

'Twice?' Shadow said. 'You saw the dream twice?'

'Well, it was like one dream, but in two parts.'

'With the same message?'

'I think so.'

Despite Shadow's expertise at hiding his expressions, he couldn't hide this one. 'If it was twice, you must obey. Do not delay.'

'What. Why?'

'Twice means the thing is sure. We experienced this too. Whenever a similar dream occurred twice, we took it very seriously. If it was just once, the thing didn't seem to be so certain.'

'It sounds like you're going to need that song,' Shua said. She sang it back –

> *I need your help now; I need you to be*
> *All that you have promised – sufficient for me.*
> *I need you, Yahweh, so walk by my side,*
> *And lead me onwards until I arrive.*

– But arrive where?' Shua asked.

Adah knew, but she needed a deflection. 'I remember now. I was looking for joy, and the man said joy was in my heart. Perhaps that's where I need to arrive – having joy in my heart.'

As Shua raised an eyebrow, Adah gave the slightest of nods. It said, *Leave it there. I can't say more.*

Fortunately, Shua seemed to understand. 'Well, I think it's time I brought you some breakfast. After all this thinking, I could certainly do with a cup of tea.'

CHAPTER 76

Chanoch was feeling his age. He used to be capable of sitting through the elders' meetings all day, keeping the excitement in his bones. Now, by noon he'd had enough. They never seemed to go anywhere, these meetings, just round in circles, occasionally spiralling on to some tangent that just brought more grief. At least they had chairs now, and shade. His newly crooked back couldn't cope with sitting on a bale of straw, nor being in the sun all day.

'I still maintain things have gone too far,' Kenan was saying. 'Plague spreads through the city again, passed around by large gatherings and immoral behaviour. There are more destitute people on the streets than ever before.'

'You can hardly claim the two are linked,' Lamech interjected. 'Those on the streets aren't the same as those at my gatherings – as you well know, Kenan, being a frequent visitor to my home.'

'Perhaps not your parties, but others follow your lead, Lamech. Others less fortunate than yourself. You cannot deny that sickness spreads from person to person.'

'I can deny it, for we have no idea where it comes from. It could be the animals people insist on keeping in their homes instead of outdoors, or the quality of their food. Anything—'

'Or it could be judgement from Yahweh!' Chanoch found himself standing. His legs had subconsciously propelled him up despite their fatigue.

Everyone seated went silent and stared at him. They were waiting for more.

'Did you not hear my father?' he continued. 'If we do not change our ways, Yahweh will enact judgement. We'll be wiped out! We must start by dealing with murder.' He sent a pointed glance at Lamech. 'Blood requires a reckoning, and the council are spilling blood at an unprecedented rate. These hangings... I... I never agreed to this.'

'The hangings are not murder,' Naman said. 'They are justice. We all agreed, Chanoch. They are aimed precisely at reckoning spilt blood. You are becoming addled, old man.'

Kenan stood and slammed his hand on his chair. 'That's enough. You, Naman, will not show disrespect to the founder of this city, or you will be stripped of your position.'

Chanoch was glad for Kenan's support, and his leadership. Someone had to have the final say, and Chanoch had long since lacked the authority. Yet he constantly worried about Kenan's connections with Lamech's family. How could he remain unsullied when his son was married to Lamech's daughter and, Chanoch recently heard, his daughter was courting Lamech's most immoral son? Though Kenan maintained integrity for the most part, over the years Chanoch had seen the steady decline of his grandson's fidelity and devotion, and that decline showed no sign of stopping.

'I suggest we put the council under review,' Kenan continued. 'There do seem to be a disproportionate number of *old slaves* found guilty of manslaughter. I shall send out the arrangements in due course. Hangings are suspended until the review is complete.'

Chanoch studied Lamech's face. It remained passively neutral. What Chanoch wanted to know was why the council had never punished Lamech? He'd admitted killing in front of them all. If manslaughter was punishable by death, surely self-defence should fall into the same category? If it was self-defence... To his knowledge, no one had properly questioned the man they held in such deference – or fear – and Kenan refused to talk about it.

His grandson glanced at him, suggesting he sit back down, but Chanoch didn't feel the matter was concluded. He'd opened the wound now; he may as well keep prodding it.

'When we founded the city and first came across thieves and people with vicious intent, we kept them under guard in cells, caring for them and trying to reform them. For years, I taught prisoners Yahweh's truth. Many repented and changed their ways. Yet this council, with its insistence on death— Don't you see that when we take life, we are removing the opportunity for mercy; we are putting ourselves in a place only Yahweh should occupy? What right do we have to remove ruach[5] from someone made in the image of Elohim? If people are genuinely dangerous, we should extend the existing cells and keep them contained for longer. Killing them should never be the answer.'

Lamech raised an arm but remained seated. 'And who is going to provide these cells and all the food to keep these dangerous people living in idle comfort? I am a generous person, Chanoch – you all know how I feed, house and clothe the destitute, as far as I possibly can – but even I do not have unlimited supplies for those who cannot work to earn their bread. What you suggest – a large scale prison – is simply not practical.'

'Prison? I'm surprised you have such an objection to prison, Lamech. For I live inside a prison myself. You have kept guards on my gate since my father visited your party!'

Lamech laughed. 'Guards? They are not prison guards, my old friend. Those men are there for your protection. You set several people against you with your little stunt. I took it upon myself to ensure none could enact retribution.'

'Several people? As I recall, Lamech, the main challenge was against you. Against your murderous actions.' Chanoch's heart flamed with the words he'd kept closed off for so long; controlling his tongue was proving difficult. 'Now I cannot go to market without someone following me. I cannot hold a conversation without someone listening. You are trying to find out where my parents are so you... so you can kill them!'

Lamech's mouth remained open in a half-smile. It was almost a look of disbelief – that's surely what he intended to convey – but the truth in Chanoch's statement belied it, and hints of a sneer hid behind Lamech's eyes and in the corners of his lips.

'I would never wish to disrespect you, my friend,' Lamech said without hurry or hesitation, 'but don't you think you're overreacting just slightly? What possible reason could I have for wanting The Wanderer dead? So long as he stays out of my business, I mean the old man no harm. Besides, everyone knows he can't be killed.' Now Lamech's mouth spread back into a full smile. 'I am sorry you feel this way; truly I am. How can I fix it?'

---

[5] Ruach is the breath/spirit of God

'By removing those guards for a start.' *Then you can set Adah free. Then you can cease your nachash-worshipping and your adultery, your murders, your abuse of slaves and every other evil you constantly devise!* Chanoch's cheeks burned with everything he wanted to say – but didn't dare say – to Lamech. He kept his trembling legs stubbornly extended but bit his tongue as Kenan spoke next.

'Sav Chanoch,' Kenan said, stretching an arm towards him. 'I understand you are upset. But think carefully about this. You are vulnerable and frail. You live with just one groom and no other security or company. Lamech is right; you need protection.'

No! Chanoch raised both hands heavenward and shouted,

> Yahweh is my light and my salvation,
> Whom shall I fear?
> Yahweh is the source of my strength,
> I shall not be afraid!
> Though the waters roar and enemies surround me,
> Yet, I shall be confident.
> For He blesses those who love him
> And protects those who draw near.

'He's gone mad,' Naman muttered. Several others talked amongst themselves too, and Chanoch's sudden burst of energy sank heavily into his bones. He grappled for a handhold and slowly lowered into his seat. Yet as he closed his eyelids against the murmurings, a tingling peace extended from his temples to his chest, then all the way to his toes, imbuing life back into his weariness.

As if far off, he heard voices again. Kenan was telling Lamech to remove the guards.

'Fine,' Lamech said. 'But if anything happens to the old man, I am innocent of his blood.'

The others were confirming his statement, swearing oaths that Lamech would not be found guilty.

Have I just made an awful mistake, Yahweh?

The tingling returned and inaudibly, Chanoch felt words impressed upon his heart.

'Peace. Be still.'

CHAPTER 77

City of Chanoch, 750th year of Wandering

'The Wanderer. Really?' Adah hears Juval's question in the dark, though she can barely make out the outline of his face. They are still beside Chanoch's dead fire, waiting for the elder to return.

'What else am I meant to do?' she says.

Juval is shaking his head. 'I thought you would find Yaval.'

'I don't know where he is. Eliana didn't want to give away his location via a messenger. It's too dangerous. She was going to tell me when I got there.'

'But surely they can't be expecting you to travel alone? There must be someone waiting to meet you. Why don't I go to Eliana's?'

'No, Juval. There's no time. As soon as Selene gives birth, my opportunity is lost. Worse still, Azurak was heading to the house. He must already know I'm gone. Any moment, he might sound the alarm.' *Speaking of which, what is taking Chanoch so long?*

'He won't do so loudly. No one is meant to know you are constrained, Ima. Abba has ensured that people think you are just frightened to leave, as you used to be. With all the violence on the streets, it's an easy tale to spin.'

'Don't underestimate Azurak. This is one of the first places he'll look.'

'But how do you know you can trust The Wanderer?' Juval's voice is shaking slightly - he is as scared as she is. Scared for her life, or scared of being found out? Should she tell him about her dream - about Yahweh's call?

Before she can decide, Chanoch returns. 'I know where they are,' he says. 'We must leave immediately.'

Adah stands and Juval follows her towards the door.

A loud pounding on the wood breaks into the quiet. 'Master. Someone else is at the gate. They demand to see you. I think it's...'

'We must go now,' Chanoch says. 'Not that way!' He stops Adah's movement with his voice and motions with his torch towards the rear of the house.

He must have a different exit. Adah feels quiet confidence building. *With Yahweh there is always a way.*

Chanoch clutches her arm and gently guides her, while his groom continues to call out, asking what he should do.

'Go,' Juval says. 'Take Ima and flee. I will stall them as long as I can.'

'But he'll know you're involved—' Adah starts, hating the thought of anything happening to Juval. Then Juval is before her, holding her tightly and kissing her. 'Go, Ima. I love you.'

'I love you too.' Her voice cracks as Chanoch pulls her away, then they are running to the rear of the house, through a door, up three steps and out into a stable area, where a kavash is ready.

'How did you know?' Adah says as Chanoch gives her a leg up.

'I always keep one ready.' He pushes a boulder blocking a small stone archway in the city wall, highlighted by the moonlight. Then he grabs the rein and pulls the kavash onwards. Adah can hear Azurak's angry voice on the other side of Chanoch's small complex. He is questioning Juval. Why is he here? Didn't he just see him at a party? Where is his mother? What has he done?

The thump of a body hitting a wall is just discernible as the kavash stoops beneath the arch. Adah ducks too, forcing herself to look ahead, though her heart screams, *Juval is hurt. Run back to your son!*

They are coming. Crashing through the unlit house; searching for the secret door. There must be several guards with the noise they are making.

Chanoch swings up behind her and urges the kavash into a run. It jolts and protests, kicking its heels.

Adah leans forward to grasp the hairy neck, half holding on, half stroking. She has never ridden before, but she's seen the way Yaval deals with the creatures many times. *Don't throw us off. Not now.* She hears a last shout as the kavash springs forward and the pounding of hooves takes over from the ruckus behind.

The animal's head lowers. It emits a soft snort and settles into a steady rhythm. Adah turns her neck slightly, venturing a look.

Three men are just discernible in the moonlight, throwing their spears to the ground in anger as she passes the boundaries of Chanoch's farmland into the wilderness beyond.

THEY RIDE THROUGH the night and only stop as dawn approaches, and the Great Lake comes into sight, mottled with the colours of sunrise. Chanoch veers towards a copse of trees from which a small stream is trickling into the lake.

'There's a spring here,' he says.

He allows the sweat-lathered kavash to take the fresh water first before tucking it behind the trees so it's invisible from the plain. As Chanoch dismounts, Adah notices he's hobbling and guilt surges within.

'You must rest,' she says, as she slides off. The aching of her inner thighs intensifies as her feet touch the ground, and she struggles to walk as well. She hadn't realised riding was so painful.

'For a little while,' Chanoch says, bending to cup the running water and splashing it over his face.

Adah lets her hood down as the sunlight breaches the leaves, promising another scorching day.

'I have no doubt that Azurak is a master tracker. He will have set out the moment it was light enough to see our trail,' Chanoch says. 'The thought of losing you in his master's absence will be enough to spur him on for days, and I haven't made nearly enough effort to cover the direction we went.'

Adah hasn't thought about that. The relief of being free from the city had increased with every stride the kavash made, but now fear comes hurtling back like a boulder running down a hill. 'You think he'll find us?'

Chanoch peers ahead through the trees, considering the lake and the various water courses that run into it. The peaceful morning so contrasts the situation they find themselves in.

'Let's approach the lake via that herd of longhorns. Their hooves will give us cover. We can wade at the edge of the lake while we make our way round, and then continue in the water upstream. It doesn't get deep for some time.'

Adah nods and kneels beside her friend, who looks a little better for his refreshment, and grasps his hand. 'Thank you for doing this. If we live through it, I'll never forget your kindness.' She offers him a slight smile, trying to quell the fear bubbling beneath the surface of his sensible plans.

Chanoch squeezes her hand back. 'The truth is, my dear, I've wanted to rescue you for a long time. I just haven't known how.'

'Don't blame anything on yourself. It's not your fault I was too weak to leave.'

'Weak? Adah, you are anything but weak. I have seen your bruises, the nervous glances, the flinches at sudden noises. I can barely imagine what you have endured these fifty years. I also saw the way you cared for my abba the night he told his story – you gave him a stool to sit on when no-one else dared to move – and I have no doubt it cost you dearly. That was not weak, my friend. That was brave. You also cared for me when Shiphrah died. I shall never forget that.' Chanoch stands and tilts his face upwards, considering the trees. 'Ah, coconuts.'

He hunts around for a long stick then begins to bash at the tops of the trees. It does look amusing, and a giggle replaces a little of Adah's anxiety.

Once a coconut is vanquished and successfully cracked open, they share the milk before Chanoch scoops at the flesh with a stone and hands her some.

'You're good at this wild living thing,' Adah says.

Chanoch smiles. 'I grew up in the wild, remember? It was a long time before anyone settled in cities. I'm not sure I've ever adjusted.'

'Nor me,' she says. 'Though I've not been here before. Yaval told me about the lake, and I've longed to see it but never ventured beyond Abba's hillsides.'

'Yaval has been here? Is he here now?'

'I don't know where he is, but he told me once about a little cave he found on his rambles, about half a day's walk north of the Great Lake, nestled into the hills. He said there were signs of habitation.'

'Did he now?' Chanoch says.

'You know it?' Adah asks.

'I do. It's where we're going.'

Soon they are mounting the kavash again and approaching the longhorns. As they get closer and the horns bigger, nerves unsettle Adah's stomach, but the herd lets them through without a fuss, beyond grunting and nudging their young away.

Once they are hoof-deep in the lake, Chanoch speaks again. 'So, are you going to tell me how you escaped your home?'

Adah had been thinking of Yaval and wondering if she might soon see him, which led to pondering Juval's fate. What will Lamech's reaction be to his betrayal?

Recent events take shape in her mind as she tries to recall the order of it all to Chanoch. She begins by telling him about Dinah's offer, then her dream. As she does, Chanoch gives the occasional mumble or exclamation of surprise.

'Well, well,' he says when she recalls the song she remembered. 'That's one of my favourites. I've sung it many times, when I've had need. *I need you, Yahweh, so walk by my side...*' he sings softly.

'I'd never heard it before your ima's story. I don't know how I remembered the lyrics.'

'Ah. Yahweh has a way of recalling these things to mind when we need them,' Chanoch said.

'So, you think it was from Him?'

'Most certainly. As was the meeting.'

'The meeting?'

'Our most recent elders' meeting. I thought I might have made a mistake asking your husband to call off the men he had watching me - I got quite cross with him, you know - but if I hadn't, you would never have reached my house or escaped from it. Instead of being met by my guard, you would have been met by Lamech's.'

Adah feels a gentle tingling in her chest. 'How interesting that you did so just at the right time,' she says.

Chanoch chuckles. 'I'm looking forward to teaching you more about our Elohim. Though the best teacher is my ima. We digress; tell me more about what happened.'

They have paddled a quarter of the way round the lake and now Chanoch turns off and the kavash picks its way over a stream, boggy at first but gradually becoming stonier and easier for the kavash to manage with two riders on its back.

'I reached out to Dinah a few weeks ago, when I finally decided I could ignore the dream no longer. Juval had hired Selene, Shadow's woman, and asked Lamech if he could buy my guard too but was refused. I almost gave up hope then, except the words in my dream kept coming back to me: *With Yahweh there is always a way.* So, I dispatched a messenger to Dinah, asking for her assistance with *the thing we talked about*. We couldn't speak with anyone else around, you see, and I'm never alone.'

Chanoch shakes his head behind her. 'I had no idea he watched you inside as well.'

'All the time. Everywhere. Two days later, Lamech announced he was travelling north the following week. "Dinah has decided she wants to move back there," he said. "She misses her children." It turns out Dinah is even more cunning than I realised, though I shouldn't be surprised - she is Lamech's sister. She requested Lamech not just escort her to Leviathan City, with Tzillah for company, but also obtain a senior role for her new husband. Never one to forsake an opportunity to install his people in positions of power, Lamech agreed. He left two weeks ago, as you know.'

'Just after the elders' meeting,' Chanoch confirmed.

'Ever since, we've been waiting for our moment, waiting for Selene to go into labour!'

'Into labour?'

'I knew it was the only thing that would tear Shadow from my side. I contacted Eliana through her youngest son, who is a market delivery boy. I happened across him delivering vegetables to Shua and whispered a message before Shadow noticed. The following day, Shua relayed Eliana's reply. She could arrange someone to take us to Yaval if I could get to her house. She lives near the wall, you see, and, with ladders and rope, I could cross to the neighbour's roof and be lowered from there.'

The kavash stumbles on an unexpected dip, and Chanoch's arms tighten around Adah. 'Are you alright?' he asks, once she rights her seat.

She nods, looking down at the aging skin on arms not much thicker than her own.

'You said earlier that Azurak was supposed to be occupied...' Chanoch continues.

'Yes. As soon as I had arranged things with Eliana, I needed my other son's help. The problem was, I didn't think I could trust Juval not to let slip.'

'He surprised me last night,' Chanoch says.

'Yes.' Adah imagines Juval's handsome face and her heart quivers once more for his safety. Has Azurak marred it? Could he be placing a noose under it right now? Even if Juval survives - will she ever see him again?

'Unless cut short through war or disease, our lives are long,' Chanoch says. 'Who knows what opportunities the future holds?'

Adah nods again, barely noticing that Chanoch guessed her thoughts.

'Juval had already helped with Selene, but I didn't want to place too much responsibility in his hands or expose him to danger–' The word hits her, and she chokes. 'Oh! What will they do to him?'

Chanoch leans in slightly closer. 'I don't believe Azurak will touch Juval. He wouldn't dare without Lamech's consent.'

'But what if Lamech is back already?'

'Do you think he'd hurt his own son?'

Adah contemplates. Lamech loves her but hurts her. He's hurt Yaval before too. 'I don't know. Love doesn't seem to determine his actions as much as hatred, and they're so often mingled.'

Chanoch hums a little. 'I think what we love can often determine our hatred.'

'Lamech loves himself,' Adah says.

She feels Chanoch shake his head. 'I have watched Lamech for a long time. I believe Lamech's first love is power. He hates whatever and whoever stands in the way of his advancement. Sometimes, even himself.'

The realisation dawns like the brightest sunlight rising in the east. Adah has never understood how Lamech can possess love and hate so passionately and simultaneously. Now she sees it – his first love isn't her. It is power, and because of that, his heart can only have peace with those who advance it.

She never has. It isn't her inherent weakness he despises – it is her lack of usefulness. The years early in their marriage when she felt idle, he adored her because she adorned him. People complimented her beauty everywhere they went, and the only thing required for his prosperity was her standing by and smiling. They loved her; he loved her.

When he decided his power was contingent on an heir that she failed to produce, everything changed. As the years went by, he saw no alternative but to replace her, and, determined not to make the same mistake twice, chose someone who entertained, someone who shared his ambition, someone who could bear a child.

Despite Tzillah only bearing two, Lamech has never hated her. For, as he once said, "She complements me perfectly." Tzillah makes herself useful by knowing his business, knowing his friends, supporting him without question. Things Adah never did, nor could do.

The same thing applies to his children. The battle for his love continues with each one.

'Juval is still useful to him, I think,' she says.

'Then Lamech is unlikely to hurt him, though I suspect he may scold him.'

'He'll certainly do that.'

CHAPTER 78

As the sunshine of her realisation fades, Adah can't decide whether she feels liberated or not. On the one hand, Lamech doesn't really hate her - at least not always. On the other hand, he never really loved her. Not the unconditional love she feels for her children. Could she have tried harder to be a better wife? Could she have satisfied him?

She doubts it. For Lamech's version of a better wife is not something she's ever aspired to, or been morally capable of, and she's failed every time she's resolved to please him.

The water deepens so the kavash can no longer wade in it. Chanoch encourages their mount out of the stream, and they begin to pick their way up the hillside. Adah glances behind, wondering how obvious their tracks will be. Might Azurak soon appear on the horizon?

The barrenness of the plain transforms gradually into greenery, yet it is mostly shrubland, devoid of much grass or land which could be farmed. As the morning wears on, exhaustion from the sleepless night hits Adah and she begins to droop over the mount's neck. Chanoch soon draws a halt and jumps from the kavash.

'Berries,' he says, pointing to a rocky outcrop with thorny vines trailing down it.

They kneel beside the stream again, now flowing quickly and steadily, and drink their fill before picking as many berries as they can find. It barely takes the edge off the gnawing in Adah's stomach, but she's so tired, the thought of eating more doesn't appeal anyway.

'If I'd known you were coming last night, I'd have packed a water skin and some bread,' Chanoch says as they mount again.

'I'm sorry. It was never the plan to involve you. You are already in enough danger,' Adah replies.

'I was concerned for my parents. Despite Yahweh's promise to Abba, I never like to give away their whereabouts. But that was all. So, you were telling me about Juval?'

Grateful for conversation to keep her alert, Adah divulges the rest of the story. 'I decided to tell Juval that I needed to see Eliana but not explain why. I suggested it was a woman's matter, and I must go alone without my shadow. He looked curious but, as is usually the case, didn't probe me further.

'We agreed that on the day of Selene's labour, he would encourage Shadow to stay by her side. Yet, I couldn't stand the thought of Tzel taking the punishment for my escape. By contrast, I had no conscience about Azurak doing so. The problem is, there is only one person in this world who has a hold on Azurak. Not even Lamech can control him as well as her.'

'Naamah,' Chanoch said.

'You know?'

'They haven't exactly been subtle.'

'Yes... well, they were at first. It has been going on for a while, and Azurak played a protracted game of conquest to get her.' Adah shivers, remembering the conversations with Lamech's enforcer years before.

'I see.'

'Recently, Naamah has pushed Azurak away as she and Eber have grown closer. This pleased me, and I didn't want to encourage Azurak again, but Juval doesn't have my scruples. He spoke to Azurak, declaring that Lamech had given Tzel permission to accompany his child's birth, as long as Azurak guarded me instead. Then he told me I must ask Naamah to invite Azurak to the festival she's been hosting this week. However, I have never found Azurak irrational, even when it comes to Naamah. I doubted it would work.'

'I suspect it didn't exactly, given he wasn't *occupied* as you expected,' Chanoch murmurs.

'It almost worked. When Selene's pains commenced, Juval sent for Tzel, who was pleased to collude if it meant being with Selene, and I sent a message to Naamah. When Azurak turned up to relieve my guard, I pretended to be sleeping. He hovered for a while, until a messenger boy came with Naamah's request, giving me a needle's eye of opportunity to escape. As soon as Azurak departed, I threw my cloak on and slipped out, praying that Avram was on the gate.'

'Avram let you out?' Chanoch asks, as the plain becomes a hillside and the mount's gait slows.

'It's something I feel guilty about. He's always been kind and made no attempt to question or stop me. I dread to think how he will explain my escape to his master.'

Chanoch nods.

Was there anything better she could have done? *Yahweh, please protect Avram.*

'So, what happened with Naamah?' he asks.

'Eber happened! He refused Azurak entry, forcing him onto the street, where he went looking for a woman to satisfy his desires.'

'Which is when he spotted you.'

'Yes.' Adah recalls how she had to change course, then how she collided with Juval. 'As he escorted me to your house, Juval confessed he'd had a premonition something was wrong - a compulsion to leave his party just as I approached.'

'How interesting,' Chanoch says.

'I expect Eliana is worried. Juval probably can't get word to her about the change of plan... Oh the more I think about it, the more I realise how many people I've put in danger with my selfish attempt at escape. I should never have left.' Adah wipes at her eyes with one hand while the other holds fast to the kavash's neck.

Chanoch halts again. 'Adah,' he says gently. 'I understand your fear, but all I'm hearing is the multiple ways Yahweh made your escape possible. Can't you see? He cares for you. You can be sure he cares for those you love as well.'

'Truly?'

'Yes.' They trudge on. 'Imagine for a moment that Selene had gone into labour a week ago. Would Naamah have been hosting a gathering?'

'I expect not.'

'Two days ago, then. Who was on the gate?'

Adah shivers. 'The watchman I don't like.'

'Exactly. And what about Eliana's son happening to deliver to your house the previous week. Does he often?'

'No!'

'So things worked out just right.'

'But I didn't get to Eliana's, and I don't know where Yaval is!'

'This is true. But I expect there's a purpose in that too. It may be to do with Juval, or it may be something we are yet to discover.'

Adah is glad she got to tell Juval the truth and say farewell, and glad her son proved loyal in the end, but that barely quells her persistent fear. They slip into silence until they come upon a meadow, at the top of which stands a solitary terebinth tree.

'This is where Ima found Abba,' Chanoch says. 'Where my uncle Shimon attacked, where Abba sacrificed with Sav Adam and where my parents married. This meadow holds many memories for them.'

Adah imagines the scenes from The Wanderer's story - considering the way Yahweh protected, forgave and blessed Kayin - and feels heartened that He might seek her out the same way. She is such a small ant among thousands; she doesn't understand why the Creator would care about her, but what Chanoch says makes sense. He does seem to. *Perhaps You have heard all these little prayers, after all.*

As they ride up the steeper hillside, anticipation at meeting her ancestors again heightens with each hoofstep. Halfway up, they dismount, and Chanoch leads his kavash through the undergrowth with Adah following behind. On reaching a circle of trees and bushes, Chanoch secures the kavash and ducks between two thickets.

It opens out into a broad place - a glade where a magnificent oak tree dominates to the right of a cave. Beneath it is a carved seat and hanging from its lower branches, swathes of laundry.

'Ima,' Chanoch calls. 'Are you here?'

There is a clattering from inside the cave then Awan appears at its entrance. 'Chanoch!'

Awan runs to her son and throws her arms around him. Adah is surprised; the last time she saw Awan, the older woman relied on a cane.

'I see the hill country suits you as usual, Ima,' Chanoch says.

'Of course,' Awan replies, 'You know how happy I am here; though we never dare stay long.' Awan turns towards her. 'Adah. How wonderful to see you again. Welcome.'

'I hope you don't mind me coming...'

'Of course not. I'm delighted. Have you had a long journey? Come sit. I was just hunting around for some food to prepare dinner.'

Adah follows her to the stone circle and lowers herself onto a boulder, stroking the smoothness from years of use and reliving the scenes around this fireplace, the stories told, tears spilt and sins forgiven. Meanwhile, Awan bustles about preparing and chatting away to Chanoch who fills her in on Adah's escape.

'Yahweh really wants you here,' her hostess exclaims, bringing her a steaming cup of drink. 'It's acorn. A bit different, but I hope you like it.'

An inhale reveals a nutty aroma.

'I wonder what He's telling you,' Awan continues, striding towards the thick branches of the oak. She's far more confident and comfortable in her own home. Well, temporary home. It makes sense she loves the place.

'It must have been hard leaving here for fear of Shimon,' Adah says. 'It's a beautiful spot. Though I imagined the oak being a lot smaller.'

From where she's folding linens, Awan releases a peel of laughter. 'It was. Seven hundred years have passed since those events and she's an old lady now.' Awan strokes the trunk affectionately. 'We've seen many winters come and go, haven't we?' Turning back to Adah, she continues. 'It is always challenging leaving here. Leaving anywhere is difficult, and it has been hardest of all for you, I expect.'

Adah finds herself nodding as tears spring to her eyes once more.

'There now.' Swiftly, Awan abandons her laundry and sits by Adah's side, entwining their fingers. Hers feel dry and coarse like Shua's which compounds Adah's emotional turmoil, for, not wanting to make her complicit, she never said farewell to her friend.

'I tried to stay with him. I tried,' Adah gasps. 'I failed. He wouldn't change, and I'm not as strong as you.'

'Dearest girl,' Awan says. 'No one blames you. From one encounter I could see your husband was a harsh man, and proud of it. Dearest, when I found Kayin, Yahweh had already prepared him. I couldn't have lived with him had that not been so. And he never abused me, nor took another. What you have endured...'

Looking into Awan's eyes, Adah sees nothing but compassion. She momentarily wonders how Awan knows of the abuse, until she spies her bare lower arm and the scars it carries. Awan continues to stroke her fingers while closing her eyes and breathing deeply.

Moments later, they flicker open again. They are sparkling as she speaks. 'Yahweh wants you to know that you are dearly loved. What Lamech offered was not true love, but what Yahweh offers is unconditional. He wants to be your first love.'

'How—?' This woman knows my thoughts, the very conversation I had with myself earlier. Can it really be true? Can Yahweh Elohim be speaking through her, as He did through my dream? Can He really give me what I have always desired?

Awan's lips mirror the smile in her eyes. 'This is what you can have too, my dear, if you will let Yahweh into your heart. He didn't create us to leave us alone. He knows each of us intimately and wants us to know Him.'

'The only things I know about Yahweh are what my ima told me, which was mostly stories about The Wanderer, if I'm honest.' Adah's confession makes her blush. 'Eliana trusts Him, but we rarely speak so deeply, and Ruhamah...' Her blush gets deeper until she feels her cheeks might turn to fire. 'Your son has taught me most of what I know. And your story, of course.'

'Adah,' Awan squeezes her hand once more, not remotely put off by her embarrassment. 'I didn't say Yahweh wants you to know *about* Him, though it helps of course. I said He wants you to *know* Him.'

'To know Him?'

'As you know a husband – though not physically. To know Yahweh is purer. Better. He has none of the failings of human lovers. He is utterly dependable and entirely good.'

Dependable. He's dependable...

'Is the tea awful? Would you like something else?'

Adah starts at Awan's swift change of topic, then glances at the untried liquid in her cup. 'Oh, no. I haven't...' She takes a sip and decides it's bearable, if not quite what she's used to. 'Lovely. Thank you.'

Awan chuckles. 'It's not lovely; you don't need to pretend. But it's warm and comforting.'

The drink revives Adah sufficiently to get through the meal, which is just as well, for Kayin doesn't appear until midway through. The Wanderer instantly dominates the atmosphere as he enters the glade carrying an infant deer on his shoulders - wounded, but alive. The nervous excitement she'd previously felt vanishes, and instead, Kayin's presence warms her like the return of an old friend.

'Another injured one?' Awan asks, getting up to kiss him.

As Kayin peers from under his burden, he seems healthier also. Though lines of worry crinkle his brow, his eyes light up on seeing Chanoch. He greets them both then shifts the deer to the floor, ties it up and disappears inside the cave. His departure feels like a cold wind, and Adah reminds herself that he barely knows her. He has no idea he 'called her here', nor any concept of the connection she feels they share. Their many conversations exist only in her dreams.

'Predators are getting bolder,' Awan says, motioning at the deer. 'They'll often attack several in a herd before settling on the kill. We do our best to help those left behind when the herd moves on.'

Kayin reappears with a small bowl, pours a splash of hot water into it, from Awan's pot over the fire, and mixes. 'Saltwater,' he says, catching Adah's eye. 'It's the best thing for wounds.'

'Of course,' Adah murmurs, remembering the story of Awan's stings bathed in the sea. The knowledge has passed through the generations and traders bringing dried salt from the Realm of Leviathan frequently sell it in the marketplace.

As Awan explains why Adah is here, she gives her husband plenty of time to absorb the information, which he does with the occasional grunt as he bathes the deer's injuries.

'You must stay with us until we can find your son,' Kayin says, washing his hands and coming to sit opposite Adah around the fire. 'Chanoch may return to judge the situation in the city.'

'It's not safe,' Adah exclaims, revisiting the desperate escape from Chanoch's house and Azurak's knowledge.

Kayin strokes his beard. 'What do you think, son?'

'Certainly it's dangerous, but there's no avoiding it; it's my home. I can ask someone to stay with me,' Chanoch replies.

'Let's give it a few days,' Awan says. 'There's no rush, and you're likely exhausted from your journey. Speaking of which, I will make up some beds.'

She never stops. Awan has barely finished eating the meal she spent hours preparing, now she's up and working again. *I wish I was capable like her.*

Kayin chuckles. 'My wife adores having visitors. For years we had a busy home filled with children, grandchildren and great-grandchildren. Since everyone has gone their separate ways, she doesn't know what to do with herself.'

'How long has it been?' Adah asks.

'Oh, I'm not sure. When you've been alive as long as me, you lose track of the years.'

'My youngest sister, Dorit, has seen nearly three hundred winters,' Chanoch says. 'I helped build her city remember, Abba? About a century ago, I think.'

'Yes, that's right.'

They spend a while talking until Awan announces the beds are ready and directs Adah into the cave. She's never slept in a cave before and is surprised by how cold it is compared to a house, but Awan has been generous with blankets and sheepskin, and Adah soon drifts into an exhausted sleep.

CHAPTER 79

The following morning, Awan's melodic voice accompanies the sunrise flickering on Adah's eyelids. She listens in a blissful state of half-sleep, only partially aware this might not be a dream.

I trust You, O Yahweh my Lord,
And I say, 'You are my Elohim.'
My times are in Your hand,
I shall not be afraid.
For You stand, You stand with me.

Rescue me from fear, from the hand of my enemies.
Cover us in Your love, casting out any unbelief.
Your abundant goodness You've stored up for me,
My Yahweh, my Elohim.

I need You, O Yahweh my Lord,
And I say, 'You are ruler of all.'
For You heard my plea
When I cried for Your aid,
And You stand, You stand with me.

Soft footsteps pad into the cave. Adah peels her eyes open to see Awan placing a cup and an oatcake next to her pallet. Then Awan lays a hand on her shoulder and sings softly.

Let your heart take courage as you wait for the Lord.
Though you feel besieged, He hears your pleas.
For He knows your name, and He hears your voice,
He is Yahweh, your Elohim.

Awan smiles and retreats, singing the chorus again as she continues her preparations outside.

Rescue me from fear, from the hand of my enemies.
Cover us in Your love, casting out any unbelief.
Your abundant goodness You've stored up for me,
My Yahweh, my Elohim.

As she tastes her oatcake, a sensation Adah has never known before washes over her, filling her chest until there's barely room for the emotions that previously warred within. Fear pales against the warmth that trickles into her fingertips and down into her toes, a warmth that tells her that whatever happens, all will be well. *Is this Peace?*

It's a completely different life - lying here listening to Awan. Everything Awan thinks, says and does is focused on her Elohim. *I've never seen this before. Those words she sang over me - were they part of that song, or just for me, like the words she spoke yesterday? What were those words? I was too tired to think at the time...*

They return to mind instantly: 'Yahweh wants you to know that you're dearly loved.'

He offers me unconditional love, like I have for my boys. Despite everything Juval has done: the evil he's committed, the times he's let me down... I still love him passionately. I am desperate for him to turn back and can't bear the thought of leaving him or losing him. And this... This is how Yahweh feels about me?

'He wants to be my first love,' Adah says aloud. She stands and glances around. Chanoch is still sleeping soundly but Kayin is gone. After ambling outside into the sunlight, she asks Awan, 'What must I do?'

'Do?' Awan is pounding dough on a large flat stone, but she looks up and considers her.

'To know Yahweh. Really know him. To have him as my first love.'

Joy spreads over Awan's face, and she pats another stone next to her. 'There is little you need to do, my dear. Yahweh's love is a gift of grace. Have you confessed your sin, like Kayin and I did in our story?'

Taking a seat, Adah nods. 'I repent regularly. Chanoch told me I must long ago, and I've never forgotten it. He claims I'm not weak, but I know I am, and I always get things wrong. I know I get angry sometimes. I anger Lamech—'

'Not all anger is bad,' Awan says. 'Some anger is righteous, like the way you feel when Lamech mistreats people. And there is nothing inherently wrong in weakness either.' Awan stops pounding the dough while Adah considers the surprise of those words. *Nothing wrong with weakness - could it be true?*

'My son is right about repentance - we are all corrupted. Were it not for Yahweh's abundant grace, I doubt we could do anything good. Yet, we are also completely loved. And what Yahweh desires above all is for you to know that. How have you felt about Yahweh in the past?' Awan asks. 'How have you considered Him?'

'Not the way you describe Him. I thought He was powerful - a protector of sorts - but He did not protect my babies. He...

He did not protect me.' She flushes as those words leave her mouth, aware that the last two days don't reflect them.

'Ah, you've lost children. That is difficult.'

'I know He had other plans. Sav Adam said there are some for whom…'

'Childbearing would not be easy. Yes, I did mention that. It doesn't make it any easier, though. Do you resent Yahweh for it?'

'I've tried not to.'

Awan nods. 'There are many sufferings in this world, Adah, and as I look around me, I see them increase all the time.'

'So do I.'

'Hmmm… what causes the increase?'

'Mostly men like my husband,' Adah says.

'Mostly. But not always. Sometimes nature or tribulations. Do you remember Kayin's struggle with this and what our brother Havel advised him?'

'I remember he felt his experiences after the wolf attack were unfair and, knowing Yahweh could have prevented them, Kayin grew to despise Him. Havel said Yahweh might be trying to train him, as a shepherd trains his sheep.'

'You listen well,' Awan says. 'Do you feel Yahweh was unfair to you?'

'No. I deserved everything I got.'

'Ah.' The dough in Awan's hands has reached the right stretch and she beings tucking it under, forming it into a tight, smooth ball. 'Then perhaps the problem is not loving Yahweh for who He is, but that you believe yourself unworthy of love.'

Adah's heart quickens. 'What do you mean?'

Awan swivels the ball of dough one last time, sealing its shape, then leans back. 'Tell me, Adah. Why does it upset you when you see Lamech mistreating the innocent?'

This is the second time Awan has mentioned mistreatment, and Adah's next question is spoken tremulously. 'How do you know about that?'

'Oh, we've had several conversations with people since your husband's party - trying to ascertain what's been happening in the city to inform our prayers.'

'I see.' Memories of Kayin's pronouncement return - about Yahweh's judgement should this generation not repent. If they were praying for the city, then judgement wasn't something they wanted. 'I suppose I dislike it because I see all people as precious, and all lives as valuable.'

'Exactly.' Awan smiles. 'And why are they?'

'Because they are made in Elohim's image?' Adah frames it as a question, unsure if this is the answer Awan wants, but remembering it from her story. It was in the same part as those words of Havel's about Yahweh being love, goodness, kindness and joy. The words from her dream.

'Adah, do you believe this also applies to you? You too are made in Yahweh's image; you have inherent value.'

'I... I don't know. I have always felt so useless. At first, I couldn't have children. Then when I did, I couldn't keep them safe—'

'What makes you think you need to be useful for Yahweh to love you?' Awan asks.

Now her heart pounds. 'Why would He want me otherwise?'

'Oh, Adah. He already has you! The entire world is His to do with as He pleases. He doesn't need anything from us.'

'I don't understand!' Adah exclaims, feeling the overwhelming desire to run into the arms of someone safe, but not knowing who is. Tears cloud her vision as she fears Yahweh's displeasure again.

Trickling water tells Adah that Awan is refilling their cups, though with her hands wiping at her tears, she cannot see it.

Awan speaks again, softly. 'Chanoch tells me you escaped Lamech once before, many years ago, but he forced you to return.'

'Yes...' The admission fills Adah with discomfort, and she grasps the offered cup, sipping it to hide her face.

'Did you love Lamech the same way when he forced you back as when you married him willingly?'

This makes her glance up, and she catches Awan's eye. Once again, compassion reigns, not condemnation. It sets her slightly more at ease. This woman is not trying to confuse or condemn her. 'Of course not. I hated Lamech for it. It took me a long time to forgive him... perhaps I never did.'

'Do you see now how Yahweh wants your love willingly? Though I suppose He could take it by force, that is not His way. Instead, He shows us His character until we love Him in return. What I was trying to say is that He made us for His pleasure, imbuing us with dignity and honour above the animals, because it gave Him joy. That includes you, Adah.'

Awan reaches a hand forward. 'He loves you and values you, and He wants you to know that - but He will not force you. He's waiting for you to open your heart and then He can fill it. He doesn't need us to do anything for Him except accept His love and His lordship. In fact, the weaker you feel, the more likely it is that He can reach you.'

The idea that weakness could be positive is entirely strange, however, the mention of joy piques Adah's curiosity. *Joy is in your heart...* Is this the way to find it?

'I want to open my heart,' Adah confesses, 'but I'm scared. I've lost many people I've loved, and others have let me down. Then sometimes, I wonder if those I love are better off without me. I know you said Yahweh is dependable, and I have always been drawn to His name but... Can it be true?'

'That is where trust comes in,' Awan replies. 'There is no substitute for it. You just have to jump and let Him catch you.'

An unfathomably deep desire to jump impresses itself on Adah's soul, yet she still feels incapable. What if she messes it up, like everything else? What if she does it wrong?

Awan stretches out her palm. 'Would you like me to hold your hand?' she says.

After releasing her cup and placing it down, Adah stretches a trembling hand towards the older woman.

Wrapping her fingers around Adah's, Awan speaks again. 'If it's helpful, I can say the words and you can just repeat them in your heart?'

Incapable of much else, Adah nods.

> Be gracious to me, Yahweh, for I am in distress.
>> My eyes are wasted from grief.
>> My soul and body also.
> I am terrified. For my life is spent with sorrow,
>> and my years with sighing.
> My strength fails.
> To my foes I am a reproach:
>> A broken vessel.
> I hear the whispering of many -

> terror on every side! -
> as they scheme together against me,
> as they plot to take my life.
> I confess I have not trusted You to save.
> It seems too much to say, 'You are my Elohim.'
> I cannot always see You.
> I cannot always hear You,
> but I want You, Yahweh.
> So now I say, 'My times are in Your hand.'
> Rescue me from my enemies!
> Rescue me from myself.
> I repent of my mistrust.
> I know You are my Elohim.
> Make Your face shine on Your servant;
> save me in Your steadfast love!
> Make me a vessel for Your grace and truth.
> O Yahweh, let me not be put to shame,
> for I call upon You -
> on Your abundant goodness which
> You've stored up for me.
> I open my heart to You now.
> My heart takes courage.
> Into your hands I commit my spirit.
> I wait.

Adah repeats the words in her heart, words that speak to the soul of her being as well as the creator of her soul. Words that say everything she has wanted to say to Yahweh but hasn't known she can. It hurts - opening up, admitting she is a broken vessel, confessing she hasn't trusted. Yet as she expresses the truths Awan speaks, things start to change.

Nature continues. Creation in its bustle, singsong and rustling of leaves presses forward as always, but Adah is still. The present is present like never before as she waits. Then, like bread rising when the yeast takes hold, her chest opens into a wide expanse, receiving the breath of life which seeps into those places of fear, unbelief and hurt, ministering to each unsolved question and unfinished story, coating each wound with the balm of Elohim's goodness.

Her eyes are closed, but they feel open as she sees – sees the vastness of the universe and the greater glory of the Creator who holds each star delicately in His fingertips as she would hold a tiny seed. The stars are not elohim, but He is.

Adah knows – with unwavering certainty – that, just as He holds those stars, He holds and watches over her.

'My eye is on you, and my ear is inclined to you.'

So this is what it's like to hear You. The words impress themselves deep, and she responds. *I know it – as surely as I know my name.*

'I made you, and you are beautiful to me. You need be no one's adornment but mine.'

Her breath catches then comes sweeping back in, filling her mouth and extending it into a wide beam. She tastes her tears but knows one thing for certain – they are tears of joy.

CHAPTER 80

'I've found your son!'

Kayin's declaration is loud, breaking into Adah's conversation with Yahweh - a long, silent conversation of tears and truth.

She hears Awan *shhh* her husband, but it is too late. The glory of the presence fades slightly, but does not leave altogether, settling in a comfortable place Adah knows she can access again. She opens her eyes to find her smile remains fixed; she couldn't reduce it if she tried.

By contrast, Kayin looks mortified. 'I just interrupted something really important, didn't I?'

Adah laughs. 'It's fine; He's not leaving. I know it now.'

Kayin's face relaxes, and he comes to sit opposite her, resting his elbows on his knees and leaning forward. A grin twitches. 'I get the impression that while I was finding your son, you found someone far more significant.'

Realising what he said, Adah's heart quickens. Could it get any fuller? 'You've found Yaval?'

'I remembered he told us he was going west towards the mountains so I left early this morning to see if I could pick up the trail.'

'What do you mean, he told you? You've seen him?'

'Oh yes, he was here when we arrived. Did I not mention that?'

'No!'

Kayin's rumbling chuckle reverberates through the stones and adds a sparkle to his eyes. 'Sorry. Yes, he was here, and thoroughly embarrassed at us finding him.'

'He said, "We didn't know if it was your cave," and intended to leave immediately,' Awan adds. 'But of course, we insisted they stay on account of the little one. They moved on a few days later.'

Ah, little Ellie. I can't wait to see my granddaughter again.

'We very much enjoyed having them around and assured them they are welcome to use the cave whenever they please.'

'Thank you for your kindness,' Adah says.

'Not at all.' Kayin continues, 'We're fortunate. It rained before they left but it hasn't done since. As large herds don't pass through this area, your family's tracks remain. Indeed, I believe the lack of herds are why Yaval wanted to move on. He was telling us about his plans to observe some of the larger species... Anyway, I digress. Their tracks head west. If we move quickly, it shouldn't take us long to catch up with them, for they'll move slower than us.'

'West - towards the mountains?' Adah remembers her dream.

'Initially. Though if they want to find larger herds, it's likely they'll veer north at some point. Do you have an interest in the mountains?'

'In a dream I had, I heard a call from the mountains. I thought it might be the place I find my joy but... I think I've already found it here.'

Kayin leans forward. 'Tell me what just happened.'

'I prayed with Awan, opening my heart to Yahweh and committing to Him. Then I felt Yahweh speak for the first time.'

'The first time?' The tip of Awan's eyebrow raises. 'I don't think it was the first time.'

'What do you mean?' Adah asks.

'For a start, He seems to have spoken in your dream and through our story. Yet, I suspect if you look back on your life, you will find other times. Have you ever felt compelled to do anything?'

Adah thinks. Several instances spring to mind, but one in particular impresses itself clearly. 'I helped those suffering from the plague. The first day I did it, I woke with conviction in my belly, which I knew wouldn't go away unless I did something. And then - this strange sensation. It sort of instructed me how to protect myself in a way no one else seemed to have thought of. They were all scared to help, but I never got sick. In fact, the action of helping pulled me out of disabling fear.'

Rubbing his scar, Kayin speaks again. 'Yahweh certainly knows how to protect us, and these could all be Yahweh speaking to you. He does it often, however, most of the time we aren't listening.'

'What else did you see in your recent dream?' Awan asks.

Adah feels her cheeks warming, not wanting to admit Kayin's involvement. 'In the first part, I thought I saw the man I loved calling me from a high peak, surrounded in mist. He was speaking these words, "Yahweh is love, goodness, kindness, joy, peace, patience. He is complete in justice and mercy, always faithful and true." He called me to come find Yahweh, to break free of the wall he could see binding me. To my doubts, he said, "With Yahweh there is always a way."'

'It seems this part has already been fulfilled,' Awan says.

'But - and this I didn't understand until just now - he told me he was not Ruhamah but Havel. Yet, you are the one who has explained those words to me, Awan. You have enabled me to meet Yahweh. It was neither Ruhamah nor Havel, but you I needed to find.'

Kayin nods and looks at his wife. She is pondering.

'I shared those words in my story,' she says. 'Though they were my brother's. They brought you here.'

'Exactly.'

'What was the second part?' Kayin asks, fixing his eyes back on her.

It's like he knows and is probing me. Is there any way I can get around telling him?

'Tell him.'

Adah takes a deep breath, and plunges in, thinking that the quicker the words get out, the quicker it's done with. 'It was you, Kayin. You stood next to me on the watchtower. You told me you had something to show me, but I was scared to step forward, for on either side of me were dead men, hanging in a noose. A noose was round my neck also, but I took your hand and stepped out of it, finding my feet were on solid ground. You said we were going to the mountains. I feared Lamech, but you told me not to look back. "Stop looking behind, Adah. To claim your future, you must look forward." Then I woke.'

Amusement tugs at Awan's lips. 'I can't believe someone else is dreaming of my husband.'

Fear jumps back in. 'Oh, no! It wasn't like that.'

A huge roar of laughter releases from Kayin, and this time it fills the glade. 'It's nice to know I'm still appreciated.'

'You're a bit old for her, my love,' Awan counters.

Adah glances between the two, resisting the temptation to stare at her feet. They are joking together; they're not angry with her. Joy floods her heart again and she allows herself to relax and join in. *Alright, Yahweh. I trust you.*

'Well, I do have something to show you - your son,' Kayin finally says, once his laughter has rumbled out. 'Perhaps your future lies ahead with him. That would make sense. I'm glad to know I was wise in your dream. That makes a change.' He grins again at his wife. 'It's important to acknowledge where we stand, but it's not good to remain there. We must move forward in Yahweh's strength rather than our own.'

Glancing back at Awan, Adah seeks confirmation of Kayin's words, but Awan is chewing her lip, and Adah gains the impression she's not sure. Then Awan smiles. 'Mountains or no mountains, it's clear that your escape was Yahweh's design. He has saved you from great danger.'

'I'm not sure I'd have survived another of Lamech's tantrums,' Adah confirms. 'Which is why I'm worried for Chanoch and Juval. Even if I'm safe, they certainly are not.'

'I share your concern,' Awan says. 'Nevertheless, you must follow the trail before it disappears. We'll leave as soon as I've put together some provisions.'

'Who's leaving?' Chanoch says, emerging from the cave rubbing his eyes.

'The three of us. Your abba has found Yaval's trail. I must accompany them, as Adah seems to have a strange fascination with my husband.' Awan winks, and incredibly, Adah feels laughter bubble instead of mortification. 'Stay here as long as you want to, Chanoch. You can look after our friend.' A delicate finger points to the fawn.

Chanoch joins them around the stone circle and considers Adah. 'You're improved this morning. You slept well?'

'Yes, though it's better than that.' She allows her smile to fill her face and Chanoch returns one. *He understands too.*

'I'll get word to you about Juval as soon as possible,' Chanoch says, placing his hand on hers.

'Thank you, but please don't put yourself at risk. Yahweh is in control, isn't He?'

'He certainly is.'

Adah washes in a nearby brook and when she borrows a clean tunic of Awan's, she recognises Manon's signature weave.

'Is this the tunic you purchased from Manon, the husband of my friend, Eliana?' she asks as she joins the others.

'Probably,' Kayin replies. 'It's old now, but still excellent quality. I like the way the brown fibres are woven into the linen; it brings out the colour in Awan's eyes.'

'It's long since I could weave. My fingers are too gnarled with age,' Awan adds.

'The weaver is Mela's abba.'

'Ah,' Awan says. 'And does Mela weave too?'

'Yes. She's excellent.'

'Even more reason to find them,' Kayin says, grinning.

Before setting off, they gather together, holding hands in a circle of four.

'Yahweh Elohim, please keep Chanoch safe as he returns to the pack of wolves,' Awan prays. 'You are the great protector.'

Next to speak is Kayin. 'Though our lives are not easy, You mark our days and hold them secure. When we are vulnerable, we have a choice – to build our own walls or to trust in Your goodness. Bless our son and the leadership of his city. Give him favour, opportunity and above all, grace.'

Then Adah listens as her three companions lift their voices in unison:

> *Yahweh is my light and my salvation,*
> *My heart shall not fear,*
> *Though the waters roar and darkness creeps in,*
> *Yet, I will be confident.*
> *For He will bless those who love Him,*
> *And protect those who draw near.*

'Be careful,' Awan says as she hugs Chanoch goodbye.

'I will. I'm sorry if I've put you in danger by coming here,' Chanoch says.

'Think nothing of it,' Kayin replies. 'I've been in danger most of my life. Every moment I continue breathing is only by Yahweh's grace.'

Chanoch nods. 'You know, recently I've been reminded of something I used to do that I've neglected. On my return, I intend to go into the prison again. Perhaps my time of influence among the elders has ceased, but I can still share Yahweh's grace with those in the lowest place. Please pray for that.'

'We will.'

A tear springs to Adah's eye as she embraces her old friend for perhaps the final time. 'Thank you for everything. I will miss you.'

'And I you,' Chanoch says. 'May you have peace when you lie down and sleep, for Yahweh alone makes you dwell in safety.'

Though saying farewell to Chanoch is bitter, excitement dominates as Adah sets off with Kayin and Awan. They take several packs of supplies, and water skins slung over their backs. Over the next few days, Kayin stops frequently to pick up the trail, but it never takes him long to find it. Yaval's family have taken an easier route through the bush and the rain continues to hold off.

On the fourth night, Kayin studies the stars while they make camp in a grove of trees. 'They've gone north now, as I suspected, moving around the mountains towards the plains surrounding the sea. If they continue north, then go west again, they'll eventually come to the river that borders Eden.'

'Is that so?' Adah says. 'I thought you had to cross mountains to get there.'

'There's a sizeable pass between the northern peaks and the sea. A few people groups live along the coast - fishermen making use of the Realm of Leviathan - but with no river until you reach Eden, the land isn't much use for farming. Cattle roam there though, ones that need little water, like kavash and gerenuk. It would be a good place to settle if you're trying not to be found.'

Adah nods. Dry plains don't sound appealing, but she can see it might be sensible for those living in fear of Lamech.

'We've avoided the northern cities belonging to the Iradites, but there is one city we'll walk close by tomorrow - that of our youngest daughter, Dorit. The one Chanoch mentioned. Her people are mostly friendly, so we'll stop there for supplies.'

On arrival in Dorit, Adah finds it strange going to the marketplace without access to Lamech's name. Several times, she almost picks something up then remembers she has nothing to trade.

'This market is much smaller than the one in Chanoch,' Adah murmurs.

'That's because this is the westernmost city in Nod,' Kayin explains. 'Although, there is a world west of Eden that we know nothing about, except what we hear from other travellers.'

'A woman who sells jewellery and ornaments in our marketplace comes from somewhere called Havilah, where there is gold, beryl and onyx,' Adah says. 'They are beautiful things.'

'I've seen some beryl,' Awan says. 'It's stunning – the colour of the sea on a glorious day. She's not here today though, this trader?'

'No, I can't see her. Which is just as well, for she knows my name and word might get back to Lamech.' Adah suddenly realises the danger of being here. 'I wonder if we should leave?'

Kayin agrees. He trades a deer hide for the items they've chosen then they depart for Dorit's home. Dorit welcomes them warmly and insists they stay the night, filling them with an excellent meal and their packs with as much food as they can carry. Adah likes her instantly and the best part is, she's never heard of Lamech.

'So, you're moving this way, Adah?'

'Yes, looking for my son. If he settles nearby, so will I.'

Dorit nods. 'It's remote here but I like that. I'll keep my people away from the sin spreading through the east as long as I can.'

Adah finds herself blushing.

'I'm sorry, did I say something wrong?' Dorit asks.

'Adah is leaving behind a dangerous family and bad people – responsible for much of the violence consuming the far east at present,' Kayin says.

'I'm sorry to hear it. It sounds like you are doing the right thing by leaving. You may be sure of a warm welcome anytime you come here – and discretion,' Dorit confirms.

'You named Dorit after your niece?' Adah asks as they leave the next day, recalling Awan's story from the night they visited Lamech's party.

'You remember that?' Awan says.

'I do. I think it's wonderful the way you prayed for her, though she hurt you.'

'Ah, I hurt her more, Adah. There are always two sides to any tale. I still pray for her daily, though I have no notion where she might be. Last I heard, Chayim and Avigail moved south-west, beyond the Euphrates, but I don't know if Dorit stayed with them.'

'I suppose I should continue to pray for those I have left behind.'

Awan takes her hand and squeezes it. 'Yes, my dear. Prayer is the best balm to heal pain and unforgiveness.'

On the sixth day, the evening sun is casting ombre and magenta hues over the clouds when they spot a group of goats, with some hens and geese, on a hillside. A howl-bark sounds before Adah spots the silhouette of a man climbing the hill from the other side.

'Yaval!'

She pelts forwards as he runs over and down the hill towards her. Meeting halfway, they throw themselves into each other's arms and do not let go until Fang, who has been yapping the entire time, starts licking Yaval's heels.

'Ima! What are you doing here?' he laughs. 'How did you manage—?' Yaval shakes his head in disbelief.

Pure joy envelops her again, as warm as her son's embrace. 'Yahweh made a way,' she says, snuggling into Yaval's chest. He smells exactly as he should - all earth and air and animal skin. Her own *wanderer*; her precious boy.

'Kayin and Awan brought you,' Yaval says, looking beyond to her guides who stroll leisurely forward.

'I would never have found you otherwise.'

'We intended to send word to Eliana with a trader as soon as we settled on a location,' Yaval says. 'We had no idea you'd be coming so soon.'

'Nor I until a short while ago. And I'm sorry to say, I don't know if your abba is hunting me.'

'Not even abba would bother coming this far,' Yaval says. 'Come, I have something to show you.' He looks at Kayin and Awan, who have reached them. 'Did you tell her?'

'Tell me what?' Awan says.

'Clearly not.' Yaval's warm grasp feels wonderful as he leads her up the hill and over the other side, where a large, rectangular structure covered in goatskin is erected beneath a tree. Adah has never seen such construction before. 'Come in - it's quite safe.'

Yaval leads her inside. 'I got the idea from the army shelters, except this is more substantial.' Indeed, large branches are tied together with rope, and covered with linen which forms the inside roof, beneath the layer of skins. There is room for all their supplies and, on a sheepskin on the floor, propped against a cushion which wraps around the central pole, is Mela. In her arms she holds a nursing baby.

'Adah,' Mela says, beaming. 'You're here? How wonderful.'

'I... I have another grandchild!' Adah's heart swells as she kneels before Mela and strokes the soft, spongy hair of the beautiful baby, then kisses Mela's cheek. 'My daughter, you are a wonder. I can't believe Eliana didn't tell me.'

'I don't think we knew when we last sent news. Gomer was a bit of a surprise.'

'Gomer... I like that,' Adah says, remembering Naamah's first love with fondness. 'But where is Ellie?'

Yaval touches a finger to his lips and points to where little Ellie is snuggled under a blanket, thumb in mouth and eyes closed.

'Come, sit,' Yaval says, shuffling some cushions to provide each visitor with one. 'I'll make you something.'

'We're well fed, don't worry,' Awan says, taking her seat.

'In that case, I'll pen the animals in.'

Kayin offers to help, and they return a while later with some hot water and slightly stale bread. By now, it is almost completely dark. Mela and little Gomer have sunk into sleep. Yaval begins to gather blankets, but Awan stops him when it becomes clear they have nothing to spare.

'Our travelling ones will do just fine,' she says, pulling hers from her pack and settling under it on the floor.

Adah, unused to the hardness of ground, is grateful when Yaval leads her by the hand through the dark to where Ellie is sleeping on a sheepskin.

'Snuggle up with her. She'll be so excited to find you there in the morning,' he says.

'She will?'

'Of course,' Yaval whispers. 'We talk about you all the time. She's constantly asking when Sava is coming.'

Adah prays as she embraces her beloved son, beyond grateful for his arms, while still yearning for his twin whom she's left behind.

CHAPTER 81

Wilderness of North-West Nod, 751st year of Wandering

Adah wakes and reaches forward for Ellie, but of course she's not there. She's outside the tent, jabbering away to Mela who, by the sound of the crackling fire and clunking pan, is preparing breakfast.

'Watch out - you're too close!' Mela says, accompanied by the scrape of heels as she presumably pulls Ellie away from the fire.

Ellie harrumphs then says, 'I'm going to see if Sava's awake.' She bustles into the tent and stands before Adah, hands on hips. 'Sava, get up quick! We have a big day today.'

'Do we?' Adah says, feigning ignorance as she leans up on her elbow.

'Yes, silly. We're moving. Remember? Come on!'

'I'm not getting up before I have my morning hug.'

Ellie pretends to look cross but then grins and throws herself enthusiastically into Adah's embrace. Adah smothers her in cuddles, but Ellie soon wriggles loose and runs back outside to bother her mother again.

'Thank you, Yahweh, my salvation,' Adah prays. 'Thank you for restoring my son to me and blessing me so abundantly. Please save Juval and redeem him. Oh, how I miss him! Guide Chanoch and protect him. It has been so long with no news...

Bless Naamah, Eber and their family. Watch over Tzillah, Mini-Kayin and Dinah. Bring them to know you. And Lamech? Well, you know best what to do with him.'

> *I trust You, O Yahweh my Lord,*
> *And I say, 'You are my Elohim.'*
> *My times are in Your hand,*
> *I shall not be afraid.*
> *For You stand, You stand with me.*

'Sava, stop singing and hurry up!' Ellie says from outside, forcing Adah to chuckle and rise, ready to face moving day. As she exits the tent, her eyes dart east. She releases a breath – no sign of her husband.

They have waited in this spot for several seasons, hoping for news from Chanoch – confirmation that he and Juval are safe and Lamech is not hunting them. No news has come and when Kayin and Awan called a few weeks ago, they advised Yaval to move on, just in case.

'They know all about being fugitives; we'd do well to heed their advice,' Yaval concluded.

It takes all morning to pack and strip down the tent. They load Yaval's kavash, and some other beasts he's acquired, with packs of belongings, leaving accessible only what is essential for the journey. By mid-afternoon they set off, heading for a man Yaval knows who trades in flax and has agreed to exchange some fibre for a goat. Mela needs it to make more linen – as a family of five, their supplies are running thin.

They spend the night in the flax trader's house. It transpires he's Dorit's son and has inherited her hospitality. He fills them with an evening meal and insists they take breakfast with him, so it is not until mid-morning of the following day that they leave and turn south. Then the mountains loom in the distance, peaks of evergreen and khaki filling a third of the sky, with white mist covering the lower half. These peaks are smaller than the ones closer to Eden which have been Adah's distant view for the past year, though she knows from Awan's story that partway across them, you enter the domain of the tanninim. She's glad they're not intending to go that far.

'Is it cold in the mountains?' Adah asks, thinking of their meagre coverings.

'In the mornings,' Yaval says, 'Hence the mist; but it soon brightens. The seasons are certainly different. We're aiming for the hills just below on this side. They'll provide good grazing without being too dense with trees. I don't want the Great Lake to be visible from where we settle - it feels too close to danger.'

'I agree,' Adah says. Though it would still be two weeks' walk from Chanoch city, any shared view doesn't appeal.

Even with Ellie riding a goat and Gomer wrapped against his ima's chest, they move slowly and must camp again before nightfall.

'I'm not cut out for this, Yahweh,' Adah says as she tosses and turns that night, trying to find a vaguely comfortable position. 'I've been pampered with soft beds most of my life. I hope we find somewhere to settle quickly, and that I can make something better to lie on than sheepskin.'

Adah has noticed her health suffering while she's been on the plains. Not just a lack of bed, but lack of a good diet. Though she wouldn't trade this for her life with Lamech, it's been hard, and her back has constantly ached. She's never mentioned it to anyone except Yahweh, but suspects Yaval has selected their next location partly because he's guessed. He heard Awan's story too - about the lower mountains being lush with fruit.

It's late afternoon the following day before they reach the hill country. Adah presses ahead, keen to see if any nourishment lies over the crest of the first mound. The air feels lighter as she climbs the grassy slope, leaving the wilderness behind. When she reaches the top, she's rewarded with both berries and beans, one trailing down the rocks to her left and the other padding out the bushes on top. *Wonderful. Thank you, Yahweh.*

The location of the plants forms a natural barrier between two meadows, almost like they were purposely located. After stuffing a decent number of berries into her mouth and stripping the plants of beans to cook later, she lowers onto the adjacent grass, revelling in the emerald softness between her fingers; something she hasn't felt for so long. It compels her to lie down, and the moment she rests her head on her hands, her eyes close and she drifts into a doze.

Adah wakes as something nuzzles her, something soft, familiar and… with teeth.

'Ouch!' Adah says, her eyes flying open to witness a goat now batting her shoulder with its horns before rummaging in her pack for beans. 'No, they're mine,' she says, snatching it back and rubbing her nose where the bite stings slightly. It was only a gentle one, but still.

'Actually, they're mine. I came here to pick some beans for dinner, only to find most of them stolen.'

That voice… She jolts and twists her torso towards it. Could it be?

'Hello, Adah.'

Her heart jumps in her chest at the man approaching with a smirk hovering on his lips. *This isn't possible.* She must be dreaming. The goat treads on her leg, helpfully confirming that she's not.

The man sits next to her on the grass, pushing the goat away. He's so close, the musk of livestock and woodsmoke reaches her, transporting her back to another life, another dream. 'I've met my niece and her family already, but I left you to rest. You looked so peaceful,' he says.

Rhythmic pounding reverberates through her chest and ears in an insistent cadence. 'It's really you. How...?'

He smiles and his eyes flicker with the same amusement. 'I live here. What about you?'

This makes no sense. 'You went west!'

His eyebrows draw together and the dimple in his cheek twitches. 'Adah, this is west.'

'But... the land between the two rivers...'

'I never got that far. I found this place...' He motions beyond the next hill – where Yaval and Mela are pitching the tent – to the first mountain peak. Adah sees smoke rising above it – several trails, like cooking fires burning. 'The village accepted me, and I liked it. So, I stayed.'

You found a wife here, then. You must have found a wife.

'You haven't answered my question,' he says. She longs to touch his face, to grasp his hands, to check he is real, but she doesn't dare. *He belongs to another. Though it looks like he's having the same difficulty...* For his hand hovers mid-air, near her cheek. 'How are you here?'

'I escaped Lamech four seasons ago. It was difficult but– I don't know if everyone is safe. I don't know.'

The tips of his fingers reach her cheek. He can't help himself either. Adah wants to lower her lashes to revel in his touch, but she won't risk it in case he disappears. Instead, she feels every work-worn callous on his slender fingers as she stares into his eyes, the flecks of green captivating her as they had the first time she noticed them.

'How long has it been?' he asks. 'Yaval must be—'

'Thirty-five,' she says. 'The twins are thirty-five. I haven't seen you for twenty-nine and a half years.'

His thumb strokes her face as his other cheek dimples. 'Not that you've been counting.' He leans forward. 'And yet, it almost feels like no time at all.'

'Ruhamah.' She breathes out his name, allowing the sound to dance uninhibited.

Now he closes his eyes, but his smile remains. 'It's so good to hear you say my name, Adah.'

No, we can't do this. 'What about your wife?'

His eyelids fly open. 'My wife?'

'You left to find a wife.'

'Now who told you that?'

'No one. I just… Everyone who goes to the land between the rivers goes to find a wife.'

Ruhamah sits back on his hands, and he laughs, allowing his shoulders to shake. Adah doesn't understand what's so funny. 'Did you hear that, Za?' he says to the goat. 'Adah thinks we could love someone else.'

The goat, entirely disinterested, wanders off to scavenge some remaining beans from the rocks. Ruhamah softens his smile, and this time, both his hands lift hers from the grass and he threads their fingers together. 'Call me hopelessly romantic, but my heart has always belonged to you, Adah. For a time, I loved Nadia as best I could, and I truly mourned her loss. But what she went through - knowing she was not the only one - I would never willingly put another through that.'

'She knew?'

'Why do you think she didn't want us to see each other?'

Oh. That makes sense now. 'So... you're not married?'

He chuckles and kisses her fingers. 'I'm not married.'

Hope flickers the flames alive. *Yahweh, can this be? Is this right? I never imagined Ruhamah being in my dream meant any more than it did with Kayin. Aren't I still married to Lamech?*

'What are you thinking?' Ruhamah asks. 'Your eyes were travelling everywhere then.'

'Sorry; I was just talking to Yahweh.'

'Now that fills my heart with even more joy than you being here.'

'Really?'

'Well, it certainly comes close. What did He say?'

'I don't know. I–'

'Shhh.' Ruhamah leans forward so their foreheads are touching, and her eyelids lower once more. 'Listen.'

Adah becomes aware of the warm breeze sweeping around them. The joy she feels every time Yahweh's presence comes floods her heart. *Is this Your will, my Elohim? I am listening.*

The breeze turns bitter. Images of her life with Lamech flash into her mind. The day they met, the wilted flowers, their marriage vows. The first time he broke them, the next and the next... Nasya. Tzillah. Tamar. Drunken violence, smashed vases, inked dancers, walls, ropes and shadows.

She shakes, suddenly feeling Ruhamah's touch like a shackle. *I cannot walk into this again.* She struggles against him as her scars throb.

'I have set you free.'

The breath breaks into Adah's mouth. It travels down her throat and swirls inside her chest, expanding the space inside once more. Then the last shackles of bondage break; Lamech's noose unravels and is carried away on the wind, split into a million pieces above the clouds. Her lungs release, and she can breathe normally again.

Adah opens her eyes. Ruhamah's greet her. However, he has moved back, and his hands are nowhere near her but are placed firmly in the grass. His eyes will not fool her, as Lamech's did. Yahweh is her dependable one now. He is her first love.

'Are you... well?' Ruhamah asks.

She studies him, watching for traces of deceit. There are none. He is as he has always been - sincere and kind.

Slowly, she nods. 'Yahweh wants to free me from Lamech; I see that now. I think the fact that he left me first, many times... Even so, I can't claim it will be easy. The years of captivity and anguish...'

'I understand,' Ruhamah says, and his face falls.

He thinks she is refusing him. Is she? Adah shuffles uncomfortably, and as she puts weight on her arm, her back twinges.

'Do you have a bed?' she asks.

Ruhamah raises an eyebrow. 'A bed? I have a house.'

'Yes, but do you have a bed? I'm desperate to sleep in a decent bed. Could you find me one?'

Mirth captures his features once more. 'Presently, I sleep in a hammock, often sharing it with a lamb, but if you need a bed, I will travel the world collecting the most wonderful materials to make you the best bed possible.'

'Don't,' she says, shuffling slightly closer. 'Don't travel. Don't ever leave.'

'I thought...?'

'I said it won't be easy. I didn't say I'm not willing to try.'

'So... where does that leave us?'

Adah doesn't answer but allows a slight smile to tug at her lips as she witnesses his discomfort.

Her love launches into an unsteady monologue. 'I'm willing to wait as long as you need me to. You can stay with Yaval, can't you? With no expectation on my part. And, I mean, if a simple bed would do for now, I can acquire one. There's only a few of us in the village, but one of them is an excellent woodworker. He could make it. We look after each other, you see. We can even place it in the tent! Just... please stay? Oh, you'll love my neighbours' children, too. We're like a big family. I almost sent word to Eliana asking her to leave the city and come here, but no messengers ever pass this way, and–'

Adah can wait no longer. She steals the rest of his words with a kiss.

EPILOGUE

The land between the rivers, 260 years later

Juval hitches his pack tighter on his shoulders. It's heavy with travelling supplies and his lyre strapped to the back. The ramshackle tavern with men lying semi-inebriated outside doesn't look promising, but he has business to address tomorrow and must stop somewhere for the night. Lamech is counting on him to secure this deal. Besides, he's heard the wine here is excellent and the women even better.

He takes a step forward.

A voice stops him. 'I wouldn't go in there.'

Juval turns to see a young man – no more than a hundred – sitting on a boulder surveying him.

'Unless you want them to rob you of all you possess during the night?'

When Juval shakes his head, the stranger stands and approaches. 'I assume from your baggage that you're seeking a room.'

'I am. Do you know of a better one?'

'Certainly. My abba has an excellent table and relishes hearing stories from other parts of the world.'

'How do you know I'm—'

'Oh, come on. You stand out rather boldly with your elegant, tasselled robe and your fine shoes. No one in these parts has anything like them. Plus, your accent. You're from Nod, aren't you?'

'I am,' Juval says, not quite trusting this astute young waif. His eyes and ears are rather too keen.

'Did you ever see The Wanderer?' the waif asks, with a wink.

Juval replies slowly as long-buried memories of that night and the resulting loss of his mother surface. 'I did once, but I don't talk about it.'

'Oooh, that sounds like exactly the sort of story my abba would enjoy. Come, friend.' The man puts his arm around Juval's shoulders in a way that seems far too familiar and leads him away from the tavern. 'You will find good sustenance for your weary bones in the house of Lamech.'

'Lamech?' Juval says.

'My abba's name.'

This is unusual. In all Juval's travels, he has never met another. 'I am also a son of Lamech.'

The young man laughs. 'Is that so? How interesting. I've never met another.'

'Nor I. It's not a common name – unlike Chanoch.'

'True. There are Chanochs everywhere. Well then, we are practically family.' The laugh continues – he's enjoying his own joke. 'Though I assume it's not the same man – in fact, it can't be – for you're a similar age to my abba, I suspect.'

Juval feels old. Though perhaps little more than a quarter through his life, it has seemed long and arduous for many an age. Oh, to be young and optimistic again like this boy.

'I have just one request,' the optimist continues, 'as you are from Nod. Please don't take offence. In my home we don't tolerate worship of anything but Yahweh. Will that be a problem?'

Yahweh. That's another name he hasn't heard for a long time. Another name that conjures up memories of his mother.

'It won't be a problem,' Juval says, reasoning that if this family follow the Creator, they likely won't rob him in the night. Nor will they provide him with a woman, though. He wishes, not for the first time, that he'd insisted Dania accompany him. Too busy with the quarry and children, his wife had refused to come. Three seasons is far too long for abstinence and though he tries to resist, the women beckon.

'What's your name then, son of Lamech?' the young man says as they draw up outside a large home, bustling with noise and laughter.

Sweet aromas reach Juval's nostrils, settling his indecision. The food had better taste as good as it smells. 'I'm Juval.'

'Pleased to meet you, Juval, son of Lamech.'

'And you are?'

'Oh yes, I never introduced myself, did I?' The young man stretches forward his palms. 'Noah. At your service.'

APPENDIX

ABOUT THE WANDERER SERIES

Although this book explores the storyline introduced in the prologue and epilogue of my first two novels, *The Wanderer Scorned* & *The Wanderer Reborn*, I wanted it to stand on its own. It is technically book three, but it could also be book one. I love an appendix, and if you find I haven't covered something you're curious about, you may find the answers at the back of the first or second book.

The series is based on a very ancient story from the Bible. I have tried at all times to remain faithful to the very small amount of information we're given in the text of Genesis 4, but having written around 300,000 words based on 26 verses, I have evidently filled in lots of gaps! I didn't do this lightly. Whilst this particular book should throw up fewer complications than the first two, there may still be some things you disagree with. That's fine. I claim no authority on the matter. Whilst I have done some research, there are so many unknowns about this period in pre-history that these books are primarily a product of my imagination and prayer. I hope there is blessing to be found in the pages, regardless of whether I have things historically, scientifically and theologically accurate.

Originally, this was intended to be Chanoch's story, as we're briefly given his point of view in the first two books. However, the initial words that sparked its writing were those now forming Chapter One, and from there, I immediately knew it would be Adah's story (and Chanoch would be a side-hustle!) When I was plotting, it all seemed straightforward, and I had no idea it would end up this length. I hope that some of the tangents and subplots blessed you, because every time I tried to cut them, my request was refused!

If you're beginning with this story and you haven't read the other two, I trust your curiosity is piqued. *The Wanderer Scorned* is the narrative Kayin relates at the fated party where Lamech finally confesses his true colours. It's based on Genesis 4:1-16. *The Wanderer Reborn* is Awan's tale which imagines the in-between of Genesis 4:17 and 25-26. *The Wanderer's Legacy* covers verses 17-24. To see how they all fit together, you'll need to read them all. When you do, anticipate several 'Oh' moments. Even so, I hope this one made sense without them!

Feeling rather sorry for Chanoch, who remained a minor character, I have now written him his own novella. *Between the Rivers* will be released at the same time as this novel.

LAMECH & THE CITY

The conundrum of Lamech's character was never how he could kill, it was always why he would admit it. The huge jump in depravity that drove us through a war with Barsabas, the establishment of a death penalty and much political manoeuvring, was all about Lamech's battle for power. For his admission to be possible, he needed a certain level of it.

When considering how on earth to get Lamech to the stage where he would tell 'all and sundry' that he'd murdered, without any fear of ramification, I was regularly listening to *The Bible Project* podcasts. In their discussions on the theme of The City, Tim and John explored the relationship between Cain and Lamech, and the power of cities to exponentially multiply both the good and the terrible things about human society. This informed much of my thinking about Lamech's downfall, the talents of his children and the corruption of the city of Chanoch. This was made more interesting by my previous decision to give Kayin a redemption story, which I couldn't now go back on! How did Cain/Kayin's legacy of murder transfer to Lamech (whose name in Hebrew is a reordering of *melek*, meaning 'king', suggesting his desire to be a ruler) even when his son (Enoch/Chanoch) was a brought up a believer?

A lot can happen in a few hundred years. Indeed, the twentieth century shows us how quickly things can escalate in a brief time, and walking this journey with Chanoch and his increasingly corrupted city has been an interesting thought experiment regarding the human condition.

PATRIARCHY

Along similar lines was the exploration of early patriarchy. Humans were created equal (from the side, not the foot, see Gen. 2:21), and both were made in God's image (see Gen.1:27, where the English translation 'man' in Hebrew just means 'human'). Equality can be accepted whether or not you believe in complementarianism.

The first hint of a change comes in God's words to the woman in Genesis 3:16, 'Your desire shall be for your husband, and he shall rule over you.' So, patriarchy wasn't the intended state of things, but a product of the fall. Yet, this must have taken some time to play out. There's no hint of it in my first two books (which predominantly consider another word of God's regarding the curse on the ground, see Gen. 3:17-19). However, by the time of Lamech, the first recorded polygamist in the Bible (and, to my knowledge, in history) it must have been present to a degree.

Therefore, this 'pre-Jewish society' series may look different from other biblical fiction you read. There is no expectation of head covering, chaperoning or dowries, and there are plenty of strong women present. However, in *The Wanderer's Legacy*, I spend some time exploring how patriarchy (and misogyny which sadly, so often accompanies it) might have gradually crept in. From an early hint (Adah's mother hiding her first flow of blood), we witness unfaithfulness, the replacement of female elders and fighters, the abuse of women, the desire for male heirs, right through to prevalent cult prostitution. These are heartbreaking things to write about, but they have occurred for millennia.

In my account it is sparked off, of course, by Methushael, who names his eldest son *Bekhor*, which is Hebrew for 'firstborn' and, in effect, calls his second son 'king'. The undercurrent of Methushael's misogyny and dissatisfaction in Bekhor's ambition, with his simultaneous respect for Barsabbas, impacts everything Lamech does – despite Lamech's determination to be *'nothing like his father'*. The sins of the father playing out in the son is another Biblical theme, and don't we tragically see it often?

TIMES & SEASONS

Time as we know it (hours, minutes, seconds) was not established until Babylonian times, and so, I have always avoided mentioning these in my novels. Months is probably a later concept also, though lunar months are fairly ancient. I generally use weeks (established in Genesis 2:2) and seasons. My characters discuss cycles of the moon for months, and throughout, four seasons (rather than two) equate to a year. In dating the chapters and ages of the characters, I have referenced years, chiefly because the biblical narrative does so (the genealogies are very precise and I have stuck closely to them.)

LEVIATHAN, NACHASH & ALTERNATIVE WORSHIP

The Hebrew *nachash* means serpent and is the word for the creature that deceives the first couple in the Garden. *Leviathan* is a related concept – a sea serpent-monster – who is altogether more terrifying. *Tannin* (pl. *tanninim*) is a general word for a monster-like creature and is also related to the two above, though in this series, I use it to refer to giant lizards, i.e. dinosaurs. In ancient literature, the sea and sea monster represent the forces of chaos that must be battled or slain by the gods to bring order and stability to creation.

In the Bible, the biblical authors have fun with this idea, asserting Yahweh Elohim's supremacy over all things by demonstrating not his need to battle the sea monster, but His complete control over it: leviathan is merely something God created which 'plays' in the sea. I explored this initially in *The Wanderer Reborn* and particularly the song, *In Wonder at Leviathan* based on Psalm 104.

In this book, I develop the idea through the emblem of nachash and the three-headed leviathan. They feature in the story as first Barsabas, and then the dwellers of Chanoch, reject Yahweh's created order in favour of the deceiver's voice. The celebration and descent of chaos, particularly regarding promiscuity, accompanies this. As I was already dealing with patriarchy, it wasn't much of a stretch to imagine the first cult prostitutes being connected to nachash.

As regards the connection with the stars, stars are another biblical metaphor, this time for the host of heaven, many of whom are a rebellious host led by 'the *satan*' (see Job 1:6, Isaiah 14:12-14, Zechariah 3:1), who is represented in Genesis 3 as *nachash*. Often, this rebellious host of heaven take possession of, or influence, the kings of the earth, such as in the Isaiah passage just referenced which is also referring to the King of Babylon, Nebuchadnezzar.

The Hebrew for 'hosts of heaven' is *elohim*, which is a plural word for 'gods' i.e. spiritual beings. I have differentiated this with Yahweh by using a capital letter. He is Yahweh Elohim, the One God (plural because he is three persons, which is only revealed much later in the Bible). Yahweh Elohim is the creator of the stars, and called *Yahweh Tsebaoth*, 'The Lord of Hosts', continually by Isaiah.

In Amos, who also refers to God as Yahweh Tsebaoth, we find a verse which establishes that the stars were often worshipped as gods: "'You shall take up Sikkuth your king, and Kiyyun your star-god— your images that you made for yourselves, and I will send you into exile beyond Damascus," says the Lord, whose name is the God of hosts' (Amos 5:27-27).

If you want to know more, there is a helpful article here https://www.jewishvirtuallibrary.org/leviathan and *The Bible Project* also did a podcast series on *The Dragon* which features several of these themes.

NAMES

You'll have already gathered that I love incorporating name meanings into my stories, and choosing names relevant for characters, following the biblical tradition. I tend to err towards the traditional Hebrew pronunciation, hence using Y instead of J and V instead of B, except where it occurs as the first letter of a word. Jabal, in our Bibles, is correctly pronounced Yaval. Juval should have been Yuval, but I used Juval for the sake of the reader. It would have been hard to distinguish them otherwise!

Adah's name meaning 'adornment' is often referenced in the text. As mentioned, Lamech למך means 'robust' but is also a reordering of *melek* מלך – meaning 'king' in the Hebrew script.

Methushael is a very interesting name. It is sometimes translated 'man of God' but that is rather too simplistic, and I clearly haven't portrayed him this way. The name can be formed as a question (like Micah which means *'Who is like God?'*) and in this sense would be *'I am man [mortal]! Where is God?'* which rather excellently fits Methushael's mysterious and abhorrent character! It could also be an amalgamation of *mut* – to die – *sha'al* – to enquire – and *El* – god, suggesting a meaning of 'they die who ask of God.'

Methushael is not to be confused with the better-known Methuselah – the longest person to live – whose name includes the popular but eponymous word 'selah' and has also had many meanings purported. The one I like best is 'When He Is Dead It Shall Be Sent' (*Jones' Dictionary of Old Testament Proper Names*) because, if you do the maths, this oldest man ever died the year of Noah's flood!

I have already referred to Bekhor. Here are a few more you may find interesting:

Tzillah	Shadiness
Yaval	Stream
Juval*	Brook
Naamah	Lovely
Tuval-Kayin	Rivulet-Acquired
Azurak	My own creation, formed from the words *azur* – helped – and *achor* – to trouble.
Shua	To be brought low
Leah	Weak/weary
Tzel/Shadow	*Tzel* means shadow. I was having a little fun with this one!
Noa	Moveable
Dinah	Judgement
Barsabas	Son of the host (see above re. the stars!)
Chanoch	Dedicated
Shiphrah	Fairness
Eliana	Light
Ruhamah	Shows mercy
Kenan	Kenan is listed in Gen. 5:9 as the son of Enosh, the son of Seth. The name likely means networker, with the root – *to weave*
Anak	Giant
Nahar	River
Selah	*Noun:* A Rock, but also used in devotional settings for a kind of reflective pause.

KAVASH

I got halfway through drafting this story before realising I'd made no mention of the cloven-hooved mounts that Chanoch rides in *The Wanderer Scorned*. Having dug myself into that difficult hole, I needed a way out of it. Suddenly, Yaval had a new job to do!

Excuse me while I go on a slight taxonomy detour. There is evidence of very early equine domestication, much earlier than that of camels etc, though of course scientific theory generally allows for far longer time periods than the text of Genesis does, if taken at face value. Moreover, I assume throughout this series that many individual *species* went extinct at the time of the flood, when only representatives from the *kinds* (roughly equivalent to *familiae*) were saved.

Equines belong to the *order* Perissodactyla which have in common hooved feet (whether one toe or several). If you go far enough back, equines have common ancestry with creatures such as tapirs and rhinoceroses. While exploring prehistoric artwork, I came across creatures such as the early equine Merychippus, with its several toes, and the Macrauchenia, of a different *order* but with the closest living relatives being of Perissodactyla. They have several features in common with tapirs.

It was this kind of creature I imagined for the kavash, which are so named because Hebrew *kavash* means to subdue/to bring into bondage. Hence, they have a cloven hoof and a long snout, but Lamech is able to describe them as almost goat like, though larger. Roughly equated, it's possible something like this could have been ridden before the modern horse evolved, but I'm only guessing, and making huge assumptions about the age of the earth which no doubt many shall disagree with. I can only claim artistic license in my defence!

METALS

We probably all know the verse about Tuval-Kayin, 'Zillah also bore Tubal-cain; he was the forger of all instruments of bronze and iron' (Gen 4:22). This provided some challenges and a deal of research to reconcile, for you are probably aware, from high school history lessons, that the iron age and bronze age were rather separate things. Fortunately, those lessons were highly oversimplistic. The 'ages' are by no means set in stone (excuse the pun) and refer to very broad periods which were non-regional and overlapped considerably. Different areas of the world did not develop technologies at the same time or rate.

This gives Tuval-Kayin some scope. Furthermore, it has been shown that arsenic-based bronze pre-dates tin-based, and the earliest bronze mixes were likely discovered quite by accident by smelting mixed ores, rather than a process of deliberate fabrication based on a considerable knowledge of metallic properties. A helpful article is here https://www.mining.com/the-metals-of-antiquity-tin/ if this kind of thing floats your boat! For the purposes of this book, I was content with Tuval-Kayin rather accidentally discovering the early bronze-making process using mixed ores.

SCRIPTURE REFERENCES

The principal text for this story is Genesis 4, as mentioned. Awan's prayer in Chapter 79 is based on Psalm 31. The song in that chapter is of my own composition, but there is biblical language scattered throughout.

Chanoch's outcry at the council, and the song sung as he leaves Kayin & Awan, is from Psalm 27:1,3 with added ideas from Psalm 46:3.

The song sung by Adah after her dream features in *The Wanderer Reborn* and parts of it are based on Psalm 43.

ACKNOWLEDGEMENTS

The Wanderer's Legacy is affectionately known as my 'epic'. I'm not sure I'll ever write another book like it! So many people have walked this journey with me, supporting me in a myriad of ways.

I am indebted to The Bible Project Podcast for this book. I was listening to their series on the theme of *The City* in Scripture while writing my first draft, and it provided so much inspiration, particularly for Lamech.

My earliest chapters were faithfully reviewed by the ACFW Scribes group. Thank you to all those who commented week after week – I am a better writer due to your feedback.

To my alpha readers – Joy Margetts, Alex Banwell and my partner in publishing madness, Joy Velykorodnyy – you are all incredible. Thanks for the recommendations to improve the storyline, even regarding the characters we had to kill (sad times!) Thank you for encouraging me that this story was worth the hundreds of hours it took to get ready.

To my beta readers – Rachel Yarworth and Jenny Sanders – thank you for your willingness to feedback on certain sensitive aspects, and the way you opened your hearts to me and corrected my style issues!

To my two picky editors – Ruth Johnson and Katy Pepper – you are fabulous. Your attention to detail is incredible, and my readers will be grateful for your keen eyes and countless hours of reading, re-reading and suggested tweaks.

To the team at *Kingdom Story Writers*, who have regularly lifted me up in prayer over the past few years – I couldn't have done it without you. To those who share with me how my books have drawn them closer to Jesus, and to those who send me little encouragements by social media, email or by leaving reviews – you are the reason I continue. Please keep on being wonderful.

My family regularly make sacrifices so I can write. To Ben, Elijah, Micah, Malachi and Boaz, I love you all so much.

To Jesus – the author and perfecter of my faith – everything I write is inspired by You and written for You. I can never thank or love You enough. I can't wait until glory!

N.W.

Get Help and Support

All forms of domestic abuse are not acceptable in any situation. If you're experiencing domestic abuse and feel frightened of, or controlled by, a partner, an ex-partner or family member, it's important to remember that it's not your fault, and there is no shame in seeking help.

Free, confidential support and advice is available to victims and their concerned family members or friends, 24 hours a day.

England National Domestic Abuse Helpline, 0808 2000 247
Northern Ireland
Domestic & Sexual Abuse Helpline, 0808 802 1414
Scotland
Domestic Abuse & Forced Marriage Helpline, 0800 027 1234
Wales Live Fear Free, 0808 80 10 100
The Men's Advice Line run by Respect is a confidential helpline specifically for male victims. 0808 801 0327
United States of America National Domestic Violence Hotline 1.800.799SAFE (7233) Or text START to 88788
https://www.thehotline.org

Information taken from www.gov.uk and www.thehotline.org

THE WANDERER SCORNED

Book 1 in *The Wanderer* Series

NATASHA WOODCRAFT

It all started with the banishment.

Kayin lives in the shadow of his parents' expulsion from the Garden of Eden and its lingering cloud of shame. He believes in the Creator but struggles for affirmation. When suffering comes and sibling rivalry threatens, Kayin wrestles with God, grasping at shards of faith. But his cries drown in the noise of his own doubts and fears, until his youthful hopes lie shattered, replaced by a twisted dance of pride and jealousy.

As Kayin spirals further, misunderstandings within the family dynamic dominate, and whispers of temptation slither through the cracks. Then a chance at redemption presents itself. With flames of forbidden love still raging hot, Kayin and his brother present their sacrifices.

No one foresees the resulting tragedy.

ISBN: 978-1-915034-82-3

Ebook: https://books2read.com/u/3GzjAK

THE WANDERER'S SISTER

A *Wanderer* Novelette

NATASHA WOODCRAFT

Avigail is stunned when her brother returns from a journey ranting and raving about her husband's betrayal.

As she digests the news, she relives key moments in her relationship with her husband, the agony of her difficulties in childbirth, and the effect of her murderous brother's actions on the family who never speak about him.

While the men stay silent, she is supported by three women, but will Yahweh join them, and heal her broken heart?

Exclusive to the author's readers' club
Get it free by signing up at:

natashawoodcraft.com/subscribe

BETWEEN THE RIVERS

A *Wanderer* Novella

NATASHA WOODCRAFT

Chanoch's family live in fear of the people dwelling in the land between the rivers – those who hunt them, seeking vengeance for old wounds. But when the time comes for Chanoch to find a wife, Yahweh's call leads him directly into the heart of enemy territory.

There he meets a woman whose vibrant spirit masks deep wounds of her own. Though love blooms between them, her belief that she is unworthy of devotion threatens everything. As Chanoch navigates his growing feelings and increasing dangers, can he learn to trust in something greater than his fears?

Journey with characters from *The Wanderer Reborn* and *The Wanderer's Legacy* in this moving story of romance, spiritual awakening, and the triumph of faith over fear.

ISBN: 978-1-915034-99-1

BROAD PLACE
publishing

broadplacepublishing.co.uk

ALSO FROM THE PUBLISHER

What do you do when your life's work lies in ashes at your feet? When your heart and body are broken and your faith is shattered?

Disillusioned, grief stricken and feeling abandoned by the God he once trusted, Brother Silas runs. He sets out on a lonely journey, not knowing where the path will take him, determined to distance himself from his painful past.

But Silas cannot escape the Love that will not let him go. Through the unexpected kindness of strangers, and a series of inexplicable events, Silas's heart begins to heal. Then an unlikely reunion puts him on the path to rediscovering who he really is. Will Silas find somewhere he truly belongs or will he remain a stranger forever?

Who is Benny Wellander?

To his mother, he's her precious baby, forever in need of protection. To his sister, he's "Pestie", the kid who destroyed her happy childhood. To his classmates, he's the quiet loner plagued by seizures. To his father, he's barely visible; a constant disappointment.

Caught in a web of insecurity, Benny defines himself by his illness and the damage it's wrought on his mind. But is he truly rubbish at everything? Or could he be worth loving?

Join Benny on a poignant journey of self-discovery as he seeks to understand his own worth. What will it take for him to break free from his labels and embrace the person he truly is?

Find out more at
broadplacepublishing.co.uk

Printed in Great Britain
by Amazon

63018420R00302